"Don't go," she whispered. "Not yet."

Her hand was warm on his forearm and a muscle worked its way along his jaw as he struggled to remain calm and in control.

"You don't know what you ask."

Her eyes changed. "I know exactly what I'm asking. I know exactly what I want."

She had no clue what he was. What he was capable of. *What he'd done in the past.*

"I'm not a nice man, Rowan. In fact I'm the most flawed creature you'll ever meet."

"In case you haven't noticed, I don't scare easy."

By Juliana Stone

KING OF THE DAMNED
TO HELL AND BACK (novella)
WICKED ROAD TO HELL
WRONG SIDE OF HELL (novella)
HIS DARKEST SALVATION
HIS DARKEST EMBRACE
HIS DARKEST HUNGER

JULIANA
STONE

KING
OF THE
DAMNED

A LEAGUE OF GUARDIANS NOVEL

AVON

An Imprint of HarperCollinsPublishers

"Wrong Side of Hell" was originally published as an e-book novella March 2012 by Avon Impulse, an Imprint of HarperCollins Publishers.

AVON BOOKS
An Imprint of HarperCollins*Publishers*
10 East 53rd Street
New York, New York 10022–5299

Copyright © 2012 by Juliana Stone
Excerpt from "Wrong Side of Hell" copyright © 2012 by Juliana Stone
ISBN 978–0–06–210231–7
www.avonromance.com

First Avon Books mass market printing: December 2012

Avon Trademark Reg. U.S. Pat. Off. and in Other Countries, Marca Registrada, Hecho en U.S.A.
HarperCollins® is a registered trademark of HarperCollins Publishers.

Printed in the U.S.A.

10 9 8 7 6 5 4 3 2 1

To all the best girlfriends out there!
I believe a woman's life is enriched
by the women she calls friend.
I'm truly blessed because I've too many to name,
but you know who you are.
Thank you for being there for me.

ACKNOWLEDGMENTS

A writer's life is pretty much a solitary journey for long stretches of hours at a time. It's family and friends who make it worthwhile, as much as the joy of the written word. I need to take a moment and thank Andrew, Jacob, and Kristen for putting up with an absent wife and mother. Dreams are as important as anything in life, thanks for letting me pursue mine.

I need to give a shout-out to my Brit, Tracy Stefureak, my beta reader . . . "WHATEVAH." The Art Department at Avon Books/HarperCollins, once again, this cover is a thing of beauty. Esi Sogah, Jessie Edwards, Pam Spengler-Jaffee, Adrienne Di Pietro, you're all wonderful ladies and I love working with you!

I wrote this book listening to Sixx A.M., Tool, Five Finger Death Punch, and the Foo Fighters. Music is an important part of my life and incredibly inspiring. May we Rock On Forever, my friends!

Lastly, to all the readers who've e-mailed and sent kind words my way . . . Thank You! It's such a thrill to know you're all reading my words and loving my characters! Kind of makes the solitary hours worth it . . .

For millennia, the struggle between light and dark, between the upper and lower realms, has been policed by a secret group of warriors culled from every fabric of existence. They are both otherworld and human, male and female. They are light and dark themselves and known to each other as the League of Guardians. Their pledge, to protect the line between dominions and make sure neither side grows too powerful. If they fall, so shall the earth, the heavens, and Hell. And there will be no more.

CHAPTER 1

There's nothing like a trail of blood
to find your way back home.
SIXX: A.M.

Darkness had fallen hours earlier, leaving only the moon's glow to illuminate the house on the hill. Rowan cut the engine of her rental, a frown furling her brow as she stared at the large, rambling home.

The wind whistled and moaned, whipping dead leaves from the ground into a chaotic dance across her windshield. In the distance a once-vibrant sunset settled along the edge of darkness that encroached from below. The day was dying, and soon nightfall would be complete.

She glanced at the parking area next to the gift shop and was surprised to see it empty. The Black Cauldron was one of the premier bed-and-breakfast stops in Salem, and there were always guests in residence. Not even Cedric's car was present. Nana's caretaker and all-around handyman usually shared dinner with her at the Cauldron and had been a fixture at the place for as long as she remembered. He was . . . like family.

Her eyes narrowed as her gaze returned to the house. The porch light was out, and though early evening brought with it a murky shade of gray mist, she saw newspapers piled up next to the door, the steps filled with leaves and debris. It looked as if it hadn't been swept for days.

She pursed her lips and frowned. It was too dark and too silent. Something was wrong.

Very wrong.

Rowan pushed the door open—ignoring the way her stomach rolled with a queasy shudder—and grabbed her overnight bag as she slid from the car. Cool wind caressed bare legs, and a shiver wracked her body as she paused beside the vehicle. She was still dressed for Southern California, not fall in Massachusetts.

She smoothed the lines of her skirt, exhaled, and strode toward the house.

Her Nana had left a message on Rowan's answering machine a few days ago—a quick hello as she had a habit of doing—a check-in that warmed Rowan's heart. She'd been in Europe on business for her law firm and hadn't gotten the message until the night before.

Her grandmother sounded as she always did though her voice held a hint of frailty Rowan hadn't noticed before. As she'd listened to the message again, something hadn't seemed right, and she'd decided to fly back for a surprise visit.

Now that Rowan was home, she was anxious to see her.

Using her toe, she swept a pile of twigs and maple leaves from the corner and bit her lip as the door opened beneath her hand. The house looked closed up, yet it was unlocked? None of this made sense, and the bad feeling in Rowan's stomach doubled. Heck, to be honest, it tripled, spreading a sheen of sweat across her flesh and tightening the muscles in her neck until it was hard to breathe.

"What the hell?" she whispered, as her eyes adjusted to the gloom. "Nana?" Her voice tentative, Rowan set her bag on the floor and locked the door behind her. Silence bore down on her ears. She swallowed nervously as she squinted into the dark. Inside the house, the shadows were thicker . . . longer . . . and more menacing.

Her hand felt along the wall and she flipped a switch, bathing the foyer in a soft glow, and Rowan relaxed a bit as she glanced around. It looked exactly as she remembered. Delicate roses adorned the wallpaper in the entry, and the floor at her feet was worn, the oak planks smooth from years of use and polish. In fact, the faint scent of lemon oil hung in the air as if it had been recently waxed.

The Queen Anne side table—the one that held Nana's guest book—sported a large crystal vase. It was always filled with fresh flowers taken from the gardens out back and, depending on the season, held either a riot of color or the fresh greens of November.

But not tonight. She frowned at the sight of dark green water and the droopy remains of a bunch of sad sunflowers that hung over the side like limp soldiers.

What the hell was going on? Was Nana ill? Why hadn't she called sooner?

She headed toward the back of the house, where her Nana kept a small apartment. As Rowan neared the kitchen the hair on the back of her neck stood on end, and a cold shot of *something* slid across her skin.

Hell, who was she kidding? She knew what that something was, and it wasn't anything good. Not in this part of Salem anyway. It was dark energy. Scratch that. Dark, *powerful,* energy.

Fear for her Nana pushed Rowan forward, and she jogged the last few steps, her out-of-place leopard-print Fendis clicking across the hardwood in a sharp staccato beat.

"Nana?" she whispered hoarsely as she rushed into the kitchen. Her heels slid across the worn wooden floor, and she barely avoided a fall as her hands grabbed the edge of the large kitchen table.

"You've got to be kidding me." She nearly went down again as she struggled to maintain her balance. "Shit!" she hissed, pushing a strand of long hair behind her ear—the wind had pulled it loose from the tight ponytail she sported.

The window above the sink rattled as a wall of rain hit the panes, while shadows from the trees shot spidery legs along the wall as the wind picked up and howled. Okay, this was not the homecoming she'd been expecting.

Rowan nearly slipped again, and her gaze fell to the floor. A large stain marred the golden hardwood, leaving in its wake a macabre splash of dark art. Nausea roiled in her gut, and her eyes widened in horror as her brain processed what her eyes were seeing.

It was blood. There was no mistaking that coppery stench. A lot of blood.

The silence was broken as music erupted from inside her Nana's apartment. "I Fall to Pieces," a sad lament sung by Patsy Cline, cut through the silence, and a sob escaped Rowan's throat. It was Nana's favorite song.

Her heart pounded crazily as she sidestepped around the sticky mess and moved toward her grandmother's rooms. The door was ajar, and soft light fell from inside, spilling into the dark like a sunbeam, beckoning her forward. She paused, fighting fear and anxiety.

She hated Salem—the memories, the nightmares, the danger—the legacy that had taken many and driven her mother mad. It was the reason she'd left. The reason her Nana had forced her to leave.

Where was she?

Rowan slipped inside and was careful to keep to the

shadows. It was automatic, the pull toward the darkness, the need to disappear—old habits died hard. The room appeared empty, but she knew that in the world she inhabited—a world most people were unaware of—looks could be deceiving.

She crept toward Nana's bed, holding her breath as she did so, eyes moving toward every corner. Her fingers grazed the stereo on the night table, and Patsy was silenced.

Rowan exhaled and turned in a full circle, taking in everything—the heavy crimson coverlet that was turned down. The robe flung across the chair at the foot of the bed. The book that lay open upon the pillow, and the reading glasses that rested alongside it.

Her hand trembled as she picked up the book, and a sad smile lifted the corners of her mouth as her fingers touched the yellowed pages. *To Kill a Mockingbird*. How many times had they read the book together?

She held the novel tight against her chest and tried to clamp down the fear that bubbled inside. The blood in the kitchen filled her with dread. The silence that echoed in her ear made her stomach clench.

"Nana, where are you?" she whispered softly.

Somewhere in the house a noise sounded—a footstep or scuff of a heel—and she froze. Her breath caught at the back of her throat in a painful gasp as she tried to squash her reaction. When she heard it again, sweat broke out on her forehead as the fear in her gut tripled with a sharp stab.

Carefully, Rowan put the book back just as it was and reached for her cell phone, cursing beneath her breath when she realized it was in her bag.

Which was in the foyer.

Back where the weird noises were coming from.

Shit.

Someone was out there—she sensed the energy and

knew it was someone powerful. Or rather, some *thing*. At this point she had no idea who or what the hell it was, but she knew it didn't belong. Not here in her Nana's bed-and-breakfast.

Rowan exhaled and centered herself. She needed to be calm.

She crossed to the sitting area beside the stone fireplace. An iron poker rested against the hearth, and she grabbed it, holding it tight as she melted into the dark corner nearest her. With her back protected, she felt more in control and had a clear view of the room.

She closed her eyes for a second, concentrated, and felt the familiar pull of energy sizzle along her fingers. There was no way she could charm or spell, her power was weak, ill-used, but it would have to do.

She heard a step echo, then another. Anger washed over her skin in a hot wave that left her teeth clenched, her fingers tight, and her resolve firm. The bastard was playing with her.

Rowan slipped out of her heels, tossed them to the side, and spread her legs as far as she could considering the constraints of her skirt. She balanced on the balls of her feet and squared her shoulders. There was a certain sort of freedom in the act, and it wouldn't be far off to surmise that in fact she relished the thought of a fight.

Come on, asshole. Let's do this.

Someone passed beyond her line of sight, then there was silence. It stretched long and thin until she wanted to scream. Rowan's heart was nearly beating out of her chest, but her eyes never strayed from the door.

She called to the shadows, coaxing them as they slithered along her flesh and covered her body with their darkness. A small thrill shot through her as the energy around her shifted. She'd denied her gifts for so long she'd forgotten how good it felt to use them.

Slowly the door swung open. Something big stood there a few feet beyond the frame. She couldn't see it, but she sure as hell sensed it. She grimaced, more than a little pissed at herself for letting her powers get so rusty.

Rowan's senses opened up, and she listened intently. She heard a scuff, like a boot scraping along the floor, and held her breath in anticipation. Who would have predicted ten hours ago she'd be hiding in her Nana's room, gripping an iron poker from the fireplace, waiting to attack?

Back in the day, before she'd reinvented herself, it had been the norm—fighting demons and monsters. But Rowan had taken great pains to distance herself from that life— she'd gone to college and now worked at a law firm. She had a gerbil. A boyfriend. *A life.*

She'd traveled halfway across the country to get away from Salem, yet here she was, back in Massachusetts, with the ghosts of her past circling fast.

A tall shape came into view. Impressively huge.

Rephrase: The ghosts of her past were about to kick her ass but good.

The door creaked as it slowly slid all the way open, the hinges dry and squeaky. Her breaths fell lightly as she struggled to keep it together, and with a wave of power, she forced them to quiet.

Rowan's eyes widened as the intruder strode into the room like he had every right to be there, and cast a long shadow along the threadbare carpet. It was a very large, very *male* form.

Denim and leather adorned his powerful frame, emphasizing long limbs and wide shoulders. He moved with the grace of an animal—a predator—and she held her breath as his gaze swung toward her.

Was she safe? Could he see her?

His face was in shadow, but the square jaw was visible.

He reeked of power; even in her weakened state she was able to sense the enormity of it, and a sliver of fear bled through her determination.

Something awful and tragic had happened in her Nana's home. Had this man been involved? If so, what was the extent of his involvement and what did he want? Why had he come back?

He took a step forward into the light and her mouth went dry. A day's worth of beard shadowed his chin. Dirty blond hair as thick as sable framed a face that was, without a doubt, the most devastatingly handsome one she'd ever seen. *Ever.* Hollywood had nothing on this guy.

Classic features aligned perfectly to create a face that was as arresting as the entire length of him. He was tall and brooding, with intense eyes an unusual shade of piercing gold.

Rowan knew she couldn't take him. There was no way in hell. The man was well over six feet in height—A) she'd just tossed her heels and at five-foot-six, she didn't even reach his chin and B) the power that clung to him was incredibly strong. It cast a fractured light around his frame, one bled through with gold and black.

She'd never seen anything like it.

The stereo erupted once more, and Patsy's mournful soprano sliced through the quiet. Rowan's heart took off, banging out of control, and she tried to swallow her fear as the stranger turned fully in her direction. Sweet Mother of God, could he see her?

For one second she thought she heard her Nana's voice whisper to her. *Always keep them off kilter. Do the unexpected.*

A shot of courage rolled through her and pushed Rowan into action. She fell from shadow and stepped forward. "Who the hell are you and where is my grandmother?"

Surprise flickered across his face though it quickly disappeared. She swallowed tightly as the stranger's eyes narrowed into twin strips of black oil. There was no trace of gold left in their depths, that ray of sunshine fled instantly. He raised his hand, and her fingers clutched the iron poker so tightly, they cramped.

She flinched as he flicked his wrist—a subtle motion—and the music silenced.

He arched a brow. "Granddaughter?"

His eyes glittered, a strange shimmer deep within their depths. His voice was low, and she detected a slight accent when he spoke. She couldn't place it.

"I won't ask again." Rowan straightened, glad her voice was firm, no matter that her insides were mush. "Who are you and why is there"—she took a moment—"blood in the kitchen?" A small tremor caressed the end of her sentence, but it couldn't be helped.

She was freaking out, scared as hell, and there was a mountain of muscle between her and freedom.

The stranger cursed. "No one mentioned a granddaughter."

"Listen—"

His hand silenced her—an arrogant *shut up,* as he cocked his head to the side and frowned. "We've got company."

He crossed to the window and yanked the drapes into place in one quick motion. At the same time the glow from the night-light was extinguished.

Rowan didn't know what to think, but she was starting to get pissed off.

"This is crazy. Where is my Nana?" She took a step forward.

"Cara is . . ." His voice trailed into silence, and he scowled as the windows began to shake, the panes rattling against a fresh onslaught of wind and rain that hit the glass like bullets against steel.

"She's what?" Rowan's eyes were huge as she stared into a face devoid of emotion. There was a coldness there that was unsettling.

"I'm sorry," he said abruptly. "She's dead."

The iron poker slipped from her fingers as she stared up at the stranger. She heard the words, but her brain wasn't translating them. Rowan shook her head, "I don't . . . that can't be, I'd know . . ." She couldn't articulate the words in her mind. None of this made sense. Her eyes fell to the book on the bed, the reading glasses at its side, and she felt something inside her break.

Nana.

In that moment she knew the truth, felt the pain and the guilt. *It's my fault.* The whisper slid through her mind. *I never should have left.*

A low keening erupted, one that shot up several decibels in seconds until the window shattered. Glass blew everywhere and shredded the curtains into billowing tatters, long plumes of crimson silk that fluttered like crazed feathers in the wind.

Rowan winced at the sharp sting of shrapnel as it sliced into her arms and legs. Searing pain ripped across her cheek, but she paid no mind. The wind pulled at her, whirling into the room with a hazy cloud of freezing mist that made it difficult to breathe.

The touch of his hand on her flesh pulled her from the darkness. The roaring dialed down, and as she stared up at him, her lungs expanded, and she was able to draw a shuddering breath.

"Who . . . who did this?" she rasped. She had no idea who the hell he was, but in that moment she knew he meant her no harm. The darkness, *the evil,* wasn't in this room. It was out there, beyond the broken window.

"I think your answer is there." His solid, flat, black eyes

were intense, and the white of his teeth flashed through the gloom as he spoke. He pointed outside, and Rowan turned to the window. Thunder and lightning had joined the chaotic dance of rain and wind. A bolt of energy streaked across the sky, illuminating the entire front yard in a flash of white.

It was a quick, precise hit, and gave just enough light for her to see seven hulking figures standing in the pouring rain.

Their scent reached her, and she nearly gagged on the thickness of it. *Demons.* Their eyes glowed red. *Blood demons.* A weird calm settled over her. She'd come full circle it seemed.

Rowan squared her shoulders and glanced up at the man beside her. "Who sent you?"

He was silent for a moment. "Someone who cared deeply for your grandmother."

She felt her stomach twist. She didn't like the stranger's vague answer. Her Nana was dead, and outside seven blood demons called—his presence was no coincidence.

A guttural cry rent the night—a harsh echo that slid like nails against chalk—and her hackles rose. She didn't have time to worry about the details.

"I'm Rowan. What should I call you?" she asked as she grabbed the iron poker off the ground.

"Azaiel."

The name whispered through her mind.

The demons howled in unison, their voices rising into a crescendo of noise that dropped suddenly until there was nothing but the rain to break the heavy silence. It was eerie.

The tallest of the demons grunted and started toward them, a deadly machete trailing behind him in the mud as it took slow, deliberate steps. Another series of lightning strikes crashed across the sky, and its ugly horned face split open into what she supposed was a grin.

"I'm sorry, but it looks like things are about to get nasty," she whispered, her gaze focused upon the gathering outside. "But then again, with a name like that, I suppose you've not forgotten."

"Forgotten what?" he asked, moving beside her.

Rowan whispered. "What it feels like to get your ass kicked."

CHAPTER 2

Azaiel turned from the woman and peered out into the dark, instantly dismissing such a notion. The ominous keening picked up once more, an off-key chorus that grated something fierce.

"Let's go." He had no intention of getting his ass kicked, especially not by the slimy bastards outside.

"The attic." Her voice was husky.

He knew she'd just suffered one hell of a shock, but there was no time for hand-holding. "Lead the way."

She ran past him, and Azaiel followed her through the darkened house and up the stairs located in the foyer. The wind and rain continued to duke it out, lashing against the brick with an intensity that screamed otherworld.

This was no ordinary storm. This was a gathering of the elements, called to this place by someone with great power.

"Wait here," she whispered. They were on the second floor, and Azaiel paused as she slipped inside a room a few feet away. A crash and shattering glass was heard below. There wasn't much time.

"This way." The woman, Rowan, had a large bag slung across her shoulders. It was old and weathered, with a well-used look to the peat-colored distressed leather. Her cream-colored blouse had come loose, the buttons half undone, the ends no longer tucked neatly into the waist of her skirt. Her feet were bare, and her hair fell from its binding, long strands of crimson that hung wildly about her neck.

Diamonds glittered at her delicate ears. She was, if nothing else, a study in contrast.

A second stairwell was located at the far end of the landing, and they slipped up to the attic. It was dark, filled with all sorts of things—boxes, trunks, books, and furniture. There was a small window located to his right, but other than that, no other way to gain access except the stairs they'd just taken.

She unpacked her bag with careful, deliberate actions. "Do you know what we're dealing with?" Her voice had changed. There was a new strength there, one fueled by tragedy. In situations like this it was the best kind, and he hoped it would be enough. One dead witch was all he had time to deal with.

"Blood demons," she continued. "They're nasty." She glanced up at him and hoisted an impressive crossbow onto her shoulders. "First off don't let them get close. Their tongues have a radius of nearly two feet, and the poison they wield"—she grimaced—"well, let's just say that pretty face of yours will never look the same."

Azaiel watched in silence. She was nervous, high on adrenaline. That was good, she'd need it.

He wasn't concerned with the blood demons—not for himself—he could eat them for lunch and go back for seconds. It was the other, the malevolent presence he sensed beyond that held his attention. It watched and waited—he felt its interest—and *that* had him concerned. The energy in the air was thick with the scent of something ancient. But what did it want?

"Here." Her voice was tense.

Azaiel arched a brow. She walked toward him, a dagger in her hand. "It's charmed. I don't know how strong it is." She shrugged, shook her head, "It's been lying in my bag for years."

Azaiel accepted the dagger and felt a jolt of energy shoot up his arm as he touched it. "I think it's still got some juice," he murmured. Her eyes widened. They were blue, cerulean blue, like the warm waters of the Caribbean.

Her eyes had been blue as well. Azaiel turned away, banishing thoughts of Toniella, the betrayer. Would there ever come a time that thoughts of his ex-lover didn't taunt him?

"They're coming." He glanced at Rowan. "Make sure you separate their—"

"—heads, or pierce the brain through the ears. I know. I may be rusty, but I remember how to kill them."

He watched her load the impressive crossbow in seconds, and she slung it across her back before scooping up extra daggers and guns. She tossed him a Glock—modified of course—and a bag of ammunition.

She squared her shoulders and turned to face the stairs.

Azaiel shoved the gun into the back pocket of his jeans and felt the familiar rush of power flood his cells. He had no need for human weapons, modified or not, but sometimes it was fun to shoot the damn things.

He glanced at the dagger in his hand. The hilt was inscribed with powerful runes, and his fingers tingled with the magick that resided there. This he'd keep. There was something poetic about using a sharp blade to slice through demon hide.

Rowan swore as five demons erupted from the hole in the floor. She shot two right away, their screams of pain as the charmed arrows ripped through their skulls, loud and abrasive.

They kept on, lunging toward her. But the little witch was

fast. She ran toward a large trunk and used it to launch herself into the air. She sailed overtop them, and the crossbow let off once more, rifling their bodies with another round of the deadly spears.

The remaining three rushed Azaiel, and a smile broke over his face as they neared. The first one stopped suddenly, nostrils flaring, and Azaiel took great satisfaction at the look of fear that crept into its eyes.

These blood demons were bottom feeders—weak, pathetic creatures. They were no match for someone like Azaiel. He flashed a smile——one as cold as a winter morn—and held out his hand, beckoning with his fingers.

Come on, assholes.

They hesitated, and Azaiel attacked. He moved so quickly, he was inches from them before they could blink. He drop-kicked the closest, grinning as bone cracked, ribs separated, and blood erupted. The demon went flying into a solid support post and squealed harshly at the force of the hit. The second was silenced rather quickly by the crushing grip of his hand at its neck. He grabbed hold of it with his other and twisted violently, separating the head from its body in seconds.

Sulfur-laced blood spewed everywhere, and the third demon howled in anger as it slammed into Azaiel. This one was a little different. It was larger, heavier, and more than a little pissed off.

Azaiel rolled with it, his body loosening as he went. They crashed into a towering pile of boxes that toppled and fell around them. The demon hauled off and swung its fist. Azaiel's head snapped back from the force of it, and he spat out blood as he rolled to the side.

Enough games. He was up in a second, his fist flying out and sending the demon flying backward. He flipped his dagger into the air, caught it, aimed, and nailed the son of a bitch to the wall.

It screamed bloody murder, curses in an ancient tongue that no one but an ancient would understand—something the bottom feeders shouldn't know. A frown fell over Azaiel's features. Who the hell did these demons answer to?

Azaiel growled as he walked toward the snarling demon. Its skin was smoking where the dagger had pierced it. The demon would have yanked it from its body, but Azaiel was there, one hand upon its forehead, the other gripping the hilt and holding it in place.

A loud crash sounded behind him, but Azaiel paid no mind. From what he'd seen, the witch could more than hold her own.

"Why have you come? Who sent you?" he asked, watching the demon closely as the monster struggled to speak.

"We're collecting." It sneered, staring at him in defiance. "Witches."

"So *you* killed the old one, Cara." Azaiel twisted the dagger some more and smiled as the demon roared in pain. He didn't mind this part—the torture—though it was much nicer to be doling it out rather than receiving for once.

Surprise flickered in the demon's eyes, and that made Azaiel uneasy. The bastard stared back at Azaiel in silence but didn't utter another word.

"You had no idea she's been murdered," he said, more to himself.

The demon hissed, its eyes now full of malice. "Doesn't matter. The bounty extends to anyone who carries the coven's mark." The demon's gaze moved behind Azaiel. "The redheaded bitch's days are numbered." It smiled, a wheezing breath escaping from its lungs. The charmed dagger was doing a bang-up job. "They will keep coming."

A bounty. Interesting.

"Who ordered the mark?" Azaiel pressed on.

The demon laughed. "Not who, but *what*."

Azaiel leaned forward and let a glimpse of his true power

show. The demon's eyes widened, and its body stilled as it stared into Azaiel's eyes.

"I know you," it said, grunting in pain as Azaiel withdrew the dagger. The demon staggered, its face pale as the charmed poison worked its way through its veins. "You're the Fallen. The ancient Seraphim who escaped the Hell realm." It gritted its serrated teeth and snarled. "Toniella's bitch—"

Rage colored Azaiel's vision. "Nice to know my reputation precedes me." He lunged forward and with one clean swipe, destroyed the demon. He watched, chest heaving as its head tumbled to the ground, followed by its body.

An image of the betrayer rose before him. Her long blond hair was all around him, her scent filled his nostrils, and for a second, he was back there. *In Hell.* Locked away in his prison for eons, with the knowledge that the betrayer had put him there—a woman he'd loved.

A woman he'd sinned for.

"Watch out!" The scream ripped him from the past into a very different reality. Azaiel whirled around and ducked, barely missing the wrong end of a machete as it swung toward him. The blade whizzed past and embedded into the wall behind him.

The fucker he'd sent flying had rebounded.

Azaiel grabbed the machete, yanked hard, and faced the demon, angry that he'd been so easily distracted. The demon snarled and lunged forward, opening its mouth, ready to let loose the poison its tongue wielded.

It had no chance. Azaiel moved with preternatural speed. He brought the machete down hard, slicing through bone and flesh with ease.

He stared down at the remains with disgust, stepped over them, and shook a few remnants loose from his boots. He glanced at Rowan. The witch's blouse was splattered with blood, bits and pieces of gore clung to her hair. At her feet lay three demons—their bodies already decomposing as the charmed poison continued to work its way through their systems.

Their eyes caught and held and for a second—for the briefest moment of time—he felt something other than the hatred and self-loathing he'd been living with for longer than he cared to remember. He looked away, cracked his neck, and when he gazed upon her once more, it was gone.

"Stay put." He nodded toward the window. "Until I'm sure it's safe."

Azaiel moved past Rowan, but her hand shot out, and she grabbed his arm. Her energy sizzled along his flesh, and he turned to her in surprise. Her eyes were now fully black, the pupils dilated. They shimmered like pools of liquid ebony.

She was no ordinary witch.

"I'm coming with you."

His eyes narrowed as he gazed down at her and frowned. "There's a bounty on your head. You will stay inside."

"A bounty." It wasn't a question, and she wasn't surprised. "No kidding." She looked away as silence fell between them. Azaiel studied the woman. She knew something—or at the very least suspected something.

Lightning cracked across the night sky, splitting through the dark and illuminating the room in a flash of white energy. It was then that he felt it once more, the probing, silent presence beyond. A small gasp escaped the witch, and he saw the way her eyes darted toward the window as a mix of emotions crossed her face. She pushed at the mess of hair around her face and wiped her mouth, avoiding his eyes as she did so. She felt it, too.

Interesting.

"Stay here and keep to the shadows. Do not show your-self unless it's me."

She opened her mouth to speak, but Azaiel was down

the stairs before she could utter a word, and he threw up a barrier of magick that should hold her for bit. How long depended on just how much mojo the young witch possessed. Azaiel hadn't been given much information but from what he gathered, the James line of witches had been blessed with powerful magick.

When he reached the bottom of the stairs, he paused. There was no power, so everything was awash in darkness though the steady strikes of lightning illuminated the dead sunflowers on the table and a bag on the floor near the door.

A ripple of energy and the touch of heat on his skin had him fully alert. His nostrils flared, and he gathered his power. Something was outside, just beyond the porch.

A thrill rushed through Azaiel, and he clenched his hands as a shot of adrenaline pumped through his body. Was it sad that he felt alive when he was about to maim or kill? Whatever the reason, he'd take it. Anything was better than the emptiness and hatred he'd felt for millennia.

He moved with stealth, melting into the shadows, and with a flick of his wrist, the door yawned open. He slipped outside between the sheets of rain and wind, his gaze moving quickly as he sought the enemy.

Azaiel hopped the railing with ease and crouched low, letting the cool water wash over him like a blessing from above. Ironic that thought.

It was eerily silent, with only the sound of rain against the roof echoing in his ear and the dance of wind through the trees. Overhead the moon was hidden, and night covered everything in a murky gray mist. Lightning struck at random, sparks of light that tainted the surroundings in fire. They sizzled along the ground, then were gone.

He blinked, wiped some excess moisture from his eyes, and focused on the small building to his left. He'd start there.

Azaiel slid through the dark, a silent assassin who blended with the shadows like a plume of smoke amongst a fire.

He felt a shift in the air, a sliver of matter that didn't belong, and changed direction, approaching a small car in the driveway with caution. Something was there, just beyond the vehicle.

Azaiel withdrew his dagger and jumped, easily clearing the car with a few feet to spare, but there was nothing for him. No demon, human, or other. He felt the barest whisper of energy against his skull, and slammed his mental barriers shut.

And then it was gone.

Azaiel's breathing returned to normal as the adrenaline inside dissipated, washed away by the cold rain. He frowned as his eyes scanned the entire area. Damn, but he'd been itching for a fight.

He turned and made his way to the porch, and once sheltered from the elements, he reached into his pocket and withdrew a cell phone.

It was answered on the first ring.

"Cale," the voice was terse.

"It's Azaiel." He knew the Seraphim warrior hated his guts, but then, every member of the League felt the same way. They all thought he was untrustworthy. A wild card. And they'd be right. Every day he fought the darkness inside and wondered what the hell Bill saw in him that was redeemable.

"You make it to Salem?" Cale asked.

"Had a welcoming party waiting for me."

There was a pause on the other end. "A little elaboration would be nice."

"A pack of blood demons. Seems the coven has been marked."

"Marked?" Cale cursed. "Who the hell would mark a coven as powerful as Cara's?"

"I don't know," he admitted. "I don't think they knew Cara had been murdered though they had no qualms about going after her granddaughter instead."

"Her granddaughter," Cale murmured softly. "The red-head?"

"Yeah."

"I thought she was out of the picture. Last I heard she'd taken off to California."

"Well, she's back." Azaiel leaned against the railing, watching the now-receding storm clouds. A clear night sky winked down at him, full of stars and black velvet.

"Was Cara marked because of her affiliation with the League of Guardians?"

Azaiel exhaled, straightened his body. "That remains unanswered." He thought of the powerful entity he'd sensed and glanced into the darkness.

"Get back to me when you've got one. And about my bike, that's a '69 Shovelhead, you bastard. You had no right to take—"

Azaiel pocketed the cell and grinned. The Harley had been parked outside The Devil's Gate when he'd been ordered to Salem a few days ago. Damned if he cared who it belonged to. That it had been Cale's was fucking perfect. They'd never gotten along. Not even when they were new and full of light, although Cale's exact origins were still a mystery, even to Azaiel.

He hopped the stairs, entered the house, and paused. A strange scratching noise echoed into the silence, and he followed it down the hall to the kitchen. The soft light from overhead illuminated the room. It was neat and tidy, with nothing out of place save for the woman on the floor.

Rowan was on her hands and knees, scrubbing the bloodstains that marred the otherwise pristine wood floor with steady, determined strokes.

She paused, dipped her hand in the soapy bucket beside her though she didn't turn to look at him. "It's not coming out." She sounded winded and upset. "It's like sticking, and this water is hot and I squirted the whole bottle of dish soap into it and it shouldn't be sticking and I"—she shook her head, her voice now tremulous—"I mean, it's blood, right? It should just come off, nice and easy." She exhaled and kept on. "I just . . . it's soaked into the wood or something, and I don't know why it won't come off. I . . ." Her voice broke, and she continued in a whisper, "I just want it gone."

She bent over once more, her slight shoulders hunched as she swiped furiously at the floor, then paused. "Do you know where she . . . where she is?" Her voice was barely above a whisper.

"No. I'm sorry."

She waited a second, then began to scrub again, her hand circling fast.

Something unthawed inside him, a chunk of ice breaking free. It had been so long since he'd experienced any emotion other than ones tinged with darkness that he wasn't sure what it was.

But he'd take it. Maybe there was hope for him after all.

Azaiel stripped his jacket off, threw it onto the table, and grabbed another sponge from the kitchen counter. He felt the weight of her blue eyes following him as he knelt beside her.

"You don't have to . . . I can do this . . ." she whispered, shaking her head.

Azaiel dunked the sponge into the warm water. "I know you can," he said gruffly, "but you shouldn't have to do it alone."

CHAPTER 3

Rowan woke with a start, her chest pounding and muscles tight. She flung her legs over the side of the bed and leaned over the edge, groaning, as the room spun. Oh God, she felt like she was going to throw up.

She pressed her head between her knees in an effort to stop the panic inside. The terror beat at her mercilessly, and she knew if she didn't get it together, she'd lose it big-time. So she squeezed her eyes shut and tried with all her might to make the panic go away.

Long seconds ticked by and eventually her breathing returned to normal, her heart rate slowed. Sweat pooled along the top of her lip, and she clenched shaking fingers into a fist. It had been forever since she'd suffered an attack.

Her lips thinned. Six years would be her *forever. Fucking Salem.*

She tucked loose strands of hair behind her ears and glanced around her old bedroom. The furniture seemed smaller than she remembered, antique white dressed in soft pastels that were heavy on the pink. Hot tears stung the corner of her eyes, and she wiped them away angrily.

A long, shuddering breath escaped as her thoughts turned to her grandmother.

Rowan's clenched hands tightened, the nails biting through skin until she drew blood. The pain was good. She deserved it.

Her grandmother had died alone. Violently. That was on Rowan, and one day she'd grieve properly. But not now. There was no time. She had much to do.

Her overnight bag was on the floor beside the bed, her bloodstained skirt and blouse stuffed in plastic nearby. She grabbed a change of clothes, groaning as she stood. God, she ached all over. Clearly she was out of shape, no longer the lithe, demon-fighting witch of the past.

Considering she had a shitload of hunting in her immediate future, she sure as hell needed to work on that.

Rowan drew back the blinds and winced as piercing rays of sunlight rippled into her room. She glanced down, arched a brow at the sight of the large motorcycle parked beside her rental, and sighed.

It must belong to the mysterious stranger who'd shown up at her door. *Azaiel.*

She mouthed his name, her lips moving slowly as the syllables rolled off her tongue. The name was familiar, but she couldn't place it. If only Nana was here.

After offering to help her, he'd not said a single word. The entire time they'd washed the blood from the kitchen floor—nothing.

He was different from anyone she'd ever met. It wasn't just his silence, his lack of words. It was something in his eyes—something she recognized. *Pain.* A soul stained with a darkness that lingered. Seemed he was just as damaged as Rowan.

She sighed and pushed away from the window. The man had an overabundance of testosterone, and the intensity she sensed beneath the surface put her on edge.

He was otherworld, but what the hell was he? Demon?

Shifter? Magick? It was weird that she had no sense of his origin.

All she knew for sure was that he was a complication, and that's something she could do without. There was no way he could stay. Not with what she had planned. She needed to be on her game one hundred percent.

She let the blinds fall back into place and headed for the bathroom. Maybe he'd be gone by the time she was showered.

A half hour later, she was dressed in boots, jeans, and T-shirt. She headed downstairs, her fingers trailing along the railing, a bittersweet smile on her lips as a kaleidoscope of memories danced in front of her. This had been her home once. She'd been happy here, back before her mother had gone crazy.

She grabbed the vase off the table in the foyer and headed toward the kitchen. She stopped just outside the room, her gaze drawn to the now-pristine wood floor. There was nothing to indicate murder had occurred in the house. No tremor of darkness in the air. Nothing to show that her Nana was gone.

"Dead," she whispered softly, wincing at the coldness of the word.

She gritted her teeth and stepped into the kitchen though she was careful to avoid the area that had been scrubbed clean the night before.

Rowan tossed the limp flowers into the bucket beneath the sink, rinsed the vase, and placed it on the counter. Outside the window, sunlight danced upon Nana's pond, sunflowers swayed in the breeze, and to the left, her pumpkin patch was ripe, ready to be harvested.

A nervous flutter messed with her stomach, and a wave of nausea rolled through her. Samhain was only a few weeks away. She didn't have much time. She needed to gather her

coven, spring her mother from the loony bin, find the grimoire . . .

And then she needed to hunt.

"Was wondering how long you'd sleep."

His voice was deep, husky, and she froze at the sound
of it.

Rowan took a few seconds to gather her thoughts and
turned. His shoulder rested against the doorframe, his long,
denim-clad legs crossed casually. The jeans he wore were
faded, well used, and rode low on his hips, held in place by a
wide leather belt. His black T-shirt was formfitting, stretching taut across wide shoulders and muscular arms.

His strange golden eyes were intense as he stared at her.
He was without a doubt visually stunning—perfect even—
with his square jaw, chiseled nose, and full mouth. The day-
old shadow along his cheeks only added to his sex appeal.

But perfect didn't belong in her kitchen, especially the
kind that was wrapped in danger and smelled like sin.

"Why are you still here?" she asked roughly, making no
attempt to mask her irritation.

"I'm not the enemy, Rowan," he said simply, pushing
away from the doorframe as he moved toward her.

Rowan. The way he said her name sent shivers running
along her skin.

She eyed him warily and fought the urge to step back.
"Just because you helped with the"—she gestured wildly—
"blood and stuff, and wasted a few demons . . . that doesn't
make us friends."

His eyes narrowed, and he stopped inches from her.
Damn, but she wished she'd gone for her six-inch boots instead of the comfy Docs that adorned her feet. They were
old, well-worn, but gave her no advantage when it came to
height.

The man in front of her was well over six feet. And he

was dangerous. His energy was strong, lethal, tinged with something she'd never felt before.

Not good.

She glanced up into his eyes. "Let's cut the bull. Why are you really here?"

"I told you last night, Rowan, I was sent by someone who—"

"Yeah, I know what you said, someone who cares about my grandmother." She shook her head. "Well, my Nana is dead, so their fucking concern is days late." She shrugged. "I'd rather have a name. I'll ask again, who sent you?"

Rowan didn't like the way he went silent. His eyes shimmered as he stared down at her, and she took a step back, needing some distance between them.

"You're not safe." His tone was matter-of-fact, and his eyes never left hers.

"Wow, that's pretty goddamn observant." She arched a brow. "Again, why do you care?"

He opened his mouth, but Rowan had had enough. "Never mind, I don't want to know. Let me be blunt, Azaiel. *I* don't want *you* here, and I'm asking nicely for you to leave. This is my problem, and I'm going to take care of it."

He stood with his arms crossed and glared at her, which only managed to piss her off more than she already was. A thread of pain weaved its way through her skull, and she winced as it settled behind her eyes. Great. A migraine in the works.

The phone rang, a shrill alarm that cut through the tense air with the subtlety of a sledgehammer. On the third ring, the answering machine cut in, and bittersweet longing clutched at Rowan as her grandmother's voice filled the silence, her tone cheery.

Hello, you've reached The Black Cauldron. Please leave a message, and I'll get back to you shortly.

A beep sounded, followed by a man's voice, heavy with a slow Californian drawl.

"Hey, ah . . . this message is for Rowan. Babe, you're not answering your cell, and you were supposed to check in last night." There was a pause. "Call me when you get this."

She turned from Azaiel, exhaling loudly as she ran fingers along her temple. Crap. Mason.

"Who's that?"

"No one," she answered a little too quickly and knew she was losing her edge. Azaiel threw her off her game. "You need to leave," she said once more.

A tingle of energy slid across her skin, and she froze. He was right there, so close the heat from his body teased the coolness of her flesh.

"I'm not going anywhere until I get some answers."

There was an arrogant tone to his voice that pressed hard on Rowan's last button. Anger unfurled, deep in her gut, and her fingers tingled as a shot of energy sizzled through her veins.

She whirled around, chest heaving and eyes blazing.

"I don't have time for this shit." She pushed him, hard, and felt a sense of satisfaction that she was able to move him back a few inches. The man was a solid mass of muscle. Score one for the witch.

"My grandmother is dead—gone forever—*murdered*." She let out a ragged breath and tried to get hold of her emotions. She wouldn't break down in front of this man. "I've got two weeks to find the bastard who's responsible. So I suggest you get the hell out of my way or else."

"Two weeks?"

"Samhain is in . . ." she shook her head, mad because she'd already said too much. "Forget it."

"Who's marked your coven?" He moved closer, and her hands itched with the need to zap him once more, this time with ramped-up juice. She clenched her fingers as she fought the urge.

"It's not about the coven." She took a step back, frustrated and filled with anger. "Nana was just collateral damage, and if I don't deal with this soon, there will be more bodies." Oh God, to hear the words was like a punch to the gut.

"If not the coven, then what?" His arm shot out, and he grabbed her wrist.

She glanced down. His hand was large, his skin golden against her paleness. She felt his strength; it had a subtle hum of energy that slid over his flesh and melted into hers.

"Let me go." She barely managed to get the words out. She felt her temper tickling the edges of her mind and clamped down quickly. She needed to keep a cool head—*needed to stay in control*. Bad things happened when she wasn't.

Silence filled the space between them as she stared up in defiance. The gold of his eyes shimmered, and she watched as small rivers of black bled through them.

"Don't make me hurt you," she whispered. The slow burn of energy in her gut erupted and slid over her body in a seductive crawl. It infused her cells, electrifying them.

His grasp tightened, and his eyes were hard as he glared at her. "Why do you defy me?" His voice was low, controlled. "I'm offering to help, and you would turn it away."

She yanked her hand from his. "For Christ sakes, can we not do this?" Rowan snarled, her anger bubbling over into ugly. She was done. Her pin had been pulled, and there was no going back. "Why do I *defy* you? What are you, a fucking Neanderthal? You hiding Tarzan's balls in there?"

Her gaze fell to the crotch of his jeans.

"There's no room for anything that's not mine," he answered dryly.

Her cheeks reddened as a slow smile drifted across his face, and her hand rose, the tips of her fingers sizzling with a blast of energy. She wanted nothing more than to wipe the smile from him, in the most painful way she could.

"Do it." He was goading her.

Fuck you.

Rowan ducked, blasting a shot of energy at him as she twisted, her booted foot aimed for his gut. Unfortunately, she came up empty and would have fallen on her ass, except two strong arms slid around her midsection, pulling her from behind.

Goddamn but he's fast. What the hell is he?

She cursed as the released energy exploded into the wall and watched as bits of plaster crumbled to the floor, along with the cuckoo clock—the one that hadn't cuckooed since she was ten. It crashed to the floor and, wonders of wonders, let out one sad "cuckoo" before the little blue bird was silent once more.

She tried to wiggle free from his grasp—even considered biting him—but gave up. He was too strong.

"Who watched from the shadows last night?" His breath was hot against her neck, and shivers ran down her spine as he spoke. His body was hard, harder than she'd imagined, and she bit her lip at the realization her ass was tucked securely between his powerful thighs. "I know you felt it."

She shifted, and he stilled, his right arm underneath her breasts as the other moved down to her hip. Something changed; the air thickened as the energy between them darkened.

"Look, nothing personal, but this is not your fight." She shook her head. "It's never been anyone's but mine." The anger left her suddenly, like air whooshing from a balloon. She would have stumbled if not for his arms. "I thought I could outrun it." She exhaled a shaky breath. "I thought I could disappear and live someone else's life—*a normal life.* Go to college, get a job . . . and I did for a while."

She leaned back against him, resting her body upon the solid wall of man behind her. It was nice, to have that security, even for only a few seconds.

"It felt nice for the two minutes it lasted." There was no way to keep the bitterness from her voice.

"Who are you running from, Rowan?"

Rowan glanced toward her Nana's rooms. If only she'd come sooner. If only . . .

"Rowan?" he prompted.

"Let me go," she whispered.

He released her, and she moved a few feet from him. Outside, a ribbon of leaves blew by as the wind picked up, gold, reds, and shit brown. In a few weeks, the trees would be bare, the ground covered in early-morning frost. Where would she be?

"My family has lived in Salem since the early 1600s. Our coven fled Europe when the witch trials were at their bloodiest." She shook her head. "Was it bad luck they ended up here? Or was it fate?"

What are you doing?

Rowan ignored her conscience and turned to Azaiel. She saw his strength. His warrior soul. His arrogant attitude.

He wanted to help? He was going to need all of that and a shitload more.

She carefully lifted the heavy mane of hair off her neck and turned just so. She knew he'd see the mark clearly. It wasn't hard to miss.

When she couldn't stand the silence any longer, she let her hair fall and turned to him. He stared at her, his mouth tight, eyes hard. Something stirred within him. She felt the shift.

After a few moments, she spoke. "Now do you understand?"

CHAPTER 4

The mark lay at the base of Rowan's neck, a coiled snake ready to strike, its long, forked tongue pointed upward. It appeared dull, not at all like the luminescent ones he'd seen in the Hell realm, and there had been many. Azaiel frowned. The mark belonged to a demon lord—of that there was no doubt. But who? And why?

He thought of the powerful presence he'd sensed earlier. Azaiel ran his hands over the day-old beard along his jaw. This wasn't good. Things had just become a lot more complicated.

"You must explain," he said finally, as she let her curtain of hair fall back into place. She moved away from him, her limbs long and graceful, and leaned her hip against the kitchen table.

"No." She gazed at him, eyes as huge as saucers, her mouth pinched in anger. "I'm done sharing." She folded her arms across her chest. "It's your turn."

"My turn?" Her attitude intrigued him. "Is this a game?" He considered her words—knew he was going to have to give her something—but what to share? The League's protection was paramount.

"If this were a game, I'd have kicked your ass out of here last night, and you would never have seen it coming." Her eyes flashed. "If this were a game, my Nana wouldn't be dead, and my mother . . ." She shook her head savagely. "This is no game. This is life and death, and the curse ends here. Right now. With me."

"Curse?" Azaiel didn't like the sound of that.

"Shut up. I'm asking the questions." Her chest heaved, and Azaiel couldn't help but notice the strain of the thin T-shirt against the soft roundness of her breasts. She was slim, with the lines of a dancer, but her curves were all woman. Breasts that were more than a handful, hips that rounded nicely, and a butt that filled out the worn jeans in a way any man would like.

His body reacted instantly in a way that surprised him.

He'd not felt desire—true physical desire—in more time than he cared to remember. The lust he'd felt for the eagle shifter Skye Knightly had been twisted, born from the darkness he'd fallen into. But this . . . this was something else entirely. It was not expected, and it made him wary.

It brought to mind how weak he'd been in the past and the treacherous path he'd chosen. He would never let a woman get under his skin and steal his control again. *Never.*

"Who sent you here?" She was angry. He saw this in her darkened eyes, which were now a shade past navy.

Azaiel decided it couldn't hurt to feed the little bird a few bread crumbs—a bit of the truth would suffice. "An old friend of your grandmother's."

"Yeah, I got that last night, but it would sure as hell be nice to a have a *name.*"

Energy erupted into the air around her. It shimmered around her head like a halo of red, and once more he sensed the true depth of her power. The James witches came from no ordinary line.

"You would know him as Bill."

Her brow furled, and she repeated, "Bill?" She chewed

her lip for a moment, brows furled in concentration. "Would Bill be a short, fat, round little guy? With a motormouth and an insane candy addiction?"

"That would be the one," Azaiel answered dryly. If she only knew what Askelon's human facade hid, she wouldn't be so cavalier. But he supposed that was the very reason that Askelon—or Bill as he was known in the human realm—paraded around in such ill-equipped human skin. He wanted no one to know what really flowed inside his veins.

"I haven't seen him in years." She ran her fingers along the top of the kitchen table. "I just thought he was some eccentric guy who was sweet on Nana."

Rowan looked up at him suddenly. "What are you?" There was suspicion in her voice. He heard it in her words and saw the way it colored her eyes even darker. "You're otherworld, but I've never met anyone like you before."

Outside, sunlight played upon the window, casting vignettes of shadow that fell from the trees to parade across the windowsill. It was a beautiful fall day. Not a cloud in the sky, and the sunshine was golden. The brightness of it called to a part of his soul that was long dead. The part of him most thought was beyond redemption.

Except for Bill, of course.

"Hello?" Rowan spoke sarcastically and waved her hand in front of Azaiel's face.

"I am Seraphim."

She was surprised though quick to hide her reaction. "Seraphim," she repeated. "As in Angels?"

Azaiel's face darkened as his thoughts turned to his past. "Humans would call us that, but simply put, Angels is too broad a term. Like the humans who populate this realm, we are many different kinds—different breeds if you will." He shrugged. "Seraphim are the most powerful sect in existence, and I'm one of the original seven." He said the words not to be boastful but because they were the truth. The thought of his betrayal and subsequent fall drew a scowl. His eyes flashed, and he took a step toward her. "There is nothing angelic about me."

For a moment only silence accompanied the whistle of wind and the moaning protest of the old house.

"Bill sent you here because he knew my grandmother was already dead." She gazed at him intently, blue eyes glued to gold.

"Yes," he answered simply. "Bill asked me to find the person responsible for your grandmother's death. He cared deeply for her, which is why I won't leave until I have an answer for him."

And until I know Cara's death isn't related to her association with the League.

"Is he . . ." She frowned. "Is he like you? How did he know she'd been killed?"

Azaiel shook his head. "That I can't answer, but it should be enough that I'm here and willing to do whatever it takes to keep you safe."

She bristled at that. "I don't need you to keep me safe. In case you didn't notice last night, I'm more than capable of kicking ass when I need to. I might be a little rusty, but it won't take me long to get up to speed."

The lady had spunk. Azaiel had to give her that. He nodded. "I meant no disrespect." He took a step toward her. "It's my turn, no?"

She shrugged but remained silent.

"Who placed the mark upon you?"

Azaiel watched the curve of her cheek as she turned to look out the window. She leaned her hands upon the faded, rust-colored countertop and sighed. It was a deep sigh, one filled with resignation, but judging by the jut of her chin, it was also filled with determination.

She tucked a loose strand of hair behind her ear. "My ancestors fled Europe to avoid persecution and as fate would have it they ended up in Salem." She snorted. "Can you believe it? And only a few months before the Salem witch trials broke out. I can't imagine what it would have been like to live through that. The ignorance. The hatred. The fear. A whisper in the right person's ear, a nod in that direction . . . a nudge." She shook her head. "That's all it took."

"So your family came under suspicion. Were they accused of witchcraft?"

"No," she said softly. "It never got that far. Agatha didn't let it happen." Rowan turned back to Azaiel. "Our family has gifts that are special, power that is stronger than most, but as I'm sure you know, everything comes with a price. To save us Agatha did something desperate. She called forth a demon. Of course, not just *any* demon would do." She arched a brow. "Mallick."

Azaiel's jaw clenched. In all the years he'd been below, he'd never met the mysterious demon lord—but he knew that Mallick was a sadistic son of a bitch. Even in his gilded prison, deep in the bowels of Hell, Azaiel had heard rumblings about the scope of his power.

"She made a deal with him, and we've been paying its price ever since. He marked our coven."

He thought of Rowan's words the night before. "So this *is* about the coven."

"No, not entirely. It involves only our line—the James witches." Rowan's eyes were bright yet they were filled with a sadness that weighed them down. "He claimed Agatha that night, and has come for one of us every generation or so."

His eyes narrowed. "For what?"

"Our blood and magick. He feeds from us. Uses us. Claims us in every way."

Azaiel swore, ancient speak that rumbled from his chest.

Why would someone like Mallick need these witches? He was a powerful demon lord. It made no sense.

Rowan ran her hand along the tabletop and gazed at the polished floor beneath her feet. The oak was buffed to perfection thanks to their efforts the night before. "The thought of him filled my mother with terror because she knew he'd come for her. There was no one else. My grandmother was too old for his purposes, and as you can imagine, our line thinned. Some of my ancestors refused to have children." She laughed—a harsh echo that slipped into the empty air. "I can't blame them. Why would you bring a child into the world knowing it might end up in the Hell realm, slave to that evil monster?" She was lost in thought, haunted by memories. "My mother was a bit of a rebel, which was Cara's way of saying that she was a boozer and loose—if you know what I mean."

Azaiel didn't know how to respond to that, so he remained silent.

"She slept around. Didn't look after herself." She shrugged. "Marie-Noelle lived life like she was starving and the only thing that would fill her up were men, booze, drugs, and sex. She lived like she had no future and subsequently lost her reality. She did things . . ." A painful sigh escaped. "Things that no mother should ever do." Her voice was wooden. "And now, here we are."

"You've been marked." His words were not a question but a statement of fact.

Rowan nodded. "By the time I was thirteen, she was really bad. Her mind wasn't strong, and her body was weak from years of abuse. She'd disappear for days, and none of us knew where she'd been. Cara was more a mother to us than she ever was."

"Us?" he asked, but she continued as if she'd not heard him.

"When he came for her, she was wasted. High on something illegal." She paused as if lost in a memory. "He was so angry with her, and afterward, she wasn't the same. I don't know what he did to her exactly, but it scrambled her brains even more than they'd already been."

"Where is she?"

"We locked her away, somewhere safe."

"And where would that be?"

"An otherworld asylum. At least there they can deal with her special needs, and she won't hurt anyone."

Azaiel understood. "So Mallick marked you instead."

"He *would* have taken Nana, but I begged him not to. How could I live without my grandmother?" She smiled—a bitter whisper of a smile. "Nana was furious with me, but it wasn't the first time I defied her. I was a bit of a bad seed myself." She hunched her shoulders. "The apple didn't fall far from the tree."

He found that hard to believe. The woman before him seemed well put together and in control.

Silence fell between them, and Azaiel let it pass as he watched Rowan closely. Her young face was tight with memory and tragedy. The tears that reflected like mirrors in her eyes remained unshed. The girl was strong, and considering what she'd just imparted, she was going to have to remain so. Mallick was no bottom feeder. He was pretty much the top of the food chain down below.

It changed everything.

"He marked me as his property." She sneered. "Said he'd come for me when I was older." She ran her hand through the tumble of hair at her nape, her voice bitter as she spoke. "He was gracious enough to let me have more time to develop my powers."

"A demon's mark, especially the kind put down by one with as much power as Mallick, can't be denied. And yet he searches for you." Azaiel thought of the dullness to it and arched a brow. "How have you managed to hide from him?"

"Nana," she whispered, "was exceptional. She conjured forth such magick I can still feel the caress of its power." Rowan blinked several times and cleared her throat. "She closed the eye, and Mallick's mark has been blind ever since. We thought . . . we hoped that it would be enough. That if he couldn't find me, he'd turn his attention elsewhere, and we could find a way to break his claim on our family."

"Mallick is a formidable demon to call enemy."

She nodded. "He killed my grandmother because I was too weak and pathetic to stand up for myself. What was I thinking? I never should have left. Deep down I knew he wouldn't stop until . . ." Her voice trailed off, and Azaiel stepped forward.

"Until what?"

"Until he finds me," she spit out. "He's hunted my family down like we're animals, feeding off our blood and magick for hundreds of years, but it ends here."

"What are you planning?" He didn't like the light that shone in her eyes. It spoke of pain, reckless anger—and that could prove dangerous.

Rowan pushed away from the table, crossed to the sink, and ignored his question. She grabbed the empty vase off the counter and headed toward the door. Azaiel let her leave and once she was outside grabbed his cell phone. Bill needed to know what they were dealing with.

The phone was answered before it even had a chance to ring.

"Cale."

Azaiel frowned. "Are you now Askelon's secretary?"

Cale ignored the sarcasm. "What did you learn?"

"I need to speak to Bill." Azaiel owed his life to the head of the League. Simply put, he would do anything for the powerful Seraphim leader. His brother.

"He's no longer at The Pines and will be off the grid for a while. He's doing a little digging of his own."

The Pines was a protected sanctuary, close to the Canadian/American border, where members of the League could gather in safety. The town wasn't large, barely two hundred humans called it home, but it was their base in the human realm.

Azaiel's lips thinned. The less he had to do with Cale, the better. None in the League had welcomed him with open arms. He knew of their animosity—their distrust—and sadly couldn't blame them.

"We've got a problem."

"Azaiel, there's always a problem. Some just matter more than others." Azaiel's frown deepened. He was going to have to adjust Cale's attitude. He clenched his hand and smiled—a dark, dangerous glint lighting up his eyes at the thought.

"Mallick is our problem now." Silence greeted his words, and Azaiel knew the severity of the situation was not lost on Cale.

"Shit," was the gruff response.

"Thought that would get your attention."

"Has the League been breached?"

"I don't know. At this point the only thing I'm sure of is that Cara's granddaughter has been marked by Mallick, and he's coming for her. Whether Cara got in the way and was murdered in anger is anyone's guess."

"We need to know if Mallick has more than the granddaughter on his radar."

"Agreed."

"Damn, but I'd love to kick that son of a bitch's ass."

"Sounds personal."

"It is." There was no hesitation, but then a pause. "Did you have dealings with Mallick when you were on vacation in Hell? Is your identity safe? Wouldn't be smart if he finds out *the Fallen* is prowling the streets of Salem."

"I've never had the pleasure."

"Good. You're not going to be able to deal with this on your own. If he wants Rowan James, nothing will stop him, and I'm sure you can appreciate the kinds of monsters he has in his employ. Unfortunately, I can't join the party as he and I have an interesting history."

"Care to share?"

"Not a chance."

"Glad to see our lines of communication are so open," Azaiel murmured.

"I'll send backup as soon as I can. Just not sure how long it will take to rustle up a crew."

"More like, no one wants to work with the Fallen?" Azaiel responded dryly.

"Well, there is that. Hold on." Cale yelled to someone in the background, and Azaiel heard shouting, some loud grunts, and a crash that had him holding the cell phone inches from his ear.

"Trouble?"

"Nah, just a couple of blockheads reenacting the latest UFC fight. Samael is bored."

Azaiel didn't reply because he had no clue what UFC was.

"All right. I'll see what I can dig up on Mallick and the James witches. In the meantime, hold tight, and I'll send a team ASAP."

The line went dead, and Azaiel pocketed the cell phone. He moved toward the sink and peered out the window. Sunshine spilled through thick, fluffy clouds, finding its way to the earth and kissing the vibrant colors of fall in a soft glow.

Vines crawled along the trellis, their once-soft green leaves already turning dull brown, and in the corner of the yard, large stalks of corn swayed in the breeze as pumpkins littered the patch beside them. It was no longer a time for flowers and soft pastels. The yard was filled with oranges and reds of every shade. Leaves whistled by the window, falling from the huge oak trees that bordered the property. In the distance he spied Rowan, vase in hand, filled with cattails, twigs, and sunflowers.

An interesting combination.

Her hair looked as if it were on fire, and he found himself mesmerized by the fluid movement of her limbs as she meandered through the garden. There was a loneliness to the picture she presented, and it pulled at a melancholy rooted deep within him.

Azaiel pushed away from the counter abruptly. It was time to come up with a plan, but first . . .

He turned around and came face-to-face with an elderly black man. The newcomer's short, coarse hair was peppered with gray, and his small frame was lean and whipcord hard. He wore a bright red-and-white-checked shirt tucked into faded jeans held up by a thick leather belt that had seen better days. His nose was sprinkled with dark freckles, his mouth thinned into a grimace.

Azaiel glanced at the rifle he held—the one aimed straight for his heart—and then back into coffee-colored eyes that were full of distrust and anger. He wasn't afraid of the rifle—normal bullets would hurt like hell, but he'd survive. For curiosity's sake, he'd play along.

Azaiel raised his hands into the air and nodded toward the weapon. "I'd be careful where you point that thing." Azaiel's mouth tightened as the older man lowered the muzzle so that it was now aimed directly between Azaiel's legs. He wasn't so sure a shot in *that* particular area would heal satisfactorily.

"Don't think I won't shoot you down. And just so you know, this here rifle is loaded with the kind of ammo that does damage to your type." The voice was gravelly, and Azaiel knew that the gentleman meant business. "Who the hell are you, and where is Miss Rowan?"

CHAPTER 5

A small orange tabby weaved its way around the pumpkin patch, its lithe form navigating the large pumpkins with predatory grace. Its belly hung low, heavy with life, and Rowan figured the animal was about to give birth.

"You'd best find someplace safe to have your kittens." The cat meowed, a loud, plaintive howl, then slunk between the cornstalks. Rowan glanced back at the house. "Because it sure as hell isn't here."

She closed her eyes and let the early-fall sun soak into her skin. Wind whistled in her ear, a soft breeze that caressed her hair and left a crisp feel in its wake. Birds sang to each other, quick, excited chirps that shouted, *Winter's on its way*. In the distance, the sad drone of an airplane drifted across the robin egg blue sky.

Fall had always been her favorite time of the year, but living in Southern California, while it had its own merits, just didn't touch her soul the way Massachusetts did. Pain spiked across her chest, and she nearly dropped the vase as a myriad of memories and images assaulted her.

She both hated and loved this place. The twist of emotion left a bittersweet ache in her heart, but Rowan had no time to tread down that path. There would be time to process them and grieve later. At the moment, there were other things to worry about.

She needed to warn the coven, gather her troops, and spring her mother from the asylum. Marie-Noelle might be crazy, but Rowan needed her magick . . . and the knowledge buried inside her head. She clenched her teeth together. She wouldn't fail this time.

She had two weeks until Samhain. Two weeks to prepare. And then she'd deal with Mallick once and for all.

Her hand was upon the door when the small tabby surprised her once more and slid between her feet. She nearly fell over and muttered, "What the?"

Rowan glanced down and tried to move the animal with her booted toe, but the little devil wasn't having any of it. "Who are you?" she murmured, balancing the large crystal vase in her hands while pushing on the door with her hip. "Were you a friend to Nana?"

The cat darted ahead, and she followed it inside, nearly dropping the vase when she spied the older man. "Cedric!"

Her Nana's oldest friend and caretaker stood defiantly in the middle of the kitchen, rifle raised threateningly toward Azaiel. He looked as if he'd not slept well, with several days' worth of scruff dressing his chin in a brush of gray. The sadness that softened his eyes was heartbreaking as he turned his gaze toward her.

"Miss Rowan," he said simply, and she noticed how the rifle shook. The damn thing looked to be an antique and most likely was. Rowan doubted it would fire even if he tried.

"It's all right, Cedric." She nodded toward Azaiel. "He's . . . a friend."

Cedric hesitated, distrust heavy in his eyes. "He's not human."

"No, he's not, but you're going to have to trust me."

Slowly the man lowered his rifle and let it fall to his side as he eyed Azaiel warily, then walked toward her. He stopped a few inches away, his slight shoulders hunched forward. Cedric's gaze fell to the floor, and he moved gingerly, as if he knew Cara's life's blood had slowly drained from her body in that very spot.

Patsy Cline erupted into the silence, and the hair on the back of Rowan's neck stood on end. Her eyes widened as a realization hit her.

"She's still here." The words were whispered, and her legs felt like jelly as she crossed the kitchen and stood in the entrance to her grandmother's rooms. It was empty, of course, but she closed her eyes and concentrated, opening her senses and searching.

How long she stood there, Rowan couldn't be sure, but the vase grew heavy in her grip, and her shoulders ached from the strain. And still the music played on for several seconds until it stopped abruptly.

A whisper of energy slid over her skin, and she shivered at the power she felt. He was there, just behind her. Azaiel.

"Can you see her?" she asked quietly.

There was a pause. "No."

Disappointment rushed through Rowan, and she pushed past Azaiel, setting the vase on the table before turning toward Cedric. She hugged him fiercely, not caring as the tears that had been threatening for hours fell unchecked down her cheeks. His body, frail with age and—shock filled her—disease, swayed in her embrace. She smelled the sickness inside him, and it only added to her grief. *How much am I going to lose?*

"Miss Rowan, she's gone."

They clung to each other for several more minutes before Rowan wiped away her tears and stepped back. "I know." She took the gun from him and placed it on the table. "Where were you . . . do you know what happened? Who did this?"

Azaiel moved to her side, and she was conscious of how large he was. How incredibly *male* he was. She couldn't lie. There was a certain comfort in that, which surprised her. She'd only had herself to count on for so long, it felt strange to think there might be another to share the burden.

"I had a suspicion but wasn't sure, Miss Rowan." Cedric's soft Southern drawl had never left even though he'd lived over half his life in Massachusetts. His eyes were wide. "She came to me in a dream two nights ago. Told me to make sure you were safe and to keep you away from Salem. I wasn't sure if it was just a bad dream, so I came home right away but . . ."

Rowan digested Cedric's words. "Did she . . . did she say how . . ." She paused, not wanting to verbalize what was in her head.

"Did she say how she was murdered?" Azaiel interjected, his voice level and matter-of-fact. "Or more importantly, did she say who and why?"

Cedric's eyes narrowed as he swung his gaze toward the tall man. "I'll ask again. Who are you?"

"Azaiel. As Rowan's already told you, I'm here to help and will do whatever I can to keep her safe and find the bastard responsible for Cara's murder."

Cedric ignored Azaiel's comments and arched a brow at Rowan. "And you believe him?"

Rowan hesitated. She still wasn't a hundred percent sure about the mysterious stranger's agenda, but she knew he meant her no harm. "He says he's a friend and at the moment our allies are few and far between."

"Huh." The old man shoved his hands into the front pockets of his jeans. "Surely you don't think it's a coincidence that he's here now."

"He says that Bill, you remember him, don't you? Nana's friend? Azaiel said that he sent him." She watched closely as Cedric digested that bit of information.

"Huh," he said once more.

"Where were you when Cara was murdered?" Azaiel spoke, and she jumped slightly, hating the way her stomach tightened at the sound of his deep timbre. Hating the way he stated the facts so coldly. But then, why shouldn't he? It's not like her grandmother meant anything to him. He was only here as a favor to Bill.

Pain lanced across Cedric's features. "I'd gone to Louisiana for a few days to visit my granddaughter. She'd just had a baby you see, and Cara insisted I go seeing as I'm . . ."

"Sick?" Rowan inserted gently.

Cedric shook his head. "Yes." A muscle splayed across his jaw. "Damn cancer." He glanced toward the floor. "Damn smokes. Cara had been on me for years to quit you know and last summer I finally did. I let her do some of her magick you see, and the craving went away." Cedric snorted harshly. "Too bad the damn things left a little present behind."

"I'm sorry," Rowan said softly.

"Well, I've lived a long time and though I've not got many good days left, I sure will use what ones I have to make things right." His dark eyes were lit with a feverish light. "Whatever you need, Miss Rowan. We'll get the son of a bitch who hurt our Cara."

"Okay," she said softly. "Have you talked to anyone from the coven? Mariah? Abigail? Do you know where they are? Do any of the others know what happened to my grandmother?" She paused and swallowed heavily. "What about Hannah?"

"I'm sorry, Miss Rowan, but we haven't heard from any of your kin for, well, a long time now and Hannah, well, she comes around now and again, but I've not seen her in months."

Damn, how could she have let the coven get so fractured? Rowan flushed a deep red as she arranged the flowers in the vase. She knew why. *Because I was too selfish.*

"Does Hannah still work at that bar in Ipswich?"

"She owns it now." At Cedric's nod, a thought crossed Rowan's mind. She turned quickly, and her nose smashed into the hard wall of Azaiel's chest. "Jesus. Didn't anyone ever teach you the rules about personal space?"

His scent filled her nostrils. It was earthy, full of spice and something wholly male. The energy that slithered over his skin was potent, and it only added to his attraction—not that she was interested, of course.

She didn't give Azaiel a chance to reply but pushed past him. He wasn't her type. That's if she was looking for a type. She glared at the answering machine and shot a look of resentment at Azaiel. Which she wasn't.

The light was flashing, and the number indicated there were several messages. Rowan exhaled, squared her shoulders and pressed PLAY. Azaiel moved up beside her as did Cedric, and the three of them listened as three customers called to confirm their canceled reservations.

She bit her lip and frowned. Weird.

The next message was from Cedric, checking in to say he'd made it to his granddaughter's and would call again in a few days. Rowan grabbed Cedric's hand and squeezed as they listened together.

Two messages were left, and she knew the last one was from Mason—damn, she needed to call him back before he started to worry.

"Cara?" She gripped Cedric's hand tighter as the soft voice sounded. It was her cousin Hannah. "Cara, pick up?" Static played over dead air, and her cousin exhaled loudly into the phone, a quiver of fear lacing her words as she spoke. "Cara. I . . . I'm just worried and a little freaked-out. I felt something tonight and I'm not sure what it means exactly but when you get this message, please call me." Another pause. "Okay, uh, make sure you call as soon as you get this."

The line went dead, and Rowan erased Mason's message.

Silence weighed between them all, and after a few moments Rowan let go of Cedric's hand and stared out the window, not really seeing anything, but she let her mind work its way through some things, and when she turned around a plan was forming.

She glanced up at Azaiel, more than a little startled to find his light eyes focused on her. He was much too quiet. Much too intense. The man made her nervous in all sorts of ways. If she was going to get through the next few weeks with him around, she was going to have to learn how to deal with that.

Starting now.

"Cedric." She turned to her old friend. "I can't tell you to leave or to stay. You have to make that decision on your own." He would have spoken, but she shushed him gently. "I'd rather you leave because danger is heading our way, and I don't know if I can live through someone else I love getting hurt." She smiled sadly. "But I know you have the heart of a warrior and that you loved Cara very much."

"This has to be made right," the elderly man said quietly. "You need to be protected. He won't stop."

"I know." Rowan smiled bitterly. "Seems as if we've come full circle." She nodded. "All right. Good."

"What do you have planned?"

Rowan turned to Azaiel. "I need to gather the coven."

"What of your mother?" Cedric looked worried.

"Once we're organized, we'll get her," she answered carefully, not liking the way Cedric's eyes narrowed. "Mom may be damaged, but her power is still strong. It's locked away somewhere inside her, and I need it." She was aware of Azaiel's gaze and turned back to the window. A squirrel rooted through a pile of leaves, its tail the only part of its small body that was visible. "We need as much

James mojo as we can get our hands on if we're going to end this."

Rowan pushed everything from her mind but the task at hand and went into battle mode. It slipped over her skin with an ease born of the past, and for the first time in a very long while she just let it be. She accepted what she was with no guilt and no fear.

She was a powerful entity, a warrior made of flesh and bone—but above all else one hell of a witch. Her fingers clenched tightly, and she closed her eyes.

She would face Mallick but not until she was ready—not until Samhain—she needed her circle to be at its strongest, and before that could happen, she had much to do.

Rowan James was no one's prize, let alone that of a demon lord from the Hell realm.

She *would* end this. Or die trying.

CHAPTER 6

Azaiel followed Rowan out into the crisp fall morning. It was later, closer to noon, but the urgency of their situation wasn't lost on either one of them. She cleared the porch, taking the stairs two at a time, and headed toward the parking lot. Her denim-clad legs covered the distance in no time until she reached the blacktop, where his bike and her car were parked.

They'd breakfasted—Cedric had insisted no foray into the supernatural could be successful on an empty stomach—and the elderly gentleman had created a tasty meal of bacon, eggs, toast, and sausages. Azaiel observed the easy warmth between Cedric and Rowan in silence as he made quick work of his plate. Neither one of them engaged Azaiel in conversation, but he was more than content to listen.

After millennia of existence, he'd learned many times over that actions belied a man's innermost thoughts. And that more often than not, words unsaid spoke louder than those uttered. So he'd observed the two and learned enough.

The fact that Cedric kept himself between Azaiel and Rowan showed not just distrust for Azaiel—he was highly protective of the young woman. Cedric had served the James witches for most of his life, and the love the man felt for Cara and Rowan was as strong as any familial bond. The man would do whatever he could to avenge Cara's death.

Azaiel also noticed that Cedric's hand trembled though he tried his damnedest to hide it. The elderly man was much sicker than he wanted them to know.

As for Rowan, her pain and guilt at her grandmother's death had been pushed aside, hidden away in some secret part of her soul, where it would fester. She covered her pain with false smiles and an overly happy voice. Azaiel knew from past experience that the witch was going to have to deal with it sooner rather than later. If not, it would eat away at her and do the one thing she wanted to avoid—impede her judgment and ability to complete her mission.

"You've got to be kidding me."

He'd followed Rowan across the parking lot and paused beside the small blue car. The door was open, and she was behind the wheel, cranking an engine that didn't want to turn over.

She looked up at him in frustration. "This thing is a new rental; how the hell can it not start?" Her tone was almost accusatory. Did she actually think he'd toyed with the machine? Not that he was torn up over it. The thought of folding his large frame into the confines of the small vehicle did not please him. It brought to mind a gilded cage and endless centuries upon centuries of imprisonment below.

He nodded toward the motorcycle he'd "borrowed" from Cale. The open road and wind on his face was much more to his liking.

"We'll take the bike."

Rowan slid from the car, her brows furled into a frown.

"You afraid to ride?"

She looked startled at his question and shook her head, moving away from him toward the motorcycle. "No, of course not, I just . . ."

"You just?" he prodded, noting the tightening around her mouth.

"I prefer to drive."

It seemed the little witch liked to be in control. Azaiel shrugged and nodded toward the bike, holding the key aloft. Hell, if she wanted to drive, he had no problems whatsoever climbing on board behind her. In fact—his gaze rested upon her rounded hips—it might be somewhat entertaining. "Fine by me, if you're willing."

"No," she answered quickly. "I don't want to be responsible for something this expensive. Is it yours?"

"Nope."

Her eyes narrowed. "Did you steal it?"

Azaiel paused. "I borrowed it."

She threw her hands into the air. "Great, so you stole it. Anything else you willing to share? Because now would be a good time."

Azaiel ignored her question. The secrets that darkened his soul were not for anyone's ears. Those he would keep close.

He settled himself onto the seat, his long legs easily gripping the machine, and waited for Rowan to climb up behind him. He wasn't prepared for the energy that slid over his skin as she did so. It startled him, and for a moment he gripped the handlebars tightly, not caring for the sensation. Not caring for what it represented—a connection.

Azaiel wasn't looking to connect with anyone. He'd do what he could for the League, but there was room for nothing else.

A soft grunt, or maybe it was a sigh of surprise was heard as she inched forward, and Azaiel wondered if she felt the connection as well. She muttered under her breath and wrapped her arms around his midsection, holding tight to him. "Let's go. We've got a lot of ground to cover in the next few days."

Azaiel revved the engine and let all thoughts of doomsday fly away as the powerful machine between his legs begged to be let out on the open road. The throttle growled, a low rumble that sounded sweet, and they sped out of the driveway, turning right as Rowan directed, toward Ipswich, a small New England town thirty minutes north.

The air was fresh, the streets of Salem busy. Tourists by the hundreds walked the sidewalks, shopping, laughing, drinking in the ambiance—some dressed in witch costumes, others in casual clothes and comfortable walking gear. All seemed more than happy to open their wallets and spread the kind of cheer that made the local businesses happy.

He spied a young mother pushing her child in a stroller along the sidewalk. They stopped to admire a large pumpkin decoration, and the mother reached for her child's face and stroked the ruddy cheek affectionately. They looked happy. Content. So did the group of elderly women who elbowed their way through a crowd of youths.

Not one of them had a clue what hunted amongst them. On the short drive through town, he'd felt the presence of several demons meandering through the crowds, sniffing out any who might fall easily into their embrace. By nightfall, the number would double.

With Mallick's eye turned this way, Salem would be overrun within a few days. If Azaiel and the League weren't able to contain the bastard and his legions, the quaint little town would never know what hit it. The monsters and demons that they dreamed about—the ones they immortalized in movies and books—would show themselves.

And they wouldn't play nice.

His gut tightened, and the lightness that had only recently settled in his mind was long gone. It was replaced with the weight of an almost impossible situation. And yet he knew it wasn't time to despair. Not yet. Azaiel was living proof that hope flourished even when all was lost.

It was some kind of miracle that he—the Fallen—had managed to find some bit of grace and come back from the darkness. If not for Bill, he would have perished, and for that he was grateful. He knew he wasn't yet whole. The road to redemption was littered with the sins of his past, but he would walk it—one step at a time.

Whether he was strong enough to reach the end . . . well, that was another question entirely.

For a few moments, as the sun shone on his face, and the warmth of a woman crept up his back, Azaiel let the darkness inside him dissipate. He let the freedom of the road infiltrate his cells and gunned the motor, laughing at the squeal of protest that sounded on the wind.

Rowan dug her hands into his sides, but he paid no mind. Hell, he could close his eyes and drive the damn thing safely if he wanted to. A little bit of otherworld mojo, and he'd be all set. Instead, Azaiel let the beauty that existed in this corner of the world—the burnt oranges, fiery reds, and brilliant golds—touch his soul, and he found that it offered some sort of comfort to the heaviness that weighed on him.

They rode in silence for nearly thirty minutes, and as they approached Ipswich, Rowan's hands tightened.

The small New England town was old—older than most in these parts, and its history bled through like a living, breathing entity. If ever a place had "character," this was it. From the architecture of the stately homes, to the old stone bridge, to the greenery and the water beyond.

"Take the next right." Rowan's shouted words dragged him from his thoughts, and Azaiel maneuvered the bike around the corner, expertly guiding the motorcycle down a tree-lined street until he spied the bar at the end, on the left. *Brick House.*

He pulled into the parking lot and drove the bike to a secluded spot where he could secure it. It wasn't his bike, and he sure as hell didn't give two shits about Cale, but he'd grown fond of the motorcycle on the drive up from The Pines, and it would piss him off if someone were to damage the shiny metal beast.

Rowan slipped off once they were stopped, muttering the whole time. "Might as well have parked on the other side of town. Not like we have time for a leisurely stroll around Ipswich."

He ignored her mumbling and glanced up at the Brick House. The long, rambling building wasn't a house, and there was not one brick to be seen.

The parking lot was fairly full, but considering it was Saturday, that probably wasn't surprising. Music drifted from inside—live music, the heavy bass beat told him so—and the swell of laughter followed in its wake.

Rowan was tense. It was in the way she carried herself, the frown that furled her brows, and the thin line of her mouth.

"You all right?"

She seemed surprised at his question. "I'm fine. It's just been a long time since I've seen Hannah." A small smile curved her generous mouth, and Azaiel's gaze settled there. It was a mouth meant for passion—for kissing and nibbling and sliding across skin. Not for the first time he wondered about the man who'd called for her. Mason. Were they lovers?

He found he didn't much care for the thought though he was quick to toss it aside. What was the point?

"We were pretty tight, like sisters really, and trouble always seemed to find us." She chuckled softly. "Though I was always the one to get caught." She bit her lip and sighed. "God, I miss those days."

Azaiel let Rowan lead the way inside, all the while his senses scanned the immediate area for anything out of the ordinary. Other than one witch inside, he felt nothing—no otherworld presence was detected.

The interior of the bar was much like any other he'd seen both here in the human realm, and below in Hell. Darkly lit, with low-slung heavy wood beams across the ceiling, it was a cluttered mess of tables and bodies. Shadows filled in the corners, and neon-lit signs hung on the walls as well. Various witch paraphernalia were strewn throughout— broomsticks, hats, black cats, and even a stuffed white owl that rode the coattails of some small, bespectacled boy in a cape.

The room was filled with a few overly drunk patrons near the stage, dancing to a live band that played a mixture of blues rock with a hint of jazz thrown in for good measure. It was the kind of music fit for a Saturday afternoon, one meant for laziness and drink.

The bar itself was hopping, with a host of men and women enjoying their cold brews, settled on the high chairs, while a couple played darts in the far corner. A smattering of people ate at the tables near the back, with several waitstaff seeing to their needs.

A large mountain of a man tended the bar, and Azaiel was aware that his bushy brows were raised in their general direction even as he carried on a conversation with a young blond waitress who waited for her order.

As he and Rowan approached the bar, the bartender filled her order and sent the waitress on her way. He rested his meaty hands on the bar and glared at Azaiel. "We don't want any trouble."

"Good to know." Azaiel smiled, though the warmth never left the general area of his mouth. "We're trying to avoid it ourselves."

The bartender's eyes narrowed into twin balls of gray. "Don't be an asshole." He clenched his fists. "I don't like assholes."

After his trial and subsequent punishment in the upper realm, Azaiel had been stripped of some of his powers. If not for Bill, his brothers would have left him as helpless as a newborn. As it was, he'd been banished from the upper realm for an undetermined time and left with only a few of his former powers. He could no longer travel through time and space at will, delve into the minds of humans, or— Azaiel eyed the arrogant bartender—kill with the blink of an eye.

He flexed his long fingers and squared his shoulders. He was, however, stronger than any human, and in fact most otherworld creatures, and he couldn't be killed. If need be, he had no problem at all demonstrating how quickly he could crush the bartender or any who dared give him attitude.

"Boys, let's calm down." Rowan leaned toward the bar. "I'm Rowan, Hannah's cousin. She around?"

The bartender's gaze moved from Azaiel and settled on Rowan. He studied her in silence for a few seconds, then smiled, his large, beefy hand stroking the thick beard that covered his chin.

"You're Marie-Noelle's daughter. You look just like her."

Rowan stepped back and nodded. "You knew my mother?"

The man nodded. "I did." A sad smile now graced his rough-hewn features. "Back before she had her, ah, breakdown. She was full of fire that one." His face darkened as he looked at Azaiel. "I don't think she'd like the thought of you running around with someone like him."

Azaiel arched a brow and stepped up beside Rowan. He was close enough to the bartender that if the man decided to insult him again, he could easily snap the man's neck and be done with it. "Someone like me?" he asked, his voice dangerously low.

The bartender, however, refused to back down. "Yeah, someone like you." The man shook his head and took a step back. "Far be it for me to advise you on your choice of company." He nodded to Rowan. "But you're asking for trouble with him around. The kind of trouble that got your mom all messed up."

Azaiel would have moved forward, but Rowan's hand on his arm kept him still. "You don't know anything about my mother."

"I know more than you think I do," the burly man growled.

"Who are you?" Rowan's voice rose.

The bartender didn't skip a beat. "I'm a soldier in this war, same as you. I might be human, but that gives me more of a stake in this mess, don't you think? My family, my wife and kids, are everything to me, and I'll do whatever it takes to keep them safe." He sneered as his gaze settled on Azaiel. "Safe from the likes of him."

"Look, I don't have time to debate the war or the baddies you're not keen on. If you really want to help, then tell my cousin I'm here."

Several long seconds passed before the bartender reluctantly reached beneath the bar and grabbed a phone. He turned, but Azaiel heard his words nonetheless. "She's here, and she's not alone."

He then turned back to them and gestured toward a table hidden in shadows near the exit. "Hannah will be out in a minute. We had a cook quit earlier in the week, so she's filling orders and helping out in the kitchen."

"Thank you," Rowan murmured.

"You can thank me by keeping your pet on a tight leash."

Azaiel ignored the taunt and followed Rowan to a table. He was aware of the eyes upon them—of the interest they generated, and the lust that filled the eyes of the woman two tables over. She smiled as Azaiel passed, her shoulders hunched forward, her breasts on display.

And he felt nothing.

Rowan followed the line of his gaze as she slid into the seat opposite him. "If we had time, I'm sure you could score some of that."

"Not interested."

"Really?"

He settled his large frame into the smallish wood chair. "Why do you find it hard to believe I don't want to have sex with that woman?"

Her cheeks flushed pink at his words. "I didn't mean . . . ah, I wasn't talking about sex."

His eyebrow rose, and the flush in her cheeks darkened even more.

"What I meant was that most guys would be all over a woman like that."

Azaiel leaned closer, his elbows on the table. "What kind of woman is she?" He slid a glance sideways, vaguely disgusted by the provocative display as the woman in question licked her lips and smiled at him.

Rowan's eyes were on the woman. "She's obviously the kind of woman who doesn't care that you're with someone. She wants you and wants you to know it." Her blue eyes settled back onto him. "Most men would follow her up on her offer, or at the very least be somewhat flattered."

"There you have it," he said softly, enjoying himself.

"Excuse me?" Her arched brows furled, and once more, his gaze was drawn to her mouth.

"I'm not most men."

They stared at each other for a long time. Or at least it seemed that way, but as with everything of late, things were about to get dicey.

"I'll give you ten seconds to get your ass out of my bar and take your new boy toy with you." The unmistakable click of a gun sounded, and they both looked up at a small, blond, pixie of a woman. That she'd managed to sneak up on them without either Rowan's or Azaiel's notice said something.

Azaiel just wasn't exactly sure what that something was.

She wore faded jeans that were so tattered they looked as if they'd been dragged behind his bike—all the way from Salem. A tight, bright pink tank top—with MOFO emblazoned across her chest—showed off trim, muscular arms that were covered in tattoos, or, on closer look, runes of some sort. Her short, spiky, platinum hair topped a face that was almost elfin in feature, wholly feminine, with large expressive eyes and a generous mouth free of gloss.

The look in the woman's clear blue gaze, however, was anything but friendly. She was pissed as hell and aimed the gun in her hands directly between Azaiel's eyes.

"Hannah." Rowan stood, her face pale and lips tight.

So this was the cousin. Another surprise. And it seemed to him, Rowan and Hannah hadn't parted on good terms.

"Don't push me, Rowan." Hannah moved closer. "You know I won't hesitate to shoot."

"For Christ sake, Hannah. It was six years ago. Are you still mad?" Rowan made a disgusted sound. "*How* can you still be mad?"

Hannah cocked the gun in answer and squared her shoulders. A loud gasp echoed in the bar, and Azaiel realized the band had stopped, and all eyes were on them.

"The bullets this baby is packing are special if you know what I mean, so if Mr. Blond God means anything to you, you'll convince him to leave." Her mouth thinned. "Now."

Neither Rowan nor Hannah was focused his way, and that was fine—the gun was the only thing paying attention to him. Azaiel knew a bullet wouldn't kill him—special or otherwise—it would just hurt like hell. He settled back into his chair, long legs stretched out casually as he gazed up at the two women.

This was going to be good.

CHAPTER 7

Rowan stared at her cousin and fought to keep some sort of control. Energy burned inside her chest and gathered there, growing in strength with each tortured breath she drew. She needed to get a handle on her emotions, or the damn gun was going to be the least of her problems.

She was too rusty to control her magick, and there were too many innocents in the bar. Rowan took a deep breath and stepped back though she let a flicker of power light her eyes crimson.

It was enough to let Hannah know she wasn't going down without a fight, and though the cousins were both from the same bloodline—the James witches—Hannah's magick wasn't anything like the monster that Rowan commanded.

She eyed her cousin. How dare Hannah stand in front of her, a gun pointed at Azaiel, while the world as they knew it was gone. Could she not feel the empty space left by Rowan's grandmother?

Mallick had flexed his muscles with deadly consequences, and Hannah had done nothing. Why hadn't she gone to Salem as soon as she'd known something was wrong?

She thought a phone call would suffice? Had their family become that disinterested in each other? That fractured?

The empty beer glasses left on the table beside them began to shake, the light fixture overhead flickered and went out, while the oak floorboards beneath her feet creaked and moaned—a few split apart in protest to the anger she projected. Whispers floated on the air—or maybe they were screams—and several patrons left quickly, money thrown on tables and food left untouched.

The giant of a bartender moved toward Hannah, but with one flick of Rowan's wrist, he stumbled and nearly fell.

"Don't," Rowan warned, as one of the glasses crashed to the floor.

The bartender cursed and motioned toward the door. "Maybe you girls should take this outside." He glared at Rowan. "Not exactly good for business."

Rowan glanced at Azaiel. His gold eyes had an amused look to them that pissed her off even more. "Give me five minutes." She spoke curtly and gave no chance for his reply.

She turned and strode through the door, inhaling a crisp shot of fall air as she walked along the worn wooden deck that ran the entire width of the Brick House. It was a weather-beaten gray building with cream trim and lots of fall displays. Pumpkins, cornstalks, and sunflowers filled the corners of the veranda, while bales of straw were scattered about. It seemed as if Hannah still had a soft spot for All Hallows Eve.

Rowan lifted her face to the sun and closed her eyes, suddenly so weary and tired of it all. Which was stupid. There was so much to do and tons of ground to cover, but the weight of her situation had been heavy for years, and she realized she might not be strong enough to do what needed to be done.

Sure, she'd fled to California, but had she ever truly believed her family could outrun Mallick? That he wouldn't find a way to get to her? It had always been at the back of her mind—she'd just learned to ignore it and, as it turned out, had paid a very high price.

An image of her grandmother floated behind her eyes, and pain lanced across her chest. Her throat was tight, and her heart hurt. It was times like this a girl wanted her mother, and for Rowan, that had been Nana. God, how she'd love to rest her head against her grandmother's breast. Feel the wiry fingers run through her hair, hear the beat of her heart—smell the soft vanilla scent of her bath oils.

But that was to be no more.

The pain in her chest grew sharper and though it hurt, she drew strength from it. It was a reminder of what she'd lost, and Rowan wouldn't rest until Mallick paid.

The sound of a boot scuff tore her mind from the darkness, and she whirled around to face her cousin. Hannah still had the gun in her hand though it was held loosely and pointed to the ground. A couple had followed her out and stopped just shy of the steps leading to the parking lot. She waved the weapon toward them, and they didn't hesitate. The man yelled, "crazy bitches," as he hopped down the steps, dragging his lady behind him.

Rowan watched them slip into a faded, black, rusted Chevy and turned back to her cousin. *You're not far off, Mister.*

The two women stared at each other in silence. It stretched long and thin, like a weakened spider's weave about to snap.

Where to start? She squared her shoulders and kept her voice level. "I see you cut your hair."

Hannah snorted. "Are we really going to do this? I told you six years ago that we were done, and I meant it. Nothing's happened to change my mind."

Pain, mingled with a pulse of power, surged down Rowan's arms and settled into her hands. It was hot—white-hot—and she stretched her fingers to alleviate the stress. Or maybe it was a warning. Either way, she was done playing games.

"Cara is dead." The words spoken were wooden, without a hint of emotion. That she kept inside. Nothing good could come of it if she unleashed her rage on Hannah.

Her cousin's face whitened, and she took a step backward—her blue eyes wide and frozen, the pupils bleeding through with the sifting blackness of an oil spill.

"No," she whispered. Hannah took a step toward her and faltered, her boot scraping the deck. "How?" she said hoarsely.

"Mallick, of course. Who else?"

Hannah stared at her for several long moments, tears filling the corners of her eyes, which she made no effort to wipe away. A visible shudder rolled over her body, and she clasped her arms around her chest.

"The other night I felt something but I . . ." She paused and fought for control. "I had no idea Cara was in trouble."

Rowan leaned her hip against the railing. "Knowing my grandmother, she shielded you and the rest of the coven. She wouldn't want you anywhere near The Black Cauldron when Mallick attacked."

"I should have gone to her. I knew something was wrong."

"Yes, you should have."

Hannah's eyes darkened with hurt, but there was something else there. Accusation.

Rowan shook her head and looked away. Hannah was right. "*I* should have been there, too." The fist of pain in her chest tightened even more, and Rowan leaned both her hands on top of the railing. God, she felt like shit.

Two scuffed-up boots stopped beside her, and though Rowan wanted nothing more than to hug her cousin tight and cry for all things lost, she couldn't. There was no time.

"How has it come to this?" she whispered instead.

A rumble in the distance signaled a turn in the weather, underscored by a sudden gust of wind that blew thick ropes of her hair into the air. The sun disappeared, and her chilled flesh gave credence to the quick drop in temperature.

"Rowan."

Rowan stared down at the wandering vines that crept along the foundation of the Brick House. The edges were no longer green but crap brown, ruined from cold nights and the blankets of frost that accompanied them. She didn't know what to say and needed a moment to collect her thoughts.

"Rowan, please look at me."

I can't.

She took a moment, gathered her strength, then carefully pushed away from the railing before turning to Hannah.

"I'm sorry," her cousin whispered, bottom lip tremulous though she managed to keep her voice steady. "So, sorry."

Rowan nodded. "I know."

"Six years ago—"

"I can't talk about that, Hannah," Rowan interrupted. "It's in the past and right now those ghosts need to stay there. There's no time for stuff that doesn't matter anymore." How could she make her understand? "A war is coming our way, and we need to prepare."

"I don't understand." Hannah frowned.

Rowan turned and glanced at the gathering clouds. "He's marked the coven."

"Mallick? But why?" Her voice gained some strength. "It's you that he wants."

"But he can't find me. The mark is blind, remember?"

Hannah's face whitened. "But why would he mark the coven? What good would that do? None of us are the kind of witch that he wants." Her tone was harder.

You are.

The words weren't spoken, but Rowan read them in Hannah's eyes. It seemed old wounds were still raw, but she chose to ignore the obvious dig.

"I don't think he cares about that. I think Mallick wants to make the James witches pay for keeping me from him, and if it takes eliminating the entire coven to get to me, that's what he'll do."

"Mother-trucker," Hannah bit out. "So what are we going to do?"

Rowan met her gaze full on and welcomed the fire that burned in her gut. It was the one what was going to get her through the next few weeks. The one that would get her to the end.

"We fight back. We need to gather the coven. Right now we're scattered across the state, and we're weak."

Hannah nodded. "All right. I can make some calls."

"Good, because I have no idea where anyone is."

"I think Abigail is still in Canada, but Auntie Dot will know for sure."

"Canada? Seriously?" Rowan frowned. "Why would she leave Salem?"

"Why else would a twenty-nine-year-old single woman leave her family and friends?"

"A man."

Hannah nodded. "Bingo. She met him out on the water. The boat he was in nearly cut hers in half. There were injuries and blood and lust. They bonded in the ER." Hannah's eyes widened. "Auntie Dot is horrified. *Horrified.* Abigail had been dating an Ivy League professor from Boston, and I'm sure Auntie Dot was already planning the wedding. But now she's shacked up with some Frenchman in another country." She giggled then. "Living in sin as they would say."

"Wow." Rowan exhaled. She'd certainly missed a lot.

"Wow is right." Hannah paused. "So who's the tagalong?"

"What?" Rowan had forgotten how fast Hannah changed gears.

"The blond guy with the tight abs and weird-ass energy. You guys been together a while?"

Rowan blushed at the suggestive look in Hannah's eyes and shook her head. "It's not like that."

"Well, what's it like?" Hannah wasn't giving up.

"It's"—Azaiel was hard to define, and for a moment she was stumped—"he's complicated, and honestly, I don't know much about him. He showed up at the Cauldron last night."

"Last night." The teasing tone fled, and Hannah's hands gripped tight around the gun once more. "Rowan, I know he's one hell of a looker, but seriously, how do you know you can trust him?"

"I don't really, but he helped me slay a pack of blood demons."

"What?"

Rowan nodded. "It was a great homecoming," she said bitterly.

"Well I hate to be the one to point this out, but how do you know he's not the one who killed Cara? Maybe he's trying to win your trust, so that he can hand you over to Mallick himself. His energy is way off. Like out-of-this-world off. I've never felt anything like him before." Her eyes narrowed. "What is he?"

Rowan shuddered as another strong gust of wind whipped along the veranda. She thought of how he'd gotten down on his hands and knees the night before and scrubbed her grandmother's blood out of the floor. She sensed something dark in him, but there was also good. "He's not the enemy. That's all you need to know at this point. He's a . . . a friend, I guess."

"A friend."

"Not that kind of friend." Rowan's cheeks were hot, and her thoughts turned, however briefly, to the ride in from Salem and how good it had felt to hold on to something so solid. So incredibly male.

"That's what you said about Danny Bagota, and we all know how that ended," Hannah said dryly.

"Look, we don't have time to discuss Azaiel—"

"Aza—what?" The expression on Hannah's face was near comical. "Shit, Rowan. Does he come from the land of the ice and snow? What the hell kind of name is that?"

"A—zee—el." She pronounced the name slowly, an irritated frown furling her brows as she stared into the amused blue eyes of her cousin.

"Got it." Hannah's smile disappeared. "Okay, *that* doesn't look good."

Rowan followed Hannah's gaze. A swirling black mass of something strange hung in the sky, off in the distance. "What is it?" she murmured, wincing as the bad feeling that had never really left her stomach returned with a vengeance.

"I don't know, but I can tell you one thing. That sure as hell ain't a storm cloud. It's carrying full-fledged storm babies that are gonna drop a shit-ton of crap on top of us."

The two of them studied the darkened mass for several moments until the door slammed open behind them. The shaggy bartender stood there, chest heaving, a worried expression on his face as he stared up at the sky.

"That there is trouble." He ran his fingers through the greasy mess of salt-and-pepper hair atop his head and clenched his hands. His steely eyes settled on Rowan, and she felt his anger as clear as day. "Seems to be following you."

Rowan bit back the pulse of irritation that throbbed near her temple. "The only thing that's following me is your bad attitude." She strode toward him. "And that's going to change. I won't work with someone who's got his head so far up his ass, he can't see the big picture."

The bartender stared at her in shock, then a slow grin spread across his face. "You really are Marie-Noelle's daughter."

She arched a brow. "And?"

He stroked the beard that hung inches past his chin, his intense eyes never leaving hers. He nodded. "It's about time you showed up."

CHAPTER 8

Azaiel was on his feet when Rowan pushed back into the bar. The blond woman who'd been eyeing him up was no longer content to display her charms from across the room. She stood inches from Azaiel, her overly large breasts near to bursting from a low-cut cream blouse that barely kept them contained.

Rowan eyed the long length of trim legs exposed by the short, charcoal-leather skirt she wore. They, of course, were enhanced by six-inch candy red stilettos, and Rowan had to admit, the woman's curves were enviable. She *was* attractive—in a dirty, skank, biker kind of way.

The woman turned, and the edges of a tramp stamp showed along her lower back as well as the top of her scarlet-colored G-string. Rowan made a face—the look was so yesterday.

Azaiel caught sight of Rowan and turned without another word—brows furled, eyes dark with frustration.

"I'm not keeping you from anything, am I?" she asked softly.

A scowl crossed his features. "Not at all. She's annoying."

Rowan glanced at the woman, who was now shooting daggers her way. "She's got a great rack, though."

She turned back to Azaiel, and her mouth went dry. Slowly he dragged his gaze from *Rowan's* chest and gazed directly into her eyes. "I hadn't noticed."

Bartender man cleared his throat and stopped beside them, with Hannah close on his heels. "Hate to break up whatever the hell this is between the two of you, but like I said out there"—he nodded toward the door—"trouble's on its way and we better come up with a plan or the shit's gonna hit before we're ready."

"Trouble?" Azaiel barked. He shouldered between them and strode outside.

Rowan turned to the bartender. "You didn't introduce yourself, so unless you give me a name, I'll have to call you bushy bartender guy."

"Bushy?" He smiled and ran fingers through the hair on his face. "I've been called worse." He cocked his head. "Frank Talbot."

The name suited him. "Nice to meet you, Frank." Rowan turned to Hannah. "We have any idea what that dark cloud is all about?"

Hannah shook her head. "I've never seen anything like it." She tugged on Frank's arm. "We need to clear the bar. Get everyone to go home."

Frank nodded and turned, cursing under his breath. "This is really gonna hurt our bottom line this month." He put his fingers to his mouth and whistled long and loud. "Everyone out!"

A few groans met his command, but nobody jumped to do his bidding. He turned in a circle and grabbed Hannah's arm. "You want the crazy lady with the gun to ask? 'Cause I don't think she'll be as nice as me."

Within seconds, the place was hopping with patrons throwing cash onto the tables and leaving.

Azaiel came in from outside, his face hard as stone and eyes full-fledged black. The power inside him was hard to miss. It rolled off his tall frame in waves, and Rowan realized that for the most part he kept it hidden.

"Holy crap," Hannah whispered. "He's hot as hell, but seriously, he scares me more than anyone we've hunted in the past. Are you positive we can trust him?"

I wish I knew.

"No. But at the moment, he's all we've got."

"Great." Hannah took a step back. "Good to know."

Azaiel stopped a few inches from them, his gaze sweeping the now-empty bar. When his eyes rested on Rowan, the intensity in his eyes touched her as if he'd taken his hand and run it along her cheek. It made her nervous—scared her even—this connection she felt to him.

"Do you know what that cloud is?" Thank God she sounded somewhat normal.

He nodded. "First wave."

"First wave?" Hannah asked, a touch of fear in her voice. "God, do I want to know what that means? Sounds like a mother-trucker of a sci-fi movie or something."

"Okay, I can't let this go again." Rowan turned to her cousin. "*Mother-trucker?* Really?"

"Look, I'm trying to curb my potty mouth, all right? You got a problem with that?"

"No, I just . . . it's not you."

"Well this is the new me. So get used to it."

"More like Simon Bayfield's idea of a new you," Frank snorted.

"Who?" Rowan asked.

"He's no one," Hannah answered a little too quickly. "First wave?" she prodded.

"The first of many if I'm reading this right," Frank answered. The burly man heaved a sigh and shook his head. "This is worse than I thought." He looked at Rowan. "It's him, right? Mallick?"

Startled, Rowan glanced at Hannah, but her cousin shrugged. "He knows everything."

"That is a family secret." Rowan was incensed. "Only the coven knows. Only the coven is *supposed* to know."

"I didn't tell him." Hannah's chin rose defensively. "Your mother did."

Rowan opened her mouth but didn't quite know how to respond. It seemed as if Frank Talbot knew her mother a lot more intimately than she'd realized.

"None of that matters now. That cloud dispatched several assassins, who are now looking for"—Azaiel's gaze swung to Hannah—"you."

"Me? But I'm not the one they want . . ." Her voice trailed away as she fisted her hands, the gun still held within her grasp. "Right. The entire coven is marked. I guess they don't really care who they take out."

Hannah's gaze swung past Azaiel until her electric blue eyes rested on Rowan.

"Hannah—" Rowan started.

"It's okay, Rowan." She shrugged, nonchalantly, but Rowan knew it wasn't. Her cousin was scared, and so was she. Neither one of them had faced something like this before—and they'd faced a lot in their day. For as long as Rowan could remember, the James witches had protected Salem. Ever since the infamous witch trials of the 1600s, the entire area had been a hotbed of demon activity. But this? This was unprecedented.

"It's been a long time since we've gotten out of hand, don't you think? And I don't know about you, but I'm kinda looking forward to kicking some demon ass."

Rowan stared at her cousin, helpless anger bubbling to the surface. She couldn't stand to lose anyone else. Not Hannah. Not Abigail. *Not anyone.* There would be no more James blood spilled. She glanced at Azaiel. Or anyone else's for that matter. Not if she could help it.

Hannah tucked the gun inside the waistband of her jeans and grinned. "So what's the plan?"

"We leave this place," Azaiel said. "There are too many innocents, and if we stay, there will be casualties, of that you can be certain."

Rowan nodded. "The Black Cauldron is where we need to be. It's where we're the strongest and because it's on the outskirts of Salem, it's isolated. There's less chance of any civilians getting hurt. I don't think a second wave will look there again. Not yet."

"So that leaves the first wave to deal with," Hannah inserted.

"Sure does," Frank answered.

"It will be dangerous." Rowan needed him to understand the severity of the situation.

Frank's pale eyes glistened with a fire that she recognized all too well. He was a *warrior,* and it was obvious that he wanted to fight.

"Call your family and get them as far away from here as you can."

"Already done."

Rowan nodded. "Okay. Let's head to Salem." She turned to Azaiel. "Do you know how many we're dealing with?"

He nodded. "I saw four lightning bolts." He cocked his head, put his finger to his mouth, and for several tense moments there was silence. "One is already here."

"Shit," Hannah whispered, her hand on the gun once more. "Frank, get our gear."

The bartender disappeared into the kitchen just as the lights flickered and went out. It was early afternoon, yet the darkness that surrounded the bar was as thick as night. Outside, the wind howled and moaned, lashing at the Brick House with a ferocious slam of power. Otherworld power. The air was rancid with the smell of it.

Rowan threw her hand out and called forth an illumination spell—even then she held her breath, not sure if it would work or not, which for a witch was sad indeed. She exhaled in relief as a warm glow fed from her fingers to light up the darkened room.

Eerie shadows flickered in the dark as she turned, throwing grotesque images along the wall. The Harry Potter replica that hung from the ceiling became a macabre monster with horns and long, spidery legs. A shiver rolled over Rowan as she gazed at it.

"Here," Hannah whispered.

Rowan accepted a large modified rifle, as well as two sharp daggers with intricate charms carved into the shiny blades. Power emanated from them.

We're going to need it.

"Where's the big guy?" Frank asked.

Rowan whirled around, her eyes moving quickly as she scanned the entire room. What the hell? Azaiel was nowhere to be seen.

"He's gone," she whispered, unsure if that was good or very, very, bad.

"Crap," Hannah said roughly. "I knew he was too good to be true. He probably led the bastards right to us."

"No. He wouldn't do that." Her spidey sense was going haywire, her heart beating like a jackhammer inside her chest. She set the rifle on the table beside her. "It's here." She turned in a circle, both hands gripping daggers, her feet planted apart.

"I feel it, too. But where is it?" Hannah whispered.

"Right here, you dumb bitches." The voice was rough-hewn, like amplified, thickened nails being dragged across a chalkboard.

Crimson light emanated from within thin air, a spiraling dirge of bloodred energy that solidified into a tall, gruesome-looking creature. Its thin frame was draped in several layers of robes the color of wet clay, and they swept along the ground, billowing outward as if riding an invisible breeze.

It pulled a long, luminescent hood off its head and snarled at them, flashing huge fanglike teeth that dripped crimson liquid onto the worn wood planks of the floor. Several thick, gooey drops splattered at its feet, and smoke rose into the air as the liquid melted through the wood.

Its eyes were merely sunken holes of swirling mist, and its long tongue darted out, twisting in the air as if seeking something. Rowan stared at it in disbelief. She'd never seen anything like this. Never even dreamed up anything like this before.

Its gaze settled upon Hannah, and Rowan realized in that instant that it had no idea Rowan was a witch—the one they were hunting. With the eye of Mallick's mark closed, she was in fact hidden in plain sight.

She aimed her dagger, dead center of the back of its head, and fired it hard, only to watch it bounce off an invisible wall and fall to the ground several feet away.

Its head swiveled around, and what looked like rotting flesh appeared from inside its gaping hole of a mouth. Rowan hazarded a glance at Frank, but the bartender was eyeing up the demon, eyebrows twisted in concentration, hands holding tight to an impressive-looking shotgun.

The air around the demon swirled in a flash of crimson light. It was so bright that for a second, Rowan was entirely blinded. Panic ate at her, and she stumbled backward, trying to gain some equilibrium. How could she kill something that she didn't understand? Or more importantly, see?

She shook her head hard, and when she was able to see, the sight wasn't exactly what she'd hoped for. Three of the massive creatures now stood in front of them.

"Mother-trucker," Hannah said as she took a step back and tossed a wild look at Rowan. "What the hell are these?"

"Replicatus." Frank cocked his rifle and moved forward. "Demons that have the ability to replicate into as many versions of themselves as they need. I've never seen one before, but I've done some reading on them."

"Really?" Rowan cocked a brow, finding her strength. "And it thinks it only needs three of itself to take us out?"

Frank grinned at her. "Apparently, so. The only way to kill them is to cut their heads off." He aimed his rifle and fired point-blank into the face of the demon closest to him. Sparks flew everywhere as the bullet cracked the shield that somehow protected them, and the demons screeched in anger.

"Now!" Rowan shouted, and all three sprang forward, daggers drawn and guns at the ready.

The original demon ignored Rowan completely and turned toward Hannah, its focus solely on the only witch it could sense. That was fine. She'd help her cousin out as soon as she took care of the ugly-looking bastard whose toothless, rotted mouth smiled down at her.

She called up the energy that waited inside her chest—felt it scald her skin with power—and crouched in a defensive position as the demon moved toward her. Her rifle was on the table to her left, locked and loaded, and she held her remaining charmed dagger loosely in her hands. She needed to get close enough to cut its head off—but she also had its shield to deal with.

Another shotgun blast rent the air, and the smell of gunpowder slid up her nostrils. It was followed by grunts and a string of profanity that was familiar.

"I'll rip your head off you fucking piece of filth.

"Really? You think that punk-ass mouth of cockshit is going to scare me? Are you for real, you ball-less fuckwad?"

Rowan dared not take her eyes off the advancing enemy, but she smiled nonetheless—Hannah's foray into a world without potty mouth had ended. It was somehow comforting.

A sliver of energy rippled through the air, and Rowan realized she'd lingered too long. She leapt for the rifle and twisted in the air so that she slid across the table on her back, the gun held in front of her as she blasted away at the thing's head. The shield cracked into a shower of light, and she fired once more, yelling as its body fell backward.

"Take that, dickhead." Guns had always been her cousin's specialty. The charms she infused them with were unparalleled.

Rowan jackknifed her body and landed on the floor in front of the demon, bending backward just in time to avoid a large, clawlike fist to the face. She slid to the side and nearly lost her balance but was helped up—by the demon's fist in her hair. Long talons curled along the curve of her scalp and dug in painfully.

The demon held her aloft, several inches off the ground and only a few inches from its face. The putrid smell that fell from its mouth made her want to puke. Its rotted flesh quivered in anticipation; its blackened, empty eyes seemed to focus solely on her throat.

"You smell different," it whispered slowly, and its smile widened. "Better than the witch."

The demon was puzzled—hence the hesitation—and Rowan knew this would be her only chance.

The sounds of battle faded into the background as all her focus shifted to the demon that held her. It brought her closer still, and when its tongue flickered out to touch her, it took everything in Rowan to remain still. She needed to get as close to it as she could because the dumb bastard didn't think she was strong enough to use the dagger that she still held.

Pain sliced across her cheek as its tongue slowly traveled the length of her face. Her stomach roiled, and she thought for one moment that she was going to lose her breakfast. She knew the moment when it realized the truth—that she was, in fact, the witch they sought—but by then it was too late.

"Suck on this, asshole!"

Rowan gripped the knife with both hands and, as she dangled in the air, still held by the Replicatus demon, the power inside erupted from her fingers, fueling her strength and that of the dagger. She plunged it inside the demon's mouth, withdrew just before it dropped her, and on her way down sliced cleanly through muscle and bone.

Rowan rolled to the side, gagging on the odor that surrounded her as the head landed a few feet away, and its body tipped forward. She screamed at Hannah, who was pinned beneath the original demon. Its large hands were wrapped around Hannah's neck, and she struggled to breathe, unhealthy gasps escaping her lips as she jerked about like an insane puppet.

The demon's swirling gaze focused on Rowan, its long tongue testing the air, twisting slowly like a snake in the grass. A growl rumbled from its chest, and it bared its fangs, obviously displeased it had been duped.

Crimson energy surrounded the demon once more, but before it had a chance to replicate itself, its head was severed from behind. It was a clean swipe, and as the body tipped forward, Frank Talbot helped it down with a well-placed kick to the shoulders.

Hannah rolled over and coughed hoarsely, inhaling deep gulps of air as she slowly got to her knees. For several long moments, the three of them stared at each other, their faces lit by eerie shadows—and then Hannah laughed. It was a full-bodied, near-hysterical giggle that was infectious.

Her cousin's eyes were wide as she looked across the room at Rowan. "Holy fuck, but that kinda rocked."

"Potty mouth banished?" Rowan asked.

"What?" Hannah made a face and grabbed her gun. "Like any addiction, it'll take time to overcome." She leapt to her feet, and, as she stepped over the body on the floor, the door to the bar crashed open, and Azaiel strode inside.

Hannah reacted instantly. She yanked Frank's rifle from his hands and, before Rowan could stop her, aimed both weapons and fired.

CHAPTER 9

The bullets punched Azaiel in the left shoulder, and the force of the hit lifted him off his feet several inches. It took him backward into the wall, and for a moment he saw nothing but stars as he slid to the ground, pictures crashing around him. He lay there, senses dulled, body aching, and realized he was on his back, splayed out on the ground like a helpless child.

He grimaced and stifled a groan. Son of a bitch, but it hurt.

Azaiel took a moment, eyes closed, as he focused his energy on the wounds—and they were significant. What the hell kind of bullets had the witch used?

"Oh my God, Azaiel!" Rowan was at his side, and she sounded frantic.

Fingers ripped through cloth—cool air caressed his bare skin, and, judging by the gasp that escaped Rowan's lips, he was guessing the wounds were as bad as he'd feared. It would take a lot longer than normal to heal, and time was not something they had a lot of.

Hands weaved their way across his chest, and he clenched his teeth as they gently touched his neck, his temple, and his jaw. Energy tingled along his flesh, awakening long-dormant emotions. The sensation left behind by her touch was exquisite—it had been millennia since he'd felt anything like it.

And yet, it was not the time to deal with a tangled mess of want, need, loss, and desire.

Rowan bent over him, once more dressing him in the heat of her body. He was so damn cold.

"Are you alive?" The whispered words blew across his cheek, slightly tremulous, wholly feminine.

Slowly his eyes opened, and he exhaled roughly as he tried to push her away. She was much too close and smelled too damn good.

"You're hurt." She was anxious and more than a little rattled judging by the flushed hue to her cheeks.

He grimaced and, refusing Rowan's help, sat up with more than a little effort. He leaned against the wall, winded and in extreme pain. A harsh light entered his eyes as he glared up at her cousin, Hannah. "A couple of bullets will do that."

"That ammo should have killed you." Hannah was surprised. She stood beside Rowan—with Frank a few steps away—her spiky hair even more askew, her expressive eyes shiny with an adrenaline afterglow.

"Lucky for you they didn't." He glared at the blond witch and winced as Rowan ripped the rest of his shirt from his body.

Her fingers trailed along his collarbone as she studied the damage.

"You're losing too much blood." Rowan leaned forward, her head in the crook of his neck as she gingerly felt the back side of his shoulder. His first instinct was to push her away, but something about her touch held him still.

"There's no exit wound. We have to get the bullets out."

Azaiel inhaled sharply as her fingers poked at both of the ragged wounds, and he hissed. All right, the touching could stop.

"Sorry," Rowan whispered. "I've never been good at this kind of thing."

"I take it you're not a nurse in your other life," he said dryly as he shifted and eased a bit of the pressure.

Rowan shook her head and offered a half smile that in no way hid her anxiety. "No. Far from it. I'd rather fight a pack of nasty demons than deal with pain and blood."

Her eyes hung like luminescent sapphires, all shiny and big, as if they held a host of secrets.

"That's good to know." What was it about her eyes that was so compelling? Witch, he reminded himself. She was a witch.

Her gaze lingered a moment longer, then she said in a rush, "We still need to get them out."

He shook his head. "There's no time. I took out two of the Replicati while you dealt with this one, but there's still another out there." His lips thinned. "They're tenacious sons of bitches. It will come for you." He directed his last comment toward Hannah, a cold smile claiming his lips. "Maybe this time he'll be successful."

His gut roiled, and a wave of dizziness rifled through his head. "Damn, what the hell did you spike those bullets with?" Eyebrow arched, he glared at Rowan's cousin.

"Son of a . . . ah, I'm sorry," Hannah whispered. "We thought . . . *I* thought you'd led them to us."

Azaiel straightened, teeth clenched. "And why would you think that?"

"I . . . well, you just left and . . . you're not human and . . ."

Rowan's mouth thinned into a tense line as she turned to her cousin. "You *still* shoot and ask questions later. That's not smart, Hannah, and we need to be smarter than them."

"There was a time when you did, too," Hannah said defensively. "Or don't you remember? No demon fighting for you in college? And here I thought Buffy was a way of life in Southern California."

Rowan ignored her comments though her anger bled through in her tone as she spoke. "Those were your extra-*special* specials?"

Her cousin's gaze faltered. "Extra extra specials now. I've juiced them up with belladonna. Sorry. I only keep the deadliest bullets in stock. I mean, what's the point in using something that will only stun?"

"Right." Rowan stared down at him, eyes huge with worry. "Azaiel, this doesn't look good."

The little witch sounded like she actually gave a damn. "Azaiel?"

"Yeah." His shoulder hurt like a son of a bitch. His head pounded, and the taste of cloves and something he couldn't quite pinpoint sat heavy in the back of his throat. It left him with the unwelcome feeling that at any moment he'd heave all over his boots. Or maybe hers.

Rowan shook her head. "Azaiel, we have to get the bullets out. You won't survive with them inside you."

"I'll be fine." He nailed her with a look that brooked no argument. "Help me up." His eyes softened a bit, more than a little surprised at her concern. "I'm not going to die on you. I promise. But if you could cauterize the wounds, that would go a long way toward helping my situation."

"Cauterize the . . ." She bit her lip and sat back on her haunches, her blue eyes now a shade darker than charcoal.

Sweat beaded his brow, and he tried to shift, but the pain was too intense, and as a fresh batch of blood poured from his shoulder, he cursed.

She held his ruined T-shirt tight to his shoulder. "Give me a second." She cocked her head to the side and bit her lip. In the space of twenty-four hours he'd seen her do this several times—when she was upset or unsure. He kind of liked it.

"Hannah, get all the ammo you have. Weapons . . . anything we can take. Do you have a vehicle?"

"I've got my truck around back." Frank stepped closer,

wiped a meaty hand across his brow, and nodded to Azaiel. "You took out two of those bastards?"

At Azaiel's curt nod, Frank grinned widely. "Impressive. Well, it's going to be a pleasure working with you my friend. We can always use an extra set of hands, especially when they seem to carry a lot of weight." The bartender paused, a shadow crossing his face as he glanced at Rowan. "He *is* gonna be all right . . . right?"

"I'll be better once we get the hell out of here." Azaiel hissed as another wave of pain sliced across his shoulder.

Rowan jerked her head, a quick affirmative. "Grab whatever you can. He'll be fine."

Frank and Hannah disappeared, leaving him alone with Rowan. He stared up at her, but her eyes darted away, and he realized for the first time that she was nervous.

"Are you sure you can you do this?" he asked softly, hoping like hell she could, or else the trip back to Salem promised to be as painful as his first trip down into the bowels of Hell.

She nodded and removed the wadded-up T-shirt. Her face was pale—he saw that clear as day. "Yes. Absolutely." She smiled at him, an overly bright attempt to make him feel better, and Azaiel played along. It was the least he could do.

She swallowed, like a lump was stuck in her throat, then closed her eyes. Within seconds, the edges of her fingers glowed, spreading light until the two of them were cocooned in a bubble of heat.

She made a noise, and he looked up, every muscle in his body tightening as their eyes connected. Rowan bent toward him, and he held his breath, suddenly thinking that maybe this wasn't such a great idea. The thought of her hands on him again filled his heated bones with a sizzle of red-hot energy that had parts of him excited—parts that might be considered inappropriate given the circumstance.

He couldn't help it. He was on fire, filled with pain and desire—a deadly combination that made him growl in agitation.

"This will probably hurt," she said softly.

"I'm sure it will," he bit out.

"I'll try to be gentle."

"Please do."

Her fingers touched his flesh, and he grunted as red-hot energy surged into the wounds. The pain was immediate, and he cursed in ancient speak, spewing words that no one would know but his brothers.

Gone were the days when pain was nothing more than a notion. As Seraphim, he'd been endowed with unparalleled powers and magick that was unlike anything found in the human realm. Pain was not something he'd ever given much thought to until he'd fallen and been stripped of most everything he'd claimed from his heritage.

Still, it was a sad blow to his ego that a weapon made by a witch could fell him in such a manner.

Gradually the pain subsided as the wound closed and the heat from her fingers sizzled to nothing. Azaiel wasn't sure if it was because his shoulder was numb or because she'd charmed the pain away.

Either way he had no time to dwell on such things.

"We've lingered too long," he said roughly. Rowan's mouth was inches from his, the small pink tongue he'd grown to appreciate licking her generous bottom lip as her forehead crinkled in concentration.

"Let me help you up." Rowan hooked her arms through his, but he shrugged out of her grasp, swearing once more as he did so. Son of a bitch. So much for the numbed shoulders.

Once upright, he cracked his neck and for the first time saw a deep laceration down Rowan's right cheek. Unbidden, his hand rose.

"Seems as if you've a war wound as well."

She took a step back, cleared her throat, and his hand fell back to his side.

"Its tongue got me," she said huskily. "I'll make a salve when we get back to Salem." She offered a nervous smile. "It will be gone by tomorrow."

Hannah and Frank appeared, arms laden with weapons of all sorts and large bags that were equally full strung from their shoulders. "We're ready."

Azaiel turned. "Let's head out."

"Holy Mother of God." Hannah's whispered words stopped him cold.

Azaiel cocked his head to the side, anger coursing through him as he caught sight of the horrified look on her face. "You've never seen a tattoo before?"

"That's a tattoo? I've never seen one like that before. Dude, I hope you got your money back," Hannah answered.

Rowan stepped beside him, her pale features pinched. "Azaiel, who did that to you?"

Images of his body suspended in the air flashed before his eyes. Memories of the cold. The wet. The miserable. The desolate.

The pain had been incredible, the sorcerer Cormac O'Hara who'd wielded his tools of torture, insane, and yet Azaiel was the Fallen—it had all been deserved.

He stared down into her heart-shaped face. "No one you would know."

The door opened and he escaped into the cool air that lingered outside. The freshness of it slid over his heated flesh and for a moment he basked in the comfort it offered.

Azaiel was bare from the waist up and though it was as cold as a winter morning, he felt nothing but fire. Whether it was fueled by the poison in his system or the rage that simmered beneath the surface was anyone's guess.

Azaiel had no time for a walk down memory lane. There would be all the time in the world for that later. At the moment, they still had a demon problem, and he knew that by nightfall, it would be much worse.

The unnatural darkness still lingered, bathing the parking lot and Brick House in a thick blanket of mist. Frank and Hannah walked past him and stowed their gear in a shiny black pickup truck parked near the building. He nodded to Rowan. "Ride with them. I don't want you exposed."

"No."

He turned to her, and lucky for the little witch he was able to clamp down on his anger. "You will do as I say and not question my authority."

Rowan hopped down the steps, grabbed an impressive-looking gun from her cousin, and started toward the far end of the now-empty parking lot, to where he'd parked the bike. "First off, Tarzan, you're not the boss of me."

In two long strides Azaiel was beside her. "You will listen to me. Out in the open you're a sitting target."

"That's a lame-ass excuse, and you know it." They were beside the bike now. "The demon can't see me, Azaiel, remember?" She pointed to her neck. "The eye is closed. It makes more sense for me to ride back with you, so that when the bastard goes for Hannah, I can take him out."

She thrust her chin out as if daring him to take her on. The little witch was itching for a fight, and if he had the time, it would give him great pleasure to show her *exactly* how things were going to work.

"This is my turf, Azaiel. *Mine*." She squared her shoulders. "I didn't ask for your help. Hell, I'm not even sure that I trust you one hundred percent, but if you're determined to stick around"—she heaved an exasperated sigh—"if I *let* you stick around, you need to remember that I call the shots. Got it?" She jerked her head toward the idling truck. "They take orders from me, not you. Do you really want another shot of extraextra special? Huh?" Her eyes flashed with a dangerous glow. " 'Cause next time, you might end up with a couple of bullets in the ass instead of the shoulder."

Azaiel had had enough. "We'll finish this conversation when we reach Salem."

The air around him shimmered, and the ground at their feet shook as several large cracks split the concrete around them. He would lay things out for the witch, nice and simple-like, just not right now. There was no time. The remaining Replicatus was nearby.

He tossed her a *don't fuck with me look* and straddled the bike, the pain in his shoulder, the nausea, long forgotten as a wave of anger rolled over him. He nodded, a quick jerk of his head. "Get on."

She opened her mouth, but something in his eyes must have conveyed the danger in that action because she didn't say a word and, instead, jumped on behind him. She signaled for Frank to move out, and Azaiel followed though he kept a good distance behind. Hopefully when the demon showed itself they'd have a good vantage point to take the damn thing out.

The streets of Ipswich were strangely silent, and it seemed as if they were the only souls on the road. Thick, cold, gray mist covered everything, its long spidery fingers slithering along the ground like tentacles . . . tasting, searching.

Azaiel's skin was flush with sweat, and he gritted his teeth, fighting the nausea that still bothered him. Extraextra special my ass, he thought. Didn't even come close. At the moment it felt like he'd been hit with Thor's hammer.

The truck turned left and as Azaiel approached the turn, the Replicatus demon swooped in from the shadows above and hovered overtop the Chevy. Rowan raised herself behind him, using her legs to steady herself as she aimed the rifle toward it.

He kept the bike steady, watching as the demon's robes began to bubble, and he knew they had seconds until the damn thing replicated itself, which would make the whole exercise much more dangerous.

His eyes widened as Hannah slid halfway out the window, motioning toward the demon—taunting it—and as he approached rapidly from behind, he saw that she was giving it the one-finger salute that was widely used in the human realm.

The demon's mouth opened wide, and it bellowed, its focus only on Hannah. It never saw the shot. Rowan's hand gripped his shoulder after she let two rounds go, and for a second the bike skittered out of control.

The demon roared as they hurtled down the road, its safety net shattered, its anger unparalleled. It lunged toward Hannah, but she was ready and with one well-played swipe of a long, deadly saber, she separated the head from the body.

Azaiel watched the head roll off to the side as the body exploded into a mess of demon roadkill. Within seconds, it would turn to ash.

He gripped the handlebars, fingers so tight they cramped, and clenched his mouth tightly as the taste of cloves intensified. He would hold on, but damn, it was going to test his strength.

As the bike sped through the late afternoon, behind them the strange cloud that had hovered over Ipswich and beyond slowly evaporated, leaving all as it had been.

CHAPTER 10

They pulled into The Black Cauldron about forty-five minutes later. Driving through Salem had been a chore. Traffic was thick, hordes of tourists littered the sidewalks, and a general sense of chaos prevailed. It wasn't in-your-face but had a more subtle vibe—hidden in the smiles, shouts, and overanimated actions of many of the townspeople as well as the tourists.

There was nothing natural about the atmosphere in Salem, and Rowan knew it signaled that the game had changed. Demons were close by—their presence was enough to ramp up the darkness that lingered in the air like a seductive whisper.

And it was the whispers that humans found hard to resist.

Have another drink and make sure you drive home, no one will get hurt.

Take the woman up on her offer, your wife won't know.

Why should you pay for this? You deserve something for free.

Things were happening much quicker than she'd anticipated. The sooner the coven was gathered the better. And then there was her mother to deal with.

Rowan had clung gingerly to Azaiel the entire way home.

He was still in pain—it was pretty obvious he favored his left shoulder—so she took care not to hurt him any more than he'd already been. She knew what magick charmed the bullets he'd been hit with—it was Hannah's specialty—and she didn't want to think about the kind of power it would take for someone to overcome that.

Rowan made a silent vow to find out as much as she could about Azaiel and what he was capable of. She didn't like being in the dark, and with the stakes so high, it wasn't a good plan to enlist the aid of someone she wasn't entirely sold on. She wasn't scared of Azaiel, she just didn't trust his motives—not yet, anyway.

Her eyes rested on the wings that had been carved into his flesh. The macabre rendering stretched across the width of his shoulders—a raw, angry etching that drew a wince as she gazed at it.

She couldn't imagine the pain it would have caused, or the evil mind of whoever had done this to him.

"Looks like we've got company."

They'd pulled in behind Frank, and the bartender frowned as he glanced toward the main house.

Hannah hopped from the truck, and Rowan carefully slid from the Harley, careful not to touch Azaiel any more than she had to. There was a large, shiny, black Suburban parked beside her rental, and it sure as hell wasn't Cedric's. His small red beater was closer to the house.

Rowan cocked the rifle in her hands and made sure her dagger was still tucked into the waist of her jeans. Power was close by—ancient power that reeked of otherworld. She glanced at Hannah just as two men appeared on her porch as if from thin air, their tall frames falling from shadow.

The first one stepped down, and she eyed him with suspicion. He was large, broad of shoulder, with lean hips and long, muscular legs tucked into black boots. A distressed black-leather jacket, black T-shirt, and worn denim jeans dressed a body that was impressive. There were strange markings along the right side of his neck that drew her eyes. Tattoos of some sort, but from this distance she couldn't make them out. Tribal perhaps?

His features were bold, rugged—his eyes intense— but it was the blue Mohawk he sported that garnered the most attention—that and the piercings in his nose and ear. He was like a big-ass version of Gibson's Road Warrior only ten times as dangerous. Ten times sexier. And he was otherworld.

Rowan's gaze penetrated his energy—shapeshifter to be exact.

The second man moved past him, and Rowan swallowed slowly. He moved with predatory grace, his steps sure, his gaze unwavering.

"Sweet Jesus." Hannah shot a look toward Rowan. "What the hell is going on?" Hannah pointed toward Azaiel. "There are three of them? *Three?* Are we in some weird supernatural version of *The Bachelorette* or something?" Her cousin turned back to the strangers, who remained silent and more than a little intimidating. "They're hot. *Really hot* . . . in a scary I'm gonna eat you for dinner kind of way." Hannah grinned. "Do I get to pick one?"

Rowan grimaced. Six years gone and Hannah hadn't changed at all. At this point Rowan wasn't sure these men were friendlies, and she was more than a little concerned about Cedric. Where the hell was he?

She didn't take her eyes from the tall, dark-haired man who slowly made his way toward her. He was strong-featured, with prominent cheekbones and a square jaw. More than a day's worth of stubble graced his chin, and the thick head of hair, while dark, was shot through with strands of gray. His eyes were so light they appeared white, but as he moved closer, she saw the merest whisper of ice blue in their depths.

He wore a long duster that swept the ground near his feet—it, too, was leather—seemed as if men who looked like *that* had some kind of dress code. Underneath he wore black military-type pants, heavy kick-ass boots, and a plain T-shirt with Five Finger Death Punch across his chest in large, red, metallic font.

Rowan gripped the rifle in her right hand and squared her shoulders as he stopped in front of her. The energy inside her pulsed, and she let it simmer beneath the surface, ready to call upon in case she needed to. Her cheeks heated as he held her gaze for several long seconds, and she jumped when Azaiel spoke, his voice strained and rough.

"Priest."

Rowan glanced back toward Azaiel. He'd slid from the bike and stood several feet away. With the late-afternoon sun shining down on him, dusting his thick blond hair in a halo of light, he looked exactly like what he was—a fierce warrior with ties to the upper realm.

"Damn, this is like my birthday and Christmas morning wrapped into one yummy present," Hannah said gleefully. "I haven't seen this much beefcake since the last time Abigail and I went to the Foxes Den for her roommate's bachelorette party. Mind you none of that beefcake can compare to—"

"Seriously, Hannah?" Rowan glared at her cousin, aware that blue Mohawk man had descended the stairs as well and was only a few steps behind the man Azaiel had called Priest. "Can we tone it down? There are no hidden cameras, and this sure as hell isn't a game."

"You look like shit," the shapeshifter growled, his eyes cold as he glared at Azaiel.

"I've had better days." Azaiel's words were frosted, and

judging by the closed look in Priest's eyes, there was no love lost between these men.

An uneasy feeling coiled in Rowan's gut. She didn't much care for the mixed signals, and she *really* didn't care for the overabundance of testosterone that littered her front yard.

Azaiel was beside her, and her heart lurched when she glanced up at him. His face was pale, a shade past gray, that left no doubt the man wasn't well. She needed to get him into the house and treat him with something. Nana always kept healing potions and herbs on hand. There had to be something she could use to draw out the poison. If not, it was going to be a long night for him.

Her eyes narrowed as she glanced up at the house. Cedric would be able to help.

"I don't know you," she said with more than a hint of anger coloring her words. "But you're uninvited, and as you can see, The Black Cauldron is closed for the next few . . . weeks."

"Penance is a bitch, whose master is Regret." The man called Priest ignored her completely, his eerie eyes focused on Azaiel.

"Trust me. Penance has nothing to do with this," Azaiel hissed.

"*Hello.*" Rowan pointed her gun toward the two strangers. "I'm standing right here." Nothing pissed her off more than being ignored simply because she was a woman. She'd dealt with that kind of nonsense at the law firm and knew it needed to be nipped in the bud right away.

"Either you tell me who you are and what your business is here, or I'll introduce you to my friend Mr. Extra Extra Special." She waved the rifle once more. "And then maybe you'll understand the kind of pain Azaiel is feeling."

"She shot you?" Blue Mohawk grinned widely at that though his eyes remained hard, the color of golden topaz.

"Actually," Hannah interrupted, and stepped forward, her large shiny eyes gleaming, "I shot him."

Blue Mohawk's focus shifted, and Hannah's words dried up as the full power of his gaze rested on her. "Well then, I'm impressed. It's not every day someone can impart such pain on a creature like him."

Rowan cocked her rifle and aimed it directly between the shifter's eyes. "I'm not asking again." Frank had moved closer, his weapon drawn as well, and it seemed that Hannah finally got it—these men were dangerous. She pulled out her Glock with a smile and held it aloft.

Priest didn't look worried. In fact he stared at the four of them with an amused look on his face. "Save your impressive ammo for later. Darkness has already descended on your town, witch, and it plans on having one hell of a party."

"Who are you, and why are you here?" Rowan asked pointedly.

The stranger's eyes lingered on Azaiel for several more seconds, then he turned his full attention to Rowan. "I'm called Priest, and my friend here"—he nodded toward the shifter—"Nico."

"No kidding. Please tell me you're not really a priest," Hannah interjected. " 'Cause that would be a total waste."

Rowan ignored her cousin and narrowed her eyes as she faced Priest. "And you're here because . . ."

For a second she caught a flicker of something almost human in his eyes—a shadow of pain, or sadness—but then it was gone, and she wondered if it had ever been there. "We're here for Cara. To invoke justice in her name and to find the persons responsible for her murder."

Surprise clogged Rowan's throat, and she worked hard to clear it, aware that Hannah had taken a step closer. "You knew my grandmother?"

Priest nodded. "I did. I know you, too, little witch, though you were but a child the last time I visited."

A groan escaped Azaiel, and all thoughts about the newcomers and her grandmother fled as she turned to him. A thick sheen of sweat glistened against his skin, rivulets of it sliding down his chest and abs until they disappeared beneath his low-slung jeans. The path drew her eyes, and she swallowed thickly as she dragged her gaze back up, frowning at the wound on his shoulder. It oozed blood once more, the vibrant red liquid harsh against his pallor, which was awful—the color of dirty dishwater.

Rowan slipped her arm beneath his, and when he would have shrugged away from her help, she clasped him harder. Azaiel glanced down at her, and the dullness of his golden eyes was troubling.

"If you're really here to help, then someone get the damn door. Your friend here is about to pass out."

"He's no friend of mine," the shifter muttered harshly.

Rowan glanced up sharply. She had no idea what was going on between the three of them and at the moment didn't give two shits if they were enemies or best friends. She glared at Mohawk man—or Nico as Priest had called him—took in the scowl and disdain in his eyes, and let her anger boil over.

Something rose up inside Rowan—something fierce that she had no way of controlling, and truthfully, in that moment, she didn't want to. It was a familiar, scary feeling, and judging by the wary look that crept into Hannah's eyes, it was ready to explode.

A cold wind whipped along the ground hurtling dead leaves and sharp stones into the air. They flew at the newcomers, like bolts of lightning flung from the sky, and pushed the men back a few feet off the path that led to the house.

"Ah, guys, I'd move out of the way if I were you." Hannah

ran past them and up the steps to the house. "Looks like she's about to blow, and it ain't exactly pretty."

Rowan's eyes were fully black, and her hair swirled around her head, long ribbons of crimson that looked like blood against her pale skin. She tugged the hair from her eyes and spoke calmly though the ground rumbled beneath her feet, and the wind continued to push at them with great force.

She focused on the two men and, for one small moment, let a touch of the real power inside show through. It's not something she'd done in years—tapped into that part of her that not even her Nana knew about. It felt wicked and hot and wrong and powerful all at once.

Priest's eyes widened, while Nico remained stony, his eyes a glacial shade of winter.

"I'm going to tell you what I told Azaiel, so you'd better listen closely. This is my turf. *My war.* Got it?" The men's gazes were long as they stared at her in silence.

The porch light flickered erratically, then went out.

"Shit." Hannah's hoarse whisper floated down from the porch. "Here we go."

"I don't care who you are or where you've come from. But if you want to stay—if you really want to help this situation because of some loyalty to my grandmother—I suggest you do two things." Rowan moved forward, and by now Azaiel was leaning on her so much that she wasn't sure she could make it up the steps.

"What's that, witch?" Priest spoke quietly, a dangerous edge to his voice that seemed to alarm everyone except Azaiel—who was nearly passing out—and Rowan.

She paused inches from the tall stranger, who now stood blocking her path. "Move the fuck out of my way and show this man the respect he deserves. I don't know much about him, but that's a whole lot more than I know about either one of you."

"The Fallen does not deserve such loyalty," the shifter spit.

"Loyalty is earned," she replied carefully. She thought of how he'd helped her clean up the evidence of Nana's murder. Of the painful carving across his shoulders. Of how good he felt as she'd pressed against him on the Harley. "Azaiel has proved himself to me. Taken a bullet for Christ sake. That means something."

She pushed past them, her anger fueling her forward so that she had no problem at all getting the large man beside her up the steps. With relief she saw Cedric in the entrance, his face full of worry. When he saw the condition of Azaiel, fear filled his eyes.

"We're fine, Cedric." Rowan nodded. "But we need Nana's special healing herbs and some tools."

"What happened to him, miss?" Cedric asked.

"I shot him with an extraextra special," Hannah said sheepishly. "Twice."

Cedric studied Azaiel closely. "Well now, it didn't kill him outright, so that's good."

"Hurry, Cedric."

"Of course, Miss Rowan. Where are you taking him?"

Frank had come inside and slipped his shoulder under Azaiel's other arm. They both winced at the grunt of pain that fell from the tall Seraphim's lips.

"He's burning up," Frank acknowledged, and Rowan shot a worried glance toward the bartender.

"Nana's room." It was the closest, and she didn't think they'd be able to get him up the stairs.

She started forward, down the hall, but paused at the sound of booted feet on the porch. She cocked her head to the side.

"One more thing, boys. If either of you call me *witch* again, I will hex a part of you that neither of you wants hexed. Got it?" She nodded at Frank, and they started forward, the anger in her voice unmistakable.

"My name is Rowan, and you'd both be smart not to forget it."

Priest stood on the porch and watched the witch drag Azaiel down the hall until they disappeared from view. He leaned against the railing and grabbed a cigar from his pocket without offering one to the Jaguar.

The wind continued to howl, carrying bits of debris and dead things into the air. The long fingers of sunlight were fast disappearing—evening came early at this time of the year, and he knew once nightfall descended the danger would triple.

A smile crept over his features as he lit the cigar. He was fine with that. As much as his life was a lonely existence—had been for centuries—he enjoyed the battle when it came his way. Of late, he'd been pretty fucking busy.

"It's gonna be a long night." Nico cracked his neck and stared off into the distance.

Priest let the sweet tobacco settle on his palate—the Montecristo's unique blend of cocoa and coffee was something he'd never get tired of. It was a smooth taste of heaven, here amidst the drudgery found in the human realm.

He nodded but remained silent as wisps of smoke drifted in front of him. He'd never been a man of words, not even centuries earlier when he'd been made a Knight Templar. Priest had always been a man of action, and words seemed to get in the way.

He glanced at Nico. The shifter was new to the League, and they'd only just met. Only days earlier, Nico, Declan O'Hara, and the vampire, Ana DeLacrux had been key in keeping the Mark of Seven contained—for now—and his initial impression of the shifter was that of a man on the edge whose loyalties ran deep and whose strength was impressive.

But he was also dangerous and could prove volatile.

O'Hara and DeLacrux were on another assignment for Bill—something to do with the Mark of Seven—and when Cale had put out the call for extra bodies to help out in Salem, there were only he and Nico. Priest preferred working alone, but in this instance, he understood that numbers would count. He only hoped they had enough.

An owl hooted, an eerie cry that echoed into the coming dusk. Priest clenched the cigar between his teeth and spoke quietly. "Did you see the power that lives inside her?"

Nico squared his shoulders and nodded. "She isn't your everyday witch, now is she?"

Priest pushed away from the railing and took the steps two at a time, his long legs eating up the distance to the black Suburban in seconds. "No." He shook his head and opened the driver-side door. "She's not. This complicates things."

"What is she?"

"I don't know, but you can bet your ass I'm going to find out."

Nico slid in beside him, and Priest glanced toward the house once more before he put the SUV into gear and pointed the vehicle toward town. This was more than just complicated, and he made a mental note to fill Cale in on everything as soon as he got the chance.

Priest would do whatever it took to keep the witch from Mallick's grasp.

Even if it meant he had to kill her himself.

CHAPTER 11

Azaiel woke with a start, heart pounding, body bathed in sweat. Unclear images wavered in his mind—ghosts from the past no doubt—and he pushed them away angrily, hating the weakness. He swung his feet around and groaned—his head swam, and his gut roiled. His shoulder throbbed like a son of a bitch, and for a few seconds his eyes were unable to focus.

Remnants of the nightmare rolled around his head and though he couldn't remember specifics, it always left him feeling the same. Hopeless. Ashamed. Betrayed. Furious.

Where the hell am I?

He forced himself to calm down as the darkness that slept with him fell away. Eventually his breathing returned to normal, and he opened his eyes as memory returned.

Salem. Demons. Rowan. Her crazy cousin and a couple of—he winced and gingerly touched his shoulder—extraextra specials.

Damn, it felt as if he'd been put through the ringer and thrown back in for a second round. His mouth was dry, his tongue swollen, and the taste of cloves still clung to the back of his throat.

A poultice of some sort pressed into his wounds—he

grunted and wrinkled his nose. The smell alone should have been enough to chase away the poison inside him. He supposed it had done much to ease his suffering; he just wished it didn't smell like the back end of a dead rat.

Slowly his eyes adjusted to the gloom, and he realized he wasn't alone. He got to his feet and sucked in a harsh breath, stretching out tight muscles as he walked toward the overstuffed floral-patterned chair tucked into the corner on the other side of the bed.

He recognized the room—it was Cara's—and glanced toward the window. The shattered pane had been boarded up with plywood, and the remnants of broken glass were long gone. The flimsy bloodred curtains dressed each side of the window, their tattered ends trailing along the wooden floor like whispers of silk.

He thought of Cara. He'd never met the woman, but judging from the pain in Bill's eyes and that of the League members, she was much loved. He hissed as a wave of pain skittered along the side of his neck. All this was wrong, and he gritted his teeth as he stared down at the foot that hung over the edge of the chair. It was covered by a fuzzy pink sock that sported a small hole along the underside of the big toe.

Rowan was asleep, curled up like a child, a quilt of many colors pulled up to her chin as she rested her head on the faded, worn armrest. A soft glow from the night-light plugged into the wall beside the chair caressed her features with shadow. She drew long, even breaths—seemed no demons stalked her dreamland.

Azaiel ran his hand over the rough stubble along his jaw and frowned. At least not yet.

She moaned softly and turned, her tongue darting out as she settled herself once more, her head at an awkward angle that couldn't be comfortable. Judging by the grimace that touched the edge of her mouth, she was going to be stiff for sure.

The clock on the table near her glowed 5:15, and the sight of it filled Azaiel with frustration. Damn, he'd been out for hours. Once more his gaze rested upon the sleeping woman.

A large leather bag lay a few feet from her chair, and he spied the unmistakable hard lines of several daggers as well as the barrel of a rifle. She'd been hunting while he'd been passed out like a weakling.

He eyed the bed once more and before another thought entered his brain crossed to the chair and carefully scooped Rowan James into his arms. The pain in his shoulder was ignored, and for one small moment he stilled. Everything inside him quieted.

He held her close and took in her warmth, savoring the feel of her against his cool flesh. She was small and tucked into him perfectly. Her scent drifted in the air, invaded his body, and filled up the spaces that were empty—the spaces that were dead.

He closed his eyes, aching with a hurt that he didn't understand. He barely knew this woman, yet she touched the dead places inside him. He didn't deserve to feel. At least, nothing like this.

Something broke then, a crack in the wall he'd built around his soul. It was a sensation unlike any he'd felt before—a slow surrender from the inside out. It caught him by surprise, and for a moment he did nothing—he let the wall of feeling engulf him. He was hungry for her, aroused, and hard. A wave of hot need rolled through him, and he nearly stumbled.

What the hell?

Azaiel swore beneath his breath, ancient speak that sounded rough and belligerent. He ignored the erection that strained against his jeans and gently placed Rowan on the bed. The patchwork quilt was once more tucked under her chin, and he paused for a second, then—because he was weak—took the time to caress a silky strand of hair from her brow. She sighed, turned onto her side, her fingers clutching at the pillow, and buried her head in its softness.

He gazed down at her, took in the tumbled hair, candy red mouth, and creamy skin. Her long lashes swept downward, casting inky shadows onto her cheeks, and her mouth parted slightly as she exhaled. She was earthy, sexy, fierce, and loyal.

She was not meant for someone like him—the Fallen.

"She's a beautiful woman."

Azaiel stiffened.

"We need to talk," Priest said softly, then he was gone.

Azaiel flicked his wrist and extinguished the night-light before turning and following the Knight Templar from the room. He closed the door behind him, nodded to Cedric, who was busy at the sink, and rolled his shoulders in an effort to loosen up the stiffness that had spread across them and down his back. His chest was still bare, but at the moment, his overheated state meant the chill in the early-morning air eased his discomfort.

He grabbed a milk carton from the fridge and strode down the hall. Priest and Nico were on the porch, their low-pitched voices echoing into the still morning. He had no idea where Frank or—a scowl crossed his face—the witch Hannah was, though judging by the hour, they were most likely asleep somewhere.

He ignored the two men lounging to his left and drank the entire carton before he turned to them. Nico's barely contained hostility was palpable. The tall shifter literally thrummed with repressed anger.

Azaiel understood it. The warrior was a man of honor, and it didn't take a rocket scientist to figure out that the shapeshifter would never trust him.

"You still look like shit, Fallen."

Azaiel placed the carton on the window ledge. As it was, he didn't give a rat's ass if Nico trusted him or not, but if they were going to work together, some rules needed to be established.

"Do not call me that again." Azaiel said the words slowly so that there wasn't any confusion—the shifter had not earned the right to call him Fallen. They had no history. No connection. "I have a name." He turned to the jaguar, whose teeth were now bared. "Use it."

He might have been stripped of some of his power, but it was time for Azaiel to let the jaguar warrior know he wasn't to be trifled with. He was still Seraphim, and if the shifter was smart, he'd back off.

Azaiel took a step forward, muscles bunched, nerves tingling, but Priest interrupted. "We've no time for posturing, boys. Let's try to get along." Priest let the cigar in his mouth roll to the corner, and he glanced at the shifter. "Understand, Nico?"

The shifter growled but kept silent.

Azaiel slowly unclenched his hands and inhaled the fresh, crisp, morning air. In the distance a line of fire spread out along the horizon, signaling the imminent arrival of dawn. He arched a brow and addressed Priest, sensing it would be better for them all if he and Nico kept communication to a minimum.

"What happened last night?"

Priest withdrew the cigar and studied the red glow that burned on the end as he slowly twirled the long, brown stogie between his thumb and forefinger. "We were busy." His pale eyes narrowed as he glanced up at Azaiel. "Busier than I thought we'd be. The demon numbers were significant, and though I caught the scent of vampire, I didn't come across any." He arched a brow, his pale eyes intense. "But they're close by, and Dark fae have joined the party."

Azaiel shook his head. That wasn't good. The fae hardly ever interfered with the affairs of men. They were content to live in the between worlds and watch from afar. So why now did they think to involve themselves in a witches' war with Mallick?

"The human Frank held his own as did the other witch, Hannah. She's a little excitable, but her aim is always true." Priest's gaze fell to his shoulder. "As I'm sure you already know." He exhaled and took a few steps, turned, and leaned against the white railing that ran the length of the porch. "Rowan is impressive. She preferred to hunt alone and refused help from any of us. I followed her at a distance."

Azaiel's eyes narrowed. "And how did that go?"

"Like I said. She's impressive, and it only took her a few minutes to lose me."

Azaiel found that hard to believe. "You're a Knight Templar. How did that little slip of woman evade the likes of you? Witch or no?"

The air stilled around them, and Priest blew out a long plume of smoke. "Well, now. That seems to be the question of the hour, don't you think?"

An uneasy feeling rolled through Azaiel's gut. What the hell was Priest getting at?

Priest butted his cigar, leaving a long line of gray ash on top of the railing, and cocked his head. "Mallick can never be allowed to claim her."

Nico moved forward, and the two of them stared at Azaiel, their faces intense, their eyes dark with hidden meaning. Something wasn't right.

"What are you not telling me?" Azaiel stretched out long fingers in an effort to release the tension that held everything inside him tight and uncomfortable.

Priest looked off into the distance. "Do you know who her father is?"

Azaiel frowned. "She hasn't mentioned a father." He didn't like the look that passed between the two men. "What the hell are you getting at?"

Priest opened his mouth to retort but slammed his mouth shut before uttering a word, his pale eyes glittering harshly as he gazed behind Azaiel.

Azaiel felt her presence before she stepped foot onto the porch, and when he turned to her his chest tightened in a way that was becoming all too familiar. She was barefoot, must have lost the pink fuzzies that had adorned her feet, and even though frost covered everything in a thick coating of white crystals, she didn't seem to notice.

Her plain pink T-shirt clung to her curves, and he felt his heart quicken as he took in the faded, worn jeans that hugged her hips and followed the sleek lines of her legs. Long strands of hair hung in disarray, curling past her shoulders, and her sleep-heavy eyes widened, their navy depths filled with concern as she walked toward him.

It hit him then. She cared. About him.

Azaiel didn't know how to react and stiffened as she paused in front of him. She bit her lip and had to stand on tiptoe as she carefully inspected the wounds on his shoulder. Again, her scent filled his nostrils, and he tensed, bending his head back as if he hated her touch. It was in fact quite the opposite though he didn't miss the slight tensing of her mouth or the shadows that crept into her eyes.

"They look good." She nodded and glanced up.

"Thanks to you they're healing well."

She shrugged. "It's my Nana. Her herbs and poultices are legendary."

For a few moments there was no one but Rowan, and everything faded to gray except the two of them. It was like a physical tether had woven them together. The connection was that instant. That intense.

He drank in her pale features, and his hand rose to her cheek. The wound from the day before had already faded, thanks to her healing magick no doubt, but there was a new bruise along her jaw that traveled nearly to her ear. It was a mottled purple mess that brought anger to him.

She winced as his fingers ran over it and stepped away, clearly rattled.

"Who touched you?" he asked flatly, not liking the fact that someone had done so with a violent hand. Some protector he was, laid out flat on his back, as sick as a newborn. The thought fed his rage, but he knew better than to place the blame anywhere other than where it belonged.

Firmly on his shoulders. If he'd been stronger, this wouldn't have happened.

She licked her lips and ran fingers along her temple, her brow furling into a frown. "I'm not sure. It was something I've never encountered before. I can't even tell you if it was male or female or animal. There were layers to it that kept shifting, and it was a fast, slippery thing." She shrugged her shoulders. "I think it was surprised that I saw it." She sighed. "I guess it was a demon of some sort, and I'm pissed that it got away."

Azaiel watched her carefully. "From what I understand, it was you who got away."

Rowan glanced toward Priest and Nico, cheeks coloring slightly as if just realizing they weren't alone. When she finally spoke, she was all business. "You boys are up early."

"I don't sleep much," Nico answered tersely.

She arched a delicate brow at his ill-concealed hostility. "From the look on your sourpuss face I would have guessed you got up on the wrong side of the bed." She smiled then, a sweet, fake grin, and Azaiel stepped back, enjoying the show. "It might do you good to get some shut-eye." She shrugged. "Salem isn't for everyone, and I'll be honest, shifter." She paused, brow arched. "That is, if you want me to."

Nico's stony countenance was near comical. With clenched fists at his side, he growled. "I'm a big boy. There's no need to hold back."

Rowan nodded and took a step toward him. "I don't like you."

Surprise narrowed Nico's eyes, and Azaiel didn't think the shifter had expected such brutal honesty.

"Your attitude sucks. I don't know what your problem is with Azaiel and frankly, I don't care to. None of your private shit concerns me." She jerked her head toward the road. "Salem, the people that live here . . . my family . . . they concern me. The fact that I've got a deranged demon gunning for my ass." She glanced at all of them. "*That* concerns me. So check the ego and learn to get along because if you can't, *Nico*"—her eyes flashed as she emphasized his name—"maybe you should leave."

Priest tucked the remnants of his cigar into his pocket. "We're not going anywhere."

A subtle shift in energy flew from Rowan. It was a quick, silent attack that no one but Azaiel noticed. Rowan turned to the tall Knight Templar and glared at him. "Then I suggest you keep your overgrown kitty on a tight leash and discuss the consequence of his bad attitude."

For the first time in ages a genuine smile parted Azaiel's lips. The look on Nico's face was thunderous, the veins in his neck strained with the need to vocalize his displeasure, and yet he stood, glaring at the witch in silence.

He couldn't speak. Azaiel's grin widened even more.

"Or I will personally kick his ass all over Salem and back." She shifted her gaze toward Nico. "I told you last night. This is my war, and I'm calling the shots. There's only room for one alpha in this pack, and it sure as hell isn't any of you. I'll accept your help because I'm not stupid. The shit is about to hit, and it's going to hit hard." She gestured toward all of them. "Know this, gentlemen. If any of you get in my face, I'll not hesitate to rethink our arrangement." Her voice lowered then, a hint of menace in the tone that drew Azaiel's attention. "And don't make the mistake of thinking I won't back up my words with action." She flicked her wrist, and Nico choked, curses flying from his mouth as he clutched his throat.

Seemed to Azaiel the little witch had wasted no time reconnecting with her powers. He was impressed. The woman was nothing like the one he'd first encountered nearly forty-eight hours earlier, and it was good a thing. She'd need a tough skin to get through what was headed their way.

Rowan rotated her head and glanced at Azaiel. "You must be hungry." Gone was the warmth that he'd seen earlier— her dark blue eyes were hooded, and the garish bruise along her cheek more pronounced. He nodded, surprised at the pangs of hunger that sat low in his stomach.

"Let's eat. We've got lots to get done before nightfall."

CHAPTER 12

Azaiel stared down at the orange tabby and frowned. The damn thing wouldn't leave him alone, and he'd tossed it from his lap several times already. He'd been gentle—the little cat was obviously pregnant—but still, there was something unsettling in its long, slow blinks as it stared up at him. It looked almost . . . human in its regard and made him uncomfortable.

"I think she likes you."

He glanced at Rowan. "If it liked me, it would go find a corner and relax."

"She's not an 'it' Azaiel. She's a little tigress and needs a name." Rowan finished her coffee and placed the cup in the sink. They were the first words she'd spoken since they'd come inside.

"Then give her a name."

Her brow furled as she concentrated. "A name is so important." She glanced up, and the smile that lit her eyes was something to behold. "You get it wrong, and the poor thing could be scarred, you know?"

Azaiel's mood lightened. "Do you actually believe that the little fur ball knows the difference between a good name and a bad one?"

Rowan stroked the animal behind her ears, her long, delicate fingers massaging the tabby's neck in slow, methodical strokes. As he focused on them, his mouth went dry, and his mind went south.

"Of course she'll know." Rowan glanced up. For a moment their eyes locked, and he was sure her heart beat as fast and hard as his.

He cleared his throat. "Well, then. You'd better get it right."

"I'll try my best."

"Oh, Lord."

They both glanced toward Cedric, who stared back at them from his perch near the stove. His warm, chocolate eyes narrowed, and his lips pursed. "Uh-huh. You two best forget about that there feline and get some food into you."

Cedric had cooked up a feast of eggs, bacon, toast, home fries, and the sweetest strawberry jam ever. Azaiel and Rowan dug in, and the quality of the food was more than enough to make up for the strained atmosphere—if anything, it kept conversation to a minimum though the covert glances were hard to ignore.

Nico wasn't in his happy place, and the shifter had no qualms about letting everyone know his state of mind. He sat at the large table, legs stretched out in front of him while he stared out the window, looking like he'd rather be anywhere but where he was. His mood was foul, and not even Hannah's attempts to engage the shifter worked. The little blonde had given her best shot and now chomped her way through a bowl of cereal as she glared at the Jaguar.

Priest returned to the kitchen and stood alone, his face expressionless, though his eyes touched them all. He'd left to make a phone call, choosing his cell over the landline—which meant the identity of whoever he was calling wasn't meant for public consumption.

Azaiel caught Rowan's eyes upon Nico several times,

and, for whatever reason, he didn't like it. He knew Rowan was full of questions—the jaguar warrior's dislike wasn't exactly subtle—but he was in no hurry to explain the sins of his past.

They were a sorry-ass bunch and needed to gel somehow, or they wouldn't be successful. The thought of Rowan in Mallick's clutches made him ill, but the questions Priest had posed earlier were troublesome. What had the Knight Templar been getting at?

Rowan pushed away from the counter, bent slightly, and scratched the little animal behind her ears. "What shall we call you?" She glanced up and caught Azaiel's eye, a soft blush creeping up her cheeks before she straightened and looked away.

The last half hour had been an almost surreal expanse of time. There'd been no replay of the night before, and from what little he could see, a lot had happened. Aside from the bruise on Rowan's jaw, Hannah sported several cuts along her forearms, and her middle finger was broken. She'd laughed about it and said she didn't need the middle finger to unleash her extraextra specials. Azaiel had remained silent. He didn't find the joke funny.

Frank seemed to be all right though he was limping a bit, and Nico and Priest remained unscathed.

The words unspoken, the plans that needed to be addressed were like a weight across his chest, and Azaiel opened his mouth, intending to do just that, but the phone rang, and he didn't get the chance. For a moment startled silence followed its shrill sound. And then Hannah jumped off the counter where'd she'd been eating a bowl of Lucky Charms and scooped it up.

"The Black Cauldron, Hannah speaking." Her light brown eyebrows bunched in concentration, and she turned slightly, as if she didn't want anyone to hear her words. She listened for several seconds, and Azaiel noticed that both Priest and Nico watched with undisguised interest.

Rowan's eyes were trained on her cousin as well though her expression was hard to read.

"Abigail, you *have* to come. Oh good." Hannah's eyes darted toward Rowan, who'd pushed her chair back from the table. "What? No! Seriously you can't—"

Hannah bit her lip and shook her head. "I don't think that's a good idea." She spoke lower, though Azaiel had no trouble hearing her. "I told you we've got some extra bodies, and once the rest of the coven is here . . ." She darted another look at Rowan. "Yep, sure, I'll let her know. See you tonight."

She hung up, straightened the ceramic lime green frog that was near the sink, returned a plastic red sponge to its mouth, and, with a bright smile pasted to her face, nodded.

"What's the matter with you?" Rowan took a step closer. "You're acting really weird."

"So that was Abigail." Hannah's face looked pained as the smile forced upon it tightened even more.

"And?" Rowan prompted. She grabbed the ketchup off the table and threw it in the floor-to-ceiling pantry that stood beside the back door.

"She's coming," Hannah replied brightly.

Something was at play, and Azaiel studied the women closely. All was not good news.

"I got that."

Hannah rinsed out her cereal bowl and carefully dried it before she continued.

"She's uh, not coming alone."

Rowan swore. Loudly. "She better not bring her Canadian lumberjack. She knows better than that. Humans just get in the way." Her eyes darted toward Frank. "No offense."

The bartender nodded. "None taken."

Hannah's eyes glittered strangely, and she swallowed carefully before clearing her throat. "Ah, nope. Actually, they broke up. This whole freaking—she made quotation marks with her fingers—*legions of doom thing,* really worked out well for her . . ." Hannah's voice trailed off. "I mean, timing-wise that is."

"Really," Rowan answered softly. "So who's she bringing? Cousin Terre? Maybe Vicki?" There was a dangerous edge to her voice, and Azaiel glanced at her sharply.

"She was pretty upset last night when I told her about Auntie Cara, and she's really scared for you."

"That's nice, so who's she bringing?" Rowan wasn't fooling around and glared at her cousin. The tension in the room was palpable, and all the men had come to their feet.

"Oh Lord." Cedric sighed. "I knew this was coming."

"Don't be mad." Hannah's voice held a pleading note.

Rowan's frown deepened, and the two women had the undivided attention of every male in the room. Even the orange tabby jumped from the kitchen counter and weaved its soft length between the two women, as if trying to calm them both.

"Hannah," Rowan warned.

"Don't be mad," she said again.

"She called Kellen didn't she?"

Hannah nodded and winced.

Azaiel's ears perked up at the name, as did Priest's and Nico's. He watched Rowan closely, his muscles tensing at the look of . . . was that pain in her eyes? His jaw clenched tightly, and he narrowed his eyes. What did this man mean to her? Not that he should care . . . not that he *did* care, he just needed the witch focused.

Keep telling yourself that, my friend.

"He's not going to stay away, Rowan. Not when your life is on the line. Just because the two of you . . ." Hannah cleared her throat and stopped abruptly, obviously uncomfortable. "Just because the last time you were together all hell broke loose. And, let's be honest here Ro, you were a bitch."

Rowan froze, and absolute silence ruled the kitchen.

"Hey, don't get me wrong, Kellen was a total dick as well, but I don't think he deserved . . ." Hannah bit her lip and cleared her throat. "You two belong together. You always have. *Especially now.*"

Azaiel's eyes went flat as he stared at Rowan. Her back was rigid, her shoulders tucked in as if she were trying to gather what comfort she could. But it was no use. The woman was in pain, and he was pissed that he cared.

Rowan carefully closed a cupboard. She was silent for a good long while, her fingers absently running along the top of the tabby's back as its small body purred furiously.

Hannah glanced over to Cedric, but the old man was busy with some invisible speck of dust in the corner. Frank's face was white, which didn't bode well as far as Azaiel could tell.

He couldn't be quiet any longer. "Who the hell is this Kellen?" His words sounded a whole lot harsher than he'd meant them to. He ignored the sharp glance Priest sent his way, as well as the smug grin that lightened the jaguar's craggy features. To hell with them.

Rowan exhaled and ran her fingers through the loose hair at her shoulders. She, too, glanced at Cedric, who'd turned back to them, his dark eyes wary.

"Kellen is . . ." She scooped up the cat and held on tightly, so tight that the small tabby squirmed, and she let her hop back onto the floor.

Azaiel leaned forward and found himself hanging on, wanting to know and afraid to hear her answer at the same time. He thought of the man who'd called the first night,

Mason, and narrowed his eyes as he studied Rowan. Did the woman have lovers wherever she laid her head?

She glanced around the room once though her eyes skimmed them all as if she were searching for a place to hide. A shadow crossed her face, and she shrugged. "Kellen is a ghost from my past that I'm not sure I can face."

She was bitter.

Azaiel watched as she walked past all of them and slipped out into the backyard.

Bitter and hurt.

Rowan held her arms tight around her body, seeking what warmth she could even though inside she was as cold as ice. The sun was up and had burned off the frost that had coated everything only an hour ago, leaving the brown, dead things that littered the ground in warmth.

She kicked at a pile of shriveled leaves and watched them tumble and scatter in the breeze. She'd always loved fall. The turning of the seasons . . . it was one of the things she missed most about living in Salem.

But now? She watched a large maple leaf swirl in the air before it fell back onto the gray cobbled stone path. Now, she felt as dead and empty as the leaves seemed to be. Dislodged from their anchor, they went wherever the wind took them, wandering aimlessly. Lost. And in the end, they died alone.

Rowan's chest tightened, and she bent over to pick up the large leaf. It had turned a vibrant yellow, yet the frost had edged the tips with brown, and it was no longer soft but had a hard, crisp texture.

It was already half-dead, and by Samhain, would be nothing more than a shriveled-up piece of waste.

She held the leaf up to the sun, letting the anger inside

rush through her veins. Was this to be her fate? To wander the next few weeks anchorless? Would she perish, a prisoner of a demon lord? Destined to spend her youth and whatever she had left deep beneath the human realm, ensconced in the underworld?

The leaf fell from her fingers and drifted away, catching a tide of wind that took it high into the sunshine, only to disappear beyond the gardens.

Would she survive Mallick's onslaught? Would she have the chance to grow old and have children? She thought of Azaiel and her cheeks flushed crimson. She shook her head and squared her shoulders. Why the hell would she think about him? Sure, he was gorgeous with his abs of steel, wide shoulders, long legs, and to-die-for mouth.

But he was also dangerous. She knew this. She felt it in her bones. And Rowan had vowed never to involve herself with a man who was otherworld. What was the point? It only complicated things, and her life . . . her very existence . . . was complicated enough.

Besides, she had Mason waiting for her when this whole crazy mess was over. So he'd not seemed overly concerned when she'd called to tell him she'd be staying a few extra weeks. He hadn't even asked why. It wasn't their way. They didn't have an intense relationship. It was calm. Comforting. Trusting.

With his lazy Californian way and slow kind of charm, the man was kind of perfect. He never got in her face, or asked questions about her family, or left the toilet seat up. He was stable. Had a good job and with his bookish ways, loved the quiet life, which for Rowan had been the prize she'd sought after such a tumultuous childhood.

She bit her lip. So maybe the sex wasn't all that great, but it wasn't bad either. Okay sex was better than nothing. Wasn't it?

I bet sex with Azaiel would be mind-blowing.

Rowan swore and banished all thoughts of Azaiel and sex from her mind. Why would she even go there? *Because he's got a killer body, and you're dying to see him naked.*

She whirled around, eyes narrowed as she gazed at the house. Dammit, was Hannah putting these thoughts into her head?

Rowan sighed. There was so much to think about. So much to plan, and now with Kellen coming back . . .

She sniffled and wiped at the corner of her eyes, wincing at the pain that crept along her jaw. She couldn't think about Kellen right now. Couldn't think about the way they'd parted. The anger, harsh words, mistrust, and, ultimately, the disappointment that was between them.

If he was coming—and she'd believe that when it happened—then they'd have it out, but right now there were more important things to do. Time was ticking away, and she needed to put the first part of her plan in motion.

Rowan pulled up her big-girl pants, turned her butt around and headed back inside. There was no time to wallow in self-pity. No time to dwell on memories filled with ghosts and bad tidings. If she lost this war, there'd be time enough for all of that, but right now, she needed to gather her troops.

Everyone was in the kitchen when she entered. Hannah was deep in conversation with Priest and Nico. She looked up quickly, a guilty look on her face, and Rowan's eyes narrowed. If Hannah was putting sinful inappropriate thoughts in her mind, she'd deal with her later.

Cedric and Frank were cleaning weapons—the kitchen table was overloaded with them—and Azaiel leaned against the counter, trying like hell to ignore the orange tabby, who seemed determined to win him over.

Rowan took a second and glanced at all of them though she didn't quite meet Azaiel's gaze. With the lusty thoughts and fresh images of his naked body still burned into her brain, she didn't think it was a good idea. For all she knew, he had mind-reading capabilities.

Wouldn't that be an awkward thing to explain?

"Have you contacted everyone in the coven?" She directed her question to Hannah, and her cousin nodded vigorously, moving away from Nico and Priest.

"Yes, they'll be here within the next few days. Terre and Vicki should be home by tomorrow. Clare is in Europe, but she's catching the first plane from Dublin, so a few days at most, and I've not heard back from Simone though I left a message. Abigail and"—she stumbled—"Kellen will be here tonight."

"Good." Rowan nodded to Cedric. "Okay, it's time."

Cedric carefully placed the gun he'd been cleaning back on the table and slowly got to his feet. He walked with an uneven gait—his arthritis was worse in his right leg—and as he left the kitchen she caught the look that passed between Hannah and Frank.

Azaiel pushed away from the kitchen counter, muscles rippling across his shoulders as he stretched. You really could bounce a damn quarter off the perfection that was his abs, and if those jeans slipped any lower . . . She shot him a look of irritation.

"Can you not put a shirt on?" she snapped, eyes stormy, temper rising.

I did not just say that out loud.

His golden eyes darkened, and she hoped like hell he wasn't going to acknowledge her comment.

"What's it time for, Rowan?" Priest asked quietly.

Rowan exhaled and squared her shoulders. Saved by the priest it seemed. "We're going to spring my mother from the asylum." And break a few dozen laws along the way.

Nico moved forward. "Mental institutions have security, yes, but it's minimal at best."

Rowan studied his dark, fathomless eyes. "You were locked up?" The question was more of a joke, but the jaguar's eyes flattened, and his mouth thinned.

"Yes."

"I'm sorry to hear that." And she was. When the shifter wasn't being an arrogant asshole, there was substance there that held a whole lot of pain and hurt.

"It shouldn't be hard. Not for us." Priest flashed a smile. It was obvious he was eager to do something more than sit around her kitchen table waiting for the enemy to come to them.

"Shit, you have no idea," Hannah muttered.

"Mother's not in a human institution." Rowan paused. How could she make them understand? "It's more like Azkaban." At the blank looks on both Nico and Azaiel, she shook her head, clearly disgusted. "Harry Potter anyone? Seriously? Where the hell have you guys been hiding?"

Priest stepped forward. "You don't want to know. I, however, am more than familiar with human pop culture. What's the story with this place?"

"There is no way in other than by blood, and since I'm banned from the island, that won't work," Rowan replied.

"Why are you banned?" Azaiel asked.

"You really don't want to know." Hannah shook her head.

Rowan shot a look at her cousin that said zip it before meeting Azaiel's probing gaze. "It's not important. It just is."

"So we break in." Azaiel moved closer.

"Yes." Rowan nodded. "But it's not that easy."

"Nothing ever is." His eyes were still flat, and, for a second, she thought that maybe he was angry with her.

Priest spoke up and motioned around the room. "Trust me. I don't think this group will have trouble breaking into an otherworld insane asylum."

Rowan didn't bother to answer. The man had no clue as to the real power that existed amongst sorcerers and witches.

If he did, he wouldn't have made such a flip comment. She decided there and then that at some point over the next few weeks, she'd make sure Priest understood it. Fully.

There were those who knew, those who would take . . . those like Mallick.

"*If* we make it into the asylum and right now, that's a big if, there's the whole problem of actually getting back out . . ."

"If we can get in, we'll make it out," Azaiel cut in.

Rowan took a second. Breathe. "I've no doubt we'll find a way out once inside. I was more concerned with keeping my mother unharmed and making sure we have all of our body parts intact."

Priest frowned. "Okay, just so we're clear. What's the reason for this breakout?" He glanced around the room. "If the shit is coming down here in Salem, won't your mother be safer inside some heavily protected asylum?"

"I need her," Rowan answered. "She may be crazy, but she's still a James witch, and her power is impressive."

She didn't like the way Priest's eyes narrowed. He didn't believe her. Rowan held his gaze for several seconds before looking away. Screw him. The fact that he was right to be suspicious only made her more defensive. She *did* need her mother's power, but it was the other reason she needed her that mattered more.

Rowan just hoped Marie-Noelle's mind wasn't so far gone that she'd be useless.

Azaiel nodded toward the door. "Let's go do it then. There's no point in just talking about it." A frosty smile crossed his features. "I'll even put a shirt on for you."

"If you must," she replied with equal coolness. "We'll go, but first . . ."

"But first?" Priest prodded.

Rowan's attention turned to Cedric as he walked back

into the kitchen with a large scroll in his grasp. He also clutched something under the crook of his right arm.

Frank and Hannah removed all the weapons from the large table, and Rowan helped Cedric spread an ancient map on the table. Her fingers trailed across the tobacco-colored paper and followed lines that had been etched centuries earlier by a relative . . . a woman whose blood she carried in her veins.

Pretty powerful stuff. It was but one piece of her history— one piece of her soul—and she was filled with emotion.

She glanced at Cedric, and mouthed, *"Thank you."*

She eyed the faded parchment, then turned to the men, and whispered, "First we have to find it."

CHAPTER 13

"You have to find it." It was a statement, not a question. Priest no longer looked like he was in his happy "we get to go hunting and possibly kill things" kind of place. "How can you not know where it is?"

Rowan gave Priest an irritated look, which she then passed to Nico—in case he had any ideas of getting in her face. For the tenth time that morning, she thought about how much men complicated things. They were always second-guessing, throwing their weight around, and trying like hell to take over.

She just wanted them to ease up and give her a little breathing room.

Mostly, she wished that Azaiel would move the hell back. The Seraphim had stepped closer, to get a look at the map no doubt, but it was much too close for comfort. *Her comfort.*

"Step away, people. This is a valuable James family heirloom, and if any of you so much as breathe on it, I'll give you the worst case of face warts ever."

Frank and Cedric moved back immediately, and they both looked at the three remaining men as if they were crazy. Cedric tugged on his chin. "Just so you boys know, the last time Miss Rowan spelled a case of face warts, the entire football team was quarantined." He paused dramatically. "For two whole weeks."

"Crap, I forgot about that, though it could have been worse," Hannah agreed. "She was so pissed at the quarterback that I thought for sure she'd make their peckers fall off too."

Nico, Priest, and Azaiel moved back.

Rowan ignored all of it. Her focus was clear, and she was more than a little anxious to get started.

"Cedric, can I have it?"

Cedric nodded and withdrew a plastic Ziploc bag.

"Hannah, get the candles. They're in the walk-in pantry, on the last shelf, tucked away near the back. Behind the big blue water jug." She looked at Cedric. "At least that's where they used to be."

"Nothing's changed, Miss Rowan." A sad smile crossed his face as he carefully unzipped the plastic bag and grabbed the hairbrush. "Your grandmother was a creature of habit."

"Good." A thought crossed her mind, and she turned quickly. "Hannah, don't forget to—"

"Mother-trucker!" The shriek was instant, followed by a string of cusswords that weren't anything like the G-rated version.

"Ask the goddess for permission to enter," Rowan finished lamely, wincing as she glanced back toward the pantry.

"Is she all right?" Nico asked gruffly.

Rowan turned to Nico in surprise. "She'll be . . . fine." The shifter didn't reply but relaxed against the doorframe. She wasn't fooled. The jaguar was strung tighter than a yo-yo, and she got the impression that maybe Azaiel wasn't the only thing making him uncomfortable.

She looked pointedly at Azaiel. "I'm going to need you and Priest for this spell. Without the coven present I need more power. I'll be tapping into yours if that's all right."

Azaiel nodded. "Fine with me."

Priest agreed as well. "Whatever you need."

"Good. I promise to be gentle."

Priest's eyes darkened. "Don't be gentle on my account. I like it a little rough."

"That, I don't doubt." She tried to be sarcastic but failed miserably. There was something about the tall man that made her nervous. An edge that was raw and secrets that were painful. How could you be flip with someone like that?

Azaiel remained silent, but she didn't miss the narrowed eyes or the muscle that flexed across his jaw. She turned quickly, wanting out from under his gaze. He was a whole new can of worms entirely.

She glanced at the shifter. "*You* need to stay the hell out of the way. Understood?"

"Yes, ma'am."

She ignored Nico's sarcasm and tried to ignore Azaiel, but he'd moved closer to the table, his brow furled in concentration as he studied the old map. His jeans hung way too low on his hips, the wide belt doing nothing but drawing the eye to the thin brush of hair that shadowed his taut lower belly and disappeared from sight.

Keep your eyes above the neck.

She gave herself a mental shake, and when he bent forward her eyes climbed higher until she settled upon the scars that graced the tops of his shoulders. Even though they looked painful, there was something striking about the way they cloaked Azaiel. The more she studied them, she realized they were not so much a reflection of violence but one of the power within him.

He cleared his throat, and she glanced into his eyes, startled and embarrassed that he'd caught her staring at him like a goofy teenager. All thought fled her mind, leaving only a blank canvas, and she blurted out the first thing that popped into her mind.

"It will take us a few minutes to prepare for the spell, so . . . now would be a good time to throw on some clothes."

Priest snorted, and though Azaiel's eyes darkened—the gold much diminished as black bled through—he gave her a look she couldn't quite read.

"Sorry my state of undress offends, but at the moment, I have nothing to wear."

She'd insulted him. She saw it in his eyes. "Azaiel, you don't offend me, really. It's just, well everyone else is . . ." She gestured toward Priest and Nico. "I just prefer . . ." Oh God, Rowan, shut the hell up and stop babbling. "I prefer you in clothes, that's all."

"You're probably the only female in the county who would," Hannah said in disbelief.

Rowan ignored her cousin and was thankful when Cedric intervened.

"Come with me." Cedric nodded. "We've got a trunkful of clothes that have been left behind over the years. I'm sure we'll be able to find you something."

Azaiel's eyes lingered for a moment too long, and she looked away, hating the flush that crept up her cheeks. He followed Cedric from the room, and Rowan didn't know she was holding her breath until it escaped in a rush.

Hannah frowned and held up her hands. "Look at these." The tips looked raw, and several small blisters were forming.

"Suck it up. That's what happens when you don't—"

"Respect the goddess," Hannah finished. "I know, but sheesh, she doesn't have to be such a bitch about it."

Rowan took the candles from Hannah as well as a small dagger that was no longer than the tip of her fingers to the edge of her wrist. The handle was delicate, an antique cream ivory that felt smooth in her hand. The shiny blade was charmed with several intricate etchings that darkened the silver and climbed up the hilt.

They were druid markings and held much power.

She put the dagger down and unwrapped the candles. They'd been stored in a plain beige-linen cloth that unraveled with ease. Carefully, she placed the candles at each corner of the map. They represented the four elements that she commanded and would tap into their power to fuel the spell.

The blue one in the east—water. The red one in the south—fire. The white one the north—air. And the green one to the west—earth.

When she was done, she accepted a bowl from Cedric—one that was older than anyone cared to remember—its clay facade was a faded copper color, with large, dull brown, spidery cracks lining the sides. She carefully set it in the middle of the map next to the dagger and blew out a strained breath.

Sunlight fell in from outside, spilling over the large kitchen table and showering the map in fingers of gold. It looked . . . beautiful. Nervous energy rolled through her body, and she brushed back a strand of hair that stuck to her sweaty neck. Her stomach felt queasy, but she gritted her teeth and tried her best to focus.

She couldn't screw this up.

"Hey." Hannah's warm hand on her shoulder felt like a memory—a wonderful, warm-you-to-your-toes kind of memory. How could she have let the two of them grow apart? She'd given Mallick too much power, and it was going to stop.

"You'll be fine. Trust me."

"It's just been so long." Rowan tried not to let her fear get the best of her, but the damn doubt weasels were circling fast and hard. "And this is so important." She bit her lip and shuddered. "If I don't get to her, Mallick will." Her eyes widened, and she did her best to stop the hot prick of tears. "I can't let that happen. I can't lose my mother. Not after everything I did to keep her safe. Not after Nana." Her voice broke, and she inhaled a ragged breath, trying hard to calm her out-of-control nerves.

"You won't." Azaiel's low timbre sent shivers rushing across her skin.

Rowan turned in a rush, her hand skimming his taut chest. He was much too close—again—but as she stared up into his fathomless eyes, for one moment of clarity she knew it would work. She saw the power that lived inside him—it was reflected in their depths—and she drew from that. She nodded. "Okay. Let's do this."

"What the hell are you wearing?"

They both turned at Hannah's shocked exclamation, and Rowan followed her cousin's gaze, for the first time seeing what covered up the broad chest she was so close to.

"It was all that fit," was Azaiel's terse reply.

Behind them, Nico guffawed, and Priest snorted.

"It's . . ." Rowan's mouth twitched. "It's very *pink*."

Azaiel wore a tight-fitting V-neck T-shirt with a jewel-encrusted HELLO KITTY logo across the chest. The cloth had a shiny texture to it—spandex maybe—and did more to enhance the six pack he sported than anything else. He looked both ridiculous and hot all at once.

Cedric hid a grin. "I forgot I'd donated everything at the beginning of summer. There were only a few items of children's clothes and . . . this."

Azaiel scowled. "Can we get this done? Tick tock and all that."

"No sense of humor, Seraphim?" Nico gloated.

Rowan turned to the jaguar, her hand raised. "Are we going to go there, Nico?"

The shifter's grin died slowly, replaced with a scowl that was fierce, and he stepped back, arms crossed over his chest.

Rowan exhaled, her voice barely a whisper as the heaviness of the situation pressed on her. "Let's do this. Hannah, Priest, come." She directed them around the table, Azaiel to her left, Priest on her right, and Hannah across from her. Once they were in place she cleared everything from her mind and went to work.

She reached for the bowl, set it before her, and stared down at the dagger as her heart beat hard inside her chest. She was so damn hot. *So damn scared.* A week ago she'd been in Europe, flush with the excitement of her job, of being entrusted with an overseas meeting—and the lights of Paris. She'd had Mason waiting for her at home, Monday night cooking classes, and now . . . now her world was tilted, its axis spinning out of control, and she had no clue if she had what it took to set things right.

Hannah pulled a strand of her mother's hair from the brush and dropped it into the bowl.

"You can do this Rowan." Azaiel spoke quietly.

She nodded okay and grabbed the dagger, slicing through her palm without hesitation. The sting was instant and the burn harsh. Sweat broke out on her forehead as she held her hand over the bowl and watched her blood drip downward.

Not a word was spoken.

When enough had fallen, she placed the dagger beside her and wiped off the excess blood with the linen cloth used to store the candles. She touched her finger to the wound in her palm, closed her eyes, concentrated, and recited a healing charm. It was one of the first her mother had taught her—a simple spell used to heal scrapes and bruises.

And it was enough.

Rowan held out her hands, and their small circle was completed. She felt the strength, the well of power that the men on either side of her harnessed, and she saw how Hannah's eyes widened. She felt it, too.

Blue eyes met as the two women gathered their own strength. Tapped into their wells of power and deep-rooted beliefs. Took from the goddess, whose spirit watched over them all.

The candles erupted in fire, each one burning brightly, as Hannah and Rowan began their spell.

Travel through the sands of time
Find us that which is mine
Allow the sight to reach its goal
Bind to us our long-lost soul

The bowl rose into the air, and Rowan watched it closely, sweat dripping from her brow as she concentrated and held the power still. She couldn't lie—the thrill she felt as her energy connected with Hannah's was intoxicating. The conduit of power from Azaiel and Priest electrified her cells in a way she'd never felt before.

For one brief moment as the connection between the four of them solidified, images and emotions assaulted her. It was a heady mixture that left her panting. A cross. Instruments of torture. Fire. Rage. An eagle. Despair.

They were gone as fast as they'd come, but a lingering touch stayed behind—an intrusion inside her head. Rowan gritted her teeth and slammed her mental doors shut—the ones that protected her innermost secrets—and pushed back. Hard.

Someone wanted something from her, but who? Irritated, Rowan easily cleared her mind. She'd deal with it later.

As she and Hannah continued to chant, the bowl turned in the air, slowly to the right four times, then back to the left the same number of turns. It hovered over the map, seeming to drift aimlessly. The weight of that bowl in the air was like a slab of stone pressed against her chest. It seemed to hover forever, but she knew that, in fact, mere minutes had passed.

All eyes were on the bowl as it slowly stopped turning, and the cracks that ran along the circumference liquefied into long, spidery arms of black. Blood seeped through. One single drop slipped out and fell onto the map.

Rowan tugged her hands from the men, grabbed the bowl from the air, and set it beside her. She pushed several strands of hair from her neck, hating how they stuck to her slick, sweaty skin. She was light-headed and jittery, but all was forgotten as she gazed upon the map. Hannah studied it closely as well, her eyes alive with a fever that Rowan knew all too well. Magick was like a drug, and the euphoric feeling that accompanied its use was indescribable.

It had led many a weak witch to an early grave.

Cedric, Frank, and Nico moved in closer, and they all stared down at the table. Rowan's fingers trembled as she pointed toward the map. "There," she whispered.

Frank leaned in and nodded. "Okay then. Guess we're headed to Maine."

Azaiel nodded to Priest. "A word?"

Priest and Nico followed him outside. They left Rowan and Hannah quietly packing up their tools of magick, while Cedric and Frank had disappeared into the basement to check out the weapons situation.

Azaiel's long strides didn't stop until he'd reached the far end of the property. A large oak tree spread its branches above him, most of the leaves dead and missing. The sun still shone—he felt the warmth on his face—but coldness settled inside him and left a bitter taste in his mouth.

Priest lit the end of his cigar, his eyes hard as he clenched the cigar tightly between his teeth. "You felt it? You saw?"

Azaiel nodded. "The power inside her is impressive. Above the norm even for a James witch."

Soft swirls of smoke blew between them. Nico glanced back toward the house, eyes flat, voice subdued. "What the hell is she?"

"I have no idea," Priest offered up, his gaze sharp as he stared at Azaiel. "But this changes things. A lot."

The coldness inside Azaiel fisted. He knew what the Templar was getting at. And he knew Priest was right.

"Yes." Azaiel nodded. "It does."

Azaiel followed Nico's gaze and exhaled a long, slow breath. Mallick would never stop searching for Rowan. She held something inside her that made it impossible for the demon to do so—which meant that the demon had to be destroyed. He could not be allowed to claim her. The balance between the realms would fall apart and plunge their worlds into chaos.

But Mallick was a demon lord. Destroying him wasn't going to be easy. If only . . . Azaiel turned away in disgust, his hands clenched into fists, his jaw sore with tension. If only he had the full extent of his power, it would be within reach. But he'd been cut off, and rightly so.

"If we can't defeat Mallick . . ." Priest said, the cigar held tight in his mouth.

"She'll have to be destroyed," Azaiel finished. Hearing the words spoken filled him with anger, and he rolled his head, stretching out the muscles in his shoulders and neck.

"A shame," Nico said grudgingly. "Even though the witch hates my guts, there's something about her I like."

The coldness inside Azaiel evaporated, leaving a rush of heat that electrified his spirit and mind. He might be weaker than any other of his kind, but he was still Seraphim. He could still do damage. And he wasn't alone.

He addressed the two men, for the first time really feeling his own power—one that was fed with purpose.

"Remember that, shifter, because I have a feeling this is

going to be the toughest assignment you've had, and I"—his eyes bled black—"don't intend for her to die."

"Well then." Priest tossed his finished Montecristo into a pile of browned, dead leaves. "Let's get this done."

They turned toward the house. "But Seraphim, one suggestion?"

Azaiel paused, brow arched in question. He didn't like the Templar's tone.

Priest grinned widely and pushed past Azaiel. "A change in wardrobe might be a good idea. I don't relish the thought of storming an otherworld asylum beside a man wearing Hello fucking Kitty on his T-shirt."

CHAPTER 14

They arrived on the coast of Maine at nightfall.

A cold wind blew off the water, carrying with it a hint of darkness that immediately had everyone on edge. Overhead a moonless sky held up a blanket of diamondlike stars though their light was muted and did nothing to penetrate the inky black that hovered over them. Large swells of water broke against the shore, a melody Azaiel had not heard in eons, and though it was a crisp, cold, fall evening, there was something soothing about the sound that warmed his soul.

"Goddamn, it's miserable out here." Frank shivered and pulled his thick black sweater closer to his burly frame.

Nervous tension hung in the air—so thick you could cut your teeth on it—and Azaiel knew there was good reason for it. The otherworld asylum was well guarded with both protective spells and who knew what else. This was not an easy task.

Their plan was simple in theory. Gain access to the island and split into three teams. The locator spell had given them the island, but it wasn't an exact science, and Rowan's mother could be anywhere. Once her mother was located and extracted they'd fall back to their boat and head to the mainland, then to Salem, where several of the coven were due to arrive.

They'd decided to go ahead with the extraction and not wait for any members of the coven due in to Salem—time was their enemy, and the sooner they retrieved Rowan's mother, the better. They'd left Cedric at The Black Cauldron, safe behind a heavily fortified protective wall that Hannah and Rowan had worked on for several hours. The charm should be enough to keep anything that didn't belong out.

"There's the boat." Priest nodded toward the dock. He'd made a few inquiries and found someone willing to take them out to the island—but more importantly someone willing to wait for their return. Who knows what the hell they faced.

"Let's go." Rowan led the way, and several moments later their boots treaded soundlessly across a rickety dock until they stood before a tall man Priest addressed as Scar.

He was otherworld, there was no mistaking the scent of it, but exactly *what* he was remained a mystery. Priest hadn't offered up that information, and no one had asked. It was enough that he'd been willing to get them to the island though apparently he owed Priest a favor. Judging by the scowl that settled on his craggy face, it most likely was the only reason he'd agreed to it.

Scar stared at them in silence for a few moments, eyes narrowed. Each of them had charmed guns strung across their shoulders, as well as daggers tucked into scabbards tied to their waists and boots.

"Time to do this." Scar motioned toward the boat.

Azaiel waited until all were on board, then hopped over to land a few inches from Rowan. She'd been quiet since they'd located the island though he'd caught her eyes upon him a few times. Questions hung there and maybe . . . fear?

He thought of the mysterious Kellen, who most likely would be waiting for them when they got back. He didn't like it. Didn't like that this Kellen meant something to Rowan.

His mouth tightened, and he looked away. He sure as hell didn't like that he was thinking about her ex-lover when he should be preparing for what promised to be an intense mission.

Scar was aptly named—a jagged raw line ran from his temple down his cheek and disappeared beneath the edge of his coat. His expression sharpened as he settled in behind the wheel. "Hold on. These waters are rough, and I'm sure you can sense the ill wind that blows."

Azaiel drew his jacket closer. The man was right. He didn't like the feel of things out there and knew by the way Rowan kept biting her lip, she felt the same.

Silence fell between them all as the boat slowly moved away from the dock, and, once clear, Scar gunned the motor.

The ride was rough as they navigated their way through several islands. Some of them were nothing more than large rocks protruding from the water, while others were miles long and sported luxury hotels or private homes.

After nearly twenty minutes the boat slowed as thick fog rolled around them in waves of cool mist that swirled crazily, pushed along by the wind. There was no sound other than the motor, and Azaiel's heart beat against his chest, a strong pounding that fed the adrenaline inside.

They were close. He felt it.

He glanced down at Rowan and, without thinking, his hand rose, his fingers dragging softly against her cheek. For one brief moment, she leaned into his touch, and something inside him unraveled, filling him with such intense emotion that it startled him, and he pulled back.

"Stick with me, and you'll be fine," he said roughly.

She cleared her throat and shot him a grin, answering cheekily. "More like the other way around, I think."

"If you say so."

"I say so."

He nodded. Good. She was going to need all the spunk she could handle in order to make it through the next few hours.

"Something's not right." Nico stared into the darkness ahead, and they gasped as the mist evaporated, and the craggy shoreline of the asylum island came into view. Huge swells of water rushed against the rock, spilling massive fists of foamy water into the air, threatening to crush anything that came close.

But it wasn't the near-impossible landing that grabbed everyone's attention.

"Holy fuck." Hannah's tortured whisper pretty much said it all.

A lighthouse perched overtop the edge of the island was in darkness, its shape only discernible because behind it, all the buildings that made up the asylum were in flames.

Like the turning of a page, reality bled through the charms that hid the island from human view. Chaos reigned, and shouts of pain and anger colored the night sky.

"Hurry," Azaiel barked. He glanced at Priest. "Is he here?" And cursed his need to ask. As Seraphim, he should know if the demon lord Mallick was close. He hated that he'd been blinded in this way . . . that he could sense something dark but had no clue what it was.

"No," Rowan answered bitterly. "He's still hiding, but it's obvious he knows my mother is here."

Priest's terse nod confirmed her answer, and he breathed a bit easier. If the demon lord had decided to come on this raid personally, that would open up the whole can of worms regarding Rowan's need to live. Or die.

Azaiel wasn't ready to deal with that just yet.

"We need to get to her before they do," Rowan said quietly. He nodded and turned.

We will.

Scar guided his boat around the top end of the island and brought them in alongside several boats already moored in place at a large, rickety dock. Frank and Priest jumped onto the platform and tied up the boat while Rowan, Azaiel, Hannah, and Nico followed them onto the dock.

"Well, now, at least we can thank these dumb bastards for one thing." Frank adjusted his rifle and waved his Glock toward the asylum.

"What's that?" Priest asked, his eyes trained on the chaos before them.

"They pretty much took care of security. There's no one here."

Rowan exhaled. "We stick to the same game plan and use the craziness up there to our advantage. As soon as we locate my mother, signal the rest of the teams and fall back. Hannah and Nico take the left side, Priest and Frank the right. Azaiel and I will take the center." She glanced at each and every one of them, and it struck Azaiel how easy it was for the woman to take command and be a leader. "Remember, we're cloaked under a powerful invisibility charm, but I have no idea how long it will last. We need to make this quick."

Azaiel nodded. "We all set?" he asked. The jaguar was still, his eyes narrowed as he studied the terrain before them.

"Nico?"

"Sure." Nico smiled harshly. "Hundreds of crazy-ass otherworlders on the loose, a pack of who the hell knows what waiting for us . . . we're outgunned and outnumbered . . ." The shifter grinned, his eyes lit with an unholy fire. "What the hell are we waiting for?" Nico pushed Hannah forward. "Let's go."

The two of them disappeared from sight as they scrambled up the steep steps that led to the top of the island. Frank and Priest followed suit. Azaiel looked down into Rowan's tense features. He knew how hard this was for her. It wasn't just another mission to run. This wasn't just another target to retrieve. It was her mother.

"Ready?" he asked softly.

Rowan nodded, eye focused on the steps. "More than ready, but the question is"—she arched a brow and smiled, a bit of crazy lighting her features—"are you?" Rowan took off at a run, leaving him to follow in her tracks as she followed the others. Once they cleared the steps that led from the shoreline up the cliff, he was greeted by a sight that was sobering to say the least. It looked as if the entire world was on fire.

Bodies littered the immediate area—some demon, but most were guards. Nico was right. The outer security detail had been decimated.

Cries of anguish ripped through the night, followed by screams of pain and bellows of rage. "Hurry!" Rowan shouted, and she was off running full tilt for the largest building in the center of everything. Its shell consisted of large slabs of slate stone, but the roof was awash with flame, and through the windows, more of the same was visible, with the added bonus of billowing black clouds of smoke.

Azaiel followed on Rowan's heels, his large sword unsheathed and held in his right hand, while a deadly modified Glock in his left pointed ahead. The bullets were freshly charmed and would rip apart anything—human or otherwise.

They zipped past an intense battle between a pack of blood demons—the aggressive creatures seemed to be Mallick's demon of choice—and a security detail of mixed otherworld creatures, including magicks, vampires, and a couple of gargoyles. The blood demons were ferocious creatures, and he understood why Mallick cultivated their loyalty. Death was the only thing that stopped the damn things.

The large door to the building was open, barely hanging from its hinges, and thick smoke continued to erupt from inside. Rowan dove in without pause, Azaiel inches behind.

Fear was as thick as the smoke that clogged his throat, and Azaiel stared into eyes half-crazed from the weight of it. A female werewolf, howling in pain because her body was caught in half shift—her bottom half lupine while the top still human—stumbled past him and disappeared into the chaos outside.

He and Rowan moved with quick precision through the main lobby, dodging the flood of demons and inmates who roamed about crazily. It was like a scene from one of the horror movies that humans seemed to love so.

She made a quick turn to the right, slicing off the head of a demon as she went by, and disappeared down a dark corridor. The fire continued to rage over their heads, and the moans of pain and fear sounded vaguely familiar—raw and animalistic. It was the music of choice below, deep in the bowels of District Three.

They entered a long, dormitory-type area, with cells lining each side. Several of the cell doors hung wide open, and the small rooms were empty. Demons were everywhere and Rowan was like an avenging angel as she made her way toward each and every one of them, calling for her mother and slaying anything that stood in her path. The dumb bastards had no chance as they couldn't see her, but a few of the demons sensed her presence just seconds before she separated head from shoulders.

Azaiel took the left side, and the two of them made quick work of it. They liberated poor souls still trapped as they made their way down the long rows, but when they reached the end, there was no sign of Rowan's mother.

"She must be in one of the other buildings." Rowan's voice cracked, and he knew how hard it was for her to be there. To do this. Hell, less than a week earlier, she'd been playing the part of a normal human, safe and secure in her life on the West Coast. And now? Now she was an executioner, a demon-fighting queen with a master of darkness hard on her ass.

Her eyes met his then, and his breath caught in his chest. She was magnificent.

A small man darting through the chaos caught his eye, and he leapt forward, hands nearly crushing him as the small weasel tried to escape. He looked up, startled, eyes wide and arms flailing.

"Who's there? What madness is this?" He was dressed for bed, his small, round body cloaked in red-and-gold brocade. One foot still wore a slipper while the other was bare, the fat, stubby toes pale in the dull light. The man coughed furiously, his body shaking as he tried to clear his lungs.

"Where is the James witch?" Azaiel growled, leaning forward and willing his face to bleed through the invisibility charm so that the little man could see exactly who held him.

The man stopped moving as his watery blue gaze stared into Azaiel's features in astonishment. His energy shifted, and Azaiel realized he was fae. Dark fae . . . and the mention of the James witch filled the man with fear.

Interesting.

"Where is she?" Rowan moved in closer, and the man's head whipped around crazily.

"Who are you?" he shouted into the darkness, while all around them demons continued to flood the room, searching for the same prize that Rowan so desperately sought.

"I'm going to be your worst nightmare if you don't tell me where my mother is." Rowan was inches from the man's face, and though he couldn't see her, his fear was palpable.

"Her line ended. The mark died out." The whites of his

eyes bulged, and a whimper fell from his lips. "We would never have taken her otherwise."

"Her line has been remade."

Rowan fell from shadow; for one brief moment, the small fae went limp in Azaiel's hand.

"How can it be?" he whispered hoarsely. "I would know. Surely, Darrak would have . . ." A sob caught in his throat. "Sweet goddess, but you look so much like Marie-Noelle." He paused, and something akin to fear crept into his eyes. "God help us."

"News flash, buddy." Rowan smiled harshly. "God isn't here, and he sure as hell isn't helping you, so listen closely. I will only ask one more time. Where is she?" Rowan held her bloodied and well-used sword aloft, and it seemed to Azaiel that she enjoyed the fae's fear immensely.

"I knew it was a bad idea to take her. All those years ago. I knew this and now . . . now Mallick knows." The little man gulped for air and coughed crazily as he struggled to breathe. "You must take her from here." The smoke was thicker, and Azaiel knew they were nearly out of time.

"Where is she?"

"In the dungeon rooms on the other side of the island."

Rowan raised her brow and sneered. "If she's damaged in any way, I will rip your insides from your body and feed them to the blood demons who seek you." She nodded. "Show us where the dungeons are."

Azaiel tapped his com unit. "Priest? Nico?"

"Copy." Priest's voice sounded forced. "No luck here."

"She's in a dungeon on the far side of the island. We'll get her and bring her to you. Keep the path to the boat clear."

"Done." A rush of static filled Azaiel's ear. "I'd hurry it up, princess; looks like another boatload of baddies has landed. Human soldiers mixed with otherworld. We'll keep them busy, but don't take all night."

Azaiel turned to Rowan. "Let's go."

He half carried, half pushed the small fae along, taking out several demons as they made their way from the burning building out into a night sky that was on fire.

Rain had started to fall, thick, cold sheets of it hitting his face like bullets. Already the fires that raged along the tops of the three main buildings were starting to wither though the heavy smoke still billowed upward.

They ran through the chaos—the noise and the wall of pain that hung over the asylum—the small fae's legs pumping as if the very devil were on his heels. Up ahead, through the torrent of water that fell, a small shape loomed against the dead gray sky.

The three of them arrived just as Nico and Hannah did. Both the witch and the shifter looked a little worse for wear—clothes ripped, skin covered in thick, dark soot.

"The roof caved in overtop of us just as we were about to leave. Took out at least six bloodsucking demons," Hannah said breathlessly. "Unfortunately, I was underneath them all." She cracked a grin and winced as she clutched her side. "Nico saved me."

"It was nothing," the shifter said gruffly.

The small fae had no clue who or what surrounded him, but he pointed toward the building. "She's in there, but it's charmed against intrusion."

Rowan snarled and smacked the little man. Hard. His head rocked backward, and he howled in pain, turning wildly, trying to see her.

"You think that will stop me?"

The tone of her voice changed. It was subtle, but the hairs on Azaiel's neck rose, and he caught the look that sat, however briefly, in Hannah's eyes. Concern? Surprise?

They started forward, Rowan still in the lead, and she stopped in front of a large structure built into a massive hill.

The rain had let up somewhat, the sheets of water now more a gentle fall than the furious deluge they'd experienced earlier.

"Can you see the charm, Hannah?" Rowan asked. "It's unbelievable."

Hannah nodded. "Yes, but it looks weird. Like nothing I've seen before and it feels . . ."

"I know," Rowan whispered.

Azaiel glanced at Nico. He could see nothing. The shifter shrugged and watched as the women moved closer.

"It's been reinforced by fae magick," Rowan murmured and pointed. "See the double ring that binds it all? It mimics the power, hiding in the shadows, yet it strengthens the charm tenfold. It's incredible. I've never seen anything like it."

Azaiel's mouth tightened. The fae seemed to be up to their asses in this whole mess, and they rarely interfered in the affairs of others. It raised the question—why?

CHAPTER 15

"**F**ae?" Hannah was surprised. "How can we break through a fae spell?"

Rowan's hand reached out, and sparks shimmered in the air as she came into contact with the wall of energy. Her fingers glowed, a deep crimson color, and cracks spread along the wall—a conduit of energy that infected the entire area. The cracks crystallized, and small bits of the ward shattered, falling to the ground in clumps of dust.

"I can do this."

"I don't get it." Hannah glanced at the men, obviously uneasy. "How?"

Rowan exhaled. She shook her head, and whispered, "I don't know." The words slipped easily from her lips though the taste left behind wasn't pleasant.

But really, what was one more lie amidst all the chaos?

Rowan stared up at the massive protective spell. It sparkled and shone like a wet, translucent bubble, one that encompassed the entire hill—very much like a snow globe. Again she reached her hands outward, and an incredible jolt of heat hit her as she connected with its power. It traveled up her forearms, leeching into her cells, sizzling across her flesh, until it settled in her chest. There it pulsed, and she lost her breath for a moment.

Behind her, screams, moans, and shouts of anger filled the air. It was a near-deafening cacophony of noise. She shut everything out, clearing her mind so the canvas was blank, then concentrated as hard as she'd ever done. This was crunch time, and there wasn't room for mistakes.

The signature in the spell was old—there was weight to it—it felt almost familiar. She pursed her lips. Something about the way the lesions of energy flowed. About the design and pattern. Rowan frowned. It *was* familiar. She knew this charm. She'd seen it before . . .

"Stand back," she whispered hoarsely.

Rowan closed her eyes and held her hands aloft, drawing from the center of her own unique power. Energy sizzled along her fingers and sparked ferociously against the charm, sending showers of light into the air. She winced, felt the heat of it on her skin, but held her ground.

Her magick rolled overtop the fae charm, invading, feeding, duplicating, and eventually weakening. She wove intricate patterns, carefully dissecting the fae magick until it wavered. Until it frayed along the edges.

Until the beauty disintegrated and fell away like the tide leaving shore.

Inside, down in that part of her soul she kept hidden, something stirred, and for a moment Rowan faltered. Fear, thick and acrid, clogged her throat, and she sputtered, stumbling backward, and would have fallen if not for Azaiel.

"Let me help you." Azaiel's voice sounded near her ear—his arms were secure around her shoulders, his warmth caressed her skin, and her heart calmed as the darkness evaporated.

"I'm good." Rowan pulled away and nodded toward the door. "We should be able to get inside now."

Nico passed them and walked up to the door. He squared his shoulders, cocked his head to the side as he studied the frame for a moment and kicked it in. It shattered down the center, and he took a step back as the door fell to the ground, splintered in half.

"You probably could have just, you know, turned the handle," Hannah said wryly.

"I know," Nico replied, and disappeared inside with the blond witch following on his heels.

Rowan hesitated, rubbed her hands along the side of her neck. She was tense, her chest tight.

"Let's get this done." Azaiel grabbed her hand and nodded toward the bunker. "We need to go."

His hand was warm . . . and soft and hard all at once. She felt his touch deep inside, as if his energy penetrated the layers of her soul the same way her charm had defeated the fae spell. The connection was strong, and for one brief moment she let it linger. Wash over her like a gentle caress.

There was strength there, honor and courage. There was also much pain.

Azaiel leaned forward, his dark eyes glittering, his expression hard to read. "There's no time for holding hands. We must do this now."

Rowan yanked her hand from his, cutting the connection. The heat. "You think I don't know that?"

He paused. "I think you're afraid of seeing your mother again."

"I think you need to step back. If I need a therapist, I'll call a real one." She whirled around and jogged toward the gaping hole left by Nico, drawing her dagger as she did so. The Seraphim was much too intuitive for his own good.

Rowan ducked to avoid a low-lying beam that had broken away from the doorframe and plunged into the waiting darkness. Azaiel was inches behind her; it was pitch-black, but she heard him. She called forth an illumination charm and held her left hand aloft.

They were in a narrow entrance, one carved from the rock that existed beneath the grassy knoll. It was rough-hewn and damp, with moisture sliding amongst the many crevices that lined the dull gray limestone, like wrinkles on leathery skin. It was a steady drip that fed the ankle-deep puddles at her feet.

The ceiling was low, and she glanced back at Azaiel. This dungeon or whatever the hell it was, wasn't made for men of height, and yet he slid through with ease. He didn't make a sound as he followed in her footsteps, his eyes flat, his expression grim with determination.

She broke into a run, and a wave of claustrophobia rolled over her as the passage narrowed, and the ceiling dropped even more. Behind her Azaiel grunted and cursed—from the sounds of it he'd smacked his head on something hard. She knew it wasn't an easy task for him to keep up with her in such a confined space.

As they forged deeper into the tunnel Rowan began to sense different energies ahead. Hannah and Nico, of course, but there were others, including one like a song from her past—a memory newly awakened. The dread in her gut churned harder, and she swallowed bile.

She thought of the day they'd sent her here. Marie-Noelle had been out of control, piss drunk, and nasty. She'd been dragged home from Ipswich by Hannah's mother after using magick in public, which in their world was a huge no-no. The bartender had cut her off, and she'd hexed him—a painful spell that took his voice and eyesight.

Marie-Noelle had always been weaker than most, a beautiful woman whose fragile spirit couldn't handle the threat of Mallick's curse. She'd used drugs and alcohol to get by but eventually her mind was so far gone, that even after Mallick had rejected her, she couldn't recover.

Cara and some of the coven had taken her away and had her committed to the otherworld asylum. Of course, the warden hadn't wanted anything to do with a James witch, and Rowan knew they'd resorted to dark means of magick to make sure Marie-Noelle was accepted.

They'd left her there and hoped that she'd find some kind of peace. And she had. She and Kellen had seen it firsthand six years ago.

Guilt hit with a hammer of pain, and Rowan winced. No one but Hannah had known of their clandestine trip to the asylum. Kellen had planned to liberate Marie-Noelle though Rowan's agenda had been much darker. In the end, Marie-Noelle had stayed behind, a much more fragile flower than the one who'd greeted them both with open arms.

No wonder Kellen hates me.

She thought of the crazies she'd seen outside. Of the loneliness, the darkness, and the isolation of this place.

What was she walking into? What kind of mother would greet her? Had she recovered yet again? Was she the crazy lady from her teen years or the wonderfully whimsical creature from her youth? They had been happy . . . once, before her mother's weakness and Mallick's darkness had leeched into their world.

Rowan sighed and pushed such thoughts from her mind. There was no point. There would be no happy ending for her family, and if Rowan's plan didn't work, there would be no family at all.

She slowed as beams of light from her fingers cut through the inky darkness ahead. Water still dripped, oozing from the rocks like blood seeping from a wound, and the air was so cold she saw her breath in front of her face. Cautiously, she and Azaiel crept forward, both with weapons drawn and ready to fight.

The light grew brighter as the passageway opened up until Azaiel could stand without his head smacking the top of the ceiling. She hesitated as a wall of cold slithered over her flesh, and she shivered, a violent shaking that left her teeth chattering.

Azaiel stepped in front of her, his large body blocking the light, and she was struck at the massive expanse of his shoulders. At the larger-than-life air about him. At the fierceness that clung to his frame and the power that resided there.

And she was grateful he was there.

"Azaiel." Her whisper sounded on the air, a slight murmur, and at first she thought he hadn't heard her. She was fine with that. What the hell was she going to say to him? Rowan's chest tightened, her heart was pumping blood like she'd run a freaking marathon, and when he turned slowly, when his golden eyes glittered down at her, she felt as if time were suspended.

The space between them widened and lengthened, stretching out until her every cell thrummed with energy— his energy. Her dry lips parted, her tongue moistened, and his eyes darkened, the gold gone as the blackness swept over.

She wanted to run into his arms, bury her head against his chest. Feed from his strength and pain. She wanted to crawl inside him, experience his soul, taste his darkness, and touch his flesh.

She wanted him to say everything was going to be all right. That her mother would forget the past and welcome her with open arms. That she'd be able to forgive herself. That Kellen would see she'd had no choice. That Mallick would be defeated. That no one else she loved would die. That she'd grow old and have babies and grandbabies.

Rowan wanted everything from him in that moment, and the intensity of those emotions left her breathless. She couldn't speak. Could barely breathe. How could she?

"I know." His voice was like a rough whiskey-soaked kiss.

She exhaled a long, shuddering breath. "Thank you."

He nodded as if they were having an everyday conversation, and she followed him toward the light.

They paused at the entrance to what seemed to be a large chamber, and Rowan held her dagger in her left hand, while in her right she grasped her Glock. She nodded to Azaiel, and they both entered quietly.

The chamber wasn't overly large, and the light source was nowhere to be found. It glowed as if the very rock that it had been carved out of was charmed with the sun. The effect was eerie, a translucent wash of illumination that bred shadow and light.

Two glass-encased cells were built into the rock—one on each side—but they were empty. The one to Rowan's left had a small cot, a table and chair and a row of books stacked neatly on a shelf above the bed. The blankets were rumpled as if there'd been someone there recently, but other than that, there was no sign of life. No color. No pictures or anything personal.

The cell to her right was as empty as the other, but the glass had been shattered. Something had escaped. The question being . . . was it her mother or something else entirely?

Ahead were two passageways, and both were in darkness. Above them runes were carved into the stone, but the scripture was ancient, and Rowan wasn't familiar with it.

"Nico and Hannah have taken the right," Azaiel said. "We'll take the left."

He stood aside, and Rowan passed through the entrance, her skin shuddering as she did so. There was a ward in place—some sort of spell—but it had already been breached and was weak.

Again she held her hand aloft, the light from the ends of her fingers throwing beams of light ahead. From what she could see it was very similar to the passage they'd just traveled except the elevation was dropping as if they were going deeper into the earth.

What if this was a trap?

Unease rolled in her gut, cold fingers of it that made her stomach roil. She broke into a sweat and found that she was holding her breath, ears straining as she listened for any clue as to what lay ahead. She was wound so tight her jaw ached with tension, and the beginnings of a headache pinched behind her eyes.

"Not much farther. I sense a presence ahead," Azaiel said quietly.

Rowan paused and nodded. "I feel it, too. We need to hurry." She broke into a run, Azaiel close behind. She was glad he was there with her and not just because he was a big, strapping warrior, but because . . . she just didn't feel so damn alone.

They would do this. They would get the job done.

The tunnel veered to the left before straightening once more. The glow of a light shot weird shadow caricatures along the walls, and Rowan extinguished her own charm, plunging the immediate area into darkness.

She knew Azaiel was at her side, but for a moment it felt as if nothing were there. She was disoriented—it was so black she couldn't see her own hand in front of her face. Her stomach rolled, and she felt as if she were spinning in place. The sensation passed just as quick, and they moved toward the light—which grew brighter the closer they got. She and Azaiel were at least twenty feet away when she heard voices—one a female's. Her mother?

Rowan's heart quickened, and she ran, not caring about the darkness or the uneven terrain, or the unknown—and nearly landed on her ass. Would have landed on her ass if not for the strong arm that grabbed her.

Azaiel righted her, his whisper harsh against her ear. "Are you crazy? Caution is a must."

She yanked her arm from his grasp and whispered harshly, "I'm fine." Then she stood back and barely caught her breath when a blinding light erupted from the blackness, a piercing strobe that had her wincing and shielding her face.

When the intensity subsided, Rowan blinked rapidly and widened her stance. She still couldn't see shit—nothing but stars and haze—but she knew someone was there.

Scratch that. *Two someones.*

Rowan fisted her palm against her eyes, trying to clear them, and stepped to the side. She banged into Azaiel's hard body and moved forward, trying in vain to see what was there.

Suddenly the dagger was wrenched from her hand and an iron grip closed around her neck. She was lifted several feet off the ground and slammed into the wet rock at her back.

Stars danced inside her mind, and she struggled to breathe, her fingers clawing at the large hand around her neck. Azaiel made an inhuman sound—a bark or a cry of rage—and charged forward only to stop dead in his tracks when the owner of the iron grip spoke.

"One more inch and I take her head off." His words were heavily accented, and he spoke slowly, with careful enunciation, so there was no mistaking his intent.

The fact that he squeezed harder drove his point home with a vengeance. The man would not hesitate to snap her neck. Rowan was furious—at herself. How could she have let this happen? The bloody cloaking charm must have failed.

Cold steel pressed into the base of her neck and sent shock waves of pain dancing across her skin. Azaiel growled like an animal—a sound that would make most take notice—yet the knife pressed in harder. It drew blood. She felt every single drop that dripped down into the crook of her neck. The blade was charmed—heavily so—and the burn was fierce.

Slowly the gray haze faded from her vision like fog rolling away at dawn, and her sight cleared. The man who held her wasn't a man at all . . . at least not in the normal sense. He was massive—had a few inches on Azaiel—with skin the color of peat moss and eyes as yellow as a sunflower in bloom. From the chest down his body was humanoid—powerfully so, with muscular shoulders and arms of steel—and what appeared to be wings hovered behind him. Yet his face was definitely not human.

Her eyes widened, and she squirmed as his eerie yellow ones studied her. His features were demonlike, with a wide forehead, small horns protruding from his skull, and fangs peeking from between his generous mouth. Two large silver rings pierced his nostrils, and an intricate marking, or tattoo, was etched from temple to jaw. He sported a mane of hair that was thick and wavy, hanging well past his shoulders.

He was beautiful and repulsive at the same time. Rowan's vision blurred once more as she struggled to breathe.

He was also strong as hell.

"Gargoyle," Azaiel spat. "Take your hands off her now, or I will destroy you."

The creature smiled—a macabre caricature that stretched his face tightly. "You could try, but she would be dead before you moved." The smile left, and he loosened his hold. "Who are you and why are you here?" he growled.

The light from behind him grew bright just then, beams of energy falling over his shoulder and blinding Rowan with its intensity. The gargoyle snarled and dropped her to the ground like a piece of garbage.

"You've got to be kidding me," Rowan spat as she struggled to her feet. She had no idea what the hell was going on, but she was pissed. Pissed and tired and pretty much fed up. The ominous darkness that pressed on her was too much. Something was coming, and she didn't need two fucking guesses as to who it was.

They needed to get off the island. Like yesterday.

The gargoyle stared down at her, the dagger clutched in his hand, his eyes confused. "What trickery is this?" he said harshly.

Rowan pushed her hair off her face and glared right back at him.

"Who the hell are you?" she rasped, rubbing her hands along the tender skin at her neck.

"I am . . . Mikhail."

Azaiel was at her side in an instant, his hand warm against her cheek. His eyes were full-on black, and the energy that slithered across his body was just as dark.

The Seraphim was livid. Blood would be spilled.

He whirled around, slammed his fist into the gargoyle, and both of them tumbled to the ground inches from a slight figure draped in long robes that once were ivory yet now were yellowed with age.

"Rowan?" The voice was tentative. Strained. And so very familiar.

The gargoyle and Azaiel rolled away from her, both on their feet in an instant, squaring off in silence as the woman stepped closer. Her long auburn hair was shot through with bolts of silver—it hung to her waist in tangled waves. A face so achingly familiar stared at her in wonder.

It was a face that was older—more wrinkles and a softening of features—yet the glittery rage of crazy wasn't there. Her eyes were clear and more than a little wary.

Rowan stood on shaky legs, feeling all her strength waver as she looked upon a ghost from her past. Her throat constricted. Tears pricked her eyes.

Mother.

She supposed if she were eight again, she would have run into her mother's arms. Laid her head on her breast and let the warmth of her mother's embrace seep into the coldness inside her. She would have clung to the woman with all the mad longing of a child who didn't know better. One who still believed in fairy tales at bedtime, and hot chocolate and giggles and hugs.

Rowan cleared her throat. Too much had happened. She was none of those things.

"We need to go, Marie-Noelle. He's coming for you, and I won't let him win."

For several seconds there was nothing. No noise. No air. No color. No sound. Just the four of them staring at each other.

Marie-Noelle nodded. "I know," she whispered. "I feel him. But why? He refused me . . ." Pain tightened the woman's mouth, and she lowered her eyes. "It's you he wants. Why have you put yourself in his path?" Marie-Noelle's brows furled, and she took a step toward Rowan. "Why would you risk capture for me?"

Rowan held her mother's gaze steady. "This has nothing to do with you, Mother." She ignored the wince and flash of pain that crossed her mother's face. "For once."

Mikhail growled a warning, and Rowan turned to him. "You'd best keep it under your hat, Mister. I'm calling the shots." The temper that simmered beneath the surface flushed her cheeks, and her chest burned with nervous energy.

Azaiel butted in and turned to the gargoyle. "You are a watcher?"

The tall creature moved toward Marie-Noelle, his stance protective as he glared at Azaiel and Rowan. He nodded. "She's my ward, yes." He then motioned toward Rowan. "Is this her daughter?"

"I am," Rowan answered defiantly. "And I'm right here, so don't talk as if I'm not." Rowan held her hands up and threw a burst of energy toward the gargoyle. He deftly avoided it, but the stone wall behind him wasn't so lucky. Large slabs of gray rock crumbled to the ground.

"Holy Mother of . . ." Azaiel turned eyes as black as oil on her. "We've no time for childish games."

Rowan's temper fizzled and left in a rush. He was right. She glanced at her mother, feeling utterly defeated and not knowing why. "Let's go.

The woman eyed her for a moment, then whispered, "I'm not leaving without Mikhail."

Rowan arched a brow at that and shrugged. "Fine by me, but I suggest you keep your little pet on a leash, or, next time, I won't miss." She tilted her chin. "And it won't be his butt-ugly head or shoulders I'll be aiming for . . ." She nodded to the impressive package between the gargoyle's legs. "I'll hurt him where it matters most to the both of you."

Mikhail took a step toward her and growled.

Here doggie. She wanted him to come at her. She wanted to hurt him.

Marie-Noelle's eyes widened at the insult—for just a moment—and then she nodded but remained silent.

A tumble of emotion ran riot inside Rowan, and her chest felt as if it were going to burst with the heaviness of it all. She pushed past Azaiel, not really trusting herself with words or actions at the moment.

She felt no different than she had as a child. Confused. Ashamed. Scared.

And how sad was that. Rowan James. Self-appointed executioner of the demon lord Mallick. All twisted up over her crazy mother.

Except her mother didn't seem crazy at all.

And maybe *that* was the scariest thing of all.

CHAPTER 16

Dawn was breaking by the time they neared the outskirts of Salem. Rowan sighed and rested her forehead against the cool glass of the window as they drove down the mostly quiet, mostly deserted streets. The odd group of partiers were still out, weaving along empty sidewalks, their loud, animated conversations echoing into the silence. With Samhain two weeks away, the town was overflowing with tourists.

Halloween decorations blew in the wind, hung from various businesses that lined the streets—witches on broomsticks, bats, skeletons, and vampires. Cobwebs hung from doorframes—eerie wisps of smoke gray silk, while bales of straw and pumpkins were everywhere.

It was a beautiful fall scene straight out of a Norman Rockwell painting—and one that was false. If only the regular folk knew most of what they fantasized about was all wrong—that the monsters, the vampires, and the demons who populated their highly rated television shows and movies *really did exist*.

And they sure as hell didn't glitter.

The human population wouldn't romanticize these creatures if they really knew what hid in the shadows. They'd freaking pack their things and flee.

She settled into her seat as best she could and watched closely as they drove through town. There was nothing dark lurking amongst the shadows that she could see. Seemed as if the filth of the underworld had retired early this night.

Whatever the reason Rowan was grateful. She wasn't in the mood to bash demon heads. She was bone tired, and a nasty headache had fingered its way up her cranium, squeezing hard until it hurt even to blink her eyes.

Bed was looking pretty good right about now. She glanced at Azaiel, startled to find his golden eyes fixed on her. Immediately her cheeks stung red, and she gulped air, embarrassed at her reaction.

She was very much aware of Azaiel's warm leg pressed against her own—with the added body count of her mother and the gargoyle—they were pressed together like sardines in a can. She wriggled slightly, but it didn't help.

Damn but the man ran as hot as a furnace. And he smelled way too damn good for someone who'd just run crazy through an otherworld insane asylum. She shivered at the thought of what they'd left behind. Of how they'd hacked their way back to the dock.

When they'd finally reached the boat, it looked as if Armageddon had visited the island. More mercenaries had shown up—human and otherworld. Priest and Frank had used them for target practice, clearing a path for the six of them to make it to the boat. While they'd scrambled aboard, the heaviness inside Rowan had pinched hard, and she'd had the disturbing notion that someone was there, just on the other side of reality, watching her.

It wasn't Mallick.

As they'd pulled away the feeling eventually subsided, but for one brief moment the terror she'd felt had nearly brought her to her knees.

"Are you all right?" Azaiel's low timbre tickled her ear, and she shuddered.

"Of course," she answered abruptly. *No, not really. How can I be all right? We just sprang my mother from an insane asylum, and I hate the fact that she doesn't even seem insane, which makes no sense. She's brought along a fucking frog-man-gargoyle thing and. . .*

"You seem tense."

"Well, you would be, too, if you knew." She changed the subject.

"Knew?"

"If you knew what the hell is waiting for us at The Black Cauldron." Their whispers drew the curious gaze of Hannah. She was on the other side of Azaiel.

"You don't think they brought the donkey, do you?" Hannah leaned toward them.

"Oh God, I hope not." Rowan made a face.

"Donkey?" Azaiel arched his brow.

"Don't ask," they answered in unison.

"Pea-knuckle." Hannah laughed.

A smile cracked Rowan's stiff features, and she felt a bit of the heaviness dissipate. Hannah held her gaze and reached across Azaiel to squeeze her hand. "It will be fine, Ro. All of it."

Rowan nodded, not trusting herself to speak as she cleared her throat of the lump that had suddenly appeared. She was pretty sure they wouldn't be fine, but at the moment, that was the least of her worries. The more pressing question was where the heck was she going to put everybody? Sure, the Caldron was a bed-and-breakfast, but there were only so many beds to go around, and if Abigail and the others had arrived, who knew where they'd lay their heads.

She groaned and tried to relax. *Almost there.* But it was too hot. Too confined. And Rowan would have cut off her right arm to be anywhere but pressed up against the Seraphim, with only the back of her mother's head to look at. Over four hours of driving, and she was ready to go mad.

Azaiel made her feel things she had no time for, and Marie-Noelle . . . Rowan closed her eyes, hating the taste of bitterness that clung to the back of her throat. It was full-bodied and ripe.

Her mother opened up a lot of wounds she wasn't sure she wanted to deal with. Ever.

It wasn't just the abandonment issues. Or the fact that Rowan's life had become forfeit the moment Mallick had chosen her. Sure there was resentment and anger toward a mother who'd boozed and drugged her way through most of her child's younger years.

It was more than all of that. It was . . . she bit her bottom lip and glanced down at her hands. Her mother had given up. Taken a long vacation on the island of looney and left Rowan and Cara to deal with the fallout.

Marie-Noelle *should* be buck-crazy. She should be a shadow of her former self. She should be on her hands and knees, begging forgiveness.

And yet she was none of those things.

Rowan peeked at the huge gargoyle. What was his story?

They passed a gift shop, and for a second she thought she saw a reflection in the glass—a strange man with glittery glass eyes, dark hair, and striking features. She sat up a little straighter and narrowed her eyes, but when she focused once more, there was nothing.

Priest turned left onto Millen Road—it led to The Black Cauldron—and as they came upon the laneway, she groaned.

Good God . . . it looked as if a gypsy caravan had set up camp. Two large RVs were parked off to the side, near the old oak tree. One was laden with several bicycles—not sure when there would be time for a leisurely ride through New England, but hey . . .

A beat-up jeep was beside her rental, its rusted back bumper held tight with lime green twine. The faded red paint wasn't much different in color than the rust that ate up a good portion of the side panels.

Shit, Abigail had been driving the damn thing since before college but then she was a girl who never threw anything away. Well, except for boyfriends. Those she went through on a regular basis, which made the thought of her settling down north of the border that much more interesting. As if it would have lasted.

"Oh God," Hannah groaned and pointed.

Rowan followed her gaze and shook her head. "Great." A large black donkey stood next to the largest RV, it swiveled its head slowly their way as they pulled in behind it.

"Well, they don't usually leave home without it," Hannah observed dryly.

"A warning?" she said pointedly to Azaiel. "Don't piss that thing off."

He looked at her as if she'd lost her marbles.

"It's not just a donkey," she reiterated.

Azaiel looked as if he was trying his hardest not to laugh. "It's not," he said carefully. "Just a donkey."

"Nope," Hannah answered. She pounded the seat in front of her, earning a growly acknowledgment from Nico. "That goes for all of you. The donkey needs to be treated with kid gloves, and if it talks to you . . ."

At the expression on Azaiel's face, Rowan laughed, feeling a sense of lightness for the first time in days.

"If it talks to you," Hannah continued, "ignore it."

Nico turned around and gave her a "what the fuck" look, his eyebrows fierce in his rugged, handsome face as he glowered at the blond witch.

"I'm serious," Hannah retorted, opening the door. She slid out and shrugged. "That donkey will fu—"—she grimaced—"will screw with you, and the damn thing has a nasty side that makes Lucifer look like a mother-truckin' angel." At Nico's huff, she shrugged. "Don't say I didn't warn you"

"Warning noted," the jaguar answered silkily. It was obvious he thought the girls were jerking him around.

"And I'm pretty sure Leroy doesn't like cats."

"Leroy?" Nico looked incredulous.

Hannah, blew out hot air. "The donkey? They call him Leroy, which is ridiculous considering he's fecking Satan's spawn.

"You two are serious." Nico glanced from Hannah to Rowan.

"Dead serious." Hannah arched a brow. "Don't talk to it, don't answer any of its questions, don't humor the damn thing." She bit her lip, brows furled. "Actually, don't even look at it."

"It's a donkey," Azaiel said.

Rowan snorted and shook her head. "It's one mean son of a bitch. If I were you guys, I'd do as Hannah says and ignore Leroy."

The SUV's passenger door opened, and Rowan moved out of the way, sliding alongside Azaiel. She then turned and watched in silence as Marie-Noelle exited the large Suburban and stared up at the main house. Mikhail was at her side, and Rowan assumed by the way he hovered over her that their relationship was more intimate than watcher and . . . and what? What exactly was her mother to this creature?

Marie-Noelle turned then, and Rowan's throat constricted as she observed the many emotions that ran across her mother's face.

"Something's wrong," Marie-Noelle whispered harshly.

Rowan opened her mouth, but before she could say anything, her mother tugged her hand from Mikhail's and ran toward the house, a tortured cry drifting back to them.

"Mother."

The fist that had been playing havoc with Rowan's guts all evening turned, sharply and with a heavy hand. She clenched her jaw tightly, hating the dread that now kept her company. She'd not told her mother about Cara.

Marie-Noelle yanked on the door and was immediately greeted by Cedric. The old man's arms wrapped her in a hug that lingered, as if the woman were his own child. His gnarled hands held her tight, and he whispered into her ear, drawing her close when she would have collapsed.

The gargoyle stood to the side of the steps and seemed unsure, while Priest and Nico stood in silence beside him.

The woman's sobs were heartbreaking, her small wails quieted by the whisperings of the man who held her. They cut through the gray morning like a blade through flesh, and it hurt to listen to her pain.

Azaiel couldn't watch, and so he turned, his eyes wandering over the tops of the trees that lined the property. He wanted to look anywhere but up to that porch. Her pain reminded him too much of his own . . . of things lost and regrets that would never heal.

"Shit," Hannah whispered as she ran past Azaiel toward the house.

"She doesn't know." Rowan's voice was subdued. "About Nana."

It said something, that Hannah and Cedric comforted Marie-Noelle while her own daughter watched from the shadows.

A light went on in the RV that tethered the donkey, and seconds later a petite brunette appeared. She pushed small, round glasses off the end of her nose and tucked a wild strand of hair behind her ear. A riot of shoulder-length curls framed an interesting face—wide forehead, small bow mouth, and large, expressive eyes.

"Terre." Rowan took a step forward and halted. It was obvious she was unsure, and once more Azaiel was reminded that the family dynamics at play here were convoluted.

Terre stepped down and glanced toward the house, sniffling as she did so and wiping her nose with a Kleenex.

"You didn't tell her?" Accusation rang in Terre's voice, and something puffed up in Azaiel's chest when he saw pain flicker across Rowan's face.

"There hasn't exactly been time for niceties," he inserted as he took a step forward.

"Niceties?" Terre turned incredulous eyes his way. "*Niceties? Are you kidding me?*" She shook her head and looked at Rowan. "How could you *not* tell Auntie Marie that her own mother was dead?"

The woman at his side was silent, but the pain in her eyes was long gone and had been replaced with a coldness that didn't belong. It sucked the warmth from her, turning the azure blue of her eyes into winter cold.

"She isn't just dead, Terre. She was brutally murdered." Rowan gestured toward the house. "In that kitchen with no one there to protect her." Her voice trembled slightly. "She was slaughtered like an animal, and I don't even have a body to hold. I don't have anyone to say good-bye to." She arched her brow. "Though they left behind a lot of blood in case you were wondering. I should know, I had to clean it up." She cocked her head and smiled, cruelly. "Nana meant more to me than anything else in this world. Do you understand what that means? Did you really think I was going to discuss her murder on a ride back from the insane asylum?" She clenched her hands, and the ground beneath his feet shifted. "With the woman who gave up on all of us years ago?"

Terre's chin went up, and Azaiel realized these women were not afraid of confrontation. In fact, it seemed as if they sought it out.

"I think," Terre began carefully as she flexed her fingers and moved forward, "that you want your mother to hurt more than she already does."

"You're full of shit," Rowan said stiffly.

"Am I?"

The ground quaked some more, while overhead, clouds erupted with flashes of energy. Azaiel heard rumblings from Priest, and Nico swore. He stepped between the two women, hoping like hell neither one made a move that would burn his ass.

"I don't think now's a good time to point fingers," Azaiel said as he glanced from Rowan to Terre. "Especially fingers juiced up with witch mojo."

"And you are?" Terre bit out.

"A friend," he answered softly.

Her eyes narrowed, but she backed away from Rowan.

A second woman emerged from the remaining RV and strolled over in a T-shirt that barely covered her ass. Long, trim legs moved gracefully as bare feet picked their way over the cold earth. DIXIE CHICK was emblazoned across her chest, the large, silvery letters doing a lot to enhance her generous . . . assets.

She rubbed sleep from her eyes, stretched her arms above her chest, and Azaiel actually held his breath, wondering if the woman was clothed beneath her T-shirt, only dragging his gaze from the tops of her thighs when Rowan cursed. The woman tossed a headful of long dark hair over her shoulder—one of which was bare, showing a lot of creamy skin.

Rowan exhaled and stepped away. "Vicki, I'm not in the mood for the two of you to tag team the whole blame thing on me."

"Oh, don't worry about that." Vicki shot a dark look at Terre. "I'm sure my sister has more than enough guilt and blame to throw around for all of us. It's what she does." The woman turned his way and made no effort to hide the interest that widened her eyes to large ice blue jewels. She held out her hand and, after a pause Azaiel offered his own.

"A name would be good," she purred.

"Oh for God's sake, Vicki. His name is Azaiel, and for the duration of his stay in Salem, he's off-limits."

Azaiel glanced down at Rowan. Her hands were bunched, her face fierce. She nodded toward the RV. "And keep Leroy away from the rest of them or . . ."

"The rest of them?" Vicki moved to her right and licked her lips as she gazed behind them, a seductive smile breaking wide. "Oh my God, Rowan, did you hijack an America's Got Hot Men bus or what?"

The donkey brayed, and Azaiel couldn't be sure, but it sounded like the damn thing had said, *suckers!*

Rowan made a weird noise, muttered, "stay away from her" in his general direction, and disappeared into the darkness that still lingered around the edges of the house.

It was, Azaiel thought, one of the most bizarre evenings he'd ever known. He eyed the donkey, whose large, moist eyes had settled on him with an intensity that was unnerving, and decided that Rowan was right. He aimed to stay the hell out of its way.

"She's always been a bit overly dramatic. You need a coffee or something?" Vicki's seductive drawl was impressive. "I just put a pot on and don't mind sharing."

The invitation wasn't subtle, amplified by Terre's disgusted huff before she disappeared inside her RV.

And yet it did nothing for him.

"Thanks but I'm good." Azaiel nodded and before he'd even thought about it turned to follow in Rowan's footsteps.

CHAPTER 17

He found her among the large oak trees that bordered the back of the property. The smell of damp, rotting leaves hung in the air, while the crisp morning left a blanket of powdery white frost over everything.

She stood a few feet away, shoulders hunched forward, arms wrapped around her body as if trying to find what warmth she could. There was something forlorn about Rowan that tore another chunk of the hard part inside him away. He felt it crack like a physical snap of bones, and he clenched his hands, trying to calm whatever the hell it was stirring inside him.

He didn't much care for feelings of any kind, so he quickly clamped down on the ball inside his chest and cleared his mind.

The old trees stood like silent men at arms, their generous span of branches cloaked in shadow but illuminated from behind by the ever-lightening sky. Along the ground fog snaked across the earth, seeking shelter from the coming sun, which would dissipate the smokelike tendrils as soon as they met.

Rowan turned slightly, aware of his presence, and he was struck once more by her delicate bone structure, the high cheekbones, small nose, and graceful curve to her chin. She was wholly feminine and a study in contrast.

A beautiful princess in need of rescue. A powerful witch who could kick ass along with the best of them. It's what made her so interesting. Rowan James was made up of many, many layers, and lucky was the man who'd one day have the time to delve through them.

The mysterious Kellen entered his thoughts, and Azaiel frowned, wondering once more as to the nature of their relationship. The thought of intimacy between the two left a taste in his mouth he didn't like, which was ridiculous. He had no claim on Rowan.

"I'm going to apologize now for my family, then you'll never hear me speak to their craziness again, because trust me . . . it's never-ending."

Azaiel paused, a few feet behind her. He cleared his throat. "They seem . . ." He thought of the donkey and an unbidden smile crossed his face. "A little eccentric."

Rowan shook her head. "You have no idea." She took a step forward and bent down—he couldn't help it, his gaze followed the line of her body and rested on the feminine curve of her butt. The jeans she wore fit her like a glove—he envisioned his hands there, him behind her, and his groin tightened uncomfortably.

Azaiel grimaced but was unable to tear his gaze away.

She righted herself, a yellowed, waxy oak leaf in her hand, and twirled it absently between her fingers, studying it closely as if it held the many secrets she sought.

She turned toward him suddenly. "We hardly agree on anything from politics to music to"—she held the leaf aloft-"what color this leaf is." Rowan stared at it closely, still twirling it between her fingers. "I'd call this butter cream, but Vicki would call it gold and Terre?" She shook her head. "She'd have some fancy name for it . . . sun-ripened ash . . . blah blah blah."

Her brows furled, and Azaiel thought he saw a hint of tears in their recesses.

"Abigail would call it yellow because at the end of the day that's what it is. And Hannah wouldn't give a flying . . . *duck*"—she snorted and muttered—"because she doesn't swear anymore."

She looked up suddenly. "Do you have family? Brothers? Sisters?"

The question took him unaware, and, for a moment, Azaiel was silent. He thought of Askelon and the others from the original seven. They were family. Blood of his blood and yet, he'd not felt a connection to them in eons, save for Askelon. But even that connection was tenuous. Untested. Askelon believed in Azaiel, it's just that Azaiel wasn't sure he deserved such devotion.

"I have . . . brothers but my situation is complicated."

She nodded. "Oh I get that, trust me. Families are messy. Just when I think I'm fine on my own, something like this happens, and I realize when all is said and done, family . . . blood is the only thing that matters." Her eyes dropped to the ground. "I haven't seen much of my cousins over the last five years, and yet our bond is as strong as ever." She paused, chewed her lip, and frowned. "I didn't know that until now."

She glanced up, and he was struck by the sharpness in her glittery eyes. Her hair hung past her shoulders, a riot of crimson tangles that set off her creamy skin to perfection. She was earth and sun and moon all wrapped into one hell of a sexy package.

"I've missed them so much. I know it doesn't seem like it because all we seem to do is bicker but . . . Terre and Vicki are twins, which I'm sure is hard for you to believe. They shared the same womb, the same DNA, but not much else. Terre studied botany at Stanford while Vicki danced on Broadway in New York. She has a weakness for musicians." Rowan's eyes darkened. "Or any male who's a plus five."

"Plus five?"

"Her standards have never been, shall we say . . . high."
Rowan smiled. "When we were teens, we'd rate guys, with
everyone starting out as a one and we added points. You
know, body, smile, hair, personality . . . of course." She
raised an eyebrow. "We could always take away points,
too."

"So a plus five is in the middle?"

"You got it. Plus ten is the highest you can score." She
shrugged. "There weren't a lot of plus tens in Salem, that's
for sure." She paused and nodded toward the house. "Abigail
is as crazy as Hannah."

Great. As if one crazy witch wasn't enough to deal with.
"I hope she's not packing a bagful of extraextra specials."

Rowan laughed at that. "No. That's not Abigail's thing.
She's more of a healer. I think she would have just about died
if she'd shot you the other day."

Good to know. He decided he liked Abigail, sight unseen.

"And Kellen?" He asked the question that had been at the
back of his mind all night and watched her closely.

Her expression changed—she glanced away, lips tightened. Gone was any lightness that had been there. His jaw
clenched as he waited for her answer. The man meant a lot
to her.

"I don't want to talk about Kellen," she said carefully.

Small puffs of mist shot from her nostrils, and as his eyes
adjusted to the changing shadows her features sharpened.
Their eyes met and held, and the silence became a heavy,
living thing that wrapped them both in a cocoon of their
own making. It was intimate. Secretive.

He was aware when her breathing changed. When her
pupils dilated and her heart rate sped up.

"Rowan—"

"Have you ever felt like doing something you know you

shouldn't?" A long wisp of hair blew across her face. His gaze lingered there as she tucked it behind her ear.

He knew where she was going. Hell he wanted to follow her, but it was a dangerous path—for both of them. Azaiel paused for a few seconds. Gathered his thoughts. "If you have to question whether something is right or wrong Rowan, always go with wrong."

She licked her lips, slowly, with care, and still their eyes never left each other's. "Why does wrong feel so . . . right sometimes?"

They were approaching a line that shouldn't be crossed. He felt it. Rowan knew it, and she didn't give a damn. It was in the way her body moved as she took the remaining steps that separated the two of them, a graceful, seductive glide over the cold, wet leaves at her feet. Her scent reached his nostrils, and his body tightened even more, the blood rushing through his veins like a drug from a needle.

"Wrong always feels right," he answered woodenly. "It's why hell is full of lost souls who weren't strong enough."

Her mouth opened slightly, in a provocative, feminine way that drew his attention like a heat-seeking missile about to launch. He caught sight of her even, white teeth and the small, delicate, moist tongue that teased him with a peek. Her mouth was meant for sliding, for licking, nibbling, and moaning sounds of pleasure into a lover's ear.

Such need arose in Azaiel that the heat of it, the very rush of it through his body, was painful. He clenched his hands into fists as muscles tightened and strained even more. He grimaced—wanting her to leave—wanting her to slide against him and prolong the torture. It had been so long since he'd felt this kind of pain.

This kind of need.

He took a step back, suddenly thinking his chances were a hell of a lot better with the damn donkey. An arrogant ass he could handle, but Rowan? She was a different animal entirely, and this was a very, very bad idea. He'd hurt her. It's the one thing he managed to do without fail. Hurt and disappoint.

"I won't do this Rowan."

She reached for him, and he watched the leaf she'd held dance in the air, twirling slowly as it fell to the ground between them.

"Don't go," she whispered. "Not yet." Her hand was warm on his forearm, and a muscle worked its way along his jaw as he struggled to remain calm and in control.

"You don't know what you ask."

Her eyes changed. "I know exactly what I'm asking. I know exactly what I want."

"I'm not a nice man, Rowan. In fact I'm the most flawed creature you'll ever meet."

"In case you haven't noticed, I don't scare easy."

She had no clue what he was. What he was capable of. *What he'd done in the past.*

Her eyes were luminous, huge jewels hung in a face so exquisite he knew he would never forget her. How could he? She was perfect. Just as she was. Right now. At this moment.

She stared up into his eyes, then slowly dropped her gaze to his mouth. Azaiel's groin tightened even more, and he inhaled sharply as she moved closer. He needed to stop whatever the hell this was before it was too late.

"Move back," he bit out.

"No."

Anger boiled inside him. She was just a little girl playing a game she couldn't win. He was Azaiel, one of the original Seraphim. There was no middle ground with him, and his passions ran hotter than she could handle.

"What game are you playing, Rowan?"

"I'm not playing a game."

"This can't happen," he said through clenched teeth.

"I think it can." Her eyes focused on his lips once more, and he thought he was going to go crazy.

"Your family is right inside—"

"I don't want to talk about my mother or my crazy cousins." She licked her lips, and they glistened, plump and ripe and inviting. "I don't want to discuss the curse or Mallick or . . ."

"Kellen?" The man's name on his tongue was bitter, and he scowled down at her.

Rowan's hand crept up, and, when she touched his cheek, energy rolled over his tall frame in a wave of hot need. She stood on her tiptoes, and if Azaiel were smart, he would have disengaged himself from Rowan's touch and stepped back. He would have put some distance and perspective between the two of them.

But Azaiel wasn't smart. Or even in control. He was under a spell. Rowan's spell.

And at the moment she was all that mattered.

"I especially don't want to talk about Kellen."

Her mouth was open, ready and wet. "I want to feel something other than the cloud of doom that's been hovering above me my entire life. I want to feel alive." Her hand slipped along his jaw and crept into his hair. "I want to feel something other than dread and fear and anger. I want passion, Azaiel." She paused, the tip of her pink tongue edging out from between her teeth. "Can you do that for me?" She shuddered.

Move away. The thought roared through his mind.

Her body slid up along his hardness, and he knew she felt his arousal. In fact the little jezebel worked it, her softness rubbing against him provocatively. "Please?" she whispered, her breath hot against his skin. "Just for this moment?"

Maybe he should give her a taste of just how much of a bastard he really was. That should put an end to her feminine games. Azaiel had always run hot. Where Askelon had been cautious, he'd jumped in without thought. It's what had gotten him into trouble all those centuries ago. Mad passion combined with absolute power was not something he'd handled well.

He'd paid the price. He just wasn't sure he'd learned the lesson.

"I think you could make me lose my mind," she whispered.

Her lips were near his mouth, and her scent was driving him crazy. If Azaiel were a stronger man, he'd pull away. He'd tell the woman to leave him the fuck alone and concentrate on her problem.

His fingers slid up her face until he cradled her head between his hands. For several long moments he stared down at her, willing his body to relax. To obey him, not the witch.

When he had a handle on his emotions his thumb gently swept toward her mouth, and he sank into her warm wetness. It was time to teach Rowan a lesson better learned now than later.

Azaiel was no gentleman. He was not her knight in shining armor. He would kiss her until her knees buckled, and she was putty in his hands. He would make her want and rage with need.

And then he would leave her. And if she were smart, she'd never come to him looking for comfort again.

"I think," he said finally, his voice rough, "that it's time for you to stop talking."

What the hell am I doing?

Rowan paused, for one breathless moment, and let the situation roll over her. She was throwing herself at someone she barely knew. Sure he was a "hot as hell" someone, but still. Rowan didn't do shit like that. Not anymore.

Rowan had perfected the masquerade that had become her life over the last six years. She'd grown into the skin of someone who bore no resemblance at all to what she'd been. In California Rowan James was average. Ordinary. Less than ordinary. She'd morphed form a hell-raising teenager into the kind of woman who dated someone like Mason and had a pet gerbil named Tiger.

She'd not used magick in years, and she sure as hell hadn't contemplated getting naked with a tall, god of a man who held more secrets than she did.

And yet there she was. Back in Salem, knee deep—hell, ass deep—in magick, men, and danger. And she liked it. The thrill. The power.

It was as seductive as she remembered.

But Azaiel . . . she gazed up into golden eyes shot through with black . . . he was more dangerous than all of that. She should be running the other way, yet . . . her fingers trailed over his taut, hard chest . . . she couldn't move.

He made her feel things that she shouldn't. Not with the threat of Mallick hanging over her head. Not with her mother returned to Salem. Not with Samhain so close.

And yet . . . it felt amazing to *feel* again.

Azaiel shuddered beneath her fingers, and as she slid along his body, the evidence of his passion was hard to ignore. He wanted her as much as she wanted him, so what was the problem? He was a man. She was a woman. They were both adults.

For a second reality punched her hard, and she paused, breath held in her throat. He wasn't like anyone she'd met before. She felt his power. Felt how his energy bunched and pulsed with something she'd never experienced before. What *was* she doing? Was she as crazy as her mother?

But then his hands were on her body, traveling down her back, past her waist, until he cupped her butt and pulled her in closer. She gasped at the intimate feel of him. He was hard, unyielding. One hundred percent male.

Rowan opened her mouth—to protest? To pull away? But it was too late. Azaiel's lips descended, and he opened her mouth with his own, his tongue probing, seeking the heat inside her.

He tasted like heaven, and waves of hot, wet need rolled over her, weakening her limbs until she leaned into him. Until her breasts were crushed to his chest, and that moist, throbbing place between her legs was intimately introduced to the hard bulge at his groin.

His large hand kept her anchored, fingers splayed across her butt, while his other sank deep into the thick hair that clung to her neck. He held her so that she couldn't move—a little too tightly, truth be told—so that when his lips trailed red-hot fire across her neck, she could do nothing but whimper. When his tongue licked and suckled near her ear she surely would have fallen if not for his ironclad grip.

Shivers of delight wound their way across her skin, and she shuddered as his mouth clamped down near the pulse that burned at the base of her neck. Her hands crept up, and she clung to his powerful shoulders, animalistic sounds falling from her lips as she moved against him.

And when he licked his way back to her mouth she opened wide and claimed him. Tongues slid, teased, and tasted. They heaved against each other and, with a growl, Azaiel picked her up, and they moved deeper into the shadows. He shoved her against the shed, his large frame hovering against hers as his tongue swept along her mouth before plunging deep inside once more.

Rowan's head spun. Her insides were hot, like molten lava, feeding the ache between her legs until she could barely stand it. She tried to close her legs, tried to put out the fire, but his knee was there, pushing into her, rubbing against her . . . and warmth flooded her in a wet weep of desire.

"Oh God, Azaiel," she whispered, her hands capturing his face so that he stilled for a moment. So that her eyes connected with his and said the words she couldn't. *Stop. This is crazy. This is amazing.*

His had morphed to full-on black but they glittered, as if backlit with specks of gold. Thick strands of dark honey-colored hair fell over his brow, and she brushed it back as she gazed up at him. Their hearts pounded heavy, a rhythm that was in sync, and the thin sheen of sweat that coated his skin only emphasized the perfect features of his face.

The man was the most beautiful thing she'd ever seen. He looked as if he'd been carved from angel's stone.

His gaze never wavered, and she caught a glimpse of the intensity that ruled the man who held her. It scared her. His strength. His total control.

Suddenly a tingle of apprehension shot through her. A warning that maybe she was pulling on the tiger's tail. It was a cold shot of reality, and her heart turned over. Shame scorched her cheeks.

What the hell am I doing?

Rowan's throat constricted, and she pushed against his chest, but his large frame didn't budge. She needed to jump off the crazy train and get away from him. She needed to clear her head.

"I warned you." His voice was harsh and held a hint of something that was dark.

Rowan opened her mouth, wanting to explain. Wanting to apologize for her behavior, but he gave her no chance. His mouth was on hers once more, and he moved so that she was crushed between the shed and the hard wall of muscle that was his large body.

His hands were everywhere, on her face, in her mouth, caressing her breasts, and flickering along the quivering muscles in her lower belly. His mouth wreaked havoc, his long, sensuous tongue spreading fire across her neck, and she shuddered when he blew against her ear and suckled the tender spot just below.

"I warned you," he repeated, his hands tugging at her shirt, and with a curse he ripped it from neckline to hem. She froze when she felt cool, crisp air rush across her naked skin.

"Azaiel," she whispered.

Then his mouth was at her breast as he pushed aside her bra and enveloped a turgid peak deep into his warmth. He teased and suckled, each draw hitting her hard between the legs. Never had she experienced such sensation. Such raw passion.

The man was a bloody plus eleven if that was possible.

Her hands were anchored in the thick hair atop his head, holding him steady as he fed from her breasts, while his free hand sank into the hot crevice between her legs. Even through her jeans she felt the burn of his flesh, and each stroke of his finger drew such friction across her that she ached with pleasure and rocked into him. Pushing. Straining. Groaning.

Deep inside her body, a tremor grew—a spiral of pleasure that quickly spread. He rubbed and sucked and tugged at her, and it expanded into a ball of exquisite pressure that spun crazily, each pass of his hand stoking and intensifying. She moaned, her hips bucking as the tidal wave built and rolled through her, faster and harder until it broke, and she was limp in his hands.

Slowly he pushed her bra back into place—though his right hand still cupped the juncture between her legs as he gazed into her eyes. His expression was unreadable, and she swallowed, suddenly uncomfortable and ashamed. She'd literally thrown herself at him. What did that say about her?

She watched as the black slowly faded from his eyes, leaving only the eerie gold that was so unique.

"I only wanted a kiss." She was horrified to hear her whispered thoughts echo between them. Her cheeks burned scarlet, and her hands crept up to her chest.

"I could have had you, right here against this shed." He paused, his gaze running from her head to her toes. "*If* I'd wanted to."

The inference wasn't lost on Rowan. "You're an asshole," she spat, her anger overriding anything else.

Azaiel nodded. "I've been called a hell of a lot worse, but you should remember, I did warn you." His voice lowered. "I'm not a nice man, Rowan. I haven't been for a very long time. You would do well to remember that."

A throat cleared behind them—a masculine, pissed-off kind of sound—and Rowan froze.

Azaiel's eyes widened for just a second before he straightened his body though she noted he was careful to keep her concealed as he cocked his head to the side. "Enjoy the show?"

"Not particularly."

Rowan banged her head against the shed and squirmed so she could see around Azaiel. A tall man glared at her, his handsome face familiar . . . as was the expression that sat upon it. Anger. Pain. Disappointment.

"Kellen," she said hoarsely.

Azaiel stiffened. She stared up into a face of stone, the warmth they'd shared only moments earlier long gone. He stepped away, and Rowan glared at him, hating the way his control had never wavered. Hating the way he'd made her feel. Hating that he appeared to be not affected at all.

He nodded toward Kellen. "She's all yours."

And then he left her alone in the early-morning gloom with the twin brother she'd nearly killed six years earlier.

CHAPTER 18

She watched Kellen warily. From her vantage point she didn't see any weapons, but that didn't mean he wasn't packing. In fact it most likely meant he was armed to the teeth. He wore a plain black T-shirt and military-style pants in the same shade. The boots on his feet could hold a dagger . . . or two, and she knew from experience Kellen's pants were usually weighted down with a host of weaponry—all of it aimed at killing.

She clutched the edges of her T-shirt, tied them together, and zipped her leather jacket tight. Behind him lights from inside the house glowed softly, and she noticed that the light in her Nana's rooms were lit as well. Small darts of it filtered between the boards that had been pounded across the shattered glass window.

Was it less than a week ago she'd been in ignorant bliss?

"What are you doing?" Kellen asked harshly.

His anger was palpable. She got it. But she sure as hell didn't plan on taking the brunt of it.

Rowan pushed away from the shed and shoved her hands into the pockets of her jacket. The gloom was considerably lighter than only fifteen minutes ago, and she knew sunrise wasn't far behind. She cracked her neck. God, she was so tired.

"Just getting some fresh air. You?"

His face darkened. Okay, maybe he was more than a little pissed. "I don't care about your fucking boy toy, Ro. Let's talk about our mother."

Her heart clutched at the sound of her nickname and, for a second she thought that maybe things would be all right. That maybe he didn't hate her as much as she feared and that he'd forgiven her for the last time they'd been together.

"If you've harmed one hair on Marie-Noelle's head, I will make you pay." Kellen spoke slowly, enunciating his words so that there was no doubt as to the depth of his anger toward her. His eyes flashed, and he took a step toward her. She noted the way his right hand was loose near his pocket. That wasn't good.

Okay, so the whole hate thing was still ongoing.

Rowan studied her brother. He wasn't the lanky young man from her past. A natural athlete who'd excelled at foot-ball, he'd always been tall and sported a fluid grace that had earned him a full ride to Harvard. Handsome and a born leader, his dark hair, vivid blue eyes, and absolute charm had made him very popular with the ladies.

But that was a long time ago. Back before Mallick and his curse and their mother's downward spiral had created a rift so wide, she was pretty sure nothing would be able to fix it.

Gone was the young, easy-going man he used to be. He was now a hardened, powerful man whose body had ma-tured into that of a soldier who could dish out a hell of a lot of hurt. There was a cruelty to his eyes now, and she didn't doubt he could kill with his bare hands.

Didn't doubt that he *had* killed with his bare hands. Demons, of course, nasty otherworld creatures for sure, but still, killing changed a person.

"You don't have to worry about that, Kellen. She's good. Even has a bloody gargoyle protecting her." She held her hands apart. "Big, nasty-looking thing."

Kellen's mouth tightened even more. "She has a name."

"Marie-Noelle is fine." Rowan nodded toward the house. "Go see for yourself."

"Why did you bring her here?" he bit out. "It's dangerous."

Her own anger thrust against her chest, and that part of her stirred—the one that she mostly kept hidden. Heat rushed through her veins as she stared at a brother who, spiritually, was so far away from her, he could be living on another planet. She took a second and sought the control inside of her. This would not be a good time to go off half-cocked and start something with him.

"She's damn lucky we went after her last night. Didn't anyone fill you in on what the hell went down?"

He ignored her words. "You should have called me the minute you got back to Salem."

"Really?" she snorted. "Because we've been so incredibly close the last six years?" Oh God, why did it still hurt so much?

"Because I wouldn't have let you anywhere near her."

Rowan ran her hand through the tangled mess of hair at her nape, not wanting to acknowledge the fact that his words pained her. More than she wanted them to. Suddenly, she was so tired of it all. Of the past and how it constantly bit her in the ass. Chewed her up and spit her out like yesterday's meal.

"I don't want to fight, Kellen. You know she's safer here with us than anywhere else."

"That's bull." He took another step closer until she could have reached out her hand and touched him. "There's another place she can be."

Her lips whitened, and she shook her head violently. "No." She would not send her mother there, to the in-between world.

Something shifted in his eyes as he studied her, and when

he spoke his tone changed. "We've never asked him for help. Maybe now's the time."

"No! What happened to the promise we made to Nana? She said that he was more dangerous than Mallick!"

His face whitened. "Nana is gone, Rowan. Everything's backward. Messed up."

"Kellen, we can't."

"I know you must be scared, Ro."

"Don't." She shook her head and took a step back. "Don't patronize me. I'm not scared, Kellen. I'm furious and tired, and I've fucking had it." She blinked back hot tears. "Don't you get it? Mallick killed Nana. *Our Nana*. He won't stop until he claims his prize, and the last time I looked that effing prize was *me*. I'm done running, Kellen, don't you get that? Why won't you trust me enough so that we can get this done?"

"How can you be sure it was Mallick?"

His attitude pissed her off. "The coven has been marked, of course it's Mallick. He's pissed at all of us because his mark is blind, and he can't find me."

"I don't like any of this."

"I don't see that you have choice." She lifted her chin and uttered the words she'd thought but hadn't spoken aloud. "Why weren't you here with her? The only reason I agreed to leave Salem was because I thought it would keep her safe. That if I was gone, nothing bad would happen to her, and with you around . . ." Her chest heaved, and she took an aggressive step forward, her fingers outstretched as a surge of power rushed along them. "Where were you, Kellen? Why did you leave?" Accusation rang in her voice, breaking her words and tearing at her heart.

His eyes glittered as he stared down at her, and the ache in her heart tripled. There was so much anger and mistrust in them. And pain. "Nana meant the world to me, and the fact that I wasn't here when she was attacked is something I'll carry to the grave." He glared at her, though the bleakness in his eyes shone through. "You have no idea what's going on with me, and that's fine. My life is none of your business. Not anymore. You don't get to ask those questions."

"Fair enough. I won't ask any more questions, and you'll stay the hell out of my way."

He laughed. "Don't try that crap with me, Rowan. I want that son of a bitch to pay as much as you do . . . I'm just not willing to sacrifice our mother in order to achieve that goal."

He didn't understand. He'd *never* understand.

"Kellen, I need to find the James grimoire. She's the only one who knows where it is since *she's* the one who sold it for drug money." Her voice rang bitterly. "It wasn't hers to give. You know that. She broke Nana's heart."

He swore. "There has to be another way."

"There isn't."

He expelled a long breath and shook his head. "You nearly destroyed her last time. You would have—"

"If not for you." She finished for him. Her chest constricted, and she moved, startled, as the orange tabby suddenly appeared, weaving its way between her legs. For such a small thing, it purred like a tiger.

"You lied to me, Rowan. You lied to Mom, then you nearly destroyed her. For what? A book?" He laughed, a harsh sound that made her wince. "You don't even know if it holds whatever you need to defeat Mallick."

"It does," she said stubbornly.

His eyes narrowed. "How can you be sure? Don't you think someone else would have used it before now?"

"No one was ever strong enough."

He cocked his head to the side. "And you think you are?"

"I've no choice. I have to be. He brought this fight to my

door when he killed Nana. He won't stop until . . ." She exhaled and picked up the tabby, who now meowed and rubbed its head against her chin. "I refuse to be Mallick's bitch, Kellen, and I'll die before another drop of James blood is spilled."

"You're blind to him right now. Leave and the rest of us will go underground."

"And spend the rest of your lives running?" She motioned behind him. "What about this place? It's been in our family for generations. I can't let him win. I can't let him take that from me."

"Rowan, you've been gone for six years. What do you care?"

"I care," she whispered fiercely.

He stared at her for a few more seconds, his expression unreadable. "What if you're not strong enough, Ro? What if . . ." His voice trailed off, and he glanced away, hands fisted at his side.

"Then God help us." *Because we're all doomed.*

Silence enveloped the both of them.

"Can't you use a locator spell? Like the one you used to find the asylum?" There was a note of resignation in his voice, and she glanced up, shaking her head.

"No." She grimaced. "I would have done that before, Kellen. I don't have anything to locate it with." Her voice grew steely. "Marie-Noelle needs to remember who or what she gave it to. She needs to make this right."

"Even if it means she loses her sanity again? Rowan, she's almost back. Have you talked to her?" Suddenly the man Kellen had grown into was no more, and the small boy, the brother she remembered from her youth, gazed back at her, his blue eyes earnest, full of hope.

"Briefly, last night."

His eyes darkened, his mouth thinned. "That's right. But

you didn't have the time or decency to at least let her know that her own mother was gone."

Rowan stared at her brother and saw the accusation in his eyes. For the first time a small tingle of regret tugged at her heart. She remained silent. What was there to say?

"Why do you hate her so much?" The question was direct, and by the look in Kellen's eyes he wasn't going to let it go.

"I don't hate her."

"You lie."

"No," Rowan shook her head. "I've never . . ." But as the wall of emotion inside her broke she realized that he was right. *Hate* might be a strong word choice, but it sure as hell came close to describing the complicated mess of feelings she had for her mother.

"I don't hate *her* . . . I hate her weakness. I hate that she turned to drugs and booze and men instead of dealing with her situation." She clenched her hands, heart in her throat as the words came tumbling out. "I hate that she hurt Nana. That she stole and lied and that she chose all of that over us."

The tabby meowed—she was holding it too tight—and she let the animal run free. "I hate that when you fell from the tree in the backyard and hit your head, I had to drive you to the hospital because she was passed out in her bedroom with her latest boyfriend. We were *seven*, Kellen. Seven!"

He glared at her, his expression unreadable.

"Your leg was broken. Don't you remember how much pain you were in?"

"I remember."

"I tried so hard to perform a healing spell, but I couldn't do it. I just didn't know enough. She never taught me." Her words were bitter. "Our phone was cut off. I couldn't call for help. She didn't even know Nana had come for us until two days later, when she and her creep boyfriend needed his car to buy more vodka!" She rubbed at her face, hating the sting of tears that hung in the corner of her eye. "What kind of mother does that to her children?"

He was silent for a few moments, and when he spoke, his voice rang with a note of defeat. "The kind that's screwed up. The kind that needs forgiveness."

She shook her head. "I can't do that."

"Then you've drawn a line between us, Ro. I won't let you hurt her again. That last time, what you did to her . . . I trusted you. If I'd known what you'd planned, I would never have let you find the asylum."

"You couldn't have stopped me."

He laughed. "I may not have any of your magick mojo, but don't for a second think I can't stop you if I want to." He arched a brow, his eyes cold and determined. "Don't think I *won't* stop you."

A chill ran through Rowan's body at the look in his eyes. There was something there . . . something new and dark. When had he become so . . . hard?

"When are you going to ask her about the grimoire?" he asked. "Cedric had to give her some strong meds to calm her down."

She shrugged. "As soon as possible."

"Who are these men?" He changed the subject abruptly, and for a moment she was silent.

"Friends of Nana's."

He snorted. "Sure they are. She's always hung with a bunch of *True Blood* wannabes."

Rowan made a face. "Remember Bill?"

"From *True Blood*?"

She scowled. "Don't be an asshole. Bill, Nana's friend. He'd visit from time to time and sometimes stay a few days."

Kellen's brow furled. "The little round guy who dressed funny and always carried a bag of candy?"

Rowan nodded. "Azaiel is a friend of his, and they're here to . . . make things right."

"I met Priest and Nico earlier, so I'm going to assume that Azaiel is the one you were swapping spit with?"

She glared at her brother but refused to be cowed by him. "Yes," she answered simply.

Kellen's face was unreadable as he digested that bit of information. He took a step back and issued a warning. "Don't go near Mom without me, Ro, or I swear by all that's holy you'll regret it." He left her there and disappeared around the side of the house, no doubt on his way to find Vicki and Terre. They'd always been thick as thieves—even the bloody donkey liked Kellen.

Rowan crossed her arms across her chest, trying to seek what warmth she could. The dampness had found its way past her clothes and clung to her clammy skin with an iron grip. She shivered and closed her eyes. She was surrounded by all of her family and more strangers than she cared to count yet . . . she'd never felt so alone.

For the first time since she came back and found Cara gone, the well inside broke apart. She hadn't realized until now how much she'd cut out of her life when she'd left for California.

Or how much her betrayal of Kellen's trust had cost her. She'd lost her mother through no fault of her own, but Kellen's defection was all on her.

Rowan slipped between the oak trees that bordered the property and disappeared into the early-morning mist and forest that covered acres of land behind the bed-and-breakfast. There, she finally let everything out, with only the birds, squirrels, and dead leaves to hear her sobs.

CHAPTER 19

"Are we going to discuss what happened earlier?"

Azaiel glanced back toward Rowan. She was leaning against the worn brick wall a few inches away, her hair twisting in the breeze that buffeted them. Her large expressive eyes shone in what dim light there was, and her full mouth tantalized.

Discuss it? Hell, no. The fact that he'd not been able to think of much else pissed him off, and there was no way he was going to have a conversation with Rowan James about their kiss.

It was more than a kiss.

He clenched his jaw tight and cleared his throat. He much preferred silence between them. The woman twisted him up, and he needed to stay focused.

"No." His answer was curt and left no wiggle room. Most creatures, human or otherworld, would take heed and leave him the hell alone.

"I want to talk about it."

Azaiel's face darkened. Of course, Rowan James wasn't like most creatures. He glared at her. "Do you really want to get into it right now?"

She shrugged and walked toward him, her steps concise, assured. "Nothing else is happening, so why not?"

She was right. So far the evening had been pretty slow, which was odd. They'd taken the heads of two blood demons about an hour ago, and nothing else had crossed their path.

The darkness they'd sensed days ago had descended with a bang, and currently, Salem, Massachusetts, was the hottest bed of demon activity in the country. Mallick was stretching his muscles, and it was all hands on deck. Azaiel and the others from the League, along with the coven and several bands of human demon hunters, were the only line of defense the local populace had. With Halloween closing in and all sorts of events planned the town was full.

It was a veritable feast for any demon, and the eating was good, though the diet in this part of town seemed pretty damn lean. At least at the moment, which didn't bode well for him when stuck with a female who wanted to share her feelings.

"I think you *want* me to believe you're this," she gestured wildly with her hands, "arrogant asshole. But you're not."

"I'm not?" He tipped his head back. "If I remember correctly, that's exactly what you called me."

She shook her head. "No. That's what you *want* me to think but, you see, an asshole wouldn't put his life on the line for an old woman that he's never met." Her eyes glittered, their glistening depths like jewels. "An asshole would have taken what was offered the other night, no questions asked. He wouldn't have stopped. Wouldn't have worried about my feelings."

"If your . . . if *Kellen,* hadn't shown, I'm pretty damn sure I would have gotten exactly what I wanted." Why the hell was she pressing the matter? Irritation rolled through him, and he ran his hand through his hair.

She bit her lip in that way that kinda drove him crazy. Then her tongue darted out and swept across the bottom, leaving a sheen of moisture that glistened in what little light there was.

Ignoring the obvious, which was his need for silence, she took another step forward until there was less than an inch of space between them. "Are you going to tell me why you're trying so hard to make me believe you're a dick?" She arched a brow. "Because I'm not buying it."

She was dangerous. This little witch.

A smile spread across her face, and his heart rate sped up.

And she knew it.

Azaiel bent low until his mouth was a whisper from hers. "Maybe I just don't like you all that much."

She exhaled, and her eyes widened, the dark centers thickening until the blue nearly receded. "I think you're full of crap." She made a noise in the back of her throat, and somewhere down there, between his legs, things that should stay calm and focused suddenly stirred.

"You do," he managed to get out.

She nodded. "I do."

Silence fell between them, and he found himself holding his breath. She moved again, and this time her breasts pressed against his chest. Azaiel closed his eyes, inhaled her scent, and wondered at the audacity the little witch possessed.

"I think," she continued in a slow breath, "we'd be fools not to at least explore some of the chemistry between us." She exhaled. "Don't you feel it, Azaiel? This connection?"

Her mouth was so close, her scent intoxicating. She splayed her hands out across his chest and looked so hot that it took every ounce of control Azaiel had to keep his hands off her.

Feel it?

He arched a brow. His cock was hard, more than ready, and the witch knew it. And still she pushed. All of this was wrong for so many reasons she didn't understand. Suddenly he was tired of the game and pushed her away.

"Don't ask for something you can't handle, Rowan."

She stared up at him, the teasing manner gone, leaving only a serious glint in her eye. "What happened to you, Azaiel?"

Azaiel ignored her and glanced down the alley once more. For several seconds only the harsh echo of silence was between them, and the anger that stirred within his gut churned harder, faster. "What do you want from me?"

"The truth," she answered simply.

He glanced back toward her and shook his head. "You wouldn't be able to handle my truth. It's not pretty."

"Nothing's pretty, Azaiel. Not even the shiniest, most brilliant diamond. There will be imperfections. Cracks and irregularities. At the heart of everything there is darkness. It's what you choose to do with that darkness that matters."

"You would find good in me?"

She blinked slowly and took a moment to answer. "I would."

"Why?" he asked, not so much to carry on the conversation, but because he was truly curious. In those few precious seconds, he studied her heart-shaped face intently and knew he'd never meet another woman like her, in any plane of existence.

"Because . . ."

A shadow moved, just beyond the halo of gold cast by the streetlight on the corner of Finch and Murphy, and Azaiel held up his hand, silencing her answer. Which was probably for the best.

Dark wisps of smoke twirled faster until they converged into a form that was definitely a . . .

"Sand demon," Rowan whispered.

He nodded but remained silent as he watched it solidify.

They were nasty creatures, bottom feeders yes but dangerous all the same. Once a victim was scented and lured into their embrace they struck quickly, sucking in the body whole, like quicksand. It was a fast death, yes, but extremely painful.

A human body was literally sliced apart by thousands of razor-sharp teeth that lined the sand demon's large mouth and gullet. Of course, once spit out into District One—the main processing center in Hell—it would be put back together. Lilith needed bodies that worked down there though most captured by sand demons wouldn't come close to resembling their former human form. They'd spend the rest of eternity looking like a haphazard mishmash of body parts.

"There are three more," Rowan whispered urgently, her smaller frame moving forward as she tried to maneuver past him. She was all business now, and he held out his arm to stop her.

"There's a couple walking toward them." Rowan's urgent whisper was punctuated by a tug on his arm.

Azaiel glared at her, irritated. "If you don't shut your mouth, the damn things will get away before we have a chance to kill them."

"Don't be so grumpy," she shot back.

For the hundredth time he cursed Priest's insistence that he patrol with Rowan, yet there'd been no choice. At least one of the League had to stay close to Rowan. Just in case.

His gut tightened.

Just in case Mallick himself showed. There was no way they could let the demon lord anywhere near Rowan. If he managed to get his slimy hands on her, the game would change yet again.

And it could cost Rowan James her life.

"Azaiel, we need to move out." She was much too close to him, and he moved away, wanting only distance and peace.

"Wait for my signal," he growled.

"Who said you were in charge?"

There was the attitude he'd been waiting for. He needed her to focus on the danger at hand. His arm shot out, and he gripped her tightly, turning so that she felt the full extent of his anger. He was done playing her game. Done with her fantasy imaginings. What was the point?

"I *am* in charge," he growled. "This isn't a game, witch. You may think you're the alpha in this whole mess"—her cheeks reddened at his comment—"but make no mistake, you're just a little girl in over her head. If you want to survive this . . . if you want your family, your lover"—he ground out the words—"to survive this, then you'd better learn to take orders and listen the fuck to me." Azaiel bent low until his breath warmed her cheeks. "Are we clear on this?"

She yanked her hand away. "Lover? What are you—"

A low moan drifted between them, one filled with anticipation and darkness. They both whirled around. "Shit." Rowan muttered. She took off running down the street.

Azaiel swore, several ancient words falling from his lips as he strode toward the drama now playing out. A young couple, out for a night of partying, was now surrounded by four sand demons. Their human eyes couldn't quite see what hid amongst the shadows, but they sure as hell sensed the danger.

The young woman clung to her boyfriend or husband's hand, tugging at her long blond hair nervously as they turned in a circle. They stumbled, obviously drunk, making it incredibly easy for the demons to lure them into a trap.

Rowan was almost upon them, and she yelled loudly, her voice echoing into the night wind. "Hey, assholes, why don't you pick on someone who can actually fight back?" She'd withdrawn a sidearm—one of her charmed guns from what he could see—and aimed it at the sand demon closest to the couple. She quickly fired off several rounds, and the woman screamed loudly, backing away and dragging her husband straight into the two demons behind them.

Their mouths opened wide, and a strange melody drifted in the air. It was a hypnotic blend of notes designed to lull a potential victim into a state of paralysis.

The sand demon closest to Rowan—the one she'd shot at—howled in pain, his head morphing into a swirl of sand and mist. It was a quick repair, and seconds later the demon had grown several inches and stared down at Rowan, with beady, bloodred eyes.

She was furiously drawing a charm into the air—small luminescent designs appeared like whispers of smoke—but she wasn't fast enough.

Azaiel shouted to gain its attention, as he armed himself with a couple of his own, extraextra specials. He spoke in an ancient tongue, one he knew the demon would understand.

"Leave now or die."

The tallest demon—the one closest to Rowan—paused and turned his massive head toward Azaiel. It smiled, a blatant sign that it had no fear. It was all Azaiel needed. "Actually, we're just going to go with . . . die. Open wide, you ugly son of a bitch." He ran forward and shot one of his grenades down the bastard's throat.

Rowan dove away and grabbed for the couple but only managed to get hold of the male. She rolled to the side, taking him down with her, and Azaiel scooped up the woman, as he tossed grenades at the remaining demons. He managed to get two of them, but the third whirled away, just out of reach.

The two he'd caught exploded, and force of it sent him flying though he used his body to shield the woman from the brunt of the blast. The air filled with the putrid scent of burned demon flesh, and he set the woman aside, shoving her into a doorway. "If you want to live, you will not move. Understand?"

She nodded, stunned and more than a little confused.

"Rowan!" His eyes searched the darkness—the blast had taken out the streetlights on both corners. With the swirling bits of demon remains and the massive surge of sand, he couldn't see shit.

Azaiel scrubbed at his eyes, cursing madly—pissed at his lack of skills, at the powers that had been stripped from him. In another time and place he would have been able to kill these bastards sight unseen. He would have thought it, and it would have been done.

The demon's song reverberated and crashed into his brain. He felt the pull. The strength and determination, and it chilled him. This one had some legs on it.

He charged toward where he thought Rowan might be and gritted his teeth as light filtered through the clouds of crap in the air. She was there, beams of light emanating from her hands as she shielded the man with her body. The sand demon rose above her, its mouth open wide, and the human male, so susceptible to the dark notes it sang, pushed forward, trying to move past Rowan.

"Rowan!" She turned, pushed the man to the ground, and he tossed the remaining grenade at her. She caught it, spun around and threw it up at the creature.

An incredible wailing noise erupted from within the beast, and Azaiel rushed forward, grabbed Rowan and pushed her backward as the demon exploded, blowing chunks of mist, sand, and guts all over the place.

He felt the sting of shrapnel slice into his body. And then there was silence. Only the whistle of wind in his ear.

She moved beneath him, and he rolled away, staring up at a clear night sky filled with twinkling diamonds. His back hurt like hell, but he knew it would pass. He'd been stripped of a lot of things, yes, but his ability to heal wasn't one of them.

"Are you all right?" Rowan sat up and leaned over him, her fingers on his face. The velvet sky was gone, replaced with a vision of red hair, blue eyes, and a mouth that he longed to touch.

"I'm good." His answer was curt. "Check on the humans."

She stared down at him for several seconds, then moved away, leaving only the cool wind to ruffle his hair as he got to his feet. The carnage was impressive. Azaiel reached into his jacket and pulled out a small bag containing fluid and a lighter. He bent down, aware that Rowan was somehow charming the couple—hopefully removing any remnants of memory—and he set the pile of demon waste to flame.

It didn't take long, maybe a few minutes at the most, and when it was done only he and Rowan stood on the darkened street.

"That was . . ." she began and stopped, her eyes not quite meeting his.

He reached over and plucked what looked to be bits of demon crap out of her hair. Her scent was heightened, it filled the air and his lungs, teasing his nostrils with her earthy, sexy perfume.

"That was pretty awesome," she finished, this time looking up into his eyes and smiling wide. "You have to admit, we do make a good team."

Watch yourself, Azaiel.

His gaze lingered on her lips. "Let's go," he said abruptly. He needed to move. To kill and maim. As long as he had that on his plate he couldn't think about her. Couldn't think about how she'd felt beneath him. Of how she'd tasted.

He strolled down the street, ignoring her shouts, and rounded the corner. A sliver of darkness lingered in the air. A hint of decadence that got his attention. A crowd had gathered near the far corner, their silhouettes black against the soft glow from the lights above them.

The WITCHES BREW sign flashed neon red. He headed toward the crowd and shoved his way through, aware that Rowan was fast on his heels and yelling madly.

He couldn't explain his anger. Or actions. And at the moment didn't care to. He pushed his way inside, ignored the doorman, and entered a world unlike the Salem he'd encountered so far.

The Witches Brew was located in the shell of an old building that looked to have been a warehouse at one time.

Rowan yanked on his arm. "We shouldn't be here."

He ignored her and moved forward. Neon lights in pink, green, and blue were strung along the exposed brick walls, with Gothic paintings as decor. Exposed ductwork crept across the high ceiling, and along the far wall was a bar that ran the length of the building.

The club was dark, hot, filled with all kinds of scents and all kinds of bodies. Sex and lust lingered in the air like day-old cigarettes.

He sensed several otherworld creatures right away though he focused on the closest. A tall vampire leaned against the bar, surrounded by a trio of adoring human women. One sat on his lap, her breasts nearly falling from the low-cut blouse unbuttoned to her waist. Two small puncture marks stood out along her neck, while the other women clung to his sides as if he were a rock star, waiting their turn.

The vamp nodded at him, and as far as Azaiel could tell he'd not broken any covenants. He sensed no thrall, and the women seemed willing.

"This place is a safe house," Rowan whispered. "It's been years since I've been in here, but the humans that come know exactly what they're in for. I tried to tell you . . ."

"Tell me what?"

"That we shouldn't have come here."

"I see," he said tightly, his gaze fixed upon the dance

floor and the writhing bodies that moved to the hypnotic beat provided by—what else? An otherworld band comprised of shifters and vampires.

The singer, a witch, had a voice Etta James would envy, and her coffee-colored skin glistened against the soft glow from the candles that lit the stage around her. Her hair hung down to her waist, in long strands of caramel braids, and her eyes locked onto Azaiel, their dark brown depths glittering, her plump red lips wet and inviting.

She sang a note, one that was full of rapture, and he felt the pull of her sexuality as surely as if she'd rubbed her voluptuous curves against his skin.

"She's throwing her magick at us, Azaiel," Rowan said hoarsely. "She wants you. She wants me."

He was hot and pulled his gaze from the witch, only to settle upon two shifters—werewolves by the looks of it—engaged in a very public display of sex. They were in the corner and though shadows fell over them, he knew by the way they moved—slowly, back and forth—exactly what they were doing.

Suddenly he was surrounded by bodies—hot writhing bodies—and Rowan was crushed to his frame. The music slowed, the melody became darker, more provocative, and before he could stop himself, he pulled her in close. He held her, moved with her as her arms slipped around his waist.

The beat was inside him, a living, breathing thing, and it set every single cell in his body on fire with need and want.

Rowan moved against him, sensually, her soft belly pressed tight to his erection, and he groaned as her hands slid up to his chest. He stared down at her. Into her large, expressive eyes, the small nose and lips that were enough to make anyone insane.

"This isn't a good idea," he whispered, lowering his head.

"I know." Her tongue peeked out from between her teeth,

and he sighed harshly, his hands sliding down to her rounded butt. "It's her . . . Alexis . . . the witch. She's a sex witch . . . a succubus."

"I don't care." Azaiel's lips grazed her mouth, and her scent was everywhere. Erotic images played out in his mind. Rowan, beneath him. On top of him. Naked. Writhing amongst this crowd as he entered her. As his cock swelled and filled her. As she moaned and cried out his name.

The couple beside them began to doff their clothes, and others followed suit. The woman's top disappeared, her pert breasts claimed by her partner's mouth as he grabbed at her skirt and hiked it over her hips.

Azaiel couldn't look away. He wasn't strong enough.

The woman wrapped her legs around her lover, and he entered her with one, quick thrust that brought an immediate whimper from the woman. They moved back and forth, their bodies joined. Right there beside Azaiel and Rowan.

Rowan's hand was at his crotch. Her fingers seeking, rubbing, and he swelled beneath her touch.

What the hell was happening?

"Oh God, Azaiel. I tried to warn you. I can't stop."

His tongue sought the refuge of her mouth, and he ate the words unspoken. *We shouldn't have come here.*

He slid inside her warmth, his mouth plundering, stroking, and he found that he couldn't get enough. She tasted like honey and cinnamon, and when she groaned into his mouth, he gripped her tighter and picked her up so that she clung to him, her feet several inches off the ground.

The feel of her thrilled and excited him, as did the smell of sex and lust and danger. The song in his head magnified, and as his mouth trailed kisses down her neck, he found himself reaching for her jacket. The need to both touch and see her skin clawed at him, and she wrapped her legs around his waist, very much like the couple who fucked beside them.

Each movement of the man's hips plunged his body deeper into that of his partner, and their groans of pleasure rang in Azaiel's head.

"I knew you would feel like this," Rowan whispered, her hands inside his jacket, her palms beneath his T-shirt. "So hard." She bent and kissed his collarbone. "And perfect."

"I'm far from perfect," he answered harshly as he gazed up at her. Long tendrils of hair clung to her moist skin, and he angled his head, smiled wickedly, and claimed a nipple through the thin cotton of her shirt.

Her hands crept into his hair, and she held him there, her hips gyrating against him as the music continued to swirl. The moans and cries of pleasure from everyone around him swam in his head. It intensified the need to bury himself inside Rowan, and the sensation was near painful.

He'd never wanted a woman as badly as he wanted Rowan James at that moment. Not even Toniella, the woman responsible for his stay in Hell—for his fall from grace—had made him feel like this. She'd been an obsession. Rowan was something else entirely.

The band sped up, the guitars, the bass, and keyboards, all blending into a mad, chaotic melody of sex and lust. Alexis moved through the crowd—even though she never left the stage—her voice touched them all, her sexual appetites filled everyone with the need to mate. To have sex and conquer their most base desires.

Azaiel watched the vampire feed openly from the human female upon his lap as he settled her against him. Her skirt was tangled around her waist, and the tantalizing view of her nakedness held Azaiel's gaze. The vampire glanced up and smiled at him, his hands cupping the woman's ass as he thrust into her. They rocked together in an erotic dance, and Azaiel looked away.

Highly aroused. Highly disturbed.

He gripped Rowan tightly, trying like hell to gather his thoughts. To find himself amongst the chaotic music.

This was hedonism at its finest, and it called to him with an urgency he was helpless to fight.

He set her on a table in the corner, but she squirmed away from him and knelt between his legs—her hands at his jeans, her fingers tugging at the zipper.

"I need you now," she said hoarsely, and he did nothing to stop her as she freed him from his pants. As she slid her fingers over the thick, straining length of him. As her lips, her wet, soft lips licked their way along his cock. As she took him into his mouth.

"This is wrong," he whispered, closing his eyes as she suckled and massaged him. His own words from before—his warning to her—echoed in his mind, but he paid no heed.

Wrong always feels right. It's why hell is full of lost souls who aren't strong enough.

He closed his eyes and gave himself up to the pleasure of her mouth. There was nothing but Rowan and Azaiel, there beneath the shadows and music. He thrust his hips at her. He let her take all of him into her mouth and knew he was lost. He'd never be able to stop.

And he was right.

There amongst the dark, seductive notes that fell from the succubus witch, amongst the straining crowd of human and otherworld, amongst the shadows shared by so many weak souls . . .

Azaiel lost his mind.

CHAPTER 20

He tasted like heaven, and the feel of him in her hands—in her mouth—filled her with such power that for a second Rowan was overwhelmed. The music filled her head, and each sultry note liquefied, *melted* her defenses.

Her only thought was to give Azaiel as much pleasure as she could.

She wanted to take him to the brink and fall over the edge with him. He strained against her, large, muscular, and so very, very male. He was beauty and strength. Lust and passion.

Words she didn't understand fell from him as he approached the edge, and when he climaxed—when he came for *her,* he let loose a torrent of ancient speak that made her heart beat faster.

His hands were everywhere after that, and as the pressure built inside her body, she whimpered. All rational thought had fled. There was only Azaiel. And pleasure. And the darkness that hid the music.

He ripped at her clothes, his mouth on her breasts as he pushed her back against the table. He was there between her legs, his hands beneath the waistband of her jeans, his mouth and tongue driving her crazy.

There were no words. Only his body over hers. His rough breaths as his chest heaved. The growl that rumbled in his throat as he flicked his tongue across her turgid nipples.

"You tempt me like no other," he said, then his mouth was on hers, his tongue inside. Seeking. Touching. Tasting. Her legs fell wide, and his hand was there, her zipper loosened, her jeans halfway down her hips. His long fingers sought the slick heat, which ached and throbbed, and when he plunged inside her, she lost all conscious thought.

Rowan's head fell back, and she was aware of straining bodies in the shadows. Of grunts of pleasure and watching eyes that lingered. It excited her, and the pressure built so hard inside that it made her cry out.

She wanted Azaiel inside her. Here. On this table. In this club. She felt as if she were losing her mind, and the witch's song burned into her brain. A slow, seductive melody she'd never forget.

Azaiel leaned over her, his eyes fierce, his face slick with sweat and passion. She reached up, cupped his face in her hands, and kissed him as if he were the very air she needed to live. And for that moment he was everything to her.

Something vibrated then . . . in her jacket pocket. It was accompanied by a shrill ring. At first they both ignored it. They were too busy touching and tasting and tearing at each other. But the ringtone didn't stop, and eventually the piercing key was enough to cut through the madness that had enveloped them both.

She pushed him away, slightly disoriented. "What are we . . ."

Azaiel swore, scooped her up, and moved them deeper into the shadows. He was breathing hard as he set Rowan away from him, and he turned, cursing roughly as he straightened his clothes.

"Oh Azaiel." She glanced up into dark eyes that regarded

her fiercely. "What have we . . . what are we . . ." Her head was thick, as if it were full of cotton, and she shook it aggressively, wanting the song to end.

Her breasts hung loose, her nipples hard and throbbing, the tender flesh aching. She jumped from the table, ashamed, as she buttoned her top, tucking the loose ends back into the waist of her jeans.

I can't look at him.

The phone vibrated again. She licked her lips, her mouth bruised and swollen and she reached for her cell. *Oh God, I had him in my mouth.* Never had she ever acted in such a way with a man. Christ, she'd dated Mason for three whole months before she'd slept with him.

She glanced down and ran her hands through the mess of hair at her nape. She bit her lip. "It's Kellen."

"Did anyone ever tell that guy his timing sucks?" His voice was rough, his features harsh.

She flinched. "It would have been better if he'd called fifteen minutes ago." She exhaled and read the text, hating the way her stomach clenched as she read the words.

"Has something happened?" Azaiel moved closer, and she wished he'd move the hell to the other side of the bar. Her body still thrummed and ached, and he smelled way too damn good.

She glared at the stage. And still Alexis crooned.

"I have to go and meet Kellen. Marie-Noelle is awake, and she wants both of her children."

"Both of her? Who . . ." He moved in front of her then, something new in his eyes. "You and Kellen are . . . siblings?"

She looked up at him more than just a little irritated as she nodded. "Kellen is my brother, my twin. Who did you think he was?"

Azaiel stared down at her. "I didn't know you had a brother."

Did she even hear his words? He looked like decadent, sinful, caramel-glazed chocolate. The throb between her legs burned, and she fought the urge to put her own hands there. Anything to alleviate the ache.

Shame burned her cheeks a deep rose, and Rowan glanced away, not liking the intensity of his eyes. What was he thinking? She'd thrown herself at him earlier and now . . . what they'd done here in the shadows.

She'd never lost control like that. Not even in her wild days. The last time she'd visited The Witches Brew had been ages ago. Back then, she'd come with her cousins Vicki and Hannah. To watch and titillate. But they'd always protected themselves with charms and had *never* participated.

"We have to go." She ran her tongue across her lips. "We should . . ." She glanced around, and when she turned to him, she couldn't quite meet his eyes. "We need to keep this to ourselves. Don't tell anyone we were at The Witches Brew. If Vicki finds out, she'll know . . . and I . . . I just . . ." She paused—tongue-tied and hating that he still stared at her in silence. "We need to forget this happened."

Just like that the reality of their situation smashed the sexual fantasy Alexis had unleashed in the both of them.

"This . . . what we just did isn't our fault. Not really. It's Alexis. It's what she does. We shouldn't have come in here," she finished lamely. "I tried to warn you."

He ran his hand through the thick blond hair atop his head, and Rowan tried not to think of what his hands had felt like. Of what he'd done to her this morning. Of what she'd done to him here, in this bar. *In public.*

"Oh God," she whispered, feeling slightly ill. She turned and pushed her way through the dense crowed, wanting only fresh air to clear her head.

And to forget.

* * *

"She's waiting for you, Miss Rowan." Cedric smiled though his sad dark eyes had lost some of their glimmer.

"Thank you." Rowan took a second, her hand lingering on Cedric's forearm. "Are you feeling all right? Have you been resting?"

He shrugged. "I'm feeling as good as I can right now." He nodded toward her Nana's rooms. "Go, on. You all need to say some things. Figure some stuff out."

She shook her head. "I know. It's just sometimes the doing is harder than the figuring out."

He smiled and gripped her a little tighter. "You'll be fine, Rowan. She is your blood." His eyes misted. "She is Miss Cara's baby girl, she's just not as strong as you." He squeezed her hand. "You remember that, now."

Rowan stared into his dark eyes for a few moments longer, then moved past him. She ignored Azaiel, the same way she'd ignored him the entire ride home. It was the only way she could function. The images . . . the sensations— they were too much. Too intense. Too wrong.

The small tabby appeared from nowhere and jumped onto the counter near the Seraphim. Its little body shook from the ferocity of its purring, and it butted its small head on his hip. Behind him the clock glowed 2:30, and soon the others would be back.

Her brother stood with arms crossed, a fierce look on his handsome face. She nodded. "Let's do this."

She moved toward Nana's rooms, paused with her hand on the door, and pushed it open.

Her mother glanced up from the bed, her fingers clutching the worn copy of *To Kill a Mockingbird* to her chest. Beside her, standing guard, was the gargoyle. The huge creature looked fierce, and his size only made her mother appear that much more fragile.

Rowan had pretty much had it with the kid-glove treatment. It was time for her mother to grow up, something that was way past due.

"She loved this book." Marie-Noelle's voice was like sandpaper, rough and dry, and she spoke haltingly as if searching her mind for the right words. "I can't believe she's gone. I had so much to say to her." Her mother glanced up. "I guess it's too late for sorry, now."

Rowan moved closer. "It was too late years ago."

Her mother flinched at the harsh tone, but Rowan couldn't help it. There were no warm fuzzies hiding in her heart. There was only anger, resentment, and the need for someone to pay. Kellen had asked her to be merciful. To forgive. She felt the weight of his gaze, but she couldn't do what he wanted.

There was too much pain.

Marie-Noelle stood, her shoulders hunched, her small frame almost folded in on itself. She looked pathetic, and Rowan watched as Mikhail moved closer to her, his arm at the ready in case she needed assistance.

Her mother waved him away and walked toward Rowan and Kellen, her steps little more than a shuffle. Her eyes were alive with a feverish glint that could have been her sanity leaving her or the effect of the drugs Cedric had given her to calm her nerves.

Rowan was hoping for the drugs. "Do you know why you're here?" Rowan asked.

Marie-Noelle gazed at the two of them as if she hadn't heard the question. "You've both grown so much." Pain shadowed her face, and she looked much older than her years. "Oh God, I've missed so much." Her voice broke. "I'd give anything to get it back."

"Mom, it's okay. Take your time." Kellen spoke gently, and Rowan just about pulled the pin.

"Seriously, Kellen? She's not a child, so stop treating her like one. I'm so sick of everyone walking on eggshells around her." She glared at her mother. "This isn't about you, and for the record, I don't give a flying fuck about your guilt."

"Ro!" Kellen admonished.

She turned to her brother. "No, I'm done. I'm not playing this family-reunion game. This is bullshit. There are lives on the line." She whirled back to her mother. "Lives that have been lost including the only mother I knew."

Rowan's chest burned. Her limbs trembled, and the energy inside her body tripled. The floor shook, several large planks of oak split up the middle, and a series of family pictures on the wall crashed to the ground.

Marie-Noelle flinched, and when Mikhail would have moved forward, Rowan's hand shot out, and she stopped the gargoyle. "This is our business. Not yours."

Rowan's anger filled her throat, and for a few seconds she couldn't speak—could barely breathe.

"I won't let you hurt her," Mikhail managed to get out.

"I don't need your permission to do anything," she spit out. The darkness inside her pulsed with a heavy, hot hand, and she closed her eyes, struggling for control. The gargoyle growled and managed to put one foot forward, but Rowan's hand shot up, and the creature was held in an invisible, iron grip.

"Rowan, calm down," Kellen said into her ear. He was at her side now, his hand on her shoulder, and she was aware that the door had opened. Azaiel now stood on her other side, and when he touched her hand, when that connection was made, she felt the darkness fade, and eventually she got a handle on her emotions.

Azaiel grounded her.

Sweat rolled down her back, her gut churned, and for one

brutal second the hate that she'd denied was there. It filled her body like sand in an hourglass, and her mother flinched at what she saw.

"Where is the grimoire?" Rowan exhaled and took a step forward.

Marie-Noelle's eyes widened, and fear crept into her face. "Rowan, you can't . . . it's much too dangerous."

Rowan laughed bitterly. "I'll decide what's dangerous. Getting our asses kicked every night by a bunch of demons is dangerous. Walking across the bloody street is dangerous." Rowan moved until she was inches from her mother. Until she could see the tiny veins in her eyes and the wrinkles that creased the corners. "I'd rather face a thousand Mallicks and go down fighting than to give up and become his bitch. You got that? I will steer my own ship, Mother, and it will either find safe passage, or I'll take him down with me. This has to end." Rowan closed her eyes. "It *will* end on Samhain."

Silence wrapped them all in a hot cocoon, and for several moments no one spoke. Marie-Noelle's body trembled, her fingers clutched the book tightly in her grasp, and her eyes never left her children.

"Mom, do you know where the grimoire is?" Kellen asked gently as he moved forward. "Ro, needs it." He glanced back at Rowan. "We all need it or Nana's death means nothing. I know you're scared, but we've pretty much reached the end of the road." He touched her cheek, and she leaned into his palm. "Don't you think?"

Marie-Noelle shuddered and exhaled. She nodded, her eyes lowered. "I never meant for any of this to happen."

"Never meant doesn't mean anything once it's happened," Rowan retorted.

Marie-Noelle nodded, defeat in her voice. "You're right." Her eyes cleared, and she gazed at Rowan. "You're right about all of it, and if you need to drive that point home over and over again, I won't say anything."

"There's nothing you can say."

Marie-Noelle sighed. "He was just so . . . charming."

"Who?" Kellen prodded.

Rowan stepped forward, but Azaiel's large hand swallowed her smaller one whole, and she froze. "Give him a chance," Azaiel whispered.

Marie-Noelle closed her eyes. "He was beautiful and dangerous and the sun was in his hair and he reminded me of someone."

"Where did you meet him?" Kellen asked.

"I don't remember. The forest? A bar in town?"

Rowan's stomach lurched, and her fingers dug into Azaiel's palm. *Oh God, do I want to hear this?*

"I just remember I closed my eyes, and when I opened them, he was there."

"A name would be nice. Who?" Rowan yanked her hand from Azaiel and pushed past Kellen. "Who the hell did you give our grimoire to?"

"Move away from her," Mikhail growled.

Rowan flicked her wrist, and the gargoyle was tossed into the wall as if he were a rag doll. His anger was fast and furious. Mikhail opened his mouth but was held silent by Rowan.

Her mother's eyes hardened. A ripple of energy surrounded her as she glared at her daughter. "You will show him respect, Rowan."

"Like you showed us?" she retorted.

Marie-Noelle stared up into her daughter's face. "When did you become so cold? So hard?"

"This isn't my intervention . . . it's yours. I don't care enough about you to have a heart-to-heart and relive the fabulous childhood we both know never happened. I care about the grimoire, and that's it. So tell me who has it or . . ."

"Or you'll hurt me like you did the last time?" Marie-Noelle's voice was stronger.

Rowan sensed a fight, and she smiled though her eyes remained hard, jeweled stones. "I promised Kellen I wouldn't do that to you." She rotated her wrist, and Mikhail bellowed, obviously in agony. "It doesn't mean I won't hurt your little boy toy."

"Stop this Rowan." Marie-Noelle nodded toward the gargoyle. "Now."

"Rowan!" Kellen shouted.

She whirled around, a sob escaping as she felt something inside her break. Her body felt weird. Hot and cold at the same time, but the power inside was something to behold. "Back off." She growled the warning.

Mikhail was released, and he fell to the floor, taking the bed table with him. The crash reverberated in the room, but no one paid attention. All eyes were focused on Rowan and her mother.

"Where is it?"

"I sold it to a demon."

"A demon." Rowan was incredulous. "That's just"—she threw her hands into the air, and the large watercolor beside the fireplace fell to the floor—"wonderful." She arched a brow. "This demon have a name?"

Marie-Noelle faced her daughter, head held high. "Seth," she said softly.

"Seth," Rowan repeated. "Seth have an address? 'Cause we could really use one right about now."

Marie-Noelle's eyes narrowed. "Your tongue is sharp. Reminds me of—"

"Father?" Rowan asked silkily.

The two women stared at each other in silence, then Azaiel stepped forward. "Did this Seth have Lucifer's mark on the side of his neck?"

"I don't . . ." Marie-Noelle's brow furled.

"Think, Mother," Rowan ground out. "It's the least you can do."

"Jesus, Ro. Take a seat," Kellen snarled.

Rowan ignored her brother, but she was aware that his hands were fisted, and he was itching to fight just as much as she was. They just had different targets in mind.

Marie-Noelle nodded slowly. "Yes, he had the mark under his left ear."

Rowan saw something flicker in her mother's eyes and didn't like the way Azaiel's mouth tensed.

"Do you know him?" Rowan turned to Azaiel.

The Seraphim nodded, his dark eyes somber, his mouth set tight. Rowan could tell by the look on his face that this Seth person wasn't your average everyday demon next door.

"It's not good, is it?" she said quietly, the fight in her suddenly gone. She was so tired.

"No." Azaiel glanced at Kellen. "It's not good."

"Where do we find this bastard?" Kellen asked.

"District One," Azaiel answered carefully.

"And that would be where?" Kellen asked.

"That would be a long way from here."

"An exact location would be good," Kellen retorted testily.

Rowan held her breath as Azaiel cocked his head to the side. "The exact location would be Hell."

"Wow," Rowan murmured, as her gaze swept the room. She fought the urge to laugh because she wanted to cry at the same time. "Nice. What do we do now?"

Azaiel stared down at her, his dark eyes glittering as small ribbons of gold bled through the black. "I'll look after this." He nodded toward Marie-Noelle and turned toward the door.

"Azaiel, wait! Where are you going?" Rowan grabbed his arm.

"I'll get the grimoire."

"But it's . . ." Rowan blew out a hot breath. "In Hell."

Azaiel glanced down at her, and she carefully let go of his arm. There was a hard glint in his eye—a cold wash of winter that made her shudder. "Yeah."

He turned and left her with a fractured, broken family and a big-ass gargoyle whose brilliant yellow eyes shot bullets her way. Rowan shook her head and sighed.

You couldn't make this shit up.

CHAPTER 21

It was a cold wind that whipped along the ground, churning dead bits of leaves and yanking on the wind chimes that hung from Terre's RV. Azaiel pulled the collar of his leather jacket up to his ears and peered into the gloom as a set of lights cut through the night.

It was nearly four in the morning. He'd just gotten off the phone with Cale, and the news wasn't good. Cale had managed to dig up rumors that the unclaimed James witch was the most powerful woman born into the coven—if not the most powerful witch in the human realm. It was rumored her purported father was neither human nor otherworld but something else entirely—fae. Dark fae.

Cale hadn't needed to reiterate the fact that Mallick could never be allowed to claim Rowan as his. With that kind of magick at his fingertips the dark lord's power would more than double. And that was a modest assumption. Mallick would have the ability to sway the pendulum between the realms any way he wanted, and that was something the League could never let happen.

The balance must always be protected.

Azaiel watched the large Suburban park near the gift shop and frowned. He'd learned long ago that whispers of truth lived amongst rumors, and he had no doubt that Rowan's blood father was fae. It explained too much—the fae that had been spotted in Salem. The undeniable power that Rowan harnessed. It even explained his reaction to her touch. Fae energy was unlike any other. It was seductive. Bold.

Priest exited the SUV, followed by Hannah and Nico. They didn't see Azaiel at first, and he was surprised at the light banter between the shifter and the witch. She'd somehow managed to thaw the perpetual bad mood the jaguar usually sported.

He stepped down from the porch, and Priest stopped midstride. Nico and Hannah followed suit, and for several seconds, the three of them stared up at Azaiel.

"We need to talk," Azaiel said quietly. *Not here.* He didn't have to speak the words. They were all aware of the eyes and ears that listened from the shadows. There were witches everywhere.

Priest nodded and turned, signaling for Nico to follow. Hannah would have as well, but at Azaiel's curt look she remained behind. "It's not nice to keep secrets you know," she mumbled.

The three men walked in silence for nearly five minutes until they'd cleared the James property line and were well down the country road. Out there, beyond the protection ward, the otherworld chatter that littered the wind was much more audible.

"What did you find out?" Priest ran a new cigar beneath his nose, offered one to Azaiel, and lit the end of his when Azaiel refused it.

"Cale and I are fairly certain that Rowan's father is Dark fae."

Nico shook his head and shoved his hands into the pockets of his jeans, and muttered, "Not good."

Priest blew a perfect circle of smoke and nodded in agreement. "Do we know who?"

"No."

"This changes nothing. We knew she was different from the others. Our mandate stands. She will die before we allow Mallick to take her."

Heat burned inside Azaiel's chest, and he thrust his shoulders back, widening his stance and glaring at Priest. "That is a last resort only."

Priest nodded. "I agree. But you need to know I won't hesitate to make it so."

Azaiel's voice dropped. "Are you questioning my loyalty?"

"No." Priest shook his head. "I'm questioning your feelings. I see the way you look at her, which brings to mind another point."

Azaiel didn't like where the conversation was headed. Didn't like that the Templar was hitting way too close to home. "And that would be," he bit out.

"You can't have her either," Nico butted in, his eyes hard, his mouth tight.

Azaiel turned to the shifter and took a step forward, his hands fisted, his anger instant. Priest stepped between them, cigar stuck between his teeth and his hands held up. "Come on, boys, let's keep this civil, shall we?"

Azaiel glared at the shifter. "Unless you know what you're talking about, I suggest you keep your mouth shut."

Nico smiled, a cold, calculating lift of his mouth. "You won't be able to lie to yourself much longer, Seraphim. Know this. I didn't sacrifice my life to let someone like you fuck everything up. When the time comes, if you can't take care of the witch, I will."

Azaiel stepped forward, but Priest's strong arms kept him from the jaguar.

"I'm done here," Nico spat, his dislike for Azaiel obvious. He turned and walked away, while thick tendrils of mist twirled around his legs and crept along his body. Sparks flew from within as he disappeared, and seconds later the unmistakable bark of a big cat drifted back toward them as the remaining fingers of night claimed Nico.

"You need to relax." Priest shoved Azaiel backward. "He won't stop pushing you. He can't let the past go."

"And you think I can?" Azaiel said bitterly.

"No. But you are Seraphim, Azaiel, and you fell away from all of us. You're going to have to work twice as hard as any to regain the trust that you treated so callously all those eons ago."

Azaiel turned from Priest, exhaling loudly as his gaze caught the faintest hint of light along the ridge of night sky. "Rowan needs her family grimoire in order to perform some kind of spell that will destroy Mallick."

"He's one of Lucifer's. He's protected. What power does this grimoire possess that will trump that?"

Azaiel shook his head. "I don't know. This witch magick is not something I'm all that familiar with."

"Normally someone of Mallick's stature would be protected even by the League, but he's grown much too powerful by means that are not within his parameters. I have no problem ordering his execution."

"Thanks but I wasn't looking for your approval." Azaiel rolled his shoulders. "The demon lord will die. The only question is how and who will do the killing."

Priest remained silent for a few moments. "So where is this grimoire? I'm assuming this has something to do with Rowan's mother?"

Azaiel nodded. "She sold the grimoire to Seth . . . Seth the golden."

Priest looked startled. "Seth from District One? The collector?"

"That would be the one," he bit out.

"Sounds like you've got a bone to pick with Seth the golden."

"He acquired me from District Three and was my jailer for more time than I care to remember."

The Knight Templar digested that bit of information. "Well this makes things a whole lot more interesting. How the hell are you proposing to get the grimoire from Seth? His security must be impressive."

"I managed to escape."

"True, but I've my doubts you'll be able to simply walk into his compound and take what you want. What's your plan?"

Azaiel's mouth tightened. "I thought I'd ask nicely."

Priest arched a brow.

"And if he isn't accommodating, I thought I'd kick his ass."

"Sounds like an ass kicking is pretty much the only outcome." Priest slapped him on the back, a gesture Azaiel didn't appreciate. "I just think it's going to be your ass and not his."

"Thanks for the vote of confidence," Azaiel ground out.

"You need help? I don't mind taking a trip below."

"No. I've got that covered though I do need to find the closest portal."

Priest was silent for a moment. "Samael will know. I'll call him."

"Okay." Azaiel nodded. "If you could make sure my little witch doesn't get herself into trouble while I'm gone, that would be good."

"Your little witch?" Rowan's voice slid between them, and both men were silenced as she appeared from the gloom. At Azaiel's dark look she shrugged. "I couldn't sleep."

"You shouldn't be wandering out here alone," Azaiel said sharply.

"I'm not alone." She smiled. "I'm with you."

"I've got to make a few phone calls." Priest nodded. "See you back at the house."

Azaiel ran his hands across the stubble on his jaw and stared down at Rowan. Nico's words echoed in his brain, and he clenched his teeth.

The damn shifter was right. He wanted her. God help him, he wanted her in ways that were wrong. But he was the Fallen. He didn't deserve someone as righteous and true as Rowan.

What the hell am I going to do about her? He needed to keep his perspective, or there was a very real chance he'd fuck things up.

Again.

Azaiel could not afford to let emotion rule his actions. He'd done that once and been burned badly.

"You're looking pretty grim." Her words were light, but he wasn't fooled.

"Why are you here?"

"You're doing it again."

"It?"

"Yeah . . . *it*, treading into asshole territory."

Azaiel watched as she took a deep breath and shivered. Warm mist flew from her nostrils, small clouds that dissipated in the early-morning cold.

"And we both know it's all an act."

"Rowan, go home and try to get some sleep. Let me deal with the grimoire."

"You shouldn't get to have all the fun. Take me with you."

Azaiel's scowl deepened. "Absolutely not."

"But it's *my* grimoire. *My* mess. *My* responsibility."

"Are you out of your mind?" His voice was low and rough. "Mallick, the very demon lord who hunts you, resides down there."

"In case you've forgotten, his mark is blind."

He stared at her in disbelief. There was no reasoning with the witch. Rowan James had an answer for everything. She shivered again, this time violently, which wasn't surprising as she wore nothing but a thin T-shirt and a pair of jeans. Swearing beneath his breath, Azaiel shrugged out of his leather jacket and placed it around her shoulders. It was much too big, but the sight of her drowning in his coat tore away another chunk of ice from inside him. From inside his heart.

She was dangerous, this woman, and if he let her, she'd unthaw the whole damn thing. And where would that leave him?

Totally fucking screwed.

He decided to try a different tactic. He smiled down at her as if things were just peachy; though from the wary look in her eyes, she wasn't buying it. "We should head back to the house. It will be daylight soon."

"I know what you're doing, and it won't work."

He motioned Rowan forward and fell into step beside her, matching his long strides to her smaller ones. "What exactly am I doing?"

"You're trying to change the subject, and like I said, it won't work."

"Really," he answered dryly.

She stopped suddenly and glared at him. "Yes, really."

She pushed him in the chest, and he felt the burn of magick against his skin. It stung, yet did nothing but inflame his senses. Her chin jutted out, and that delectable mouth was so close he only had to bend slightly to claim it.

"If I want to go with you, I will. End of story."

Anger sparked inside him, flushing him with heat. Azaiel had had enough. Maybe it was the way the light reflected in her eye, emphasizing her attitude. Maybe it was the fact that he was tired as hell. Maybe his fuse was running short, and it was time to blow.

Or maybe it was the fact that he couldn't decide whether he wanted to kiss her or dismiss her.

He grabbed Rowan's arm and yanked her against him, effectively pinning her to his chest. The little minx started to struggle, and even though his brothers had pretty much castrated most of his powers, his strength was still considerable, and with her hands pinned to her sides, she couldn't spell or charm.

When she finally tired and went limp he whispered near her ear. "This isn't a game. This is life and death, and in case you aren't paying attention, let me reiterate. It's your head on the chopping block, understand? There is no way I'll risk your life because you want to play the hero. And—"

"Wrong."

"What?"

Rowan wriggled her ass against him, and his groin tightened even more. Disgusted he pushed her away.

"I'm a woman, Azaiel," she began cheekily. "So, I'd be the heroine not the . . ." Her voice trailed off as her gaze dropped to the obvious bulge between his legs.

He glared at her, pissed off that she was able to get such a reaction from him without even trying.

"Details," he ground out. "Yet the only detail *you* need to focus on is the fact that you are not going anywhere near District One."

She cleared her throat before dragging her eyes back to his, her face flushed, eyes overly bright. "All right. I won't go, but I warn you, Azaiel, if you don't come back, if you fail to get the grimoire for me, I will hunt you down, and trust me, Mallick will be the least of your worries."

She started off toward the house, and he smiled at the

haughty set to her shoulders. "I don't doubt that," he called after her.

"I'm not fooling around."

"Noted."

They reached the edge of her driveway a few moments later, and she paused though she never looked back his way. "Just make sure you come back, all right?"

Azaiel didn't say a word as she slipped between the shadows and disappeared from sight.

"Who's your Robin?" Priest cut into his thoughts.

At Azaiel's confused look Priest grinned. "Batman and Robin? Superman and . . . come to think of it, Superman never had a Robin."

Azaiel shook the cold from himself. "I have no idea what that means. Kellen will accompany me."

Priest considered that and slowly shook his head. "He's strong and seems focused, but he's an unknown."

"Why does Rowan have the magick of her family, and Kellen seems to have nothing?"

Priest shrugged. "Magick is discriminate. The James witches only have female children, and therefore their magick is passed from mother to daughter with the firstborn line amped up considerably, which is why Rowan is so much stronger than her cousins. As far as I know, Kellen is the first male born into this family. I'd say the fact that they're twins has something to do with it."

Azaiel took a moment. "I find it hard to believe that as the product of both witch and fae, he's not been blessed with something extraordinary."

"I agree. But he might be more closely aligned with the fae side of his heritage. They mature at a much slower rate, mainly because they're immortal. But judging by the kind

of mojo Rowan's packing, when, or rather, *if* he matures—
Kellen James will be a formidable entity. Are you sure you
can trust him?"

"I'm not sure about anything, but it's no matter. What's
done is done, and Rowan's brother will accompany me."

An hour later Priest dropped Azaiel and Kellen in Salem
at the back of a small restaurant, something called The
Greasy Spoon North. It's where Samael had agreed to meet.
Apparently there were several scattered across the country,
and their specialty, besides the popular all-day-heart-attack-
on-a-plate breakfast, was something called poutine. Azaiel
had never heard of it before, but the thought of cheese curds
and gravy smothered over fried potatoes nearly turned his
stomach.

The place was open twenty-four hours and though it was
barely past five in the morning, The Greasy Spoon North
appeared full. Azaiel and Kellen walked in and immediately
felt the weight of many eyes.

It was an eclectic gathering of hungry souls. Some of the
patrons had been out all night partying—it was Sunday after
all—and church was definitely not on the menu. The lull in
conversation started up after a few seconds, and Azaiel relaxed somewhat. While there were a good number of elderly
folk—those used to early-morning hours, bacon, eggs, and
coffee—there was one in the back who didn't belong.

He sat in the corner, facing the door, and though the place
was lit up like a thousand-watt Christmas tree, shadows
clung to him, making it hard for the average person to see
him clearly. Azaiel had no such problem.

A large pair of aviators hid eyes not meant for humans
to see while broad shoulders bore leather easily, and denim-
clad legs stretched out in front of him as if he had all the
time in the world.

Samael.

"Kellen James." They turned as a slender woman with badly dyed magenta hair hacked to an inch past her ears walked toward them, dirty dishes and a menu in her hands. Her heavy, dark makeup hid what looked to be an attractive face, and the smile on her lips was genuine. "My God, it's been ages. Where have you been hiding?"

"Hey, ah . . ."

"Kristina." The girl's tone was a tad sharper, her smile not quite so bright.

"Right, Kristina. It's been a while. I've been in Boston."

"Boston? That's right, I think Hannah told me that last time I asked. You're attending Harvard, right?"

"I was." Kellen's reply was curt. "I'm . . . not anymore."

"Oh." His tone made it obvious the subject was closed. "I heard that Rowan is back, too? What's going on? Family reunion?" She laughed and smiled widely. "You'll have to tell Miss Cara that we're looking forward to sampling her pies and chili at the fair next weekend."

Kellen nodded but didn't answer.

Kristina turned her attention to Azaiel. "Who's your friend?" She smiled at Azaiel. "You sure as hell aren't from Salem. Heck we could surely use some more men like you around here, that's for sure."

Azaiel remained silent. Why did females talk so much?

"You guys want a table? We're a little full, what with it being so close to Halloween, but there's room at the back."

Azaiel shook his head. "We're good," and pushed past the small woman. Samael was on his feet, his tall, muscular frame unfolding from the table in one smooth motion.

"Figures you're here to see him. Just so you know, he's got a nasty temper."

Azaiel and Kellen ignored the warning and followed Samael down a narrow hallway that led past the restrooms and to the back exit.

"Don't say I didn't warn you!" Kristina's voice followed them outside.

Samael kicked the door open, and the three of them strode into the still-dark alley. A drunk sleeping it off in the corner near the large waste bin was ignored, as were the rats scurrying about.

The demon of chaos turned and flashed a smile that Azaiel knew didn't reach his eyes. The bastard hated him as much as everyone else, but for whatever reason, his vow to Askelon was solid, and Azaiel knew he could be trusted.

"Cale filled me in. You're looking for a way down?"

Azaiel nodded.

Samael turned to Kellen. "You're the witch's brother?"

"That would be me. And you are?"

"Not interested in sharing names."

Kellen folded his arms across his chest and glanced toward Azaiel. "Buddy, the guys you hang with aren't exactly friendly."

"No," Azaiel murmured. "They're not."

"This one seems more of an asshole than the damn jaguar shifter."

Samael arched an insolent brow. "I'm sure Nico would agree." He tossed a small vial to Kellen. "Drink this. It will help to mask your scent, which I've got to say is interesting, human."

Kellen's eyes frosted, and his voice held no warmth. "You and I both know I'm not exactly human, now don't we?"

Samael removed his aviators, and his shimmery eyes glowed as he cocked his head to the side and studied Kellen. "What you are, Kellen James, is a mystery at the moment, but make no mistake, mysteries are my specialty."

Kellen's face tightened. "Is that a threat?"

"No, my friend. It's a fact. You won't be able to take a crap without us knowing."

"Us?"

Silence stretched long and thin. A large dragon tattoo shimmered against Samael's neck, the colors luminescent and hypnotic. Azaiel knew what existed inside the ink and magick. The dragon was real, something Samael could call upon when needed.

It was time to go.

Samael ignored his question and turned to Azaiel. "You'll be fine, Fallen. The stench of the lower realm still clings to your flesh."

Azaiel's eyes narrowed. "Where's the portal?" Azaiel had no time for games and posturing. "We need to get this done, now."

Samael returned the aviators to his face and turned abruptly, heading toward the far end of the alley with long, controlled strides.

"Don't antagonize the demon," Azaiel said harshly to Kellen. "He may be an asshole, but you're in over your head if you think to insult him."

"Who is he?"

"He is not the person you want to piss off."

Samael held his hands palms out toward the worn, weathered brick. Several seconds passed, then the air shifted. The brick liquefied and melted into a swirling haze of red energy that pulsed and threw off an incredible amount of heat. Azaiel felt the pull immediately and clenched his hands together. He'd spent eons plotting his escape from District One and the gilded cage he'd called home.

A gilded cage that had sat prominently in Seth's courtyard, there among the dunes. He'd been like a circus freak on display for everyone to see. Seth was the largest collector in the known realms, and Azaiel had been one of his biggest prizes. The son of a bitch was able to come and go as he pleased—Lucifer placed no restrictions on his travel—and he'd often brought those from the otherworld back to the dunes to see his treasures.

Samael turned and motioned with his hands—a quick gesture—and Kellen moved forward.

"Watch your back, Kellen James. A lot of the filth who reside below are hungry for your kind of meat."

"Yeah? And what kind of meat is that?"

Samael flashed a smile and sniffed the air. "The only kind that's good. Fresh meat."

Kellen glared at the demon and stepped into the portal without hesitation.

Samael glanced his way. "Don't screw this up Fallen." Gone was the sarcastic tone. The demon was dead serious. "Mallick needs to be stopped, and if I could do it without attracting Lucifer's or Lilith's eyes, I would gladly separate his head from his shoulders and burn his remains to ash." Samael shrugged. "Alas it would raise more questions than the League can afford, so you'd best make sure your little witch is up to the task or . . ."

The words didn't need to be spoken.

"This portal opens inside the clock tower near the main square. It will only recognize your body signature for twenty-four hours, so don't linger."

Azaiel frowned. "I didn't know there was a time limit."

Samael shrugged. "What fun would there be if not for a sliver of danger? Be warned that I can't guarantee an extraction if you miss the twenty-four-hour window."

Azaiel nodded and took a step forward. He gave his body up to the pull and closed his eyes as the energy from within the portal seared his flesh. He would retrieve the grimoire for Rowan, and nothing would stand in his way.

Not even Seth the golden.

CHAPTER 22

It was nearly one in the afternoon when Rowan slid from her bed. She sat on the edge, dangling her bare feet over the worn wood floor for a long time and listening to the myriad of voices outside. It sounded like the bloody circus had come to town. The mad braying of a donkey punctuated her thoughts, and she smiled in spite of herself.

She stretched out her toes and rotated her ankle. Damn, she needed a pedicure. The blue polish she'd sported in Paris was chipped and sad-looking.

She rotated her neck and winced at the tightness that was so deep into her muscles it felt like her shoulders were going to snap. The beginnings of a headache clawed up the back of her skull, and her mouth was dry. Her window was open, and a warm breeze—at least for October—drifted across her skin, yet she shivered, cold and still so very tired.

She'd not slept well though she'd fallen into bed exhausted. How could she? Her dreamworld had been invaded by dark, erotic dreams. Dreams so intense she was sure they'd make Mr. Sandman blush.

She closed her eyes, flushed and aroused at images of Azaiel naked, his hard, lean, muscled body shifting in the shadows. Of his tongue inside her mouth, his lips on her breasts and throat. Of his hands everywhere. Of taut skin, of masculine smells, and moans of pleasure.

Rowan had never been so insanely attracted to a man before. She exhaled and ran her fingers through the tangled mess of hair that tickled her chest and bit her lip as she continued to gaze at her sad-looking toes.

The ache between her legs hadn't lessened at all—in fact it was making her crazy. She swore and clenched her thighs together in an effort to alleviate it but to no avail. If anything, the throb increased, and a whimper fell from her lips.

Not fair. Had that Alexis bitch thrown some extra mojo her way? Created a thundercloud of desire that wouldn't abate until she had Azaiel right where she wanted him? Between her legs. Inside her body.

She rubbed her eyes and forced herself to her feet. A shower was what she needed. A long, cold shower.

Half an hour later, she was towel drying her hair when a knock sounded.

"Rowan."

It was Abigail. She crossed the room and yanked her bedroom door open. Her cousin stood there, hand in the air, about to knock once more.

A streak of soft orange ran past the two of them and jumped onto the bed. The small tabby issued a sad, pathetic meow toward Rowan as it turned in a circle and began kneading the coverlet.

"Holy crap, Ro, you look like shit."

Rowan made a face—if she were ten again, she'd stick out her tongue—but stood back so that her cousin could slide past.

"Wow, this is like walking down memory lane. Your bedroom hasn't changed at all. Gosh, the stool is still next to your window. I remember sneaking in late once and I missed it and nearly broke my neck." She paused and looked around. "We had some good times."

"Yes, well . . ." Rowan didn't know what to say. It seemed like a lifetime ago.

"I guess Nana Cara doesn't use this for her guests."

Pain stabbed Rowan in the chest, but she shook her head and tried to keep it together. "No. She doesn't . . . didn't."

Abigail bit her lip and nodded silently, her large, round eyes as blue as Rowan's. Her long blond hair was much like Hannah's except the ends were dyed purple, and she had several interesting piercings in her nose, ears, and one bright pink stud in her eyebrow. Her features were pale, elfin almost, and delicate, but her mouth was generous and at the moment trembling.

"Of course. I'm sorry." Abigail was dressed in tattered jeans and a tight white T-shirt that said MOTLEY CRUE. The girl hadn't changed at all. Funny thing was, that used to be Rowan. Wild. Unpredictable. Devil-may-care. But California had changed her. *School* had changed her, and yet she'd managed to slip into her old skin without breaking a sweat. What did that say about her?

Rowan tossed the towel toward her bathroom and walked to the window. She gazed down at a sight that was not only sobering, it was impressive. The entire coven had gathered, and judging from the ragtag assortment of vehicles, sporting plates from several neighboring states, every last one of them had answered the call. All of them here to fight for her.

Did they realize how dangerous it was out there?

Her chest tightened, and she thumped her palm against the uncomfortable sensation. A lump had formed at the back of her throat, and she struggled to swallow.

"Hannah told me that Kellen and that sweet piece of ass you've been hiding left together."

"I'm not hiding Azaiel. I barely know the man."

"Uh-huh."

Rowan glared at Abigail. "They've gone to retrieve the grimoire."

Abigail was silent for a moment. "Sounds dangerous."

The worry that sat at the back of Rowan's throat tasted like crap. She swallowed and shook her head. She didn't want to think about the danger. About how the thought of her brother and Azaiel in danger made her want to hit something.

"They're big boys. They'll be fine." *I hope.*

"You're right." Abigail flopped onto the bed and scratched the tabby behind its ears. Its little body thrummed loudly as it purred and moved closer to her cousin. "So we were pretty busy last night."

"Yes. I think we all were. Salem is not a good place to be right now."

"I talked to Shane McTavish this morning . . . you remember him from high school?"

At Rowan's blank look, Abigail made a face. "He played football with Kellen. The wide receiver?"

Rowan shrugged, and Abigail made a disgusted sound. "How can you not remember him? He was the most gorgeous guy in high school. Tall, with long dark hair and the most amazing eyes."

"He sure as heck made an impression on you."

"Hell yeah. We necked at a victory game party once. It was the highlight of my night, but he was so drunk that he didn't even remember me the next day."

Ah, football and beer rarely mixed well.

"So what about him?"

"Anyway, he's on the police force now if you can believe it, which is weird because he was always in trouble."

"Must be why you liked him so much."

Abigail guffawed, a wholehearted laugh that filled up the

emptiness in the room. The sound lightened Rowan's heart a little. "He was the guy that stole the Griphon's mascot, remember? No? Well, whatever."

Rowan smiled, listening to Abigail. One thing about most James women—they liked to talk.

"I ran into him at the coffee shop this morning on my way back here. He told me they had more calls last night than ever before, and a lot of them were violent . . . domestics, etc. He also said several women had been raped." She shook her head. "It's really, really bad out there, and Samhain is still over a week away. How are we going to keep all these people safe until then?"

"We'll do it the old-fashioned way—the Buffy way. By patrolling every night and killing anything that isn't human."

Abigail nodded, her hands still stroking the satisfied tabby, and Rowan knew this wasn't the reason for her cousin's need to chat.

"So, I had tea with Auntie Marie a while ago."

Rowan's lips tightened. *Here we go.* "And?"

"Well, she seems . . . good. Really good. Her mind is clear."

"For now." Anger unfurled within her gut. "Until she decides that the bottom of a vodka bottle is something she needs to see again." Sarcasm dripped from her mouth, but she was helpless to control it. "We'll see how long this lasts."

Abigail frowned. "But isn't that what you want?"

"I only care about its lasting until Samhain."

Abigail sat up, and the cat meowed, unhappy with the sudden lack of attention. "Rowan, that's an awful thing to say. She may have screwed up a lot in her life, but she is your mother, and everyone deserves a second chance."

"You're right. Except Marie-Noelle passed her *second* second chance years ago."

"Rowan, what did she do that was so bad? The woman

had an addiction problem. A lot of people have addiction problems. It's not that uncommon."

Rowan stared at her cousin, suddenly weak from the emotion pummeling away inside her. "You have no idea," she whispered. "No one does, not even Kellen."

Abigail was silent for a moment, twirling the piece of pink hair between her fingers. "Then tell me."

Rowan sighed and glanced out the window. "It wasn't just that she had an addiction. It's what she did because of it." She wrapped her arms around her midsection and closed her eyes. "She stole from Nana. Performed illegal magick for drug money. She sold our clothes, our furniture." A tear slipped from the corner of her eye as she whispered, "She sold herself."

"Ro—"

Rowan wiped at her face angrily and turned to face her cousin. "She tried to sell me to a goblin who wanted to bed a virgin. He'd promised her unlimited access to the drug of her choice."

Shock swept across Abigail's face like a lightning strike. "Oh, Rowan."

"I was twelve."

"Did he . . ." Abigail bit her lip. "Were you . . ."

"Raped?" Rowan shook her head. "No. Kellen came home, and she came to her senses I guess because she kicked the bastard out."

"She must have felt awful."

"I don't know what she felt, and I don't care. I don't want to talk about my mother."

Abigail nodded. "Okay. Let's talk about the hot dude you were patrolling with."

Rowan had forgotten how irritating Abigail could be. "I don't want to talk about him either."

Rowan bent and slipped into a pair of running shoes,

tying her hair back into a damp ponytail. Maybe a run would do her good.

"So, who are these guys?"

"What guys?"

"The hot guys."

"My God," Rowan said, exasperated. "What is this, twenty questions?" She shook her head. "They're friends . . . of Nana's."

But are they?

Abigail stood up, and they both ignored the irritated wail from the tabby. "Don't get me wrong. It's awesome that they're here to help us, and Lord knows they're freaking easy on the eyes. Hell, Vicki is falling all over herself trying to get at least one of them into bed. She nearly had a fit when that Nico guy growled at her like an animal, but . . ."

"But what?"

"What do we really know about them other than the fact they're otherworld?"

Rowan stared at her cousin in silence. As a lawyer, she was always prepared. She researched and knew her cases from every angle possible. So why now, when she was involved in the most important fight of her life, was she clueless?

She glanced out the window and spied Nico with Hannah. The scent of sweet tobacco wafted in the air, and she knew that Priest was nearby.

"You're right."

"I am?" Abigail said warily.

Rowan nodded. "I think it's time I get some answers of my own."

She found Priest in the back garden, tending to the overgrown sunflowers that bloomed in a huge cluster along edge. He'd doffed his shirt, and Rowan watched him work for a few moments, enjoying the view.

He really was impressive. His shoulders were wide, his chest and arms muscular without being over the top. An intricate cross was tattooed across his left pectoral, the design interesting though the colors were muted, as if it was old.

With his dark hair and chiseled features he was one hell of a man; except she knew that was false. He was not your average everyday *man*. So what was he?

"You going to stand there all day or offer to help?"

His voice startled her, and Rowan nearly tripped over her feet as she picked her way through the leaves that had been raked into several huge piles along the path.

"Grab that, will you?" He pointed to a large garbage bag, and she held it open while he stuffed the refuse he'd trimmed from the tall plants. "I miss this."

"This?"

"Working with nature. Using my hands for something other than killing otherworld filth."

Rowan remained silent but watched him closely. A fine sheen of sweat coated his muscles, emphasizing their shape as he worked. Azaiel's body was much the same, though his shoulders . . .

"There was a time when I tilled the soil and answered to no one but my god." He stuffed a large handful of leaves into the bag, and their eyes met. "I miss those days . . . sometimes. Things were much simpler."

"Who are you?" Rowan asked quietly.

Priest smiled, a flash of even white teeth, and grabbed a cigar from his pocket. The black jeans he wore hung low on his hips, and his smile widened as her gaze lingered there— and how could it not? The man's body looked as if Michelangelo had carved it from stone . . . *and* had paid special attention to the abs and the hips . . .

"Don't you mean what am I?" He shoved the cigar into his mouth and lit the end, taking his time to coax the flame.

His dark eyes glittered with what Rowan called the other-world glow. It was an extra spark—an imprint of power if you will—that lit the eyes from behind.

Azaiel's was a golden shimmer. Priest's was silken brown caramel.

"Yes, that's exactly what I mean." The tobacco scent was pleasant, reminding her a little of the pipe tobacco that Cedric favored. Though she supposed he'd given that up.

Priest stuffed the bag with refuse while she held it for him, and for several minutes there was nothing but the sound of buzzing insects, the rustle of squirrels in the bush, and the echo of voices from the front of the house.

Once the bag Rowan held was full, Priest handed her another, and they moved to the large piles of leaves.

"I was human once." He shoved the last of the first pile into the bag, and they moved to the next. "A knight of the Templar, an arrogant one who lost faith." His eyes narrowed, and he gazed at Rowan intently. "When things are their darkest, that is not the time to lose faith. That's when you cling to it, when you hold it close to your heart. Arrogance and lost faith did not serve me well, and I paid the ultimate price."

Rowan was quiet as he continued to fill the bag.

"I was foolish, made many mistakes, and lost my life. I wandered the gray realm for many years."

"The gray realm?"

"Purgatory for want of a better word." The cigar was clenched between his teeth as he stared down at her. The man was as tall as Azaiel and just as fierce. "I wasn't meant to be there, so I wandered like a blind fool. I'd lost my faith and belief. It was"—he tossed a handful of leaves into the bag—"the darkest time in memory."

"I think dying would be pretty hard to beat."

Priest grinned at that, a rakish tilt to his mouth that made him look like a movie star. An action hero like Willis or Statham. "Dying is the easy part. Trust me. It's but a moment in time. It's what comes after that can be a challenge. With no purpose I was like a child, a blind, weak, sniveling child. My soul didn't belong in purgatory and there was no moving forward or backward for me."

"So what happened? How did you . . . escape?" Was that even the right word?

"There is no escape from the gray realm. You either move on, find the light as it were, or you live out your days in limbo. Never resting, always searching for something that you never really find." Priest blew out a ring of smoke. "Or you make a deal with someone who has power."

"You made a deal with someone." It wasn't a question.

He handed her the last bag. "I did."

"Who?"

Priest shook his head, and she was struck at his raw, male beauty. "We've just met, Rowan James. Don't expect me to share all my secrets with you." His eyes flashed. "We haven't even kissed."

Her cheeks blushed a deep red, and she stared at her hands. Sheesh, Priest probably thought she was flirting with him, which was absurd. Sure he was hot and sweaty and freaking gorgeous, but the only one she wanted to kiss was . . .

Rowan cleared her throat and asked the question she was most dying to have answered. "So what's Azaiel's story?"

The Knight Templar straightened, his expression no longer easy. "What has he told you?"

She shook her head. "Nothing really, other than he's Seraphim."

Preist's eyes narrowed at that. "Azaiel's story is for him to tell."

"Why don't you like him? Why does Nico hate him?"

Priest exhaled and tied up the last garbage bag. "My feelings for the Fallen are ambivalent; as for Nico, I can't really say. The shifter runs on emotion with a lot of highs and lows. There's not much in between with him."

"The Fallen? That's what Nico calls him, and I know Azaiel doesn't like it. What does that mean?"

Priest clamped the cigar tightly as he tossed the remaining bag into the huge pile of crap that would now have to be dragged to the front for garbage collection.

"It means that no matter your origin, there is always room to fail . . . to fall."

Rowan studied Priest, thinking the entire conversation had been one circle of freaking confusion. She decided to change tactics and go with a hunch.

"Why is Bill your boss? What makes him so special?"

Priest's mouth thinned, and she knew by the very silence that fell between them she'd been correct. She arched a brow and opened her mouth, but his expression changed as his eyes shifted behind her. Gone was easy, and it was replaced with something dark.

Rowan turned and spied Hannah lingering near the fountain that stood beside the garden path. Nico was a few inches behind her, as well as Vicki, Terre, and Abigail. The jaguar shifter was solemn, his hard eyes averted, but Rowan's gut twisted at the look on her cousin's face. On all their faces.

Something bad had happened.

"Ro," Hannah paused and bent over. "Oh God."

"What is it? Hannah, you're scaring me." Rowan rushed to her side and rubbed her cousin's back. Her first thought was for her mother, which startled her so much she stumbled, her feet tripping over themselves.

Hannah slowly straightened, her eyes now brimming with tears. "Clare didn't make it to the airport."

"What do you mean?" The fist in Rowan's gut churned again, and a wave of nausea rolled over her.

Hannah shook her head, her large blue eyes swimming in pain. "She was found in the city, some back alley near the downtown core. She never even made it out of Dublin."

"Found?" Rowan asked dully.

"She's dead, Ro. It was him. I just got off the phone with the police. She was . . . oh God." Nico stepped forward, his harsh features twisted as he stood behind Hannah, hands fisted, cold eyes fierce.

"The police said the attack was savage, judging by the . . . the amount of trauma, they feel it was personal. The sergeant said there was a mark carved into her chest. He described it to me." Hannah's voice broke. "It looks like your mark," she whispered. "Mallick's mark."

For a second only white noise rushed through Rowan's ears. The buzzing was intense, and Rowan stepped back, horrified. Clare was twenty-five. *Twenty-five.*

"What about Simone?" she finally asked.

Hannah glanced back at her cousins. Terre shook her head, her curls bouncing crazily around her face. "We can't get hold of her."

Hannah grabbed Rowan's hands. "It doesn't look good."

Rowan was silent, letting the pain inside expand and touch every cell in her body. Her breathing slowed, and her chest constricted. As the wall of hurt rolled through her veins she clenched her fists and took a step back. The wind picked up, tossing whatever leaves had escaped Priest high into the air.

One large golden maple leaf caught her attention as it swirled in the air—a fall jewel amidst the dreary brown and gray. She focused on it and let the pain grow as large as it could. Until she thought she would break apart from the force of it.

Her grandmother's face drifted in front of her, a hazy, familiar image, and yet it was distorted. Cara's mouth moved.

What was she saying? Was that Patsy Cline Rowan heard?

Rowan thought of what Cara's final moments would have been. What had she felt? Terror. Pain. Sadness. Where was she now? Was her Nana in this place that Priest had spoken of? The gray place? The in-between place?

The pain grew until Rowan's jaw ached from pressure. Until the ground trembled beneath her feet. Until the flag-stones cracked, and large gaping rifts sliced through the newly raked lawn. The roaring in her ears intensified until she covered them and bent over.

"Hold on to your faith, Rowan. You need it now more than ever." Priest's words filled her mind, but she ignored them, and they faded just like everything else. Except the pain.

Still the pain grew, like a worm twisting inside her. It didn't stop until she was sick all over the newly turned earth.

And then it was quiet.

She slowly straightened and wiped her mouth, her hard eyes on Priest as she walked past him without speaking.

To hold on to faith meant you had it in the first place. Rowan was empty inside. She'd lost hers a lifetime ago.

CHAPTER 23

Azaiel and Kellen arrived in District One in the middle of a storm. Such was the way of it there. The perpetual night sky was a vibrant red, with slashes of black ripping across the horizon as thunder and lightning boomed loudly.

The smell of sulfur was heavy in the air, and Azaiel wrinkled his nose in distaste. The metallic scent of it would forever be ingrained into his mind, imprinted upon his memory.

God how he hated that fucking smell.

The clock tower was where it had always been, there in the middle of the market. He paused for a moment as they emerged from the large structure and glanced down the street. Thick fog swirled lazily along the ground, hiding the cobblestone surface and who knew what else. Tall buildings dressed in shadow lined either side of the street, but it was too dark to see them clearly. Instead they stood like macabre caricatures, spectral and hollow shells of what they were.

He studied them through the cold wind and driving rain, pulling his leather coat up as far as it would go. Most were decrepit, crumbling facades, but some were in use and hid things better left in the shadows.

He thought he saw something there, reflected in the glass of one of the only windows that wasn't boarded up. A flicker of light . . . a deviation of the dark.

They couldn't linger.

To his immediate left was the hotel, Soul Sucker. It looked much the same as the last time he'd seen it. It was a tall building, but the upper floors were cloaked in fog and darkness. The paint was peeling, many windows were broken. It was as old and used as District One seemed to be, and it had stood for millennia.

When Azaiel had been a prisoner here he'd been allowed out of his cage occasionally—like a pet out for a walk—and though he could count those few moments of freedom on the fingers of one hand, all that he'd seen was burned into his memory like a movie playing inside his brain.

Club Doom was at the end of this street—a raucous gathering place where alcohol, drugs, and mayhem mixed all too frequently. The dunes—which was where he was headed—were well beyond that place.

"This looks like some fucked-up version of a Hitchcock film." Kellen was beside him, his face hard as he took in everything. "Not at all what I expected." He glanced at Azaiel. "Who knew Hell was as cold as the Arctic?"

"This place is unlike any in the known realms." Azaiel started forward. "Stick close to me. If anyone or anything gets in your face, do not challenge. If you die here, I won't be able to bring you back, do you understand? You'll be bound to this place forever."

Kellen's lips thinned. "Got it." He tucked his jacket up and squinted into the gray mist. The rain had petered off, and the wind had died down, but the mist rode the coattails of fog and created an illusion of depth and movement. "Where we headed?"

"The dunes. It's where Seth's compound is located."

They started forward. "I take it we're not going to be able to walk through the front door and ask for the grimoire."

"No." Azaiel shook his head. "There's another portal, one that will take us inside Seth's."

"And you know where this portal is?"

"I do." At least he knew where it had been located . . . if it had been moved, he was screwed. He was counting on Seth's arrogance and the fact that the demon was very much a creature of habit, not nearly as paranoid as Samael. Though he supposed playing for both sides in this war of the realms would make anyone paranoid.

They were nearly upon Club Doom; the pounding beat shook the street beneath his boots, and several demons crowded the entrance. Two of them were wraiths, their flimsy bodies transparent as they flitted back and forth, searching . . . always searching. Their large, almond-shaped eyes were hollow, and maggots squirmed from mouths that were open in a perpetual scream of agony.

In their former lives they'd been human, or demon, or otherworld until a trip below to District Three had changed them forever.

"Do not meet their gaze," he warned Kellen. "And if they sing, do not listen. Think of anything but the voice in your head."

A large crowd was gathered in front of the entrance of the club, waiting to get inside. An eclectic assortment of otherworld demons and those from the human realm—vampire, shifter, magick. District One was the most forgiving realm in Hell, and in many ways mimicked any city in the human world—a seedy, destructive, and violent city—but nevertheless it drew many parallels.

Club Doom was the only place in the entire district where one could drink, party, and do all sorts of evil, illicit things. That it was owned by Samael was no coincidence. The demon laid claim to half of District One, but Club Doom was his jewel. It provided him with both intel and entertainment.

The smell of hedonism was rank in the air, and Azaiel grimaced. It was sweet and seductive. It had called to him many a night that he'd passed down here and now . . . it made him ill. Small victory but one he clung to fiercely.

They were a block away. "Aren't you afraid someone will recognize you?"

Azaiel shook his head. "There's always a chance, I suppose, but the type of souls who haunt Seth's compound do not generally mix with the filth that inhabit this place." His gaze swept the crowd that milled about, and he drew his collar up higher as he nodded to the left. "We're headed there to Café du Blood." An alley separated the small shop from the club, a small sliver of darkness between the two buildings.

He paused, about to cross the street, when a whisper of something strange drifted over him. Azaiel glanced back toward Club Doom. A young woman stared at him with wild, beseeching eyes. Long, tangled, blond hair fell to her waist, the dress she wore, something out of Victorian England, was in tatters, and the demon who held her by the shoulders looked like a mean son of a bitch.

She appeared too frail. Too weak. *Too human.*

For one second their gazes met and held, and Azaiel felt defeated because he knew he couldn't do anything for her. There was too much at stake. He turned his back, heart heavy, and wished her well.

They'd almost reached the café when a mountain of a beast stepped directly into their path. He was demon though of a higher class than a bottom feeder blood born. A lot of the creatures felt the need to hide their true selves behind a human facade. Not this one.

His true form glittered in the darkness, the faint oil lamps from above reflecting off the shine of green, blue, and silver. His skin was like pieces of hard reptilian glass sewn together—his head sported not two but four horns, each with deadly, poisonous ends. He was well over eight feet in height, with mini tree trunks for thighs, a neck nearly as thick, and shoulders impressively wide.

His eyes glowed red, and he huffed large clouds of dark smoke from nostrils flared wide open. "The café is closed." Sharp, razorlike teeth glistened overly white as the creature bared them.

Azaiel glanced toward the dimly lit café, watched as a hunched-looking dwarf of a man poured a steaming cup of red liquid for an elegantly dressed humanoid creature.

He arched a brow and gazed up at the demon. "Looks open to me."

The demon's smile widened. "Not for the likes of you. The café only hosts those invited inside."

Azaiel glared at the beast, aware that they were attracting attention from the crowd outside Doom. It was not the time to start something. He needed to keep a cool head.

"I've business with Seth, so unless you'd like the heat of his wrath on your impressive ass, move the fuck out of my way."

The demon's eyes narrowed, his nostrils flared even more, and Azaiel kept his right hand loose, near the hidden weapons that filled his pants and his jacket. He was weak in this new skin he'd been given, and he needed all the help he could get.

If it came to a fight, Azaiel was certain he could slay the beast, but he was also certain his ass would get kicked all over the square and back before the job was done. He thought of Rowan and clenched his teeth together. He would do this for her. He would get it done.

"What business do you have with the golden?"

Azaiel was fast losing impatience. "You will move or—it pained him to play the weakling, but at the moment it was necessary—I will call forth Seth, and you can ask him yourself."

Azaiel glared at the demon, hating the impotency he felt. He would persevere, and one day his powers would be fully restored. Sometimes it was the only thing that kept him putting one foot in front of the other.

The demon glanced around, and Azaiel knew he had him when he took a step back. "I'll be watching you . . ." Its gaze swung to Kellen, "both."

Azaiel ignored the taunt, pushed past the creature, and he and Kellen entered the café. The dwarf glanced up in surprise, his distorted features wrinkling as he studied them for several long moments. The patron that sat was a vampire, an ancient from the looks of it, but the vampire ignored them all as he drank deeply of the dark red liquid. Its fangs were gone—punishment no doubt—and the only way it could feed and survive was to frequent the café.

The small dwarf set his large server on the table and shuffled over to them, limping badly with his right foot. His skin was dried and aged so that his cheeks hung like sacks of withered gray tissue paper and his dull, watery blue eyes had no pupils.

The dwarf rubbed his chin, eyes narrowed, and grunted. "Are you here for food?"

"No," Azaiel answered quietly. "We're passing through."

The dwarf glanced at the vampire, but the ancient was still engrossed in his cup. "You cannot pass unless you know the words."

Azaiel nodded, his gut clenching. Now was crunch time. If things had changed . . . if words uttered before meant nothing now, he was fucked.

He spoke in Egyptian. "Backward is forward."

The dwarf stared up at him, and the moments that passed were some of the longest Azaiel had ever spent. He didn't breathe, didn't blink . . . didn't do anything but watch the little man, hands loose at his side and ready to rock and roll if need be.

The dwarf turned to Kellen, then swung his gaze back to Azaiel. "As you wish, sir." The little man moved aside, and Azaiel moved past, signaling for Kellen to follow. The two men headed toward the back of the café and walked through a small storage room that held nothing but large glass vials of blood.

A door on the far wall opened as they neared it, and they headed down the stairs, two at a time, the same dank smell Azaiel remembered thick in the air. Water trickled down the stone walls as if they bled perpetually, and the steady drip that echoed below got louder as they made their way into the basement.

There amongst the many boxes of supplies and whatnot stood a massive oven. It was made of precious metals, the kind found only in District One, and Azaiel knew that Seth had had it forged by a powerful mage.

This was the portal Azaiel remembered. His relief that it was in the same spot was huge, as was the need to keep moving forward. To not stop. Legs without motion were legs that could be cut off. They needed to hurry.

"This is it," he said curtly. "The oven."

"Seriously." Kellen glanced around, his face dark, eyes unreadable. "This is fucking unbelievable. You know this."

Azaiel nodded and moved forward until he was inches from the large oven. "Down here nothing is impossible. In fact, most things that can be thought of . . . are." Azaiel reached out and yanked on the large handle, which stuck out two feet along the right of the round oven. The door swung open, and blue flames sizzled and sparked, sending hot flashes of ash onto the floor, where they burned to nothing within seconds.

"Seth's mind is more than a little twisted, but the son of a bitch has one hell of a sense of humor."

Kellen shook his head. "There is no way I'm getting in there. Are you crazy?"

Azaiel remained silent and watched as the door liquefied and yawned, opening as wide and as tall as it needed to. Sulfur, thick and strong, drifted toward him, and he felt the heat against his skin. The pull began in earnest, and he stepped forward, though he spared a glance backward just before the portal pulled him in.

"Stay or come. The choice is yours."

Azaiel had one moment of intense heat, then he was free-falling with the sound of wind and screaming in his head. He let go of all conscious thought, and the darkness swallowed him whole.

When next he opened his eyes he lay beneath a large fountain, one that spewed liquid gold. The tinkling sound it made as the golden showers hit the marble tub was musical, like notes falling from an angel's lips. Azaiel had listened to it many, many nights as he sat in the darkness and dreamed of a world as rich as the sound the water made.

Azaiel jumped to his feet and spied Kellen a few feet away. Rowan's brother was just coming to, and Azaiel held his index finger to his mouth as Kellen opened his eyes.

They were in the main courtyard, just outside the palatial residence belonging to Seth the golden. There would be guards, several at the very least and more than a few hellhounds, to pass in silence, or possibly ones they'd have to *kill* to silence. This meant nothing. As was the way of it here nothing stayed dead for long. No matter how badly one prayed for death once sentenced to Hell, death was an eternal state of mind there was no escaping from.

Seth's home was a vast oasis plopped in the middle of

the dunes—one of the most unforgiving places in any level of Hell. Azaiel would hazard a guess that it was akin to the Lilith's own corner of darkness, hidden deep within District Three.

He withdrew the charmed dagger hidden within the folds of his pants, and Kellen did the same. They moved forward, two intruders who didn't belong, past the ornate fountain, along the perfectly groomed grass and trees that bordered a golden path that led around the side of the main entrance.

Azaiel spied two hellhounds sniffing around the doorway, and he scooped up a handful of golden and jeweled stones that littered the walk and tossed it back behind the fountain. The pebbles echoed into the quiet as they hit the marble, and the hellhounds took off, nasty snarls rumbling from their chests.

The two men ran, silent shadows sifting through the gloom, and Azaiel did not hesitate once they were upon the door. The knob turned easily in his hands, and he and Kellen slid inside, leaving the hellhounds yapping crazily behind them. They were in a dimly lit corridor, and Azaiel kept his weapons at the ready as he strode forward with purpose. He knew exactly where he was going.

They encountered several guards along the way, and Azaiel was impressed with the way Kellen handled himself—the young man had skills, that's for sure. It made him wonder . . . what exactly Kellen James had been up to all the years he'd been estranged from his sister. Once back in the human realm, he was going to make it a point to find out.

They left behind a trail of corpses, hidden of course, but ones that would rise within twenty-four hours. Time was running out, and there was still so much to do.

He led the way down a long hall, with windows that overlooked a sea of blue. It was an illusion—this Azaiel knew firsthand—but a thing of beauty regardless. Seth the golden had an eye for it. You had to give the demon that.

When he reached the end of the corridor they turned left and came upon yet another that looked nearly identical to the one they'd just traversed.

"Are you sure you know where you're going?" Kellen sounded a little worried, and Azaiel nodded as his hand reached for the first door on his right. He clenched his teeth together tightly, felt his heart speed up, and when the surge of adrenaline shot through him he turned the handle.

The room was in darkness save for a candle burning beside the massive bed that was several feet in the air, high upon a pedestal. Pale sheets of peach-and-white gauze fell from the ceiling and caressed the edge of the bed. Several floor-to-ceiling windows brought the blue sea inside, and the breeze that tugged at the light green wisps of fabric on either side of them was sweet and warm.

A voice stirred the silence—a drowsy, feminine one.

"Is that you? Come this late to my bed? I don't know if I should be angry or insulted."

He and Kellen glanced up as a spill of long golden hair twisted in the wind, snaking outward like Medusa's pets. Azaiel felt . . . nothing. Absolutely nothing.

"Sorry to be late, but I'm here to collect a debt owed." Azaiel watched as the blond hair gave way to golden skin and eyes the color of the brightest sky, beneath the brightest sun imaginable.

"Who is she?" Kellen asked in wonder. Azaiel knew he was entranced by her beauty. By the flawless features, perfect skin, and voice full of sex and promise. He needed to nip that in the bud right away.

"She's Toniella the betrayer." He glanced at his companion. "Trust me when I say guard yourself with this one.

She'll eat you up and spit you out like yesterday's garbage and come back for seconds."

Azaiel glanced back up at the woman who'd ruined his life. He smiled and beckoned her down, his fingers motioning quickly.

Kellen's eyes narrowed. "And you trust her?"

"Hell no." Azaiel stepped back, his face grim. "But she's the only shot we have."

CHAPTER 24

Toniella stood in front of Azaiel in silence, silken hair falling to her waist, eyes wide in surprise. She wore night-clothes—if you could call the flimsy gown such. Gossamer soft, it was nothing more than a whisper of silk against her golden flesh. It did nothing to hide the perfect high breasts with their hardened pink nipples, nor the juncture between her legs, which he noted was free of hair. How could you not? Her legs were spread, just so, an open invitation by a woman accustomed to using sex for whatever it was she wanted. He knew that all to well.

She'd wanted him at one time . . . and he . . . Azaiel shook such thoughts from his mind, his eyes narrowed with scorn.

"You," she whispered, licking her lips nervously as she gazed up at him. Toniella was barefoot, her small, delicate feet, with crimson toes expertly painted, peeked from beneath the folds of her gown.

Azaiel gazed down at the woman. Her eyes were as luminous as he remembered and her scent just as sweet. Generous, ruby red lips were wet from a nervous tongue, and they were parted . . . just so. As always.

But there was uncertainty in the depths of her eyes, fear and . . . something else.

"Azaiel." His name was a whisper on her lips. "I never thought to see you again." She smiled, though the frost that she emitted was as cold as the arctic. "At least not like this. I assumed the next time I saw your pretty face it would be mounted upon the gates. Something for the guards to use as target practice . . . for the next thousand years or so."

He shrugged. "Sorry to disappoint."

"I'm not disappointed." She took a step forward. "I'm impressed."

Azaiel watched her carefully. "That would be a first."

She moistened her lips once more—when there was no need—and took one more step until he could reach out and touch her.

"Azaiel, I was always impressed by you. Don't you remember?" She stood on her tiptoes and reached for him. He let her slide her body alongside his, press her breasts to his chest, and wrap her arms around his neck. Azaiel watched through hooded eyes as she reached for him, as her mouth opened, and she pressed her lips onto his.

And still he felt nothing for her. This woman who'd tempted him from the very heights of the upper realm, who'd used her body, her voice, and her mind to lure him from his brothers. This blond viper who carried the sun in her eyes, heaven between her legs, and darkness in her heart.

He'd been damned the moment his gaze had rested upon her. There beneath the sun in the jungles of Belize and Mexico. He should feel anger. Hatred. Pain and vengeance.

And yet he felt nothing but the need to get this done. To get the grimoire back and see Rowan James again.

His hands slid along her shoulders, and the distaste he felt as she trembled against him wasn't hidden. He gripped her tightly, his fingers digging deep, until she hissed in pain.

"What's this? You like it rough these days? Has the heart of the warrior I fell in love with returned to me?"

"I need you to do me a favor," he said as he peeled Toni-ella from his body and took a step back. Time was running out, and they needed to get to the treasury. She gazed up at him, and something shifted there in the depths of her eyes. No longer were they the clear blue of a Caribbean sea. They had grown dark, fully black, and the expression on her face was one of confusion.

"What game are you playing Azaiel?" She glanced at Kellen, her face shifting once more as the sex kitten came out to play. "And you've brought me a present?" She licked her lips and ran her hands across puckered nipples that strained against the silken material of her robes.

Kellen made a sound of irritation. "Seriously?" He turned to Azaiel. "This is all we have?"

"I don't care for your tone," Toniella muttered, a petulant tone creeping into her voice.

"Listen carefully, betrayer."

"And I will not tolerate that name, Azaiel." Her tone was harder, her eyes a glint of obsidian in the flickering candle-light.

"Is *whore* a better choice for you?"

The golden glow fled as her cheeks burned red. She glanced at Kellen, but his gaze was as unrelenting as Azaiel's.

"What do you want?" she asked finally, hands clenched into small fists at her sides.

"As I said earlier. I've come to collect a debt owed."

"A debt? Since when do I owe you anything?"

"Since I shall reconsider killing you if you give me what I want."

Toniella snorted, a perfect, dark blond eyebrow raised as she glared at him. "Nothing can die down here. You know that."

Azaiel watched her closely, the charmed dagger in one

hand, the modified Glock in his other. "I've not forgotten. But I've got it on pretty good authority that it still hurts like hell and"—he pointed the gun at her—"if maimed, that pretty head of yours might not heal the way you want it. Then where would you be? Still a whore, yes but an ugly, deformed whore, and who exactly down here is going to want to fuck that?"

Her golden skin paled even more until it was as fragile as rice paper. She stared up at him and opened her mouth but had no chance to speak.

"The bottom feeders, that's who'll be waiting in line. The blood demons, the soul suckers . . . they'd all pay Seth whatever he wants for the chance to sink their cocks inside the betrayer. The bitch eagle shifter who brought the mighty Azaiel to his knees."

He was in her face now, the gun pointed directly between her eyes. "I will do this, Toniella. Do not sound the alarm, or I will rip your head off. I've been waiting millennium to destroy you, so don't give me the excuse I've been looking for."

Gone was the blank, empty void. He was filled with hatred. This woman had damned him as much as he'd damned himself.

"What do you want?" she asked carefully, her wide eyes never leaving the gun that was inches from her face.

"We need to get into the treasury."

"The treasury? But how . . . I can't get you inside. Are you crazy?" Anger underlined her words, and she pushed away from him. "Don't toy with me, Azaiel."

"I'm assuming that Lintos the keeper is still one of your weekly fucks." She flinched, and for a second, he thought he caught a glimpse of pain. It was gone just as fast, and Azaiel ignored it. What did he care? "Go to him and get the key."

"It doesn't work like that."

His expression was fierce as he returned her stare. "Make it work."

Toniella turned to Kellen. "Who are you?"

Kellen saluted her with his own modified Glock. "I'm the backup in case he misses."

Her eyes narrowed. "I see." She glared at him for several seconds. "You're not human, but I don't sense otherworld in your skin either." Her brow furled. "What are you?"

"What I am is none of your business." Kellen pointed toward the door. "I suggest you listen to Azaiel. Time's a-wasting, and we've got a party topside to get back to."

Toniella swore, a savage blending of Aztec and ancient speak, but turned and padded across the cool, marble tiles, with the two men following close behind.

They moved down the silent corridors—corridors that were much too silent—and Azaiel paused, his hand stopping Toniella from progressing.

"Why is it so quiet? If you've thoughts of leading us into a trap, know that I will follow through on my promise."

She cocked her head to the side though she was careful to keep her voice lowered. "It's your luck that Seth isn't in residence at the moment. I'm sure if he were, he'd have sniffed you out long before you reached my rooms." She shrugged and yanked her arm from his. "Several days ago, someone escaped District Three with Lilith's new pets in tow, human children from what I heard. Seth was called to Lucifer's for questioning. Everyone knows how much Seth despises Lilith, and most suspect he had something to do with it."

Azaiel smiled at that. Declan O'Hara and Ana DeLacrux had done the deed, and though he wasn't privy to the details, Azaiel wouldn't put it past Seth to help the sorcerer achieve that goal. Being called to Lucifer's court was a small price to pay. He and the dark prince shared a history not many understood, and it was rare that Seth the golden felt Lucifer's wrath.

Still, it was no reason to treat this situation lightly—

Seth's security was always top-notch, with the only fault being sheer arrogance. And this was something shared by most of the upper-echelon demons. They ruled with an iron fist and were not challenged by the bottom scum of the underworld.

The last to take from Seth had been Lilith, and that had been centuries earlier.

Azaiel was aware that because they'd arrived at eventide, it was quieter than usual, but as they trekked farther into the compound, the band of tension inside his chest tightened, so that he found it hard to breathe.

They reached Lintos's quarters, and Azaiel nailed Toniella with a glacial stare. His fingers dug into her forearm as he glared into her eyes. "You will do this for me and not raise the alarm. Understand? If things go badly, do not doubt I will hunt you down and hurt you like you've never been hurt before. I will poison and destroy the beauty you worship, and the pain will linger inside and ruin you." He saw fear in her eyes, but it gave him no pleasure. He wanted to be away from the darkness. From the sulfur and heat. "Do what you must for the key."

She swallowed and exhaled. "Take your hand off me."

Azaiel stepped back, and Toniella disappeared inside the rooms while he and Kellen melted into the shadows that swept along the corridor. Two guards passed, and they made quick work of them, a knife across the throat, a dagger through the heart. They dragged the bodies behind a set of tall planters that were home to palm trees. They'd rise soon enough; Azaiel just hoped he'd be long gone by the time that happened.

They waited in silence though somewhere in the distance a harp played, accompanied by a voice filled with melancholy. "So." Kellen cleared his throat some. "What did you do to get your ass tossed down here?"

He was wondering when the man would ask. He shrugged and peered through the shadows. "I gave in to weakness. In to pleasure. And I sacrificed all that I believe in for an illusion. For the betrayer."

Kellen frowned. "What are you? Shakespeare? Say what you mean."

Azaiel looked away, unsettled with his frankness. "I created something powerful for her. Something that could have ripped the realms apart and bled them into one. I broke every vow that I knew as Seraphim."

"Sounds to me like you used her as much as she used you."

The cold fist turned hard inside his chest once more and left Azaiel empty. He ignored Kellen and returned his gaze to the door that Toniella had walked through twenty minutes earlier. It hit him then. The thoughts he'd avoided. The whispers of regret.

He *was* no different than the eagle shifter, and yet he'd managed a second chance while she toiled below, here in the Hell realm. Was there justice in that?

No. Azaiel cleared his mind and concentrated on the task at hand. He couldn't afford to linger in the past, so much of the future depended on what happened right now.

Time ticked by, and just when he was about to knock down the door and take the key himself, Toniella appeared. Her gown was ripped, her breasts and arms marred by mottled blue-gray bruises, as were her thighs. Blood trickled from the corner of her mouth, and her left cheek was swollen below her eyes. Were those tears that stained her face?

Toniella tossed him the key. "You owe me now, Seraphim. Lintos was entertaining some friends. I had to fuck half his garrison in order to get this for you."

She looked away, shoulders hunched forward and for a second, something inside Azaiel cracked—just a little bit—

but then she tossed her golden hair behind her, the bruises already fast fading, and smiled. "No matter. At least the exercise will aid my rest."

Azaiel pointed back to where they'd come from. "You'll sleep when we get inside the treasury."

Her eyes narrowed at that. "If I get caught helping you . . ."

Azaiel was already moving forward. "Then don't get caught."

Kellen followed after him, falling in line as Toniella hastened to keep up. The three of them slid through the shadows with ease, and it didn't take long to retrace their steps though this time they turned left at Toniella's room instead of right. After a few moments they exited the main building through a nondescript doorway hidden behind a waterfall.

Once outside not more than a few steps away stood a large golden dome that looked to be the size of several football fields.

"This is not something you see every day." Kellen's eyes widened as he took in the sheer magnificence of the building. Overhead a perfect moon shone, its beams falling upon the dome in an embrace of mist that reflected back like a dazzling blanket of jewels.

It was quiet and still. Much too still. The eerie silence made Azaiel nervous.

Kellen whistled softly. "Man, I think this Seth guy is overcompensating for something." He grinned at Azaiel. "One guess as to what that is?"

He ignored Rowan's brother and crept forward, stopping abruptly. He motioned to Kellen, indicated that there were two guards straight ahead, and shot one more look of warning toward Toniella. He didn't trust the woman. At all.

Kellen went to the right and he to the left. The guards were demons, hellhound shifters—not the regular hellhounds found prowling the dunes. These were upper-echelon and from the looks of them, heavily trained in combat.

Azaiel held his dagger loosely in one hand and cocked the gun in his other. He decided that a direct approach might be the best and ran forward, firing point-blank between the demon's eyes and swinging hard with his knife hand. The shifter spun forward and took Azaiel down with him, but the knife was true, and with a mighty heave, Azaiel cut the bastard's neck clear through to his spinal cord.

He rolled to the side and strode to the door after making sure that Kellen was fine. Time was of the essence and something that moved differently down here. What seemed to Azaiel to only be a few hours could be days or even weeks topside. What if they were too late? What if Mallick . . .

He couldn't finish the thought.

The key wasn't really a key in the normal sense but more like a medium-sized trinket that fit inside a device next to the entrance. Azaiel inserted it, and his heart beat in anticipation as the doors slid back in silence. He and Kellen dragged the bodies in with them while Toniella followed on their heels.

"Holy Mother of God," Kellen said quietly, as Azaiel straightened, and Rowan's brother took in what was undoubtedly one of the most spectacular scenes he'd ever had the pleasure to witness.

The interior was a lot larger than it looked to be from the outside. Overhead lighting was muted, but it was enough to illuminate the vast, seemingly infinite number of items Seth had on display.

Kellen walked toward a massive ship and shook his head. "You've got to be kidding me."

Azaiel stood next to him and gazed up at the large craft. USS *Cylops*. "It's a boat."

Kellen snorted and shook his head. "This isn't just a boat.

It's a famous boat from World War One, though it sure as hell isn't famous for combat." Kellen walked forward and reached for the hull.

"Don't touch anything," Toniella whispered. "Are you stupid?" She glared at the two of them, but Kellen ignored her.

"This boat disappeared with a crew of over three hundred and was never found. There were crazy stories about its disappearing in the Bermuda Triangle, but . . ." He fell silent as he gazed to his left and saw five small planes parked in formation. "Son of a bitch," he whispered. "Flight 19. This is the Bermuda triangle. Unbelievable."

Azaiel was irritated. "Grimoire?"

"Grimoire? That's what you've come for?" Toniella looked confused. "Whose grimoire and why?"

"None of your business." Azaiel thought for a second. "Where would Seth keep such a thing?" There were hundreds of thousands of items to sift through, and they didn't have the time.

Toniella shrugged and remained silent, but he knew by the tilt of her chin and the slant of her lips that she knew.

He flipped the dagger into the air, caught it, and pointed it at the woman. "I warned you earlier."

Her eyes narrowed, and the stubborn set of her mouth didn't change. She wasn't going to make this easy. "I'll ask again. Whose grimoire, and why do you need it?"

"It's my grimoire," Kellen said.

"Yours?" Her brows knit together. "I don't sense magick in you."

"No," he agreed. "I don't suppose you do, but that doesn't change the fact that it belongs to my family, and we need it."

"Why?"

Azaiel strode toward her. "No more questions. Where would it be?" The anger inside bled out in his words, and she flinched as he glared at her. "Toniella, I swear on the soul of your father—"

"Enough." She nodded to a location behind him. "There's the room where Seth keeps parchment."

It was of course not just a room, but at least there was order here, with parchment, codicils, ancient scriptures, and bound books all grouped together. They found the grimoire, a leather-bound large volume, on display on a gold pedestal. An ornate lock of burnished copper held it closed, while the worn-leather binding was varying shades of amber, orange, and brown. The name JAMES was etched across the top.

"I've never seen it up close," Kellen said quietly, as they stared down at the large tome. He reached for it and paused. "Shall I?"

Azaiel nodded, suddenly wary as the silence once more weighed on him. His skin was hot, and the danger meter that he'd learned long ago was never wrong, suddenly erupted, making the hair on the back of his neck stand on end.

"Let's go," he barked. He turned, took a step forward, and froze.

A half second later an alarm erupted and filled the room with a heavy reverberating song of vengeance.

CHAPTER 25

"We're here, Rowan."

Rowan woke suddenly and glanced at the clock on the dashboard of the Suburban. It glowed an eerie green—5:15. They were home.

She took a minute, rubbed sleep from her eyes, and slipped from the SUV. They'd been out all night patrolling, killing and cleaning up one demon mess after another. Abigail nodded from across the yard. She'd pitched a tent and was about to turn in. The Black Cauldron was officially filled to the brim with both human and otherworld, all of them there to help. There was some comfort in that.

"Everyone's back, Ro. We're all good." She glanced at Priest and nodded.

Everyone was accounted for. No injuries other than a few nasty cuts and bruises. It was something to be grateful for.

Rowan said her good-nights—which was odd since it was going to be daylight soon. But the threat of Mallick's legions had turned all of them into creatures of the night.

She trudged toward the house, each step more heavy than the last, and paused at the bottom of the steps. She glanced back toward Hannah and Nico. They were beneath the oak tree out front, their bodies mere shadows among the wakening dawn. Their voices were low, but they carried, and it was obvious they were deep in what seemed to be a very intense conversation. Hannah stepped closer to the shifter, and he didn't move when her hand reached for his cheek. In fact it seemed as if he leaned into her touch.

Her cousin moved closer, and Rowan's breath caught at the intimacy of the act. She tore her gaze away and stomped up the stairs. Her chest was tight, and she felt the unexplainable urge to punch something. Anything.

With a sigh, she pushed open the front door and tossed her ruined jacket onto the coatrack tucked into the corner. A tired smile claimed her lips as she spied the large crystal vase on the Queen Anne's table. It was filled with fresh sunflowers, and the guest book was back in place. Cedric no doubt.

She glanced down at the open book, a lump forming in the back of her throat as she saw the new signatures. Priest. Vicki. Terre. Even Nico had signed the damn thing.

Her fingers traced the names, and she closed her eyes. God, she was so tired. Voices drifted from the kitchen out back, but she wasn't in the mood to talk to anyone, and though she knew she should eat, all she wanted was her bed.

And Azaiel.

The unfamiliar ache was back, inside her heart . . . across her chest. She cleared her throat and turned. What was up with that? Only then did she know she wasn't alone.

"You look like shit, James."

Her heart leapt, and for a moment she was dizzy. The dead feeling inside her chest fizzled and broke as a smile crept over tired features. "I could say the same for you."

Azaiel stood before her, shirtless, with those damn jeans that had a habit of lying so low on his hips you couldn't help but look *down*. He sported his own assortment of cuts and bruises, and someone had stitched up his left bicep. A bandage above his right eyebrow gave him a rakish, sexy air—which he so didn't need. She swallowed and nearly choked because her mouth was suddenly bone dry. Like middle-of-the-Sahara kind of dry.

His eyes glittered, their freaky otherworld coloring amplified by something other than the muted lighting in the foyer. It came from within.

She attempted to clear her throat. "What happened to you?" Damn, when had she started sounding like Marilyn Monroe? Her cheeks burned in embarrassment, but she refused to look away. Rather, she *couldn't* look away.

"We." He paused and rubbed the back of his head—which only emphasized his exquisite abs and muscular shoulders. If it were anyone else—Priest maybe—she'd think he'd done it on purpose. But it was Azaiel, and he seemed pretty damn oblivious to how incredibly attractive he was.

"Had a few issues getting out of District One."

"Oh, right." She didn't know what else to say, mostly because her eyes were still stuck on the abs. Christ, they looked like they'd been spray painted on. And then there was his stomach. And the freaking low-riding jeans.

"Kellen's fine by the way."

Her eyes flew back to his, and she bit her lip in irritation. At herself. "Good. Um . . ." She couldn't think. He was literally sucking the thinking machine that used to be her brain right the hell out of her head.

"The, ah . . ." Oh God, she even sounded like an airhead.

"Grimoire?" His voice was soft, and she detected a hint of weariness.

"Yes." The strange notion of exhilaration persisted, but suddenly the clouds parted, and her faculties returned. "Yes, the grimoire. Did you get it?"

"Piece of cake." He nodded. "Kellen has it." Azaiel took

a step forward. "Look, I'm exhausted and could sure use a bed. I just don't know where . . ."

"Oh, sure." Rowan took a step back and swore as her hip grazed the corner of the Queen Anne's table. She glanced toward the stairs.

"I don't know where there's an empty bed. I grabbed the sofa in your living room the other night, but it's occupied."

"You can sleep with me."

Holy Mother of God, did I just say that?

"I mean, not with me like sexually or anything. I just um, you know, I have a big bed, and . . ." He was staring at her as if she had two heads. *Stop talking.* "Because we can't go *there*"—she laughed nervously—"like what happened the other night kind of there . . . not here." *Oh God, stop talking.*

He was quiet for a moment though a hint of a smile played with the corner of his mouth. "That would be great." He nodded toward the stairs. "After you."

Rowan swept past him and practically ran up the stairs. Her room was the last one on the left, and she flipped the light switch as she entered, grabbing her dirty clothes from the day before off the floor and tossing them into the basket beside her dresser.

Her room was ridiculously feminine and juvenile, but she ignored the pink and white and bent over the bed. Aware that he was behind her. Aware that his silent gaze was unnerving at best. Aware that every cell in her body was on fire with the need to do something other than what she was going to do.

Which was sleep. Catch zzzz's. There would be no hanky-panky.

She pulled down the cover. And no touching.

Heavy petting leads to sinning. Christ, why was Reverend Beamish's voice in her head? She shivered and mentally quieted the voices. It wasn't that hard to do since Azaiel had managed to replace her brain cells with new and improved dumb-ass airhead ones.

She moved to the side, careful to avoid Azaiel, and nodded toward the bed.

"Take whichever side you like. I'm going to go and clean up." She took another step toward her bathroom. "I don't snore, so . . ."

Oh my God. Shut the fuck up.

His hooded eyes watched her in silence, and he didn't say anything. She swallowed thickly and closeted herself inside the bathroom, resting her head against the door until her heart slowed. Her hands trembled, but that was more from fatigue rather than nerves.

You keep telling yourself that, sweetheart.

"God, stop thinking," she rasped as she locked the door and whirled around. She grabbed a fresh towel from the shelf, turned the water on, and seconds later slipped beneath the hot spray. It felt like heaven, and for twenty minutes she was able to forget about pretty much everything, though as she cleaned herself, she was careful not to linger at her breasts or down south. No sense in getting worked up and yet . . .

Why not? Why couldn't she give in to the fantasy that Azaiel represented? She knew he wanted her. She wanted him. What had happened in the Witches Brew was only an amplification of their real emotions. It wasn't synthetic. It was organic. Real.

And damn, but it could be so, so good.

But you hardly know him.

There was that pesky voice again. She knew enough. She didn't need to know his secrets to have sex with him. In fact it would probably be best if she didn't know anything beyond the fact that he was totally, one hundred percent lick-able, and she was pretty damn sure she'd never again meet another man like him.

Besides, when all was said and done, she'd either be Mallick's whore, or if she managed to win this war, she was pretty sure Azaiel would be gone before the dust settled. Men like him didn't stay in small towns like this. Hell, she was pretty sure they didn't stay anywhere for long.

Rowan stared at herself in the mirror as she towel dried her hair. Mason had called every day, and she'd finally answered him the day before. He'd wanted to know when she was coming back and as she'd held the phone to her ear, and looked out the window at the odd assortment of otherworld—at her family . . . Frank. At the damn cat. As she listened to her mother moving about in Nana's rooms. As Cedric gathered the vegetables from the garden out back, she knew . . .

She was never going back. She suddenly realized she'd been running for years only to find out that the end of her journey was here. Right where she had started.

She'd politely told Mason as much and while he'd protested loudly . . . he'd not protested loudly enough. In the end, he'd agreed to keep her gerbil, and she promised to stop by for a coffee when she made it back to clean out her apartment.

Her large blue eyes stared back at her as she wiped the steam off the mirror. If she survived Samhain.

All the fight seemed to go out of Rowan at once. She dropped the towel and bit her lip as she stared at the bathroom door. Her feet propelled her forward, and before she could stop herself she unlocked it. Blood rushed through her veins, exhilarating tired cells and filling her brain with all sorts of erotic images.

Her fingers grazed her nipples. They were hard, her breasts full and sensitive. An ache erupted between her legs, the throb relentless as she visualized Azaiel in front of her. As she remembered what he felt like. What he smelled like.

What he sounded like as she'd taken him into her hands and mouth.

She'd been aching for days. It had been more subtle, riding beneath the surface but there nonetheless. She bit her lip, hand hovering over the door handle.

Screw it. She wanted him. The whole world was going to shit, and her future wasn't written in the stars. She had no way of knowing if she was going to survive Mallick's coming assault. This might be the only time she'd have to take something for herself. To be selfish and not worry about the consequence.

Was it a smart thing to do? Probably not, but at the moment the airhead brain cells were talking, and she didn't give a rat's ass about consequence. She turned off the bathroom light and pushed open the door to her bedroom.

Goose bumps erupted across her flesh, and she shivered—her skin was still damp, and water dripped from the ends of her hair. Her chest constricted, the muscles tight and nervous, and the ache between her legs intensified at the thought of Azaiel—of his hands and mouth.

Her heart beat hard and fast, the sound echoing in the rush of white noise that filled her ears. She took a step forward and blinked as her eyes adjusted to the muted lighting. Azaiel had flipped the switch, and it was only the gray dawn that broke through the window to touch him.

He was facedown on the bed, arms pillowed for his head, long legs hanging off the edge. His feet were bare, and for a moment she stared at them. They were big and, like everything else about him, rough and male.

She took a moment to study him, and a smile touched her mouth as she realized how ridiculous he looked. He was a warrior, made of hard lines, raw masculinity, and strength. To see him floating amongst pink and white was wrong, and yet, somehow so right.

If anything, it made him all the more dangerous. And sexy.

Rowan crept toward the bed, her tongue peeking out from between wet, trembling lips. He didn't move as she approached, and it wasn't until she was inches from him that she realized he was sound asleep. His long, even breaths indicated he was well under the spell of Sandman.

A small "meow" sounded, and she saw the orange tabby curled into a ball on the other side of Azaiel's head. The cat blinked slowly, its amber eyes wide and clear. It meowed again, stretched, and settled back into a purring ball of fur.

"Traitor cat," Rowan whispered. "How did you get in here?"

The tabby didn't answer of course, and long moments passed as Rowan stood there, naked as the day she was born, staring at a man who wasn't really a man. Not on this planet anyway. However, he was more perfect in form and in spirit than anyone she'd ever met before.

And she knew nothing about him.

Rowan bent over him and studied the wings that had been etched into his flesh. They were hauntingly beautiful and painful to look at. Who had done that to him? And why?

He murmured something under his breath and turned— Rowan's heart nearly beat right out of her chest, and she covered her breasts, a reflex action of course, but it didn't matter. Azaiel was still out cold.

His face was younger in repose, and she saw the young, adorable boy he must have been . . . however many thousands of years ago. Or longer. It was in that moment that Rowan knew she was going to learn everything she could about Azaiel. Priest hadn't given anything up—he'd said it was the Seraphim's story to tell, and maybe it was time for her to ask.

She brushed back a lock of hair from his forehead and

pulled the coverlet from the bottom of her bed over his still form. The urge to kiss him, to touch his mouth was so strong that she actually bent forward. She was inches away when reality hit, and she stepped back suddenly.

A shudder wracked her body, and she hugged herself, not liking the loss of control or the wild notions filling her head. She was in the middle of a freaking war, for God's sake. Her ass was on the line, and here she was mooning over Azaiel as if he mattered or something.

Nothing should matter except Mallick. She needed to live and breathe the bastard because if she wasn't careful, her future would never happen.

With one final glance at the hard candy in her bed, Rowan turned away. It was probably a good thing that the Seraphim was asleep.

She'd have to find another way to assuage the ache because she sure as hell knew it wasn't going anywhere.

Outside it was lighter, and most everyone at Chez Cauldron was getting some shut-eye. Rowan moved the curtains to the side and gazed down into the yard. A light was on in Terre's RV, but Vicki's was in darkness. She saw Leroy walking a path he'd beaten into the grass and held her breath as the animal glanced her way. Eventually the donkey returned to his endless pacing, and she exhaled slowly.

She'd organized several teams of human soldiers to patrol Salem during the day, and they'd be heading out soon. Most of these were from families—generations of demon hunters. She saw a few of them gathered in groups near the mess of tents that were set up near the Cauldron's gift shop. The McDaniels. The Blackstones. The Lawrences.

Lord knows what anyone from town thought if they drove by, though she supposed the protective spells they'd cast around the property went a long way to keeping most folk from coming anywhere near the bed-and-breakfast.

Rowan let the curtain fall back into place. Fatigue still haunted her bones, but she was restless as well and knew that with Azaiel in her bed she'd never get to sleep. She slipped into sweatpants and a clean T-shirt. Azaiel hadn't moved, and she hoped that he'd be out until nightfall. She needed time and space to purge her mind of the sinful, distracting thoughts that starred none other than the Seraphim.

Because, undeniably, the man was a plus ten and then some.

On quiet toes, she left Azaiel in slumber, there amongst all the pink and white, and headed back down the stairs.

CHAPTER 26

Priest held the ancient tome in his hands and felt its power. It was full-bodied, like an aged wine, and heavy with the weight of it. His fingers gripped the worn-leather binding, and he closed his eyes—visualized the many threads of power that lived within the text, each an intricate blend of genetics and magick.

There was something insanely addictive about such power, and he was careful to keep it at bay. He would observe but could never touch. He knew how corrupting this kind of power was and for the first time understood the depth of the James witches' gifts. They were undeniably a cut above all others.

Hundreds of years earlier, when the first James witch had called forth Mallick . . . *that* had been a gift to the demon. He understood why Mallick didn't want to let them go. Why he fed upon their power and harnessed it for himself. It was unlike any other organic form of power out there. Each generation of these women passed on their gifts to their daughters, and each generation was more powerful than the one before.

And Rowan was different. She was stronger, more special. Priest knew it was because of the dark fae blood that ran through her veins. It's what set her apart and held her above all others.

He'd studied the pages in the grimoire, found the spell she'd need to invoke, and knew that the chances of Mallick's defeat were slim to none. And yet there was something about her spirit that gave him hope. It wasn't a tangible thing. There wasn't any reason. It just was.

Priest's fingers loosened on the binding, and he opened his eyes. There was a hard resolve in them, a slight tightening around the mouth. He'd come to respect these witches and their strange friends over the last few days. He knew of their love and devotion to Rowan—and to Cara's memory.

So he clung to hope and the thought that maybe the young witch had what it took to defeat the bastard, Mallick. Because if not . . . if given no choice, Priest *would* do whatever he had to, to make sure Mallick did not claim Rowan as his.

A throat cleared behind him, and Priest opened his eyes. He was in Cara's room with Marie-Noelle, the gargoyle, and Kellen. Judging by the shuttered expression that crept into Kellen's eyes, as well as the not-very-subtle shift in energy, he knew that Rowan had joined them.

"Is that it?"

He turned and nodded. She looked tired. Dark smudges bruised the flesh beneath her eyes, and she was much too pale. With her wet hair thrown up in a careless ponytail and her face free of makeup, she looked almost fragile. He saw why the Seraphim fancied the witch. It was a delicate balance, her beauty and strength.

Priest exhaled and held the book out to her.

Rowan took a step forward, then hesitated, her blue eyes darkening as she glanced toward her mother and the gargoyle. The two women stared at each other, and the silence in the room grew thick with words unsaid.

"I think I'll get some coffee," Marie-Noelle said haltingly.

"Mikhail?" She quickly crossed to Kellen and hugged him fiercely. "Thank you for retrieving the grimoire. I don't . . ." She stepped back and struggled to finish her sentence. "If you hadn't, I don't . . ."

"It's all good, Mom. Get some coffee and we'll talk later, all right?"

Marie-Noelle nodded, shot a glance toward her still-silent daughter, and left. Mikhail's features were fierce with heavy, furled brows, distended fangs, and flared nostrils. He paused on his way out.

"What?"

The gargoyle leaned toward Rowan, his gravelly voice low and subdued. "Forgiveness lightens the soul, little one. You make her suffer with your eyes, your silence, and yet in the end, the one who will suffer the most is you."

Rowan returned the gargoyle's gaze with a direct stare. She was silent—no sarcastic reply fell from her lips—and after a few moments Mikhail shook his head and left.

"You need to go easy on them, Ro."

She turned to Kellen and blinked, rapidly, as her focus sharpened. Her brother stood near the bed, his left arm in a sling, handsome face a mottled mess, with numerous cuts and bruises, and when he shifted his weight the grimace that stole over his features was enough to tell her he was in a lot of pain.

Grimoire forgotten, she rushed to his side, her hands reaching out for him, but he hissed, and she held still. "Everything hurts, Ro. That hug from Mom nearly did me in." A rakish grin cut across his swollen mouth. "I'm sure I look like hell." A hoarse laugh escaped. "Literally like hell, and that's not a fucking pun."

"Jesus, Kellen. What the hell happened to you down there?"

He winced and shifted again, then slid onto the edge of

the bed. "What didn't happen?" He ran his free hand through the tangled hair on top of his head and hissed as he settled onto the mattress. "That place is . . ." His eyes met Priest's.

"I know." The Knight Templar nodded.

Rowan's chest tightened, and her hand reached for him—her brother, this man she'd lost. She wanted him to hug her, to pull her close to his chest and tell her that everything was going to be all right.

"Kellen," she whispered, voice heavy with emotion.

She wanted his forgiveness.

Her brother's blue eyes—so much like her own—stared up at her, and there was an understanding in their depths she'd not seen before.

"It's okay, Rowan. I know." He held out his free hand, and she grasped it tight within her own. His pupils widened, and for the first time she was aware of an answering surge of energy. A bolt of power she'd never felt before.

Carefully he disengaged his hand and glanced toward Priest. "I've never seen anything like him before. It was incredible."

"Who?" Rowan looked from Priest to Kellen.

"The Seraphim," Priest answered.

"Azaiel?" She arched a brow at her brother.

Kellen nodded. "I'd just lifted the grimoire from its case and the walls . . ." He closed his eyes and rubbed the skin at his temple. "The walls liquefied. I can't explain it any other way. They melted into nothing but smoke or mist. And then the smoke solidified into these things . . . these massive eight-foot-tall monsters with arms like sledgehammers. Their faces were rotting with maggots and flesh that . . . I've never seen anything like them before, and the smell . . ." Kellen's eyes flew open. "I would have died down there. Several times . . . if not for Azaiel."

Rowan didn't know what to say. She knew her brother

prided himself on being strong and smart and fierce. So to admit that someone he didn't care all that much for had saved his life told her that whatever the heck had gone down in District One must have been pretty bad.

"He was relentless, and I owe him my life." Respect echoed in her brother's words, and a lump formed in the back of her throat. She had to work hard to clear it.

"How did you . . . what happened?"

Kellen exhaled. "What didn't happen. We were outnumbered and outgunned, but somehow we made it out of the treasury, and that's when the real fun started. The place was alive, crawling with spiders the size of cars and these beast things, these hellhounds." He shook his head, his eyes glazing with the memory. "I thought my ass was toast. By the time we made it back to the portal I was dizzy from blood loss, and Azaiel, he tossed my butt inside and went back into that mess."

"What?" Rowan glanced toward Priest. "Why would he do that?"

Kellen frowned. "There was a woman who helped us, Toniella."

"The betrayer," Priest murmured.

Kellen nodded. "She was in trouble, and he went back for her—which kinda surprised me because I got the impression he didn't much care for her."

"That would be an understatement," Priest acknowledged.

Rowan felt something unfamiliar clutch at her heart. Who the hell was this woman?

"I honestly thought he was done. Before the portal sucked me the hell out of there, I saw him and Toniella pinned against a wall by a pack of hellhounds and those fucking maggot shitheads. I have no idea how he made it out of there."

Rowan's chest beat hard as she stared at her brother. "What about that . . . woman?"

Kellen shrugged. "Azaiel didn't say much other than she's alive, but then he also said that nothing ever dies down there." Her brother smiled then, a tremulous smile. "The grimoire is incredible, Ro. As soon as I touched it I knew it belonged to us. To me. I heard it whisper." He shook his head and glanced toward Priest. "I don't know how else to explain it."

"What did it whisper?" Priest asked quietly.

Kellen paused, and when his eyes settled on Rowan goose bumps erupted across her flesh. "I heard it say . . . *retribution.*"

Rowan turned, but Priest was already there, the grimoire held out. His dark eyes were intent and for a second she hesitated and she wasn't even sure why. "It's yours, Rowan. Your legacy . . . your power." He glanced behind her to Kellen. "Your retribution."

She froze, eyes glued to the old, worn, tobacco-colored leather. A large seal embossed into the cover, once golden, was now tarnished to more of a copper color. It was their family symbol—the letter 'J' interwoven with an oak tree.

Priest placed it in her hands, and for a moment everything faded to black. There was nothing. No sound. No color. No Priest or Kellen.

There was only the book in her hands. Its weight and texture.

Rowan had no idea how much time passed, but eventually she realized she was curled up in the chair beside her grandmother's bed—the old, ratty, pink, red, and blue blanket from the bottom of her grandmother's bed across her lap.

And she was alone.

Outside, the early-morning sun had laid waste to the darkness, and beams of light shone in from the newly installed window. Someone had pinned up a cotton bedsheet to one side of the window—in lieu of the ruined curtains—and her eyes lingered there for a moment. It was a gingham pattern, pink, gray, and white, and looked ridiculous. She decided that at some point over the next few days she'd make an effort to get some suitable window dressings in place.

Her gaze swept the room, this cluttered yet clean and well-worn room. It spoke volumes about her Nana's character. Her love of the color red and of texture and bold patterns. The bookshelves were full of the classics, many of them well used, with a couple of first editions in the bunch.

There was the Elvis head made of concrete that stared up at her from the corner near the fireplace. Rowan smiled. She and Kellen had found it behind Pinto's Bakery in town when they were maybe ten. It was in the alley, obviously meant for the garbage, and who knows what the heck they'd been doing out back in the first place. The nose was chipped off, and one of the ears was missing, but their Nana loved Elvis almost as much as she loved Patsy Cline.

They'd given it to her for Mother's Day, and it had rested near her hearth ever since. A place of honor she'd told them. He was the king and should be on display.

Her smile widened as she stared at the head. Elvis's mouth was open as if he was belting out a song, and with his missing nose and ear, he really did look ridiculous.

She leaned back into the chair and without pause opened the grimoire.

The pages were made of leather, or some type of leather at the very least, and they were thinner than the binding. They were yellowed with age and delicate to the touch. Woven amongst the text were drawings and runes. The colors were still vibrant, which wasn't something she'd expected after all this time.

It hit her then as she gazed upon the words. They'd been

written by another James witch—one who'd lived nearly two thousand years before Rowan's birth. The grimoire had survived time and space *and* a trip to Hell. Now it was in Rowan's hands.

She blew out a long slow breath as she carefully turned the pages, not reading things so much as feeling the power that lay there. It infused her cells and had her heart beating like a jackhammer within minutes.

The pages turned and moments passed. Long moments of studying intricate runes, eloquent passages that described many herbal remedies, potions, and charms. After a while the pages blurred, but she methodically made her way through them, turning them over and over. Eventually she stopped, and when her eyes focused and she could see clearly, Rowan gasped.

It was *the* spell. The only spell she was truly interested in. She got hot and kicked her feet out so that the blanket fell to the floor as she bent over the page and started to read. There were illustrations along the side of the text. A circle. A woman. A demon—not the human facade that so many of the bastards loved but one in its true form. An animal/human-looking monster with cloven feet, a dragon head, and a deadly, spiked tail that curled up behind it like a scorpion about to attack.

She'd only seen Mallick on one occasion, and he'd looked like any other human man—an extremely handsome one at that. She wondered for the first time what his real facade looked like. Was he a creature like this one in the book? Or something else entirely?

Rowan read the words out loud, and when she was done she read them over again. And again. And when she was done for the final time she carefully closed the book and held it loose within her grasp as she rocked in the chair.

For several long moments Rowan stared into space, not

really focused on anything. She was curiously calm. Accepting of the information she'd just ingested. Was it because she was exhausted?

A soft knock sounded on the door, and Priest entered the room. He crossed to the window and drew the sheet across it, cutting out most of the light and plunging the room into muted darkness.

"You need to sleep, Rowan."

"I know."

He tugged the grimoire from her grasp and set it carefully on the side table near the bed. His fingers lingered on it—she watched him caress the cover in a gentle, sweeping motion.

"It's not often I get the chance to see something this exquisite." He smiled at her, a wistful smile of remembering. "Time moves on, and humans change and evolve, as do those who inhabit the otherworld. It's not always for the best in my opinion. Everyone moves forward, always looking ahead and no one takes the time to appreciate the past."

She watched him in silence, not knowing what to say.

"This is a work of art. A laborious rendering of your history—your family's history and knowledge." He paused. "It really is a thing of beauty."

She nodded, still silent.

"It's also a book of great power, and it found its way back to you."

But how long will I have it? How long will I be here?

Priest knelt in front of her, and for a second it felt as if he were gazing into her very soul. "Were you able to decipher the old English in the text?"

Rowan nodded and shifted uncomfortably. His dark eyes were all-seeing. All-knowing. Did he see her fear? Did he understand it?

He watched her closely, and suddenly Rowan wanted to

look away. To be alone, so that she could rage against all she'd learned. She wanted to scream and cry and yell. But she remained silent, pushing against the darkness until a state of calm settled upon her shoulders once more.

"It's a near-impossible task," he said simply.

"I know." Rowan glanced away and focused on Elvis. Damn, what she wouldn't give for a shot of "Heartbreak Hotel" at the moment. She needed a distraction. "I'm not sure where I can find this weapon . . . this sword of Gideon." She swallowed thickly. "I've never even heard of it, and I doubt any of the others will know what the hell it is or where to find it."

"I might be able to help with that," Priest said quietly.

Elvis blurred as moisture crept into her eyes. "That would be . . ." she swallowed thickly, "great."

"So you understand the simplicity of this spell? How to vanquish Mallick?"

Rowan closed her eyes for a moment. Fought the tears that threatened, and when she was sure she'd not blubber like an idiot she nodded and spoke. "We . . . the coven, need to bind him to the circle."

He watched her closely, and Rowan started to feel a little uncomfortable beneath his gaze. He knew things . . . this man, and for the first time she was starting to grasp the depth of his power.

"Mallick is smart. How do you plan on getting him inside your circle?"

"That's the easy part, believe it or not. I know how to bring life to his mark." At Priest's blank stare she continued. "How to undo Nana's original spell. As soon as I revoke it, the eye in his mark will open, and he'll know exactly where I am."

Priest's eyes narrowed thoughtfully. "He'll come for you."

"Yes."

"Yet once inside you'll be on your own. No one else will be able to penetrate the circle."

"Yes." Her voice was barely above a whisper. "It will be only he and I."

"And the sword."

She smiled at that and nodded. "And the sword if you can get your hands on it." Rowan exhaled and closed her eyes, trying to visualize how it would look and feel. "I will use the spell to charm his essence from his body, trap it in a container." She paused. "I'm liking a big-ass smelly old pickle jar. What do you think?"

Priest's eyes softened. "I think that would be fine."

"I'll grab one of Nana's. That way she'll have a part in this." She shrugged. "Once that's done I'll separate his head from his shoulders, and Mallick will be no more than a shot of energy in a used pickle jar." She paused. "Easy enough, really."

"And yet so incredibly difficult."

Rowan arched a brow. "Anyone ever tell you, you're a real downer sometimes?"

Priest laughed. "All the time. Just ask Nico." His smile quickly faded as reality set in, and she shivered at how quickly his expression changed. "Rowan. We can't allow him to take you."

His words were like a punch to the gut. A cold bucket of water tossed over heated flesh. She shifted in her chair, and the lightness of the moment was gone.

"I know."

Priest stood. "You should get some rest."

She nodded but didn't trust herself to answer.

He bent toward her swiftly, so fast she jumped, but then his hand was on her chin, his dark eyes searching with an intensity that touched her. "We will do whatever we can to help you defeat him. Know this, little witch." Her breath caught in her throat as he lowered his head and for a moment she thought he was going to kiss her. She closed her eyes and he brushed his mouth across her forehead.

And then he was gone.

Rowan glanced at the bed and for a moment considered crawling between the soft covers. Instead she leaned back and drew the blanket up to her chin. She shivered beneath the cotton, and she thought that the cold in her bones would never go away. It would have been nice to slip into bed beside Azaiel. To melt into his arms and drink in his strength.

"Yeah, that's just a pipe dream, Ro." Her whisper faded into silence.

She'd just closed her eyes when the melancholy strains of Patsy Cline filled her ears. "Oh Nana." She tugged the blanket closer and inhaled the familiar scent of her grandmother. "Stay close," she whispered.

Rowan hummed along to the song, but within minutes sleep claimed her, and she drifted off into a dreamless state of mind.

CHAPTER 27

Azaiel avoided Rowan all day. It hadn't been hard to do. He'd crashed hard and slept until midafternoon, something he'd not done in a long time.

This new existence was going to take some getting used to. The need for sleep? Pain? He stretched tight muscles and groaned. Damn but he'd taken a beating below.

He hissed as a particularly sharp stab tugged at his side, and he rubbed the sore area just to the left of his heart. He'd been pierced by a poison-tipped spear one of the Chakra demons had thrown. It had hurt like bloody hell, and not for the first time he cursed his brothers and their need to make him pay.

Pain—physical pain—was still relatively new for him. And though he would survive a fatal wound, it didn't negate the fact that getting sliced and diced with any kind of weapon was going to fucking hurt.

"Need help with that?"

He glanced up in surprise. The entire clan was gathered outside, and he'd assumed the house was empty. Cedric had just shuffled by, arms laden with food meant for the three large barbecues that had been set up near the gift shop. One thing he'd noticed about the James clan and their human hunters was that they loved food. And drink. And sports.

All of it in excessive, copious amounts.

Marie-Noelle watched him hesitantly. She wore jeans and a T-shirt with skeletons across the chest and the words GRATEFUL DEAD in faded white. Her hair was thrown up into a ponytail, much like her daughter, the dull amber tones now softer, shinier. The woman looked ten years younger than when he'd first laid eyes on her though the haunted depths of her eyes would never change. Not really.

"I'm fine, thank you," he answered.

He was still shirtless and very much aware of the scarred artwork on his back, so he kept Marie-Noelle in view. No sense in totally freaking the poor woman out.

"You're Seraphim."

He nodded.

"You have the same look about you as Bill."

At Azaiel's arched brow, Marie-Noelle smiled, and for the briefest second he saw Rowan reflected in her features. It took his breath away. The simple, classic beauty in these women.

"Not that you *look* like him obviously. My goodness you're about as far away from Bill's physical attributes as oil is from water." She blushed prettily. "I'm sorry. I'm rambling."

Azaiel helped himself to a cold glass of water. "No. It's fine." He took a long drink and set the empty glass into the sink. Outside the long fingers of sunlight were fast leaving, and it would be time to patrol. "Bill and I are . . . well, brothers."

He wondered if they knew what hid behind Bill's human mask. *Bill*. Was he ever going to get used to calling him that? Though he supposed it fit his current state of being. He wore the mantle of small, shuffling, and plain, but he was a Seraphim, and his true visage was nothing like "Bill."

"He meant a lot to my mother," Marie-Noelle said softly.

"I never had the pleasure of meeting your mother in person, but I know a lot of people who cared deeply for her."

He watched a host of emotions flicker across Marie-Noelle's face. "I just wish . . . I just wanted to be stronger." Her eyes fell away from his, and her voice broke. "I was never strong enough." Her pain was heart-wrenching. It coated her words and clung to her shoulders, hunching them forward.

"Marie-Noelle. We all have strength within us. Sometimes it takes a while for it to grow and mature." He glanced around. "You're here. You survived. Isn't that what's important?"

"But at what cost?" She shook her head. "You've no idea the things I did. How low I stooped in order to disappear in a haze of drugs and booze. All of it because I wasn't strong enough to face my destiny and now"—she sighed—"now my children are paying the price. *Rowan* is paying the price."

When she lifted her head her eyes were haunted, and he recognized it for what it was because the same emotions plagued him. Guilt. Anger. And shame.

"How can I be happy about being here when my mother is dead, and my daughter is about to sacrifice herself to that . . . that abomination. It should have been me." Her voice was hoarse, and she put her fist to her mouth in an effort to stop the tide of emotion that threatened.

"I'm not sacrificing myself." Rowan walked into the kitchen from the front hall. Her cheeks were flush and judging by the ponytail, T-shirt, shorts, and athletic shoes, he was guessing she was just in from a run.

Rowan grabbed an apple from the basket on the kitchen table. She looked it over quickly before placing it back and grabbing another. She took a bite and stared at the both of them.

"Mallick has been allowed to terrorize the James family for generation after generation. Using us and feeding on us." She shook her head and took another bite. "It will end on Samhain."

"But, Rowan. Isn't there another way?" Marie-Noelle, wrung her hands in agitation.

"No," Rowan said quietly. "There isn't."

"We need to talk." Marie-Noelle had a bit of the deer-in-the-headlights look in her eyes, and he knew it took a lot for her to face her daughter. "About a lot of things."

Rowan was quiet for several seconds, and when she spoke her tone was . . . almost kind. "I know, and we will, but I can't do it right now."

"No, no . . . of course." Marie-Noelle took a step back.

"I need to speak to Azaiel." She paused. "Alone."

Marie-Noelle pointed to the front yard. "I was just on my way out to find Mikhail."

Rowan's mouth tightened slightly though when she spoke her voice was neutral. "He's actually in the back garden. He and Leroy got into it, and there was this scene . . ."

"I hope Mikhail didn't hurt that animal, but seriously . . . where in the world did Vicki get her hands on that thing?" Her mother shook her head and moved toward the back door. "It belongs in a barn . . . far away from here."

"Trust me, it's not the donkey you need to worry about," Rowan muttered.

Marie-Noelle left Rowan and Azaiel staring at each other in silence.

Rowan's eyes darkened, and he caught the steady increase in her heart rate as she stood there, her gaze traveling the length of him. Slowly. By the time she met his eyes once more he was hot, his muscles tight, and an unmistakable bulge was present between his legs.

That the woman could do that to him with just a look was insane.

She chucked her apple into the wastebasket and took a few steps until she was so close he felt the heat off her skin. It seared across his flesh like a caress of fire. He smelled the fresh soap she'd used to wash, the sweet lemongrass in her hair . . . and heard the small catch in her throat when she touched him.

He was mesmerized by the sprinkling of freckles that splattered across her nose, like the sweetest dusting of cinnamon.

His hands clenched at his sides as she studied the mottled bruise he'd favored earlier. It still hurt like hell, but already his body's fast healing capabilities were working, and the sting wasn't quite as bad as it had been.

"Thank you, for getting the grimoire."

Damn, but her touch was light. The pads of her fingers traveled up to his shoulder, then across and back down to his abs.

"For fighting for Kellen and making sure he came back to me." Her eyes glittered, the blue depths smoky and alluring. He'd never seen anything as spectacular as the woman before him. He'd seen her in action—knew how tough she was and yet . . . her skin was like fragile bone china, and she was so small, so feminine.

He wanted to crush her to his chest. Feel her soft breasts against him, touch the silky skin beneath her ear. Sweep his tongue inside her mouth and claim her in every way that he could.

He made an animalistic sound, and her eyes widened. "Are you all right?" Her hand fell from his chest. "Did I hurt you?"

"You need to stop," he said hoarsely.

Her tongue caressed the tips of her teeth, and the expression in her eyes changed. They smoldered. The heat between them doubled. Hell, it tripled, and the energy was intoxicating.

"Stop?" She smiled, a secret, soft smile meant for lovers. "Why?"

The little minx was playing a game, but the ferocity of

emotion that rolled through Azaiel wasn't to be trifled with. His eyes flashed in anger, and he grabbed her hand, not caring about the whimper that breathed from her mouth as he held her.

"You will stop this, Rowan, because if you don't, I *will* bend you over the counter"—he leaned forward, and his voice dropped—"and rip your clothes off and finish what we started the other night." His heavy breaths were matched equally by the woman he held. "And I won't stop . . ." Her eyes were wide navy saucers, focused on his mouth. " . . . until I'm done and sated, and you've screamed my name at least a dozen times."

"A dozen times," she said breathlessly.

Her mouth was so close to his. "A dozen," he repeated, glaring at her.

He meant every single word he'd just uttered.

"Is that a promise?"

How long the two of them stood there, staring at each other, feeding off the sexually charged silence was anyone's guess. It wasn't until Hannah spoke that they knew they weren't alone.

"Um, guys? The burgers and dogs are ready. We should eat and head out. With all this cloud cover, nightfall is coming early."

Azaiel glanced up, his expression fierce. Hannah's mouth hung open, her lips pursed into an "O." Her eyes widened, and when he scowled at her she nearly tripped over her feet in an effort to flee.

Rowan waited until the door closed behind her cousin. "My hand?"

"What?" he said gruffly.

Her eyebrows rose, and Azaiel let go. He took a step back and cursed under his breath, pissed at himself for losing control.

"Are you afraid of me, Azaiel?"

"Is that what you think? That a little slip of velvet and cream has me shivering in my boots?" His eyes darkened, and the air around him thickened. He grabbed his T-shirt off the countertop, and when he spoke again his voice held a hint of steel. "If you were smart, you'd run the other way, Rowan."

She looked him straight in the eye, in that direct way he'd come to appreciate. She paused, licked her lips, and said so softly he barely heard her, "I'm done running."

Azaiel watched Rowan follow her cousin from the house, and he let out a long, tortured breath when the door banged shut. An ache tightened inside his chest, and he knew it had nothing to do with the beating he'd taken. He stood alone, wondering what the hell it would feel like to call a woman like Rowan, his.

You can't have her either.

Nico's words echoed in his head, and the ache tightened more. If only . . . Yeah, Azaiel pushed such nonsense from his mind and headed outside. Happy-ever-afters didn't belong to him. The Fallen.

Rain started an hour after they'd dispatched teams into town. It came down in thick sheets that cut like ice and stung when it hit. Azaiel pulled the collar of his jacket up closer around his neck and blew out hot clouds of mist as he gazed upon the near-empty streets. It was damp, cold, and miserable.

What day was it? He had no clue. While he and Kellen had been in the Hell realm, at least three full days had passed up here.

"Guess the demons hate the rain as much as we do." Rowan walked at his side, and he grunted in answer. So far they'd not encountered any otherworld creatures other than a pack of drunken goblins, and they'd fled as soon as they'd seen Azaiel. "Want a hot drink?"

She didn't give him a chance to answer, so he followed her as she crossed the street and headed toward a quaint shop, The Coffee Bean. He spotted a few patrons inside as well as a man behind the counter and a woman serving tables.

He paused and glanced around. It *was* quiet. He supposed they could take advantage of the lull because it wouldn't last long. It never did.

He followed Rowan inside and shook off the wet, his eyes taking in everything as he did so. To his left a young couple held hands, sharing an awfully large mug of hot, steaming liquid as they gazed into each other's eyes. Lust hung between them, mingling with the sweet hazelnut they enjoyed. He gave them ten minutes at most before they fled, off in search of a dark, quiet place in which to act out their fantasies.

The male was stroking his lady's hand, tugging her closer. Lucky bastard.

A group of elderly men sat in the far corner, chatting animatedly about the rash of violence and what they feared would happen in the coming days leading up to Halloween and the Witches Ball. They were the only other patrons in the coffee shop, and Azaiel grabbed the booth nearest the door—the one that gave him a view of the entire room—as Rowan ordered their coffee.

She slid in across from him and set two mugs on the table.

He took a sip and leaned back, welcoming the silence and the simplicity of the place. It was clean, not overly bright, and in a town that was teetering on the edge of crazy, The Coffee Bean was a slice of much-welcomed normal.

"So." Rowan's eyes stared at him expectantly.

He was wary. Didn't like the look in her eyes. They'd danced around each other for the last few hours, and he was tense. His shoulders were as tight and sore as the wound next to his heart. Never had a woman gotten him so tangled up. Not even her. The betrayer.

"So," he repeated, deciding a different approach was in order. "Good call, the coffee's great."

"What's your story?"

So much for aimless conversation—didn't seem like a different approach was going to work. "Excuse me?" Azaiel watched Rowan's long fingers as they grasped the cup between her hands. She leaned forward and took a sip before wiping the corner of her mouth.

"Everyone has a beginning, middle, and end, Azaiel. I'd like to know your beginning and middle. For want of a better word, we're a team, so don't you think we should at least know the basics about each other?" She flashed a smile. "I'm sure that Batman knew everything there was to know about Robin."

Another Batman fan.

"Of course I'm Batman, and you're the sidekick,"

"Of course," he murmured.

Azaiel studied her through hooded eyes. Her hair was damp, and the odd piece that had loosened from her ponytail clung to her forehead in wispy curls. Her cheeks were rosy, her eyes clear, and that damn mouth was parted in such a way that his thoughts immediately went south.

His groin tightened as a soft smile stole over her features.

Way effing south, and she knew it. *Jezebel.*

"I'm not that interesting," he said stiffly, frowning through his words as her smile deepened.

"How old are you?"

He considered her question.

"Come, on. Ballpark figure." She was flirting, and some small piece of him melted. What the hell was he going to do with her?

"Rowan, I've been around for millennia." His eyes stared into hers intently. "Do you know what that means?"

"That you're really, really, really"—she paused dramatically—"old?"

He smiled; he couldn't help it. The little witch was working it, and there was nothing to do but play along. "Among other things, yes, that's exactly what it means."

"So what do you—"

He shook his head and narrowed his eyes. "No, my turn."

She laughed, a full-bodied, unconventional laugh that drew the attention of the men in the corner. She waved at them and giggled. "Oh this is a game, is it?"

"Seems fair, don't you think?"

"Sure, go for it." She took another sip of her coffee and leaned into the booth. "Ask me anything you want."

He opened his mouth, but she stopped him before he had a chance to speak. "But the only rule is that we have to be honest, all right?"

Azaiel held her gaze for several moments before he spoke. "Who's Mason?"

Rowan looked surprised at his question. "Oh." She glanced away and shrugged. "Mason is . . . or was a man that I was involved with back in California. He was my boyfriend."

"So you're not involved anymore."

She shook her head. "Nope."

This pleased him. "Just like that."

She nodded. "Just like that."

"When did you—"

"Ah, ah, ah . . . I just answered two questions." She grinned, and he found himself doing the same as she licked her lips. "My turn."

"Fine."

"Who carved the wings into your shoulders?"

His grin quickly fled, and he glanced out into the darkness beyond the windows. Christ, why had he agreed to this stupid game? *Because I like to hear her laugh.* For several moments there was silence. He should have known Rowan wouldn't play nice.

"A sorcerer by the name of Cormac O'Hara."

"Why did he—"

Azaiel cocked his head, and she made a face. "I know, your turn."

He eyed his cup, then asked a question he'd been wondering about for several days. "Who or what the hell is Leroy?"

Rowan burst into laughter once more, and he loved the way her face lit up. The smattering of freckles stood out against her pale skin, and the urge to reach across the table and taste them was strong.

Azaiel shifted in his seat, once again hard and wanting . . . and unfulfilled.

"Leroy is a goblin who was cursed by a bunch of witches juiced up on dark mojo. They were using magick illegally, and I'm not sure about the details, but I think he was being an ass . . . no pun intended." She snorted, and he found himself smiling. "They put a spell on him and turned him into a donkey. We've tried several times but haven't been able to reverse it, and it's been nearly ten years."

"That was not what I was expecting to hear."

She smiled, a slow grin that made him clench his teeth. "Leroy is a nasty son of a bitch, and I'm not saying he deserves to be a donkey, but none of us are losing any sleep over it, that's for sure."

A blast of wind slammed into the window, which shuddered from the onslaught. Out there the cold bore down upon Salem with a fury that was not entirely natural. Something watched and waited. He felt it, and if Rowan's nervous fingers were any indication, she felt it, too.

"Who is Toniella?"

His mouth tightened at her name though Azaiel was careful to keep his face neutral. He remained silent, stared into the recesses of his coffee cup for a few moments.

"Earlier this afternoon, Kellen mentioned her to me. He said that she was there. That she helped you."

Azaiel nodded. "She was."

"He said that you knew her from before . . ."

Azaiel pushed his now-empty coffee mug away and narrowed his eyes. "If Kellen told you all this, then why are you
asking me?" He shrugged. "Seems to me you know more
details than I care to give."

She moistened her lips and leaned forward. "He didn't
tell me what she meant to you."

He scowled. "That's more than one question."

"I don't care," she retorted. "What did she mean to you?"

Her breath fell in rapid spurts. He watched her small
breasts rise and fall in agitation. She seemed upset.

"Why do you care?" He watched her closely.

"I don't . . ." She lowered her lashes and stared into her
coffee cup. "I don't know why I care. I just . . . would like to
know what the woman meant to you." She shrugged. "You
don't have to answer."

"She was my lover."

Her eyes shot up, and he held her gaze steady. "She was
my obsession. My world. My curse."

Her eyes were like large round drops of liquid navy.
They shimmered when she was high on emotion, and at the
moment she was flying.

"Did you . . . love her?"

Azaiel frowned and glanced out into the darkness. He
thought he had. Lord knows he'd lain awake many a night
thinking of her smile, her hair, and her golden skin. He'd
turned his back on his brothers for her. His god. His morals.
Had he done that for love?

No.

For the first time since his banishment to Hell, he realized that it had been all wrong. Love had never entered the
equation. It had about been ego, lust, and power.

Which made his fall all the more ridiculous.

"Azaiel?"

Mist parted along the sidewalk, and his eyes narrowed as three tall forms slid into view. They held weapons in both hands and blew fire out of their nostrils. The streetlight above them sizzled and went out as they passed by. Farther down the street, totally unaware, was a group of teenagers, huddled together underneath a storefront awning, smoking and fooling around.

It looked like an intense situation was about to unfold. One that required his aid. One that required the present conversation to end. *Excellent.*

"We need to go," he muttered.

Rowan followed his eyes. "Shit." She reached for her com and immediately called for backup. They rose quietly and slipped out of the coffee shop—two lethal hunters. As they entered the street, Rowan glanced up at him, her hands loose and ready to fire energy bolts. The air surrounding her was charged, and in that moment she looked magnificent.

"Just so you know?"

He cocked his head, his thoughts grim and chaotic.

"Our conversation isn't over. You never answered my last question."

She took off running, and something inside him twisted as she threw her hands up and shot an energy blast straight at the trio of demons. One of them caught sight of her and threw a large machete in her direction. Rowan ducked and rolled to the side, a gazelle on feet as light as clouds.

The woman was crazy. She was unpredictable and fierce. She was loyal, brave, and happened to have the most delectable ass ever.

Azaiel strode toward the melee, his thoughts dark. He knew how uncertain her future was. He knew what his oath to the League meant.

If it came to Rowan's life—if she failed to defeat the demon Mallick—would he be strong enough to follow through with his mission?

He scooped up the machete and attacked with a savagery he'd not felt before. There in the darkness beyond the lamp-post, Azaiel slaughtered the enemy and showed no mercy. It was the way of it. It was how it *had* to be.

And when he was done, sorrow bled through his veins because he knew that in less than a week, she might be on the receiving end of his sword because he would not fail Askelon. He would carry through with his mission.

He glanced back at Rowan, and she lowered her eyes, but he caught sight of the wariness that colored them.

And it made him ill. She should be wary. She should be scared out of her mind. He swallowed thickly and moved into the shadows, welcoming the cool, dark caress of it.

He would do whatever he could to keep her alive, but as the heaviness of the night pressed on him and he felt the magnitude of Mallick's power he knew it might not be enough.

It left him empty, angry, and bleak. If he'd not fallen, he might have been a worthy champion. As it was, he just prayed they'd both be strong enough.

CHAPTER 28

"**Y**ou all right?"

Rowan glanced up at Hannah and shrugged, moving to the side and allowing her cousin room to sit on the blanket. She had found a patch of grass away from everyone, not far from the oak tree in the front yard.

It was, however, the day before Samhain, and she was far from "all right."

The sword of Gideon had still not shown though Priest had assured her not to worry. Pretty damn hard to do that when Salem was knee deep in demon shit, and the tension amongst her family and friends was so thick, it was choking. They all knew what was coming and were helpless to stop it. Fights had broken out—nothing serious, but still . . . morale was low.

Most of the dissension involved the volatile twins, Terre and Vicki. Rowan sighed and shook her head. Everyone needed to chill. Or find something to take their minds off the crap spot they found themselves in.

Her mother had attempted to talk to her several times, but Rowan hadn't been up for it. Not yet anyway. Though something had changed. Rowan wasn't quite sure what it was, she knew that the anger and pain she'd carried for so long was starting to dissipate. Was it the fact that her end might be so near? Was she weak to forgive a mother who'd treated her children so callously? Or was it simply human to forgive.

"I'm great," she answered, smiling at the snort that fell from Hannah's lips.

"You're so not great." Hannah bumped her shoulder and sprawled beside her. It was early afternoon, and the sun was unseasonably warm. Indian summer was lingering in this part of the world, giving way to a few nights of rain and cold, and not much else.

Though the trees had lost the majority of their leaves, the colors of fall were still in abundance, as were the horrid Halloween decorations.

God, the Halloween decorations. Rowan shuddered. Thanks to Vicki, The Black Cauldron looked as if a Halloween party superstore had vomited all over the property.

Rowan leaned back and closed her eyes, drinking in as much vitamin D as she could. No sense stressing about it now.

This could be the last hot sunny day I see.

"Auntie Marie seems happy."

Rowan grunted an answer, not because she begrudged her mother happiness but because there really wasn't much she cared to say. Marie-Noelle and the gargoyle were inseparable and though at first she'd resisted the idea—hello, a gargoyle?—she'd eventually accepted it.

If the last few days had taught Rowan anything, it was that second chances needed to be cherished and though there was still a hell of a lot of hurt between her and her mother, Rowan was willing to keep her distance.

For the moment. She would talk to her before Samhain, but every time she thought about it her belly rolled, and she felt sick. How did you reconcile their damaged relationship in one conversation?

"So, what's going on between you and Azaiel?"

Rowan glanced at her cousin and scowled. "Nothing."

"Nothing," Hannah repeated.

Rowan straightened up. "That would be correct."

"You don't sound too happy about that."

"It is what it is." Rowan shrugged. "Not that I should be thinking of sex right now."

"Sex?" Hannah squealed.

"Shut up!" Rowan hissed, aware that several of her relatives glanced their way, including Vicki. The witch was dressed in short shorts and a tank top that barely concealed her generous assets.

In the distance, Kellen tossed a football back and forth with Priest and Nico. Azaiel stood off to the side, alone. He was always alone.

Hannah followed her gaze, a silly grin on her face as she waved at Nico. The shifter seemed to be having a great time, running and playing catch. But then again, he was a cat.

"What's going on between the two of *you*?" Rowan asked, curious. Hannah had never been the sort to settle for one man. She'd always had a few in the hopper and was a terrible flirt, afraid of commitment and the big R. *Relationship.*

Hannah sighed and leaned back. "Nothing."

Rowan looked at her sharply, and the two of them burst into laughter. They fell back onto the blanket, and she wasn't sure when, but at one point her laughter turned to tears. Big fat ones that rolled down her cheeks like wet diamonds. She turned from Hannah, ashamed of her weakness.

Hell, she didn't even know why she was crying.

"Hey." Hannah's hand on her shoulder felt good, and eventually the sniffles subsided.

"I'm sorry," Rowan exhaled. "I'm just all over the place these days."

"We all are, but considering the part you'll have to play, I think it's okay for you to be an emotional wreck."

"Gee, thanks."

Hannah got to her feet. "You know what I think?"

"No, but I'm sure you're going to tell me." Rowan joined her cousin, watching curiously as Kellen had organized a bunch of the hunters and her family members into two groups.

"I think you need to get laid."

"Really," she answered dryly.

Kellen said something to Azaiel, and though she was too far from them to hear what was said, she felt his reluctance. The arms crossed over his chest was a dead giveaway. Everything about this posture said "leave me alone." Kellen tossed the football at Azaiel, and he had no choice but to catch it or deal with a broken nose.

The men began tossing the ball around, and within minutes several of them were doffing their shirts.

"Oh goodie, we're playing football." All sex talk forgotten, Hannah tugged on her arm. "This is just what we need. Everyone can blow off some steam, and we get to stare at yummy abs! Come on." Her cousin grinned at her. "Here's hoping Nico and Azaiel end up on the skins team." Hannah glanced toward the groups. "Hell, yeah. Nico just doffed his shirt."

Rowan took a step forward and paused, for the first time taking in the truly bizarre scene that was unfolding. All of the vehicles had been moved so that an impressive area of grass was open and available. Frank sat on the steps of the gift shop, a mountain of weapons on the ground in front of him. He was cleaning them, making them ready for another night of patrolling.

Not more than a few feet from him, the donkey Leroy did a patrol of his own—slowly traveling a well-worn path around the oak tree and back again.

On the field the teams were being divvied up. Demon hunters from all over the state were in attendance, as were her family members and of course the otherworlders who'd been here for days. She smiled. Even her aunt Dot was up and ready to play.

Rowan's mouth thinned as Vicki doffed her T-shirt and, clad in only a skimpy pink bra and shorts, sauntered over to the "skins" team.

Which now, she could see, included Azaiel.

Her heart sped up as she gazed upon his bare chest. Bare abs. Damn, he was wearing the jeans that fell so low they made a woman's mouth water. How the hell could he play football in that?

Her feet started forward before she even realized what she was doing and she was halfway to the field when that small, irritating voice inside her head spoke. The one that asked, what the hell are you doing?

Azaiel glanced up at that moment, and their eyes met across the field. His were intense, and even from this far away she saw they were dark, the gold much diminished. He looked pissed. Irritated. He licked his lips.

He looked fucking hungry.

Rowan's heart was beating madly, and she was flush with heat and desire. She strode toward her brother, deciding it would be more prudent for her to play against Azaiel. All the more chance at contact.

What was she doing? Rowan smiled at Azaiel and nodded, her gaze not leaving his even when Priest tried to get her attention.

She was surrounded by a large number of bodies, yet in that moment there was only Azaiel. And the desire that had settled between her legs with a heavy, throbbing weight. She knew it wouldn't go away, and Lord knew, time was running out.

She turned and followed Priest into formation.

She licked her lips as they huddled, not listening to anything Kellen said. Her eyes were focused on Azaiel. On the way the sunlight poured over the hard lines of his body, leaving him bathed in a sheen of sweat.

What was she doing? She was going to seduce the Seraphim.

Over the course of the next hour a ragtag group of warriors played a sport that transcended everything. Otherworld and human joined forces, both male and female. Though the only female who was willing to be a "skin" was Vicki. *Thank God, she'd at least kept her bra on.*

Rowan glared at her cousin, hating the way she clung to both Nico and Azaiel. Hating the way her perfect large breasts were pushed to the max in the damn pink bra she sported.

"I'm going to take her down this time," Hannah whispered fiercely. "That woman has no class. Seriously? Who the hell would even want to play football with her girls nearly falling out?" Hannah shook her head. "I'm telling you, a good elbow in the right spot might make her think twice about it."

Rowan snorted. "It's no contact."

Hannah glared. "Tough shit."

"Okay, guys, we're going deep. It's our last chance to score and break the tie, all right?" Kellen grinned like a crazy fool, and Rowan's heart lurched. It had been so long since they'd enjoyed any kind of lightness. It was wonderful to see.

Kellen turned to her. "Ro, I want you to go deep."

"Me?" She glanced at Priest. "But he's been doing the catching. I just like running down the side and maybe tripping Vicki if I get the chance."

"No, I want you to go deep. They won't expect it. They'll

watch Priest run to the left. I want you to run down to the right. I'll fake throw to Priest, then launch it down to you. All right?"

"Got it, captain," Hannah said with a grin, her eyes laughing. "Don't worry, Ro. I'll take Vicki out."

Rowan got into formation and sought out Azaiel as he stood opposite her. His eyes remained dark, his expression intense. She licked her lips and hiked up her T-shirt, twisting it through the top of her bra to form a sort of bikini top. It was the last play of the day. Her last shot.

His eyes never left hers.

Kellen threw her a "what the hell are you doing?" look, but she ignored him and kept her eyes on the prize.

On Kellen's cue, she lunged forward, arms pumping like mad pistons. She twisted and turned, avoiding everyone in front of her as she ran down the field. If she could just make this play, the game would be over, and she'd concentrate on what she really wanted. Azaiel.

She was nearly to the edge when Kellen yelled, and she turned, her eyes focused in the air, watching the football arc across the field like a rocket about to explode. She kept running and at the very last moment jumped for it—and though she would deny it to her grave—used a little bit of magickal mojo to bring the ball home to mama.

She had it, too, there within her grasp. Until a huge wall of muscle grabbed her from behind and took her down. Hard.

Arms made of steel crushed her to a chest that felt like heaven. Rowan went with him, and when they settled in the cool grass, Azaiel was on top of her, his voice harsh in her ear.

"What the fuck game are you playing, little girl?"

He was hard. She felt his erection against her belly, and gasped at the bleakness in his eyes, at the anger. At the *hunger* as his gaze settled onto her lips.

Her mouth was dry, and she had to take a moment before she could speak. Her heart was beating so heavily inside her chest that it roared in her ears, and she concentrated—a lot—and eventually it subsided.

The muscles in his shoulders strained as he held his upper body away from hers, yet his lower half was still pressed so tight to her that she felt him throb. Felt him burn against her.

"Let's be clear about something, Azaiel." She breathed the words like a harlot of old—Monroe would have been proud. "I'm not a little girl."

He didn't say a word, but something shifted in his eyes, and slivers of gold twisted in their black depths. His eyes were so beautiful, his mouth insanely hot. She wanted to feel the rough stubble on his chin against her bare skin. And all that thick, shaggy, dirty blond hair was begging for her fingers.

She felt reckless and didn't care about consequences. She shifted her hips and was rewarded with a strangled hiss as she rubbed against his hardness. Once. And then again.

"I want you," she whispered hoarsely, aware that the other players were on their way over. "Inside me."

Her breasts were engorged, her nipples hard, and the ache between her legs was unbearable. She was wet, so wet and horny that if he put his hands on her—there where she throbbed—she'd come. Right here. In front of everyone.

She leaned up and felt him tense. Saw the veins bulge in the side of his neck as she whispered into his ear. "Right now."

Rowan pushed him off and jumped to her feet. She grabbed the football from the ground and tossed it back to her brother, before turning away and wiping bits of grass and twigs from her clothes. Azaiel stood, his back to everyone—for obvious reasons. She was pretty sure he didn't want the entire group knowing he had a raging hard-on.

But she knew.

She walked toward him and paused an inch or so away. "That ache isn't going to go away, Azaiel." Her fingers traced the wings across his shoulders—a brief, gentle sweep. "The only thing that will ease your pain is sex. We'd be fools to not at least try it once . . . or twice."

Rowan walked past him and headed into the forest that surrounded The Black Cauldron. She didn't give a rat's ass what anyone thought—except Vicki. She hoped her cousin was shooting daggers at her back.

The cool shadows from the trees did nothing to douse the fire inside, and she didn't know she was holding her breath until she heard a twig snap behind her. For the first time a tingle of apprehension shot down her spine.

And yet, as she weaved her way through the tall trees, she let it go. There was nothing wrong with what she wanted. She'd lived her entire life for everyone else. Even fleeing to California hadn't cut the ties to her family. To her legacy. With Samhain coming at her fast and hard there was nothing left to lose.

Except maybe her heart.

CHAPTER 29

Azaiel lost sight of Rowan amongst the oaks and maples, but her scent lingered in the air. A tantalizing smell that fed the fire in his belly with a savagery that should have surprised him but didn't.

He'd been raging inside for days, and though he'd avoided her as much as he could—even patrolling with Nico and Hannah the last few nights—he knew all along they'd end up here. At this moment. He had to be strong enough to fight the need . . . the hunger he felt for her.

His abdomen clenched as a fresh wave of desire rolled through him, and his hands fisted as he thought of the football game. Of how she'd bent over, purposely turning her ass in his direction so that her soft curves were on display for everyone to see. Then she'd caress the damn ball with those long, delicate fingers. And stretch, just so, her breasts molded to her T-shirt in a wanton display.

Priest had grinned like a son of a bitch for most of the game, and Azaiel decided then and there that the Knight Templar needed an attitude adjustment as well.

"Jezebel," he whispered hoarsely. He'd teach her a lesson. There was no way he would make love to her. No way in hell. He knew it would be exquisite. Earth-shattering. Mind-bending.

So why would he open himself up to that? Tomorrow night he would either have to kill her or let her go. He had no future with a woman as powerful as Rowan. It would never be allowed. Not for the Fallen.

With renewed focus Azaiel crashed through the bush, his anger growing with each step he took. Where the hell was she going?

The late-afternoon sun barely penetrated the thick trees, even with their leaf loss. Through the silent underbrush there seemed to be some sort of path she was following. He upped his pace, almost to a near run, and came to a rather painful jarring halt when he burst into a small clearing.

Azaiel ran his hands through the tangled mess of hair atop his head as everything inside him liquefied into red-hot need. Rowan stood, not more than ten feet from him, naked as the day she was born. Her clothes were thrown about as if she'd tugged them off in a frenzy. He saw one running shoe, but as for the other, who knew.

Green grass, well fed by the patch of sunlight allowed into the treeless space, worshipped at her feet, and all around the vibrant colors of fall drifted in the air, clung to the trees, and blew by in the wind.

He caught her scent once more, that heady mix of lemongrass . . . as well as the musky odor of passion. Her skin was creamy, perfect, and stretched taut over young, lithe limbs. And her ass, that rounded, perfect, delectable mound of flesh teased him as she stood with her back to Azaiel, her long crimson hair billowing softly around her shoulders.

He didn't know he moved, yet seconds later found himself behind her. So close that if he wanted to, he could reach out and touch her. And Lord knew he wanted to. He wanted to touch all of her.

Rowan turned her head to the side, lashes downcast, mouth parted. She shuddered, and his gaze settled upon her slender hands. They were at her sides, and she slowly opened and closed them as the silence between them grew.

Goose bumps rushed across her flesh, and though he tried to be strong, he couldn't help himself. His gaze raked over every inch of her, and his hands rose of their own volition, wanting to touch, to caress, and to knead.

"You must be cold." His voice was hoarse, and he barely got the words out.

"I'm hot." She shook her head and licked her lips. "So incredibly hot." She lifted the heavy fall of hair from her neck and exhaled. Azaiel saw the mark on her flesh—the mark put there by Mallick, and everything inside him stilled.

He traced the simple lines first with his eyes—then with his fingers. Such need rose in him that he was glad she couldn't see that his fingers trembled. It was a need to protect, a need to touch and to make her forget.

"I won't let him win, Rowan," he said hoarsely.

She let the curtain of hair fall back until it covered his hand and the mark. She turned then, her mouth parted, her eyes misty with desire. She grabbed his hand, and he swallowed thickly as she rested his large palm against the swell of her breast.

He was helpless to look away. Helpless to do anything but stay with her and drink in her beauty—her essence and spirit.

"I don't want to talk about Mallick." She held his hand against her breast, shuddered, and moved his palm over her hard, turgid nipple. "I want to feel you, Azaiel." She glanced up at him, and the world narrowed into one hot-as-hell, sexy redhead. "All of you."

Her other hand sought out his cock, and he gritted his teeth, sweat beading along his forehead as she slowly rubbed the long, hard length of him. Even through his jeans the sensation was erotic, and he strained beneath her touch.

"I want to feel you inside me." She paused, breathing heavy as a slow, seductive smile claimed lips meant for kissing, for licking and sliding. "Hard, and full and passionate. Do you understand?"

He nodded, mesmerized by the candy red mouth. By the tongue that slid over it and by the hand that gripped him between his legs. She rose on tiptoes, her arousal in his nostrils, her soft flesh in his hands. "I don't want to make love. We can do that later. What I want is for you to fuck me, Azaiel." She slid her mouth across his neck, licked her way up to his mouth, and paused, her breath a whisper of need. "Right now."

His hand shot up and buried itself in the thick ropes of hair at her neck. Azaiel leaned down, no longer in control. He was on fire and for a second thought he saw a hint of wariness in her eyes.

"I'm on the cusp of no return, little witch. If you want this to go no further, then I suggest you gather your things and leave now while you still can." His eyebrows furled, and he bared his teeth like an animal. "You have no idea what you've awakened. Of the passions that run beneath my skin." He traced her lips with his forefinger, sinking deep into her wet warmth. "It's been so long," he whispered.

She licked his fingers, then yanked her head back so she could speak. "If that's your idea of dissuading me from what we both want"—she smiled as she rubbed her breasts against him—"you're doing a shitty job."

So many emotions warred inside him. So many voices yelling retreat, yet as he gazed down into her face he knew he'd lost. Hell, he'd given in the moment he'd followed her into the forest.

He bent low and claimed her mouth, his tongue going deep in an aggressive move. He tasted every inch of her and went back for more. Rowan swayed, and his hand slipped behind her, traveled down her back until it rested against the round, feminine swell that was there just for him. He splayed his fingers across her ass and pulled her in tight so that his erection was flush against her soft belly.

Shit, but she felt good in his hands.

She broke the kiss, and he stared down at her swollen lips and the pink tongue that peeked from between them. She wriggled slightly and stepped back, legs spread so that his eyes nearly popped when he took a second to take all of her in.

Rowan's breasts were perfect. Not overly large, but soft, and round, and meant for his hands. Her dusky rose nipples were hard and stood at attention. *His attention.* He decided he would suck and lick them until she came.

His mouth watered at the thought.

Her hands lingered near her waist, and his eyes touched every inch of her, caressing gently rounded hips and long, sexy legs that were spread. When he settled upon the narrow thatch of crimson hair between them, his cock tightened even more, and he exhaled a shot of heated air.

She was wet, glistening in the waning sunlight. So ready for him.

"You are magnificent," he managed to say, as his gaze traveled back up, and they locked eyes.

"I meant what I said, Azaiel." Her tone had changed, to an almost painful whisper. "I need you naked and inside me."

If there was a line to cross, Azaiel had left it behind in the dust. His hands dropped to the belt that held his jeans in place and seconds later it was undone and his jeans along with his boots tossed aside.

"Last chance," he managed to say though he winced as her gaze settled hotly on his straining cock.

She licked her lips and strode toward him, breasts swaying gently, mouth open and inviting. With a flick of her wrist he found himself on his back, and she was there above him, her wet, moist center open to his eyes.

Long, delicate fingers played with her outer lips, and she spread them just enough for him to know how aroused she was. Her clitoris was engorged, her skin slick with moisture. An image of his mouth there, eating, licking, and sucking nearly sent him over the edge, and he tried to move, but her magick held him in place.

She bent forward, placed her hands on his shoulders, and without pause impaled herself upon him, sliding her wetness down his length in a sheath of wet heat. She was so damn tight, and moist and hot. A heavy sigh fell from her lips, and she threw her head back and moaned.

"I knew you'd feel like this, Azaiel." Immediately, she began to move. "Like you were meant for me."

"Dammit, Rowan, slow down." He gritted his teeth and grabbed her hips, holding her in place when she would have ridden hard. He stared up at her and thrust upward, slowly letting her rise and fall with the rhythm *he* commanded. It took every inch of control he had—to keep things moving at this pace—when all he wanted to do was slam her to the ground and fuck her as hard and fast as she wanted.

But then it would be over, and Azaiel wanted this to last. He needed it to last. He nearly pulled out—let the tip of his cock rub against her clit—and held her there, watched the fire burn in her eyes. When she moaned, a deep throaty protest, he let her rock back onto him and repeated the motion, over and over. And over.

Fuck, but he needed this to last.

Her breasts swayed slowly, like a tantalizing gift, and he grabbed a turgid nipple, suckling it hard, his teeth grazing and rough. She angled her back, just so, and her fingers gripped his shoulders, the nails going deep and cutting skin.

He was sure it hurt like hell, but at the moment it only added to his pleasure.

His fingers found her clitoris and toyed with her there as she rose and fell, and every time a groan slipped from her lips, his cock swelled even more. His balls ached, and he wanted to bury himself inside her forever.

She kissed him once more, her hips urging him on, and when he would have slowed her down she bit him. Azaiel tasted blood in his mouth and swore, staring up into eyes that were stormy. Fevered.

"I can't . . ." A sob escaped. "I want . . ."

He knew then what she wanted. What she needed. To douse the fire. To quiet the hunger. To rush toward the cliff and jump off. He growled like an animal and lifted her off him, turning her in midair and pushing her to the ground on all fours.

He was behind her immediately and sank his cock into her slick, pink flesh as he bent forward, his hand rough in her hair, his words hoarse against her ear. "Is this what you want?" He thrust hard and held himself still inside her though when her muscles clenched around him he nearly lost it.

He pumped once and withdrew before plunging inside her again. And again. And again.

"Yes. *Please,* Azaiel."

He increased his rhythm, his flesh slapping against hers, and held her in place with one hand while the other ran down her spine and kneaded the ass that had been teasing him for days. There were no more words—this was no tender joining.

She fit him perfectly, and as his cock rode her, sliding in and out, his fingers continued to caress and explore. He paused near her other opening, breath ragged as he stared down and smiled wickedly, sinking his long forefinger deep within the tight pucker.

"Oh my God, Azaiel," she croaked, startled for a second, and then she started to mew as he slowly rotated his finger in tandem with his hard, deep, thrusts. He felt himself bunch, his balls tight and full as her juices ran and her muscles tightened around him even more.

"Are you coming for me, Rowan?"

"Oh God, yes," she whimpered hoarsely, as he thrust harder, and faster, and when she came, he felt her release. Felt her absolute surrender.

Only then did he allow himself to give in to his own needs. As his orgasm crashed through him, one thought rolled around his mind. After living for millennium, Azaiel had finally found that elusive slip of heaven he hadn't even known he'd been searching for.

He rolled to the side, cushioned her there in his arms, and listened to the silence around him. How long they lay there wasn't measured in time but by moments. He carefully moved long tendrils of hair from her face, and she moved into the crux of his embrace.

They didn't speak. What was there to say? Her smell was on him. It was *in* him, and he knew that if he took a hundred showers, it would never leave. He glanced down at her and felt his heart clutch.

Her eyes were large, open, glittering diamonds. Her mouth, bruised from his kisses, taunted him. Something tightened in his chest, painfully so, and he could do nothing but hold her. How could he give this up?

He was so screwed.

Overhead the first hoot of an owl sounded, and she shivered. This time he knew she was cold.

"We better get back." He started to roll away from her, but her hand was on him.

"Wait."

She sat on her knees, a fiery goddess, her nudity making

him hard once more. He wanted her again—wanted to lose himself inside her—but there was no time.

"I've never . . ." She blushed and cleared her throat. "I've never experienced anything like that before." She laughed then, a throaty note of glee and kissed him softly on the lips. "Thank you. Next time I promise we'll take it slow."

Azaiel stood and flexed his stiff muscles. "Next time?"

She stared at up him, her perfect heart-shaped face open and trusting. "Yes. Next time."

The heat inside Azaiel fled with the coming dusk. He doubted there'd be a next time, and he wanted it. Badly. He tossed Rowan her clothes, slipped into his jeans and boots. He was still shirtless and waited while she tied up her running shoes.

Just like that, reality intruded, and he felt empty inside. They had just enough time to grab some food and head into Salem. Things were heating up, and there were several events in town that would surely garner the attention of Mallick's minions.

"Ready?"

She nodded. Azaiel was just about to head down the path that led to the Cauldron when Rowan's hand wrapped around his wrist. The air stilled—emptied of everything, save for their beating hearts and something else. They weren't alone.

Azaiel peered into the shadows that blanketed the clearing and prepared himself as several figures slid from between them. Only one concerned him. The one with all the power.

A fae—Dark fae. He was tall and lean, with long, elegant lines. All fae were attractive, but this man was supremely so. His classic features, pale eyes, and long, dark hair made for an arresting face. His clothing was simple, yet the suit spoke of money and privilege. The men with him were dressed similarly as if they'd just come from a dinner party.

Azaiel watched the man closely, muscles tense and ready in case of an attack. Dark fae held many layers of magick hidden amongst the glamour they projected. Azaiel's gifts might be diminished, but the deadly power that shrouded this fae was impressive.

"We need to talk." The man's voice was melodic and enticing. His eyes were so light they were nearly colorless, with the merest whisper of blue. They glittered eerily, filled with otherworld power.

Rowan walked out from behind Azaiel and faced the group of men with raised chin and squared shoulders.

She snuck a glance at Azaiel, licked her lips, and spoke. "Hello, Father."

CHAPTER 30

Rowan stared across the clearing at the man who'd given her life. At the man she'd met fewer times than the fingers on her hands. He never changed. Darrick was still an elegant, dangerously attractive man. Nana claimed he had a mean, selfish streak and was bad news. Someone to be avoided at all cost, yet . . . there was a connection there, she felt it pulse inside.

His eyes narrowed, and she knew he was offended by what had just occurred. The smell of sex was rank in the air. Had he watched? Was he that depraved?

"Why are you here?" No need to beat around the bush.

Darrick glanced behind him, and the three fae who hovered near the edge of the forest disappeared.

He ignored her and settled his eerie eyes upon Azaiel. "You took my son from this realm and placed him in danger."

"Your son is a big boy," Azaiel responded lightly, but Rowan felt the tension. Azaiel was ready to pounce.

Darrick's gaze lingered on the Seraphim for several long moments. "I know who you are. What you did." The fae asked silkily, "Does she?"

Rowan stepped forward as anger flushed through her. She was done living in the background. "I'll ask you one more time, *Father*, why are you here?"

Darrick's glacial eyes settled on her once more, and something shifted in their depths. He studied her for a few moments, then walked toward them until he stood but inches away.

"Your mother did well. You should remember that."

"What do you mean?"

She watched Darrick warily as a smile stole over his features, yet his eyes remained frosty cold. "She chose me." He paused, watching her closely. "Did you know that?"

Rowan shook her head, confused. What was he getting at?

"She sought me out to father her children. Enticed me from the woods, then rejected me."

Rowan snorted. "*She* rejected *you*? Are you trying to say that you actually wanted us?"

His eyes narrowed, and his face darkened. "I wanted your mother and had no idea she'd been marked by the demon lord."

Rowan exhaled, aware that it was nearly dark. She and Azaiel needed to patrol. "Why are you telling me this? It's not like Kellen or I care."

Darrick's eyes narrowed, and she felt his anger. "Kellen will care one day when his legacies ascend. He'll need me. He'll need my protection." Darrick exhaled. "Right now he's vulnerable. He needs *your* protection. I can't stop what's coming. There are those who would tie my hands, but I can give you this . . ."

The fae held out his hand, and Rowan gazed upon a jeweled dagger. The hilt was inscribed with runes, and the power it held was impressive. It emanated outward, a soft glow of heat slithering along the sharp lines. "Take it," he ordered.

Rowan glanced at Azaiel, but the Seraphim's eyes were hooded, his mouth tense.

"What is it?"

"It's a little extra power that I borrowed from my queen."

She stared at it, not really sure what she should do. Her Nana had never trusted the fae, and yet . . .

"Just take it, Rowan. It may aid you in your endeavor tomorrow night." At Rowan's look of surprise her father snorted. "I know exactly what you're planning, and I know how dangerous it will be." His voice dropped. "I will do what I can to keep the demons at bay." He arched a brow. "To aid in your quest. In exchange I only ask that you keep Kellen safe. Until he ascends I can't bring him into my realm. I can't even acknowledge him or my enemies will destroy him. Do you understand?"

Something twisted inside Rowan, a slice of pain she'd not been prepared for. "This is all about Kellen," she whispered.

"Of course it is." Darrick stood back, his expression unreadable. "What did you think it was about? You mean nothing to me, child, but your brother." The fae nodded. "When he comes into his powers he will be a force to be reckoned with, and one day we will rule the between worlds together."

His words hurt. After all this time, they still hurt. Azaiel grabbed her hand, and she leaned into him, eyes never leaving her father.

Darrick stepped back, his tall form slowly disappearing amongst the gray mist that encroached from the forest. And then he was gone.

"He's one cold son of a bitch," Azaiel said quietly. She felt his eyes upon her but couldn't look at him. The dagger was heavy in her palm, and she clutched it tightly. For a few moments her gaze locked onto the empty space where Darrick had stood, then she carefully pulled away from Azaiel and nodded toward the trees.

"Time to head into Salem." Her voice was light.

"Yes."

"If anyone asks . . ." Her cheeks were pink, and she avoided his eyes.

Azaiel fell in beside her. "We were just talking."

They started forward. "Strategizing about tomorrow night."

"Going over all the details."

They entered the silent darkness of the forest.

Rowan smiled wryly. "No one is going to believe that."

Azaiel shook his head. "Nope. Not a chance."

By the time they reached the bed-and-breakfast, Hannah, Nico, Priest, and Kellen had already left for town, along with most of the human hunters. A reported riot had broken out near one of the bars, involving demon and vampire mercenaries. Vicki, Abigail, and Terre were just leaving.

Vicki ignored Rowan though she graced Azaiel with a look that could kill. Terre stuck her tongue out at her twin and winked at Rowan as she climbed into Abigail's beat-up jeep. The three of them sped into the night while Rowan and Azaiel quickly changed so they could join them.

Ten minutes later she was just about to hop onto the back of Azaiel's Harley when her mother appeared, Mikhail at her side.

Marie-Noelle's face was white, her mouth pinched. She was agitated, and the wild look that hadn't surfaced of yet was present in her eyes once more. "I felt him," she said quickly. "Darrick."

Rowan paused beside the bike and adjusted the dagger Darrick had given her inside her leather jacket. "He was here." Rowan shrugged. "You don't need to worry. He won't bother either one of you."

"I don't fear the fae," Mikhail growled.

Rowan climbed up behind Azaiel. "You should, gargoyle." She thought of the power she'd sensed and of how little they really knew about the between realm. "I think we all should."

"What did he want?" Her mother's hands twisted together, and her face was clammy with sweat.

"He . . . wants us to be safe."

Marie-Noelle was silent for a moment, but when Azaiel started the bike she rushed forward and stopped just short of the Harley. "Rowan, I'm so . . ." She struggled to speak.

The block of pain inside her chest had shattered several days ago, but Rowan still couldn't bear the thought of dealing with it. Not now. "I know," she said quietly.

Marie-Noelle took another step forward, but Rowan tapped Azaiel on the back. "Let's go."

Azaiel nodded to Mikhail. "Keep watch over Cedric and Rowan's mother."

The gargoyle nodded solemnly, then Azaiel and Rowan roared into the night.

The last night before Samhain—the possible last night of her life—was like any of the others she'd passed over the last two weeks. She and Azaiel killed several demons, dispatched a few vampires to an early grave, and restored order among the human populace. They patrolled relentlessly, hooked up with the others, and laid waste to a rabid pack of blood demons that descended just before dawn.

When it was over, Rowan was tired, bloody, bruised, and running on adrenaline that was fast leaving. She'd kept her mind empty of anything except the mission at hand, but as she rode behind Azaiel, as her hands clutched his hard warmth to her body she nearly lost it.

A wall of emotion hit her in the chest and made it difficult to breathe. Her eyes watered, and she blinked rapidly in an effort to keep them clear. In the end she lost and rested her head on Azaiel's back, swallowing the thick lump in her throat as the tears leaked from her eyes in slow rolls of sorrow.

Twelve hours to go. Twelve hours until she met the demon who'd piloted her ship—who'd steered her life with invisible hands.

Twelve hours until she either defeated Mallick or . . . she squeezed her eyes tightly and banished the thought from her mind.

They reached The Black Cauldron a few minutes later, and she slid from the Harley on legs that were weak, and if not for Azaiel, she might very well have dropped to the ground in a puddle of defeat. What kind of warrior was she?

He lifted her into his arms and held her to his chest as if she were a treasure of the utmost fragility. Her arms crept around his neck, and she closed her eyes once more. Not wanting to see anyone, or talk to anyone. All she wanted was Azaiel.

He carried her into the house, bypassed Cedric and Abigail, and took the stairs two at a time, heading straight for her bedroom. Once inside he leaned against the door and just held her. Rowan shuddered, over and over, her tight frame overcome with pain. She wasn't sure how much time had passed before the silent emotions inside her subsided, but eventually she relaxed in his arms.

She opened her eyes, angled her head, and drank in his beauty. He stared down at her with an intensity she felt in her bones. It was one of want and need and desire. At that moment he mirrored everything she felt, and a strangled noise erupted from her throat. She couldn't speak but tenderly caressed his face.

How had this man she'd just met come to mean so much to her? Was it fate that she'd only met him now? When her life was in jeopardy?

He leaned into her touch and still, with no words spoken,

he read her mind. Azaiel carried her into the bathroom and turned on the shower. As hot steam filled her bathroom they tore at each other's clothes, ripping, tearing . . . destroying in an effort to touch. To feel.

In seconds he stood before her. Six feet six inches of raw, masculine beauty, and she reveled in the knowledge that at least for today he was hers. His eyes were no longer golden but bled through with the edgy black that she loved.

"Azaiel, I . . ." Her voice caught, and she couldn't speak. She couldn't say the things that floated inside her head.

I think I love you.

I think I want you forever.

I think this is my last chance for happiness.

He lifted her into his arms and claimed her mouth in the most gentle, exquisite kiss ever. As light as a feather his lips parted hers, and he invaded with a sweep of his tongue. She groaned into him, and her head fell back as she let him take. Let him taste and caress.

He stepped into the shower, and she slid down the length of him as her fingers sought the straining hardness between them. He watched her in silence as the hot spray from above baptized them in liquid heat, and when she slowly massaged the tip of his cock and cupped his balls he clenched his teeth, but his gaze never wavered from her.

He was velvet-encased steel in her hands. God, he felt perfect, and his eyes glittered, sparks of gold lighting them each time she gripped him and massaged. The fatigue from earlier had long fled; whether it was because of the hot spray or the hot man in front of her didn't matter.

Rowan knelt in front of Azaiel and took him into her mouth. She smiled at the strangled sound he made, and when his fisted hands loosened and crept into her hair she was exhilarated by the power she felt.

She was swollen with need, her sex throbbing with an

ache only Azaiel could assuage, but first, she wanted to pleasure her man. To give him something to remember her by.

She licked and suckled and massaged until his hips jerked in tandem with her motions, and when he swore, when he lifted her away she smiled wickedly, knowing how close to the edge she'd taken him.

His eyes had turned fully black, and he looked like the fierce warrior he was. His dark blond hair was plastered to his skull, and the feral look in his eyes touched something inside her. He pulled her upward and claimed her mouth once more, his hands on her breasts, kneading, tugging, and teasing until whimpers fell from her, one after the other. His tongue probed deeply as did his fingers, and when he found her hot, wet, center and plunged two long digits deep inside his kiss swallowed a scream.

He stretched and fingered, and her hips jerked, hard, as he touched that spot so deep inside—the one that controlled her pleasure. He smiled against her, cajoling an orgasm and murmuring words she didn't understand.

Azaiel tore his mouth away and whispered hoarsely, "Come for me, Rowan. Only for me."

How could she not? Rowan clutched at him as her stomach contracted, and the ache inside her womb expanded, stretched to the limit by his insanely talented fingers. She then shuddered. Once. Twice. And still he held her gaze.

The glow of her orgasm had barely registered when he began to pleasure her in earnest. His hands were all over her body. Long, soapy fingers swooped over her waist, her hips, and down her thighs. He massaged every inch of her flesh, lingering near her butt, and she blushed when she thought of what he'd done to her in the clearing. Of how wonderful he'd made her feel.

When he shampooed her hair, massaged her scalp, every

single nerve and cell in her body was on fire. Trembling. Aching with desire.

Her chest was tight, and for some silly reason she felt like crying again. She took a moment, but when she glanced back her soul was reflected in his eyes, and their connection solidified in a way she'd not felt before.

He was hers. And she was his.

Azaiel lifted her—he kissed her again, a tender, lingering kiss that made her dizzy. He moved until she rested against the warm tiles of the shower, and his eyes held her as he adjusted her in his embrace and slowly sank his long length deep inside her.

"Oh Azaiel," she whispered, biting her lip as he pulled out, then slowly entered her again. He filled her completely, stretching her walls and hitting that spot—that special fucking spot—as he did so.

She strained against him, the ache so fierce that her body was flush with the heat of it.

"No," he said softly. "Let me love you slowly." He kissed her nose, thrust again, and was rewarded with a sob. "And thoroughly." He kissed the sensitive area under her ear, thrust again, and growled as she cried out. "But keep your eyes on me," he warned.

Rowan gazed at him, helpless to do anything else as he held her hips in place and rocked into her with a motion that left her breathless. This was to be a slow, seductive loving, and she'd have it no other way.

"Watch me, Rowan." His voice was hoarse, and he increased the rhythm slightly, his white teeth flashing as he growled fiercely. "I want to see you come. Understand?"

She nodded. Oh God. How could she look anywhere else? In that moment he was everything to her. He filled her completely—her mind, her body . . . her soul.

Her arms trailed down his back, and she cupped his hard

ass as he slowly, methodically filled her with each controlled thrust. Yet his muscles bulged, and she knew what it cost him to prolong their pleasure. He was riding as close to the edge as she.

When he captured a turgid nipple in his mouth and suckled, tugged, and teased, she thought she was going to lose it. Rowan wriggled her hips and dug her fingers into his shoulders, urging him on, but he licked her nipple and gazed into her eyes once more, a wicked grin on his face as he continued to screw her slowly and thoroughly.

"I want it faster," she begged.

Her shoulders dug into the tiles as he pushed into her. "Manners, Rowan."

"What?" He was inside her, the long length of him settled against the tight walls of her vagina. Azaiel rolled his hips, and she gasped at the riot of sensation that ran through her.

The veins on the side of his neck bulged, the lines smooth and glistening beneath the relentless hot spray of water. Azaiel rocked into her again, and again, with slow, controlled precision, his handsome face fierce as he gazed into her eyes. "Ask. Me. Nicely," he managed to say before claiming her other nipple.

Rowan let him ease out of her for the last time, and when he slid inside she anchored her right leg against his while her left hugged his hip. She leaned backward so that she could see where they were joined, and looked up at him, her mind filled with the erotic images of their bodies intertwined.

"Faster, please," she gasped.

Their gazes locked, and Azaiel obliged, with harder thrusts that electrified with every deep stroke. The ball of energy inside, the one filled with sensation and passion, unfurled and spread liquid heat throughout her body. And as they rushed toward the pinnacle of their joining, as their bodies strained and rocked together, she knew she'd found the place she wanted to be for the rest of her life.

With him. With this man. Warrior. Angel.

But did he want her?

Azaiel grunted. "Don't look away."

And there beneath the warm, wet spray they watched each other in silence as they both shattered into a million pieces.

Later, when she was tucked inside Azaiel's arms, deep within the softness of her blankets, she asked the one thing that had been on her mind for days.

"Tonight, if I'm not able to . . ." His arms tightened around her, and Rowan snuggled into the spot between this shoulder and neck. She tried again. "If I don't defeat Mallick, you will make sure he never claims me." She paused as the hurt inside filled her throat. At the thought of what might never be.

At the thought of what she wanted. "He can't claim me," she whispered.

Azaiel's heart beat strong beneath her ear, and his warmth filled her soul. He kissed the top of her head. "He won't. Of that, you can be assured."

Hearing his words was like a salve to a wound. Rowan closed her eyes and eventually drifted off to sleep. She never knew when the Seraphim left her side, but hours later it was the small orange tabby who took his place, and it was the animal's purring that kept her deep in dreamland.

CHAPTER 31

"I'm down to my last two cigars."

Azaiel turned and spied Priest in the shadows. "Are you sharing?"

The Knight Templar handed him a crisp Montecristo, stood to the side, and offered a light. It was nearing dusk, and there were but hours before Rowan would summon Mallick. Time was running out, with each passing minute bringing them closer to a conclusion that was not assured.

Priest blew out a perfect circle of smoke and leaned on the railing beside Azaiel. "We need to confirm whether the demon lord knows about the League."

Azaiel nodded.

"Do you have something in mind?" Priest asked.

"Nope."

"Good to know. I've always enjoyed a fly-by-the-seat-of-your-pants kind of operation. Makes it that much more exciting, no?"

Azaiel shrugged. "Is there any other kind?"

Priest laughed softly, but there was no mistaking the seriousness of their task. "We need to know. If the League has been breached . . ."

Azaiel straightened, letting the coffee-flavored taste of

the cigar settle on his palate. "It is the reason we came." He turned to the Templar. "Rowan should be filled in."

The Templar studied him for a few moments before glancing out toward the subdued group of hunters gathered around Vicki's RV. "She might be the only one with time to ask the questions that need to be asked."

Priest's eyes stayed on him for longer than he liked, and Azaiel looked away. His gut was churning in all sorts of directions, and he had no fucking clue what the night would bring. But he did know one thing.

In the space of a few weeks, Rowan James had insinuated herself into his life—into the air that he breathed for Christ sake—and he had no clue how he was going to say good-bye. After living for more time than he deserved. After his fall. After his imprisonment. After all of that, he'd finally found someone who meant more to him than his own life.

And for Rowan, his life was something he'd willingly give. And the thoughts that had been swirling in his head rose to the surface once more. Thoughts of a life with her. Of what it would mean. What it would *entail*.

"Thank bloody hell," Priest muttered, and strode down the steps.

Azaiel's head whipped up, and he frowned, following Priest down the steps as two forms fell from shadow. One was a small, round ball of a man and the other, a tall warrior with a powerful build and eyes as hard as steel.

"Cale." Priest shook hands with the warrior, but it was the small man who walked forward and ran his hands over his bald head in a nervous gesture that Azaiel watched.

"Askelon."

The small man shrugged. "I prefer Bill, if you don't mind." He smiled and shrugged. "At least while in this form."

Azaiel nodded. "As you wish."

"Where is she?" Bill asked quietly.

"I'm here."

All four men glanced toward the porch, and Azaiel's chest tightened as his gaze fell upon Rowan. Her pale beauty transcended the darkness that was fast approaching. Dressed in jeans and a simple white T-shirt, she did not look like the fierce demon-hunting witch that she was. Her blue eyes were on Azaiel, but it was Bill that she addressed as she slowly joined them on the grass.

"Been a long time, Mr. Bill."

The Seraphim nodded, his voice subdued. "I'm so very sorry to hear about Cara. You must know she meant a lot to me." He gestured toward Cale and Priest. "To all of us."

Rowan nodded. Azaiel saw the pain in her eyes. The slight tremble of her lips. But he also saw the strength that resided there—the determination and focus.

"I've brought you something." Bill nodded toward Cale, and the warrior stepped forward.

Cale held his hand out. The air misted and swirled along his skin, and seconds later he held a large sword in his grip, its rune-filled blade shining with a dangerous glint. The sword of Gideon.

Azaiel nodded toward Bill, grateful that he'd come through, and he watched as Rowan approached Cale. She hesitated for a moment, then lifted the sword into her hands, sweeping the air in an arc as she tested the blade.

"Mother-trucker! That looks like the freaking blade of Gryffindor!" Hannah jumped between them all, her eyes wide.

"The what?" Nico scowled as he joined her.

Hannah's blond head whipped around. "Um, dude . . . Harry Potter?"

The jaguar's scowled deepened, but he remained silent as Rowan stared at the majestic weapon. She arched a brow at Priest. "You've got some pretty heavy-duty connections, my friend."

Priest nodded, the cigar held tight between his teeth, and patted Cale on the back. "You sticking around for this one?"

Cale shook his head. The tall, dark-haired warrior grimaced. "Unfortunately not this time, though I'd give anything to kick that son of a bitch's ass." Cale's steely gaze rested on Rowan. "Good luck. He's a formidable opponent, but his fatal flaw is arrogance. Play on that." He then glanced at Bill. "We should go. I feel him lingering out there searching for her."

Bill nodded. "Of course. One minute please." He gestured, and Rowan bent forward, so that he was able to whisper into her ear, his small chubby hand closed over her own. Rowan nodded in response to whatever it was Bill imparted and hugged the small man fiercely. Azaiel heard her whisper, "Thank you."

Bill cleared his throat and crossed to Azaiel. "Let's take a walk, shall we?"

Azaiel fell in step with his brother, and they stopped just beyond the large oak tree, where dusk seemed heavier, and the coolness of twilight was sharp.

"She's magnificent, isn't she?" Bill gazed into the darkness, his voice subdued.

Azaiel nodded but remained silent. What was there to say?

"This coming war will test all of us, my friend. We'll be asked to do things . . . hard things."

"Askelon, I know what needs to be done. If she can't defeat Mallick, I will send her to the gray realm." His words were bitter and left him empty inside.

Bill turned to him, and Azaiel saw pain reflected in his eyes. "She's so like Cara, and her mother, Marie-Noelle." Bill's eyes narrowed slightly, and something shifted in his face. "She's come to mean a lot to you."

Azaiel rotated his neck slowly in an effort to loosen up the tense muscles along his shoulders. "She is one hell of a woman," he admitted softly.

"You cannot have her, Azaiel. Not as long as you are Seraphim."

There it was. Spelled out in black-and-white. "I know."

Bill held his gaze for several, long moments, then looked behind. "I must go before my presence here is felt, but know this." The small man grasped Azaiel's hands together. "I never lost faith in you. I am proud to call you brother."

Azaiel's eyes welled as Bill stepped away. He remained tight-lipped, not trusting himself to speak, and watched his brother, his mentor—his savior—retreat into the darkness, with Cale close on his heels.

"The veil is thinning. It's nearly time." Rowan's eyes were full of questions.

Azaiel glanced toward Priest. The Knight Templar clenched his cigar, nodded, and turned away, barking orders and taking charge.

Azaiel watched her closely. "It is."

Her forehead furled, and she bit her lip in that nervous way that she had. "Is there something else going on that I don't know about? I mean, I've never really pushed the issue . . . asked the question."

"What question is that, Rowan?"

She gazed up into his eyes, and his heart rolled over. "Who are you people? Really?"

He held out his hand. "I've some things to tell you before this night begins."

Rowan put her small hand in his without hesitation, and that gesture alone was enough to undo him. Inside, Azaiel's emotions twisted into a hard ball that settled at the back of his throat.

They walked until they found themselves in the back

garden and paused there amongst the pumpkins and cornstalks and oak trees bare of leaves. Rowan slipped into his
arms, and for the longest time he just held her. He rested his
cheek against the top of her head, inhaled her scent, and reveled in her warmth.

After a while she moved, and reluctantly he released her,
his dark thoughts reflected on his face.

"Just tell, me," she said simply. "Everything."

And so he did.

Azaiel told her of his origins. Of his fall from grace at
the hands of the betrayer. He told her of his weakness—how
he'd sculpted a dangerous portal for Toniella, one that would
have ripped apart the upper and lower realms. He shared his
subsequent banishment to the Hell realm and told her of his
escape. How he used an eagle shifter, Skye Knightly . . . how
his vengeance nearly ripped the world apart, again.

He told Rowan how Cormac O'Hara had tortured and
maimed him in a bid to find the portal, yet he'd taken everything and more because he deserved it. He was the Fallen. He
didn't deserve his brother's, Bill's, devotion, but he'd vowed
he would do whatever it took to help Bill, and yet now . . .

"Now?" she prompted gently.

Azaiel ran fingers through the thick hair atop his head.
"Now I don't know if I have the strength to do what needs
to be done." His breaths fell erratically. "Mallick cannot be
allowed to claim you."

"I'm totally fine with that."

His eyes pierced hers. "You know what that means?"

She nodded but didn't answer for several seconds. "I
would sacrifice myself before I let that bastard get his hands
on me, and I will trust you to do the deed if the time comes.
He *killed* my grandmother."

Azaiel cursed and shook his head. "That we're not one
hundred percent sure of."

"What?" Rowan flew at him. Pumped her fists against his chest. "How can you say that? Who else would want to hurt Cara?"

A long, shuddering breath escaped him. "We don't know."

"We?" Rowan frowned and moved away, though her eyes never left his. "Go on."

"Cara was part of a group that watched from the shadows, working to preserve the balance between the realms."

She arched a brow. "You, Priest, and the others are part of this group?"

Azaiel nodded.

"Well, how come I've never heard of it?"

"The group is secretive, with members mixing on a need-to-know basis. There are those who dwell in the lower realms, the upper realms, and beyond. Both human and otherworld. I only know the identities of a handful for a reason. Our identities must be protected at all cost."

"And yet you've just shared this with me."

"Sometimes the rules must be bent. There are those who would seek to end us, so when one is murdered, it raises the question. Has the League been breached? Does someone know who we are?"

"You're not convinced Mallick killed my Nana."

"At this point we don't know if he is in fact responsible for her death, and if he is . . . did he kill Cara because of you? Or her affiliation with the League."

"Or for both reasons."

"True."

"The dream to be free of my destiny was always an empty one." She shrugged. "It just took me six years to figure it out." She sighed and ran her fingers across the top of her temple. "Mallick's hold over my family ends tonight, and I'll find out the truth about Nana's death one way or another."

"I'll do whatever I can to help you."

After a good long while she whispered, "Okay."

She moved toward him again, put her fingers against his skin. "He won't win. I won't let him, and when this is all over . . ."

Azaiel stared down at the woman who'd claimed every single cell in his body and felt himself tremble at her touch. He heard the question in her voice, and the answer in his heart was bittersweet. He bent down and brushed his mouth across hers. "The only way I could stay is if I was less than ordinary. If I wasn't Seraphim."

"Well, then." She stilled beneath his touch. "That's that."

She pulled away and smiled. "It's time. Let's dance, shall we?"

CHAPTER 32

The night was moonless. A thick, heavy blanket of dark with only the glow from her candles to light the way.

Rowan felt ill, and every step that she took toward the clearing, she wanted to take another in the other direction and run until she couldn't run anymore. Her head was heavy, and her heart full of pain.

The information that Azaiel had imparted wasn't shocking. It wasn't a huge revelation. Hell, she'd known all along that this supernatural A-team wasn't your run-of-the-mill operation. And she was proud that her grandmother had been part of their group. Their League of Guardians.

I want him.

And that was the heart of her pain. Azaiel. In a few hours she might not even exist in this realm, and if she did succeed . . . she was bound to her family and he was bound to this League . . . this group of warriors.

They could never be together. Those had been his words. They fucking sucked.

"Miss Rowan. We're almost there." Cedric spoke quietly, and her focus shifted. The clearing was dead ahead; she saw candles burning through the trees.

"Are you sure you want to stay, Cedric?" She glanced at her mother. "Mikhail can take you back to the house."

The old man turned to her, anger in his eyes. "Now you listen to me, child. I don't need no damn coddling. I will see this ended and that abomination destroyed, you hear?"

Rowan nodded, a smile touching her lips. "I hear."

"Everything okay?" Kellen appeared at her side, his face tense, his eyes somber.

Rowan nodded. "Is everyone in place?"

"The Blackstones are in town patrolling with the Lawrences. The others are here along with Azaiel and his crew." Kellen touched her cheek. "We're ready. Let's do this. Let's end this once and for all. For Nana."

"For Nana," she whispered.

They entered the clearing, and she felt the weight of everyone's gaze as she slowly made her way toward them. Her family. Her tribe. Her people. So many faces—aunts, cousins, the entire James coven—and all of them were here for her.

Frank nodded from across the clearing as he handed out modified weapons to the hunters who would patrol the woods. His face was tense, his expression fierce, his forehead covered in sweat. He winked and continued on, barking orders to the hunters.

Hannah stepped in front of her. "Hey."

"Hey."

Her blond hair had a blue streak down the middle, and she pointed to it, shrugging. "I decided to color-coordinate with Nico, but he didn't find it amusing." Hannah's mouth tightened. "In fact he was kind of pissed off."

"Men," Rowan said softly.

"Yeah." Hannah paused for a second, her eyes misty, her voice trembling. "I want you to fry that mother-trucker. Okay?"

Rowan hugged her cousin, and whispered, "I'll do my best."

Rowan cleared her throat as she turned from Hannah,

eyes searching for Azaiel and feeling more than a little deflated that he was nowhere to be seen.

She spoke clearly as she addressed the circle. "I will bury Mallick tonight. One way or another. His hold on our family will end." She swallowed thickly as she caught sight of her mother. Marie-Noelle's face was pale, but she stood, arms linked with Vicki and Terre.

"This circle must stand strong, and I need all of you to find whatever strength you can to keep it solid. Once inside, I will summon him, and I have no idea what will happen."

Rowan took a step forward and halted when she caught sight of Azaiel on the outskirts of the circle. His expression was fierce. He exuded power, and she fed from his strength, felt his energy surround her like a warm blanket.

I love him.

He nodded as if he'd heard her, and everything fell away in that moment. *I can do this.* The invisible weight of the sword of Gideon rested against her hip while the dagger her father had given her was hidden in the pocket of her jeans.

Time was up, but she was cool with that. She was ready.

Rowan exhaled slowly, walked forward, and stepped into the circle.

Four candles in a square bordered the circle of witches. Young and old joined hands; among their ranks were Priest, Kellen, and Azaiel. The black jaguar patrolled the outer ring, his large tail sweeping back and forth as the women chanted.

Their energy lit up the night with a soft glow that hovered above them, and all around the souls of the dead came to visit. It was Samhain, the veil had thinned, and their energy was welcome.

Rowan stood alone inside the circle, seeing things she'd never dreamed of. Women appeared before her—women who she *knew*. She knew their names, their faces, and their minds.

These were her people—the many witches who'd lived before her. And there were those whose faces were rotted, maggot-filled, and sunken. They called to her for vengeance.

They were the ones Mallick had defiled. Depleted. And destroyed. Her family. Her tribe.

One face appeared and nearly ripped her heart out. "Nana," she whispered.

Cara James stood just behind her daughter and placed her hand upon Marie-Noelle's shoulder. Her sorrowful eyes held Rowan's gaze for several long moments before Cara closed her eyes and began to chant.

Rowan did the same and let her hands fall to her side as she recited the spell in her mind—the one that would open the mark on her neck. The words fell from her lips, and with each passing moment, she felt the skin on her flesh burn and recoil as Mallick's mark was restored.

A great roaring echoed in her ear, swept in by a wind that brought with it not only debris but the smell of depravity and evil. Her hair twisted above her head, and she struggled to keep her legs steady as she cleared her mind of everything except Mallick.

The howling wind intensified, and the pressure inside her head was fierce. Fog rolled in, sweeping through the clearing in waves of cold mist that dampened her clothes. Rowan's ears popped, and she cried out and fell to her knees, clutching the back of her neck in pain.

She heard nothing but her heartbeat. Suddenly the wind died down, and there was silence. It pressed upon her, and when she opened her eyes he was there. In her circle. Inches away.

Mallick stared down at her with eyes the color of glacial ice. His thick, glossy hair was pulled back, tied behind his head in a long ponytail the color of midnight. He was dressed in black. Head to toe.

Rowan smiled. They were funeral clothes. How fucking appropriate.

His handsome face changed—a subtle shift in the eyes and mouth—as he glanced behind her, then turned in a circle.

"You think to trap me?" His voice was deep, with an accent not heard in the human realm. It was not unlike Azaiel's though the demon's was thicker as if his voice box was seldom used.

"I thought we could have a chat." Slowly she got to her feet and eyed him warily.

"A chat," he mocked. "How human." He arched a brow and smiled widely. "I will enjoy breaking you, Rowan."

"Like you broke Cara? Did it make you feel powerful to maim an old woman who had no chance to defend herself?"

He laughed. A full-bodied belly laugh that reverberated inside her head and made her nauseous. Had he done the deed?

"You're a coward, Mallick. Hiding behind the skirts of my family. My blood." Rowan's fingers itched with the burn of her power. "You crossed the line when you left my grandmother to die like a piece of garbage. When you tortured and marked her."

Even now, the details of Cara's death were difficult to comprehend, and a part of her wished that Azaiel hadn't shared everything with her.

Mallick's grin widened, his serrated teeth glinting in the shadows cast by the fires that burned around them. "You think I would kill and torture someone loved by you and"—he arched a brow—"not make you watch?"

Rowan's face whitened, and she took a step forward, hands raised.

Mallick paused, nostrils flared, and his eyes widened in anger. The earth trembled beneath her feet, and she nearly fell as she struggled to keep her balance.

"You've given yourself to another." Bloodred eyes stared at her, his fury impressive as he bared serrated teeth at her. "You will pay for that. You belong to me." Mallick snarled and glanced around once more. "You all belong to me."

"No."

Mallick cocked his head and seemed surprised that she'd spoken. "That will cost you, little witch."

"No," she said again as the coven closed ranks, and their chanting increased. Their power floated in the air and slid over her skin with ease. Rowan caught sight of her mother . . . of her Nana and her cousins. Hannah's eyes were riveted to Mallick as she chanted along with the others. Their strength, their bond was inside her now. She felt it coil around her heart and soul.

A face appeared from the mist, an old, worn, tragic face. She knew it was Agatha, the one who'd called Mallick forth so long ago. Agatha nodded and screamed.

Mallick roared in anger and summoned his own army. They attacked, and Rowan knew she needed to act quickly. Her hunters could only hold them off for so long, even with the added strength of the fae, whom she felt along the fringes of the circle.

She began to recite the binding spell and sidestepped agilely as Mallick lunged toward her. The coven's power sizzled in the air, a beautiful luminescent conduit that fed directly into Rowan. She used it, smiling wickedly as Mallick struggled to get closer to her—to break through the energy that protected her.

She closed her eyes, trusting her sisters completely, and the words fell from her lips, the ones that would bind him and keep him subdued while she excised his essence from his physical body.

When the binding spell was complete, Rowan's eyes flew open, her chest rising and falling rapidly, her voice hoarse.

Mallick was livid. He glared at her with such hatred that for a moment fear sliced through her, and she thought she might be sick.

I will enjoy making you pay for this over and over, you dumb bitch.

The wind whipped at her furiously, and she struggled to keep herself upright, to keep his voice out of her head as she turned to Hannah. Her cousin tossed a large jar toward her, and Rowan caught it handily, setting it on the ground between them as she held out her hand and called forth the sword of Gideon.

Mallick's mouth frothed when he caught sight of it, and he bellowed loudly, his voice screeching as he called for his forces to annihilate the coven. Screams echoed on the wind, but Rowan dared not take her eyes from the demon in front of her.

She opened her mouth and stared directly into death's gaze as she began to call forth the charm that would pull his essence from his body. Mallick's facade wavered, and his true form shone through. It was pure darkness and evil. She closed her eyes, her stomach rolling as the horror she'd seen floated in her mind.

A scream shattered through her brain, and Rowan stumbled to the ground, rolling to the side as the circle broke. "No!" she screamed, the spell interrupted. Abigail lay on the ground, a limp, rag doll with lifeless eyes and a deep wound to the neck. All around them chaos reigned.

She felt Mallick behind her a half a second before pain erupted along her scalp. He picked her up as if she weighed nothing, and when she twisted his fist knocked the sword flying before slamming into the side of her head. Stars flickered in front of her, and the breath was knocked from her body as Mallick threw her to the ground with enough force to shake the earth.

Blood spurted inside her mouth, and for a second Rowan was confused. Everything was too loud. Too chaotic. But then she saw him. Azaiel.

He was shouting at her, trying to fight his way past several blood demons, and though she couldn't hear him, the look in his eyes was enough to clear her head. She rolled to the side, her father's dagger in her hand as she jackknifed to her feet and faced Mallick once more.

"You stupid woman." Spittle leaked from the corner of his mouth, and he bared his teeth once more. "I will kill you slowly, eat from you daily until you shrivel into nothing more than a husk of flesh. Then I will feed you to my dogs."

Rowan knew she had but one chance. "You forget, asshole." The world fell away as she lunged toward him. "I'm not a woman." She plunged the dagger into his neck and took him down, rolling with him on the ground as he sputtered in rage. He stilled beneath her hands, his veins bulging like black, spidery tattoos as she leaned toward him. "I'm the fucking witch who is going to end you."

She dug the dagger in as far as she could, watching as the fae poison spread throughout his body. Mallick's eyes bulged, and froth leaked from the corners of his mouth as he struggled to breathe.

She pushed away and began to recite once more, trusting her coven, her hunters . . . her lover to keep her safe as she completed the ritual.

She was light-headed, her voice hoarse by the time Mallick's mouth opened and his darkness erupted from every orifice, swirling in a tornado of dank, evil mist. Carefully, Rowan directed it into the large jar, and once it was captured, secured within the charmed glass, she glanced around wildly, her eyes searching for the sword of Gideon.

Her eyes burned at the sight before her. The circle was surrounded, part of it breached. On the perimeter Mallick's dark soldiers attacked with a frenzy, and she knew her forces couldn't hold much longer.

She crawled forward and spied Cedric. The old man stood beside Abigail's prone body, and in his hands was the sword. He glanced up, eyes wet with tears, and she screamed at him to no avail. There, inches away stood a massive demon, its human form long gone and in its place, a seven-foot-tall wall of scales, muscle, and evil.

Its long, clawlike hand punched into Cedric's back and through his chest like a hammer smashing into bone.

"No!" In one moment everything faded to gray, and Cedric's eyes widened as he gazed at her. She saw his love for her family, his allegiance to her Nana. She saw his acceptance of his death.

He fell forward and with a painful gasp tossed the sword into the air. Rowan leapt upward, aware the jar was cracking, shaking with the rage that it contained. Without hesitation she turned and separated Mallick's head from his body.

CHAPTER 33

He'd watched her for hours, the gentle rise and fall of her chest, the way she curled her palm into her cheek, and he'd listened to the soft sounds that fell from her lips as she twisted among her blankets. Evening shadows crept along the walls of her bedroom, and he shifted, his long legs stiff, his body aching.

It had been one hell of a battle. Abigail had been struck down, two of the human hunters along with her. Several of Darrick's fae had been gravely injured, and Cedric . . . Azaiel sighed and rubbed his forehead. The gentle old man had died valiantly.

A knock on the door drew his attention, and he rose as Priest entered.

"Has she woken yet?"

Azaiel shook his head. "Not yet."

Priest ran his hands across his temple and rolled his shoulder. "Nico and I are leaving. With Mallick gone, the threat to Salem's been greatly diminished. The Blackstones and the Morins along with the rest of the coven should be able to rout out any laggers and take care of them."

"Good to know." Azaiel paused. "There will be repercussions with Mallick's death. Lucifer will not be happy that one of his own is gone, banished to the gray realm forever."

"No, I don't suppose the bastard will like that." Priest was silent for a few moments. "I hear you're sticking around . . . for a while."

"News travels fast."

"That kind of news does."

Azaiel watched him closely. The Knight Templar was honorable. A true warrior. For whatever reason it mattered what the man thought. "You think me weak?"

Priest shook his head. "No, brother. I think you're brave." A pause. "Did you get a chance to question Rowan?"

"Not yet, she's been—"

"He didn't do it," Rowan whispered hoarsely. She sat up in the bed and pushed a mess of tangles out of her eyes. She looked from Priest and back to Azaiel. "I'm certain that Mallick didn't kill my Nana." Her eyes were shadowed with unshed tears, and Azaiel's heart twisted when she gazed at him and whispered, "So who did? Are the rest of you in danger?"

Priest swore and turned on his heel. "I've got to get to The Pines; this is not good news." He reached into his jacket and retrieved a cigar.

"I thought you were out."

He tossed it to Azaiel. "I am now."

Priest turned to Rowan, his voice soft. "What you did last night was one of the bravest things I've ever witnessed, and it's one I won't soon forget." He bent forward and kissed her forehead. "Take care, little witch. I'm sure we'll cross paths again."

Priest nodded to Azaiel. "You too, Seraphim," then he opened the door and left.

Azaiel sank onto the bed and gathered Rowan into his arms. There were no words for a very long time, and he held her until the shadows solidified, and the room fell into darkness.

She trembled in his arms, and shudders rolled over her shoulders. "Abigail, Cedric . . . oh God, Azaiel, what did I do? If I just . . . I should have just done this on my own."

"You couldn't do this on your own, Rowan."

"They died because of me."

He stroked her hair and wished with all his might that he could take away her pain. "They didn't die because of you. They died *for* you, knowing you'd do the same for them. Your circle held firm, and you defeated a demon lord who had terrorized your coven for centuries. That took a hell of a lot of guts. Most men I know wouldn't have taken the chance you took, led your people the way you did." He kissed the top of her head. "Your family is very proud of you, Rowan and now . . . now it's over."

She looked up at him, her huge eyes shimmering with unshed tears. "I should feel a lot of things, but my chest hurts, and I can't get Abigail's dead eyes out of my head."

He rubbed her shoulders and worked the knots until she relaxed.

Finally Rowan spoke, her breath warm against his chest. "Where is my mother? And Kellen?"

"They're both here. They were unhurt."

She settled against him, burrowing into his chest. "Nana was there. I saw her, only briefly, but she was there." She smiled tremulously. "I felt her warmth and her strength."

"She's inside you, Rowan. Your grandmother will be with you always. As will Abigail and Cedric."

She exhaled a shaky breath. "When are you leaving?"

"I'm not."

She wiggled in his grasp until he had to let her go, her eyes wide with confusion as she stared up at him. "I don't . . . what do you mean?"

Azaiel studied her closely, not sure of her reaction. "I thought I'd hang around for a while. Help with the cleanup. No one kills a demon lord of Mallick's caliber without consequences. There will be more attacks, of that you can be assured."

She nodded slowly, and whispered, "How long?"

It was crunch time, and his gut tightened, suddenly unsure. "How long would you have me?"

"But . . ." She bit her lip, and it took everything in him not to reach down and cover her mouth with his. "I didn't think it was possible." Rowan shook her head. "Don't toy with me, Azaiel. I've lost too much already."

He grabbed her chin and stared at her intently, his breath frozen, his heart about to explode. "How. Long. Will. You. Have. Me?"

Her delicate brows arched, and he knew she was confused. She licked her lips and exhaled shakily. "I would have you for the rest of my life, but . . ."

His mouth was on hers, a warm, gentle caress that left him aching inside. "You have me then."

Rowan broke away. "I don't understand. I thought you had to go back to Bill and the League. I thought that you and I . . . that we wouldn't be allowed to be together."

He nodded. "As long as I'm Seraphim, that is true." He brushed her mouth once more. "I'm no longer Seraphim."

She pushed at him, frowning. "What do you mean you're no longer Seraphim?"

"When I was on trial my brothers, the other original Seraphim, stripped me of everything. They wanted me to be mortal. To feel pain and to suffer. Askelon gave me my immortality back in exchange for my allegiance. At the time it was important to me." He shrugged. "That's no longer the case. I asked him to release me, and after some persuasion, he agreed. I'll still work for the League, of course, I'm just . . ."

"You're mortal."

"Yes."

"Oh Azaiel, what have you done?" The tears that shimmered in her eyes now fell freely, and she stepped back. The dead space inside him, the one that she'd filled, if only for a short while, began to crack, and his expression turned to granite.

He regarded her for a few moments, waiting until he knew he'd be able to speak without making a complete ass out of himself. Obviously he'd overstepped. By a fucking mile.

He hated the way his heart felt like it was crushing him from the inside out. How had he gotten it all so wrong?

"I thought you'd be happy," he said woodenly.

"You've given too much. It's too much, and I'm afraid . . ."

He didn't understand. "Rowan, what are you afraid of?"

She bit her lip in that way that he adored, and he rubbed his forefinger along her chin. "I'm afraid one day you'll figure it out, and you'll grow to resent me," she whispered.

"Figure what out?"

"That it was a mistake. A horrible mistake. That I wasn't . . . worth it."

He cupped her head and lowered his mouth once more, so relieved that he felt weak in the knees. "I love you, Rowan James. And I'd rather spend one mortal life span with you than countless millennia alone. You've ruined me for all others." His lips skated across hers, his voice growled from deep within his chest. "And I'm okay with that."

Her hands were in his hair, and she opened beneath him, her lips trembling, her voice shaky. "Are you sure? Like absolutely sure? Because I'll understand . . ."

"I've been unsure about a lot of things, but this one . . . this need to be with you will never go away. You complete me like no other. I'm a better man because of you, and for that I'll be eternally grateful."

The two of them clung to each other, hands running along flesh as clothes disappeared, and they fell onto the bed. They strained into each other, their mouths feverish, their hands rough with the need to touch. To caress. To linger and to grasp.

Azaiel proceeded to make love to his woman and later, much later, as he lay in her pink-and-white bed, with her crimson hair splayed across his chest, he tried not to dwell on the dire news they'd learned the night before.

But it was hard. He gazed out her window, at a starless, moonless sky, and he knew that it was shared by a murderer. A traitor. He just hoped the bastard was found before any more blood was shed.

"Azaiel?" Her voice was raspy.

He kissed the top of her head. "Hmm?"

"The day you walked into my house felt like the first day I was truly alive. I love you." She shuddered. "I love everything about you, and I'm honored to share my life with you."

He smiled, wrapped her in his arms, and let the silence envelop them whole. There would be trials ahead. A killer to hunt. An underworld that would seek vengeance for the death of one of their own. A woman to protect and a new family to navigate. The James coven, Kellen, Marie-Noelle, the gargoyle . . . Not to mention, the small orange tabby had finally given birth to seven kittens, there on the other side of the bed in Rowan's laundry hamper.

It was a complicated mess.

But, right now . . . in that moment . . . his life, such as it was, was pretty damn perfect.

Keep reading for an excerpt from
Juliana Stone's
League of Guardians e-book novella,
WRONG SIDE OF HELL,
available now from Avon Impulse

The door behind Logan Winters opened, bringing with it a gust of wind, the faint scent of pine, and complete silence. Like a ripple effect, conversations stopped, laughter faded, and eyes were averted.

Logan glanced up at the bartender, took notice of the stubby fingers grasped tight to the bottle of Canadian whiskey—the bottle Logan had been waiting for—and scowled.

The Neon Angel was a sad excuse for a drinking hole. It had seen better days, and from what he could tell, so had most of the staff and clientele. The bar was a rickety shack on the edge of a town he had no name for. It was the place he'd ended up—no reason other than timing—and for a brief moment it had been the heaven he'd been seeking.

His eyebrows knit together and his lips tightened. All he'd wanted was a drink. *Just one fucking drink.*

He exhaled and shifted slightly, giving himself more room as he pushed his bar stool back a few inches. The couple that had been sitting to his left were already on their feet, a wad of cash thrown onto the bar as they slid into the shadows that wrapped around the room.

The redhead who'd been eyeing him but good downed her wine and smiled a crazy "I'm getting the hell out of here" kind of smile before wiping the corner of her mouth and turning away.

Guess he wasn't getting laid either.

Logan swore—a harsh string of words no one would understand—and nodded to the bartender. "I'll take that shot now."

The large man ran his free hand through the thinning gray pallet atop his head and swallowed hard, his watery eyes wide as he glanced toward Logan. Thick bands of wiry gray brows curled crazily above round eyeballs the color of peat moss.

He wore a faded black wifebeater t-shirt and his soft arms were filled with tattoos that jiggled as he rubbed the scruff on his chin. "Dude . . . not sure if that would be a good . . . uh . . . idea."

Logan's ice blue eyes narrowed as a snarl caught in the back of his throat. He felt the heat beneath his skin. The burn. The itch.

"Do not," he bared his teeth, "call me dude."

A rumble rose from his chest—a menacing warning—and the bartender took heed, his body jerking in small, quick movements as he stepped forward. Logan nodded toward the bottle, his low rasp barely containing the irritation he felt. "Pour me the drink." He'd have his whiskey and then deal with whoever the hell had decided tonight was a good night to fuck with him.

The bartender swallowed nervously, his Adam's apple bobbing through the thick folds of skin at his neck. He didn't know what to do. Run from whoever—or whatever—had blown into the place or pour the damn whiskey and be done with it.

His eyes darted to just behind Logan once more but he jumped when Logan barked. *"Now."*

The bartender poured a generous amount of whiskey into

the tumbler, and though he tried to be careful, his hands shook so much it was a damn miracle he didn't spill the precious liquid all over the place.

The sound of clinking glass echoed into the dead silence, and when the bartender was done, he set the bottle to the side and stepped back. A pronounced tick pulsed near his left eye and he swallowed nervously as he stood there, shuffling his feet, eyes shifting from Logan to the door. His face was flushed a ruddy pink color, the skin shiny with sweat and fear.

Logan tossed some cash onto the dark grained bar and stood, his six-foot-six frame unfurling with the uncanny grace of an animal, which, considering his origins, wasn't surprising.

Tension settled along his wide shoulders as he reached for the glass, but along with it, a shot of anticipation. He was itching for a fight. He'd just not known it until now.

He tipped his head back. Amber liquid slid onto his tongue and he welcomed the smooth, sweet taste. It burned—all the way down—yet he closed his eyes and savored the sensation.

Logan had been pretty much everywhere—in the human realm and beyond—and he could say with certainty Canadians knew how to brew their damn whiskey better than anyone else.

He let the liquid fire settle in his belly, then carefully set the empty glass back onto the bar. He arched a brow and nodded, a slight jerk to the right.

Now would be a good time for the bartender to leave.

Sweat beaded along the man's top lip. It was quickly wiped away by a thick meaty hand, and then the bartender took a step back before he too disappeared into the shadows.

Logan slowly turned.

Two men stood just inside the door of the Neon Angel,

their tall frames bathed in shadow. They were big. Well built and muscled.

And they'd not come to socialize.

Logan had no idea who they were, but judging from the otherworld scent that clung to them, he had a pretty good idea where they'd come from. But that was the tricky part, wasn't it? Which realm did they call home?

No scent of demon twisted in the air, and yet . . .

His hands fisted at his sides. He could take them. Hell, he *wanted* to take them.

"Shit, that didn't take you boys long." Logan nodded toward the now empty bar. "You cleared the room in less time than it takes for a junkie with a needle in his vein to get high."

Nothing. There was no expression or words.

Logan remained silent for a few moments and cocked his head to the side. He studied the two creatures—and creatures they were; there was not one drop of humanity in them. His nostrils flared as the subtle scent of pine drifted toward him once more, and he frowned.

A memory stirred, and with it a flush of heat, a dirge of anger.

Slowly his fists unfurled to hang loose at his sides, and Logan leaned back against the bar, elbows resting against the edge, long legs crossed in front of him.

"I'm not much for one-sided conversation, so unless you've got something to say, I'd suggest you turn your asses around and leave." Logan grabbed the bottle of whiskey off the counter. " 'Cause I've got some drinking to do and that sure as hell *is* something I prefer to do alone."

A low keening vibration rippled through the room—an invisible thread that electrified the air and sent his radar crashing into full-on red alert.

Bright light lit the men from behind, beams so intense Logan took a step back and winced. His skin burned as if it had been touched by flames, and the control he had was fast slipping away.

Stars danced in front of his eyes and he shook his head aggressively as he moved forward, his mind emptying of all thoughts except one. Survival.

There was power here. Old, ancient power—the kind that always signaled shit was about to hit. *Hard.* Logan was determined that any ass kicking in the immediate future would not involve his own.

Sifting beams of light sizzled and popped, and for a second he saw nothing but glitter, small pulsating fragments of gold that drifted on the breeze and whirled around the shadowed forms. They merged, twirling faster as the keening vibrations became louder and they melted together into one large vortex of light.

Logan glared straight ahead, his gut tightening as the pine scent that hung in the air sharpened. It was fresh, tangy . . . and all too familiar.

His anger spiked as one form emerged from what had been two: a smallish, round bit of a man who looked nothing like what he truly was—Seraphim—and he was one of the original seven. Humans might call him angel, though in this form he bore no resemblance to the golden creatures popular in lore.

This was no fucking cherub.

"Askelon," Logan said smoothly, his anger in check, his façade calm.

"Let's not be so formal, my friend."

Glittery gold lamé lapels glistened against his gray jacket as the small man moved forward. His pants were ill fitting, a little too snug around his generous belly, and his dress shirt sported gaping holes between the buttons. Something was smeared alongside his mouth—ketchup? And in his hand he held a bag of—Logan sniffed—candy.

Good to see his sweet tooth was still intact. "A little theatrical, even for you, don't you think?"

Askelon arched a brow and shrugged his shoulders.

"Your bodyguards?" Logan continued dryly.

The small man laughed. "Ah . . . that was nothing. Parlor tricks, really. I somehow doubt this room would have emptied if I stood as myself, and I do so want a private chat. We've lots to discuss."

Logan's eyes narrowed as he watched him walk to the bar, throw his bag of candy—which Logan could now see was filled to the brim with colorful little bits of sugar—and with a little effort, settle himself onto the bar stool Logan had just vacated.

"Gummies."

"What?" He frowned, a scowl sweeping across his face as he stared at the little man.

Askelon nodded toward the bag. "They're called Gummi Bears."

Arms crossed, Logan's scowl deepened. "I hope you have one hell of a dental plan. That shit will rot your teeth out."

Askelon's pudgy fingers grasped a napkin and wiped away the stains on his face as he turned to Logan. For a second his eyes shimmered—a weird translucent silver color—and Logan saw the power that shifted within their depths.

"Please," he smiled and nodded, "call me Bill."

"Bill?" Logan's eyebrow arched in disbelief.

Bill grinned, shrugged, and proceeded to pour himself a glass of whiskey. "It's plain, I know, but suited me at the time." He poured one for Logan and handed it to him, raising his own in a toast.

What the hell do you want with me?

"I'll explain in a minute but first, let's drink, shall we? That is why you came here tonight, isn't it? To drink? Perhaps forget?"

So he was a mind reader now.

The tension that had fled moments earlier was back, pinching his shoulders as Logan reached for the glass and tossed back the tumbler full of booze.

The little round shit was responsible for his banishment as surely as if he'd . . .

"You know that's not true, Logan."

Logan's chest heaved. He gritted his teeth and slammed the glass back onto the counter.

"Stay the fuck out of my head, Seraphim." Logan moved forward until he was close enough to see the veins in the little shit's eyes. His nostrils flared and his chest grumbled. Beneath his skin, the beast stirred.

"Your banishment was unfortunate." Bill sipped the whiskey, his eyes shimmering as they regarded Logan closely. "But you knew there would be consequences when you joined the League."

Logan snorted. "Yeah, well. Your so-called League can go screw itself."

Bill set his half-empty glass onto the counter and twirled the liquid slowly with his finger as silence fell between them.

He turned to Logan and though his voice was soft, there was no mistaking the hard glint in his eyes. "That's not how it works, my friend."

Logan snarled and whirled away. He was a hellhound. His job was to retrieve souls that were beyond redemption and escort them to District Three—one of several levels in hell—for processing.

He neither liked nor hated his job, but he sure as hell was the best kind of animal for it. He was an elite hellhound shifter, born from the depths of hell and destined to straddle the realms. His hunting capabilities were legendary, his sensory skills unparalleled.

Logan's lips curled as the faint smell of pine tugged at

him once more. He stared at the mirror that hung on the wall in front of him. At a reflection so bizarre it was laughable. Askelon had outdone himself. His human façade was nothing short of brilliant. No one would ever suspect the short, round, balding man was in fact one of the most powerful beings in existence. If not *the* most.

Anger spiraled through him and Logan took a step toward *Bill*, not caring that the ancient could dish out a hell of a lot of damage with nothing more than the flick of his wrist.

He growled and passed his hands through the thick hair at his nape.

"Why are you here?" The last time he'd seen the little fuck, Logan's life had taken a header right into the fires of hell. Literally. He'd defied direct orders from his Overlord because Bill had asked him to. Logan had led a child back into the human realm—one he'd been ordered to retrieve for processing—and he'd been brutally punished.

He'd been sentenced to the Pit—*the* shit hole many leagues beneath District Three. It was the one place in hell that everyone avoided, if they were smart or had occasion to. It was saying something that he, a creature born of fire and brimstone, had nearly been broken by it.

"I need your help, Logan."

Logan paused, his face incredulous. "What part of 'shove your fucking League of Guardians up your ass' didn't you understand the last time?" He arched a brow and smiled, his lips tight in a sarcastic grin. "Or is this something else entirely? You pulling a Vader and crossing over to the dark side, Bill?" He flexed his arms—let his beast shift beneath the surface. "You want a ride down? Is that it?"

"The girl has been killed."

"What girl?" A frown crossed Logan's face. He didn't like where the conversation was headed, and he really didn't like the direction his mind was going.

"The same girl you were ordered to drag below fifteen years ago." Bill sighed, rubbed his temples. "The one we saved." If Logan didn't know better, he'd think the little shit was tired.

"We? Seems to me, I did all the work and had my ass kicked for hundreds of years because of it." Logan shook his head. No way was he getting involved again. "I'm done. I don't give a flying fuck about that girl." Did the Seraphim think he cared if she was dead? As far as Logan was concerned, she'd been on borrowed time anyway. If anything, she'd been granted a reprieve while he'd rotted beneath District Three.

Time moved differently there. In the Pit. What had been fifteen years to the human girl had been nearly fifteen hundred for Logan.

"Tsk, tsk . . . language, my friend." Bill turned fully and nailed Logan with a direct stare. "You should care. We all need to care."

"You're talking in circles, old man. Elaborate or leave."

Bill's mouth tightened for the briefest moment and Logan knew he'd overstepped with his last statement. He smiled, liking the fact that he managed to get under Askelon's skin. Score one for the hound.

"She cannot perish. Her future is hidden in the fabric that binds us all. But know this." Bill's nostrils flared as his anger thickened. "She will be protected. I will do everything in my power to keep her safe and make sure she meets her destiny."

"Seems like a moot point, considering she's already dead."

Bill's eyes narrowed. His face darkened and blurred . . . features shifting until his true self shone through. Gone was the pleasant, middle-aged human. In his stead a powerful, enigmatic creature stood. Two realities converged, and Logan had to admit the little shit's mojo was impressive.

Bill's voice vibrated, falling in layers that encircled Logan and filled his head. There was no mistaking. The Seraphim was livid.

"She is not meant to die—not yet. Someone is trying to alter her destiny and I need you to retrieve her for me."

"She's not my problem. Find some other dog."

"Oh, but she is your problem. I need someone who can track her. Someone who knows her scent." Bill leaned closer, his voice amplified even more. "Someone who's tasted her soul."

Logan had had enough. He growled and bared his teeth. "I don't take orders from you. Not anymore. I don't know why I ever agreed to it in the first place."

Bill sighed, grabbed his bag of candy, and helped himself to a generous amount of the gooey mess. "You joined the League because you knew it was the right thing to do. Nothing's changed." He chewed and stared up at Logan, his hard eyes and unyielding mouth at odds with the image he portrayed.

"You will do this for me."

Logan crossed his arms over his chest and spread his legs. The Seraphim was going to have to do a hell of a lot better than that.

Logan reached for the nearly empty bottle of whiskey and dumped the last of it into his glass. "You've wasted a trip, old man." He was dancing on the edge—tossing insults to one of the most powerful creatures in existence—and he didn't give a shit.

Such was the way of it these days. His stay in the Pit had altered him in more ways than one.

"You will do this because of your vow to the League." Bill arched a brow. "And because I know your true origins." The words slid between them—silky, dangerous. Bill's ace in the hole.

Logan paused, the glass nearly to his lips. His throat tightened and his teeth clenched hard.

"I know who your mother is."

The glass shattered in Logan's hand as a snarl erupted from within his chest. In a flash, his fist closed around Bill's throat and he shoved the Seraphim back onto the bar with such force that the walls shook sending bottles and glasses crashing to the floor.

Logan's skin shifted and the beast shone through, his eyes morphing to blood red as he stared down at the small man held tight in his grip.

Several longs moments passed and eventually Logan pulled back, curses in an ancient tongue flying from his mouth as he stepped away.

He closed his eyes, forced his body to relax, and crooked his head to the side. "Where's the girl?"

There was a pause.

"Purgatory."

Logan swore. "I don't have permission to enter the gray realm, you know that. No hellhound has ever breached it." He swore again. "And even if I did, there's no guarantee I will get to her in time or find my way out."

"This is true." Bill nodded. "But I have faith in you, Logan. I always have."

Logan clenched his lips together tightly and took a few moments to gather his thoughts. He had no choice and he hated that the little son of a bitch had put him in this situation. Hadn't he given enough to the fucking League?

He glared at the Seraphim and spoke coldly. "Where's her body?"

"The Regent Psychiatric Institute in Florida." At Logan's snarl, the round man finished quietly. "Morgue."

The word had barely escaped Bill's lips and Logan was already gone.